WE DIDN'T MEAN TO GO TO SEA

By the same author

WE DIDN'T MEAN
TO GO TO SEA

ARTHUR RANSOME

Illustrated by the Author

"Grab a chance and you won't be sorry for a
might-have-been"

COMMANDER TED WALKER, RN

RED FOX

A Red Fox Book

Published by Random House Children's Books
20 Vauxhall Bridge Road, London SW1V 2SA

A division of Random House UK Ltd
London Melbourne Sydney Auckland
Johannesburg and agencies throughout the world

First published by Jonathan Cape 1937
Puffin edition 1969

Red Fox edition 1993

Printed and bound in Great Britain by
Cox & Wyman Ltd, Reading, Berkshire

RANDOM HOUSE UK Limited Reg. No. 954009

ISBN 0 09 996350 7

TO
MRS HENRY CLAY

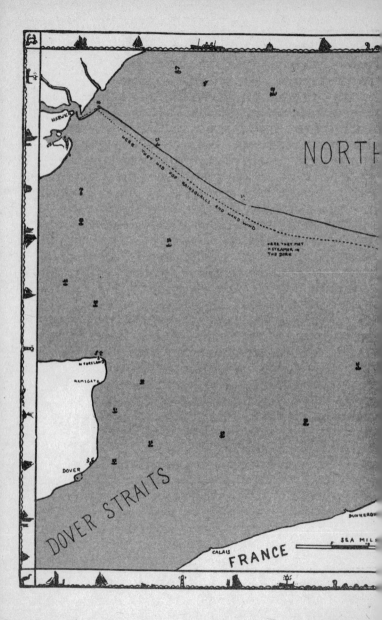

NORTH

HARWI

HERE THEY HAD FOG RAINSQUALLS AND HEAD WIND

HERE THEY MET
A STEAMER IN
THE DARK

N FORELAND

RAMSGATE

DOVER

DOVER STRAITS

DUNKERQ

SEA MIL

CALAIS

FRANCE

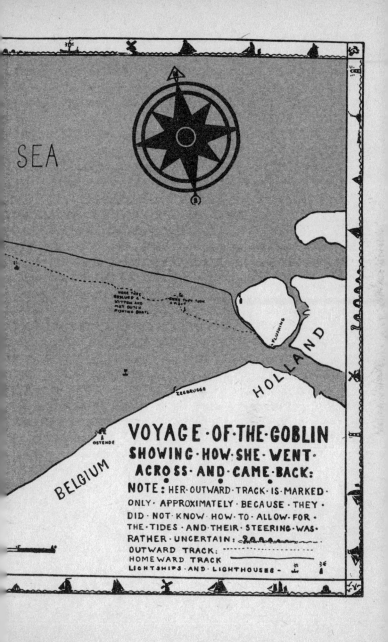

SEA

HOLLAND

HERE THEY
BOILED A
KETTLE AND
MET DUTCH
FISHING BOATS

HERE THEY TOOK
A PILOT

FLUSHING

ZEEBRUGGE

BELGIUM

OSTENDE

VOYAGE · OF · THE · GOBLIN
SHOWING · HOW · SHE · WENT ·
ACROSS · AND · CAME · BACK:
NOTE: HER · OUTWARD · TRACK · IS · MARKED ·
ONLY · APPROXIMATELY · BECAUSE · THEY ·
DID · NOT · KNOW · HOW · TO · ALLOW · FOR ·
THE · TIDES · AND · THEIR · STEERING · WAS ·
RATHER · UNCERTAIN :
OUTWARD · TRACK: ············
HOMEWARD · TRACK
LIGHTSHIPS · AND · LIGHTHOUSES ·

CONTENTS

ILLUSTRATIONS

LANDING ON THE HARD

CHAPTER I

A BOWLINE KNOT

JOHN was at the oars; Roger was in the bows; Susan and Titty were sitting side by side in the stern of a borrowed dinghy. Everything on the river was new to them. Only the evening before they had come down the deep green lane that ended in the river itself, with its crowds of yachts, and its big brown-sailed barges, and steamers going up to Ipswich or down to the sea. Last night they had slept for the first time at Alma Cottage, and this morning had waked for the first time to look out through Miss Powell's climbing roses at this happy place where almost everybody wore sea-boots, and land, in comparison with water, seemed hardly to matter at all.

They had spent the morning watching the tide come up round the barges on the hard, and envying the people who kept putting off to the anchored yachts or coming ashore from them. Then, in the afternoon, an old dinghy had been found for them, and now they were afloat themselves, paddling about, admiring the yachts in the anchorage.

It was getting on for low water. They had watched the falling tide leave boat after boat high, but, as Roger said, not exactly dry, on the shining mud. On the hard, men were walking round a barge that had been afloat in the middle of the day, and were busy with scrapers and tar-brushes. A clock chimed six from among the trees

on the further side of the river. The river, wide as
it was, seemed almost narrow between the bare
mudflats, but a tug, fussing down from Ipswich,
set the moored yachts rocking as it passed.

"Almost like being at sea," said Titty.

"Gosh! I wish we were," said Roger. "Which
boat would you like to have?"

"The big white one," said Susan.

"But look at her long counter," said John. "I'd
rather have one with a square stern, like a quay
punt. Daddy says they're twice as good in a sea-
way."

"What about the blue one?" said Titty.

"Not bad," said John.

"She's got a proper capstan on her foredeck,"
said Roger. "I wonder if she's got an engine."

"It's the sails that matter," said Titty.

"Yes, I know," said Roger, "but all the same
an engine's jolly useful."

John rowed a little harder to keep up against
the tide.

"Now, for instance," said Roger, "you'd be jolly
glad if we had one."

There was nothing to be said to that.

"What's written on that buoy?" said Titty.

John glanced over his shoulder, and pulled harder to have a look. Close to them a black mooring
buoy with green letters on it swung in the tide.

"*Goblin*," said Roger. "Funny name for a boat.
I wonder where she is."

"There's a boat coming up the river now,"
said John, "but she may be going right up to
Ipswich . . ."

"Her sails are a lovely colour," said Titty.

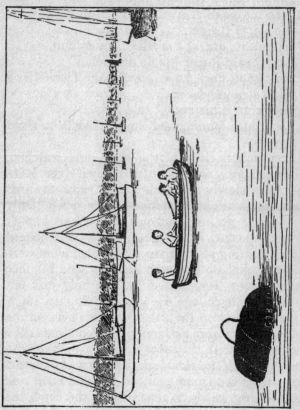

AMONG THE MOORED YACHTS

A little white cutter with red sails was coming in towards the moored boats. Someone was busy on her foredeck. As they watched, they saw the tall red mainsail crumple and fall in great folds on the top of the cabin.

"There's no one at the tiller," said John.

"I say," said Roger. "Is he all alone?"

"He's gone back to it now," said Titty. "He's heading straight for us."

"I bet this is his buoy," said Roger.

"Look out, John!" cried Susan. "We'll be right in the way."

John pulled clear of the buoy, and watched, paddling gently so as not to drift down river. More and more slowly the little cutter came towards them. Staysail and mainsail were down. Only the jib was pulling, out on the bowsprit end. It certainly looked as if there were no one aboard except that big young man, whose shoulders were so broad that no one who had not seen his face would have guessed that he had only just left school to go to college. He was standing up, steering with a foot on the tiller, with his eyes on the buoy ahead of him. Suddenly, when he was still a few yards from it, they saw him stoop and then run forward along the side deck. The jib was flapping. The young man had grabbed the boathook and was waiting, ready to reach down and catch the buoy.

"He'll just do it," Titty said almost in a whisper.

"Beautifully," said John.

"Oh," gasped Titty. "He can't reach it."

Perhaps the ebb pouring out of the river was stronger than the skipper had thought. The wind had dropped. Under jib alone the little cutter had been moving very slowly. Now, with the jib flapping loose, she lost her way. Just as the young man reached down with his boathook she stopped moving. He made a desperate lunge for the buoy but the boathook was an inch too short. He tried again and missed it by a foot. Already the tide was sweeping her back.

"That's done it!"

He was looking quickly round. There were moored yachts on all sides. He grabbed at his jib, but must have seen in a moment that he could not get his ship moving fast enough to save her from drifting down on a big black boat lying astern.

"Hi! You!" he shouted. "Can you catch a rope and make it fast to that buoy?"

"Aye, aye, Sir," shouted John.

"Sit DOWN, Roger," cried Susan.

"Duck your heads," said John.

A coiled rope was flying through the air, uncoiling as it flew. John caught it and gave the end to Roger. Three quick strokes brought their dinghy alongside the buoy, which had a rope becket on the top of it.

"Shove it through," said John urgently... "A lot of it, and give me the end."

"Aye, aye, Sir," said Roger. He pushed the end of the rope through the becket and passed it back to John, who had pulled his oars in and was waiting with a loop in the rope. He took the end from Roger, passed it through the loop in the rope, round the rope itself and back again down into the loop, and pulled it taut all in a single movement.

"All fast," he called, and hurriedly pulled the dinghy clear as the young man began hauling in hand over hand. In a moment the buoy was up on the foredeck, and the young man went on hauling in the buoy-rope, wet and thick and green with seaweed. A few yards short of the black boat the *Goblin* had stopped going astern. She was coming forward again.

"He must be jolly strong," said Roger.

"I say," said John, "she's got a square stern."

"*Goblin*," said Titty, reading her name.

Breathlessly they watched. The end of a rusty chain was climbing out of the water. It went aboard over a fairlead at the stemhead. A yard . . . two yards . . . the *Goblin's* skipper was making it fast. He stood there panting. Then he stooped, and pulled on something at his feet, and they saw the jib roll up on itself like a window blind. He stood up again, looking from boat to boat and then down at the four of them in the dinghy.

"Narrow squeak that was," he said with a slow grin. "Jolly good work on your part. Who taught *you* to tie a bowline knot?"

"Father," said John.

"He's in the Navy," said Roger.

"Lucky for me," said the skipper of the *Goblin*. "I'd have been in a proper mess if you'd fumbled things just then."

He stretched himself, dipped a mop over the side, used it to wipe his hands, black with mud from the mooring chain, and began to tidy up. John, with a steady stroke of his oars, was keeping close by. All four of them were watching. It was almost as if they had come home from sea themselves. They watched the skipper of the *Goblin* make the tiller fast. They watched him clamber forward again and turn the staysail into a neat sausage, drop it through the forehatch and disappear after it. They watched him come up again, not out of the forehatch but into the cockpit, lugging with him a huge pair of crutches, like big wooden scissors. He opened the crutches and stood them on the after-deck. Just as he went forward to lower the boom the crutches slipped. He came aft and balanced them once more.

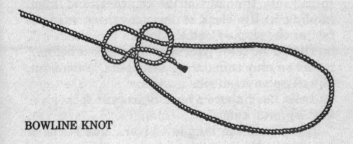

BOWLINE KNOT

"Shall I come aboard and hold them steady?" said John trying not to sound as eager as he felt.

"Wish you would. Your dinghy's got a fender round it? Have to look out for the paint."

John, careful not to bump, laid the dinghy alongside. Roger and Susan hung on to the *Goblin* as he climbed aboard.

"Good," said the *Goblin*'s skipper. "You can let her swing astern, so long as you keep her clear of the *Imp*."

"That's the name of his dinghy," said Titty,

looking at a tiny black pram dinghy that had
been towing after the *Goblin*.

"Is she the *Imp* because she's black?" whispered
Roger, "or does he have her black because she's an
Imp?"

John, standing in the cockpit, was holding the
crutches in place. The skipper at the foot of the
mast was slowly lowering the boom. John guided
it between the jaws of the crutches.

"Say when," said the skipper.

"Now," said John.

The end of the boom dropped another six
inches into the jaws of the crutches, and John,
hauling in the slack of the mainsheet, made it
fast as the skipper came aft.

"Hullo," he said, "you've been in a boat before."

"We've only sailed very little ones," said John.
"By ourselves, I mean."

"Let's have those tyers. Starboard locker . . .
Just by your hand."

John found the bundle of tyers, like strips of
broad tape. He joined the skipper on the cabin top.
Together they pulled and tugged at the great heap
of crimson canvas. "Hang on to this for a minute
. . . Hold this while I get that lump straightened
out . . . Pull this as hard as you can . . ." Gradually
the mainsail turned into a neat roll along the top of
the boom. Each bit, as they got it right, was tied
firmly down.

"Hullo! Is that the last tyer? There ought
to be one more."

"Is this it?" An eager voice spoke from the
cockpit. Roger, standing on one of the cockpit
seats, had the missing tyer in his hand. Titty was

in the cockpit, too, and even Susan, who had had
doubts about it, had not been able to stay behind.
You never knew what Roger might be doing, and
she had thought it best to follow him.

"When did you come aboard?" said John. "I
say, you don't mind, do you?" he added, turning
to the *Goblin*'s skipper.

"He said we were to let the dinghy go astern,"
said Roger. "So we did."

"The more the merrier," said the young man.
"Plenty of work for everybody. All those ropes on
the cockpit floor to be coiled."

He put on the last tyer and, followed by John,
went forward to tidy up the foredeck.

"I say, just look down," said Titty.

They looked down into the cabin of the little
ship, at blue mattresses on bunks on either side,
at a little table with a chart tied down to it with
string, at a roll of blankets in one of the bunks, at
a foghorn in another, and at a heap of dirty plates
and cups and spoons in a little white sink opposite
the tiny galley, where a saucepan of water was
simmering on one of the two burners of a little
cooking stove.

"Look here," said Susan. "Hadn't we better get
on with those ropes. We oughtn't to be here at all
really. We're going to be late for supper . . ."

One by one they disentangled the ropes from
the mass on the floor of the cockpit, coiled each
one separately and laid it on a seat. Meanwhile
John and the skipper were busy on the foredeck,
closing the hatch, coiling the buoy rope, throwing
overboard handfuls of green seaweed, dipping the
mop over the side, sousing water on the deck and

sweeping the mud from the mooring chain away and out of the scuppers. In about ten minutes nobody could have guessed that the *Goblin* had only just come in from the sea.

"This water's nearly boiling," called Susan, who had been admiring the little stove.

"Turn off the juice," the skipper called back. "Turn the knob to the right. No need to let the water boil. It's only for washing up." He was standing on the cabin top, reaching up to the screens on the shrouds, and presently John and he, one with a big red lantern and one with a big green, came aft to the cockpit.

"Well done," he laughed, looking at the neat coils of rope. "Shove them into the lockers out of the way."

"Sidelights?" said Roger.

"Yes. Empty, too. They burnt out this morning, but it was light enough then, so it didn't matter. I ought to have brought them in, but forgot."

"Gosh!" said Roger. "Were you sailing in the dark?"

"Left Dover two o'clock yesterday," said the skipper of the *Goblin*.

"He's been sailing all night," said Roger. "Did you hear?"

"All by himself," said Titty.

The skipper looked at his mainsail, at the halyards, at the decks. "She'll do," he said. "Now I'll just get through the washing up. Rule of the ship never to go ashore with washing up undone. And then . . ." he yawned and rubbed his eyes . . . "I'll see what the Butt can do for me by way of breakfast . . ."

"BREAKFAST!"

Susan, Titty and Roger all exclaimed together.

"But it's nearly seven o'clock. Haven't you had anything to eat all day?"

"Biscuits," he said. "And a thermos full of hot soup that I'd made before starting. But I never thought I'd be so long."

"We'll do the washing up," said Susan. "It won't take us two minutes."

"Come on, then." He stifled another yawn. "I never refuse a good offer."

Down they went into the cabin, climbing down the steep steps of the companion, between the sink full of the things to be washed up on one side, and the stove in the little galley on the other.

"There's an engine," exclaimed Roger, looking in under the steps. "Look here, Titty, that's my face."

THE "BUTT AND OYSTER" AND ALMA COTTAGE

"Sorry," said Titty, who had reached down with one foot and found Roger's forehead with it instead of a step.

"Come along you," said Jim. "Into that corner

so that the others can come down. You can look
at the engine afterwards."

"I'm going to sit next to it," said Roger.

Presently they were all in the cabin, sitting on
the bunks, peering forward at two more bunks in
the fore-cabin, looking at bookshelf and barometer
and clock, at the chart on the table, and at a big
envelope labelled "SHIP'S PAPERS." The owner of
the *Goblin* stooped down to reach into a cupboard
under the galley. He brought out a handful of
dish-cloths, emptied the saucepan into the sink,
sloshed in some washing soda out of a tin, and
then made room for Susan, while he put away
the Ship's Papers, cleared the chart off the table,
and spread in place of it a wide strip of white,
shiny American cloth. As fast as Susan washed
the things they were dumped on one end of the
table, seized by one of the wipers and, when dry,
put at the other end.

"You people don't belong to Pin Mill," said the
young man, who seemed to touch the roof of the
cabin when he was standing up looking down at
his busy helpers.

"We only came yesterday," said Roger.

"Stopping long?"

"We don't know yet," said Titty. "But we
probably are. We've come to meet Daddy. He's
going to be stationed at Shotley and that's quite
near."

"He's on his way home from China," said John.

"He may be here almost any day," said
Susan . . . "Roger, that mug isn't half dry."

"He telegraphed," said Roger, giving the mug
another wipe. "He's coming overland to save time."

"We're going to meet him at Harwich."

"By yourselves?"

"Oh no. Mother and Bridget are here too. We're all at Alma Cottage."

"Miss Powell's? You couldn't be in a better place. Look here, what are your names? Mine's Jim Brading."

"Walker," said John. "This is Susan. This is Titty. I'm John . . ."

"And I'm Roger," said Roger. "Does your engine really work?"

"Jolly well," said Jim Brading, "but I never use it if I can use sails instead."

"Oh," said Roger. It had been all very well for John to say that sails were the only things that mattered, but this last term at school Roger had once more begun to think a good deal about engines. He had a friend who thought about nothing else.

Titty had been making up her mind to ask a question.

"Do you live in the *Goblin* all the time?" she said at last.

"Wish I did," said Jim. "I'm going up to Oxford in another month. But I'll be living in her till then."

"Do you live at Pin Mill?" asked Roger.

"Only in *Goblin*," said Jim. "Pin Mill's her home port. She's always here when we're not cruising. I've got my uncle coming on Monday and we're going to have a try for Scotland. He always likes to start from Pin Mill. I've had her down in the South the last ten days, but the man who was with me had to go back to work."

"What's the furthest you've ever been in her?" asked John.

"Uncle Bob and I took her down to Falmouth and back one year."

"We used to sail there with Daddy when he was on leave," said John. "But only in an open boat. We never had one we could sleep in."

"Like to spend a night in the *Goblin*?" said Jim, smiling.

"Rather," said everybody at once.

"I don't see why you shouldn't," said Jim. "No. Not there. Let's get by. I know where the things go. Every plate has its place and each mug has its own hook." He worked his way past the table while they pulled their legs out of the way.

"We'd love to come, if only we could," said Susan. "Oh, I say, John, just look at the clock. Miss Powell'll have had supper ready ages ago, and we promised we wouldn't be late."

Jim's broad back was towards them as he stowed away the things in the cupboards under galley and sink. He slammed the doors to, latched them and turned round. "Well," he said. "That's that. Many thanks. Now for shore and breakfast. But what do you think? If I told your mother I wanted a crew for a couple of days? I could cram you all in, if I slept on the floor."

"Oh gosh!" said Roger.

But at that moment they heard voices outside and the splash of oars.

"They'll be aboard here, Ma'am." It was Frank, the boatman, who had lent them their dinghy.

"Oh, I say," said Susan. "Mother's had to come off to look for us."

Everybody jumped up.

"John! Susan!" That was Mother calling outside.

"Ahoy, Roger!" That was Bridget's shrill yell.

For a moment Mother and Bridget and Frank, the boatman, had been lying alongside what had seemed to be a deserted ship, except for the two dinghies astern. Now, one after another, Roger, Jim Brading, Susan, Titty and John came climbing up out of the cabin.

"I do hope they haven't been bothering you," said Mother to the skipper of the *Goblin*. "You know," she added to the others, "I didn't mean you to go and make a nuisance of yourselves to strange boats."

"We haven't," said Roger. "He's said 'Thank you' several times. He's even asked us to come and be a crew."

"They've been no end of a help," said Jim. "They've moored my ship, and done my washing up, and I've been very glad to have them."

"His name's Jim Brading," said Roger, "and he's sailed her from Dover since yesterday."

"By himself," said Titty.

"Single-handed," said John.

"Then he must be very nearly dead," said Mother, "and not wanting four of you getting in his way."

"Did you have a good passage, Sir?" asked Frank.

"Not enough wind," said Jim. "And a good deal of fog by the Sunk."

"He hasn't had anything but soup and biscuits since yesterday," said Susan.

"He's going to have *breakfast* now, at the

inn," said Titty, "just when we're going to have
our supper."

Mother looked at Jim. She liked what she saw
of him and knew very well what they wanted.

"Our supper is waiting for us," she said, smiling.
"If he'd like to come, you'd better bring him with
you. Miss Powell's sure to have given us more than
enough."

"Do come," said Titty.

"Please," said Susan.

"We'd all like you to," said John.

"I expect there'll be soup," said Roger.

"That's really very good of you," said Jim.

Frank pulled for the shore, so that Mrs Walker and Bridget might go on ahead and tell Miss
Powell they had a guest. The others climbed down
into their dinghy and followed, giving it up to
Frank who waited for them on the hard. Jim,
close after them, paddled ashore in the *Imp*. They
watched him haul the *Imp* a long way up, because
the tide had begun to come in again. Then they
walked up the hard with their new friend in the
midst of them, like four tugs bringing a liner into
port.

CHAPTER II

SLEEPY SKIPPER

"WELL, Master Jim," said Miss Powell, who was standing in the doorway of the cottage as they climbed up the steps out of the lane. "You want a bit of sleep by the look of you."

"I didn't have any last night," said Jim Brading. "How are you, Miss Powell? Uncle Bob's coming down next week."

"Do you know him?" asked Titty.

Miss Powell laughed. "Know Jim Brading? I should think I do. I've known him since he was so high and his uncle used to wade ashore from his little boat with Jim Brading kicking under his arm. You'll be taller than your uncle now, won't you, Jim? Come along in now. Supper's just ready and I dare say you'll be ready for it."

*

"Sh!"

"Don't wake him!"

Mother came into a strangely silent room.

Susan was standing by her chair, just ready to sit down. She had a finger to her lips. Titty and Roger were already seated at the round table on which a white cloth, plates, knives, forks and spoons had been laid for supper. John, holding Bridget by the hand, was standing with his back to the window. All five of them were looking at Jim Brading and keeping as quiet as they knew how. And Jim Brading, seated at the table between Titty and Roger, was fast asleep. They had chosen his place for him and sat down beside him. Jim had leaned on the table and, somehow, his head had dropped lower and lower, and now, from the doorway, Mother saw only a curly mop of hair, broad shoulders in a blue jersey, elbows wide among the plates. For Jim Brading the world had ceased to exist.

"We were talking to him," whispered Titty, "and he just flopped."

"He's tired out," whispered Susan.

Roger gently pulled a plate away from under one blue elbow that, if it had moved a little further, might have pushed it over the edge of the table.

"It must be after his bed-time," said Bridget.

"Sh!" said Susan.

John watched, wondering. So that was what you felt like after an all-night passage single-handed in a ship of your own. How soon would he have a ship himself, and sail all day and all night and bring her into port, moor her and tidy her and then, with nothing left to worry about, hold up no longer and let the tiredness he had fought for hours close happily over his head?

Mother moved from the doorway to let Miss Powell come in with the supper.

Miss Powell laughed quietly, and put the tray down without waking Jim. "He'll be all right when he's had a bit of food," she said. "Many a time I've seen him and his uncle asleep the both of them when they've come in from sea. I might

'SH! 'SH!

have known he was coming, with the supper
I've got for you ... pea soup and a mushroom
omelette ... It was what they always asked for
if they'd found time to let me know they were
coming. They would send me a telegram, 'PEA
SOUP AND OMELETTE PLEASE,' and I would know
they were on their way."

John, Bridget and Susan slipped silently into
their places as Mother sat down and began to
ladle out the soup into blue willow pattern soup
plates.

"Shall I wake him?" said Roger. "I bet he's
hungry."

"The soup's very hot," said Susan. "No need
to wake him for a minute or two."

But Jim Brading stirred suddenly, and flung
out one hand, knocking over a glass which Titty
caught just as it was rolling off the table.

"North half West for the Long Sand Head,"
muttered Jim, as if he were repeating to himself
something he had learnt by heart. That flung-out
hand was feeling for the tiller. He lifted his head
with a jerk and stared about him. "Oh, I say ...
I'm dreadfully sorry ... Look here ... I'm not fit
to ... How long have I been asleep?"

"Only a minute or two," said Titty.

John and Susan looked at Mother, almost as
if to say, "He really couldn't help it." After all,
he was their guest really.

But you could always count on Mother to understand. She was laughing.

"That's all right," she was saying. "I know just
how you feel. Why, when I was a girl in Australia
I've often fallen asleep on horseback, riding home

after a dance, and been waked by the horse stopping and snuffing at the stable door. You'll feel better when you've had some hot soup."

And really, though they did not know it at the time, Jim's falling asleep was the best thing that could have happened. You cannot think of someone as a stranger when you have seen him sprawling asleep across your supper table. There was a smile in Mother's eyes when she looked at their new friend after that. Big though he was, with his schooldays behind him, she was thinking of him much as she thought of John. Those few minutes when, with his head among the plates, he had been thinking he was still steering the *Goblin* through the night, had somehow made him one of the family.

Presently they were talking as if they had known him all their lives, and he had told them to call him Jim and not to bother about the "Mr Brading." Nor was it only John, Susan, Titty and Roger who asked questions. Mother asked them too, and Jim, waking up with the help of the soup and Miss Powell's beautiful omelette, found himself talking of his first long voyages with his uncle, and of how gradually his uncle had let him do more and more of the work of the ship, and of how at last he had given him the *Goblin* for his own, on condition that now and then, when his rheumatism let him, he might join her again and be crew for her new skipper.

"Jolly good uncle," said Roger.

"He is," said Jim. "You see I left Rugby last term and I had a bit of luck with a scholarship to Oxford, and he promised her to me if I did.

Not much rheumatism about him either. That was only his joke. He's coming cruising next week."

Not another word had been said about their spending a night in the *Goblin*. Perhaps, they were thinking, it had been just politeness when Jim Brading had said he didn't see why they shouldn't, so there was really nothing to be disappointed about. And then, suddenly, the offer was made again, and Mother was there to hear it, and somehow, now, after Jim's falling asleep on the table, it sounded different, more real, more as if it were meant, more possible altogether.

"What are you going to do till he comes?" asked Roger.

"Hang about," said Jim. "And look here, I meant what I said. Why shouldn't you join for a few days? I can cram in four of you . . ."

"Sleeping on board," said Titty. "Oh, Mother . . ."

"They'd love it, of course," said Mother, "but I can't let them go just now. Their father's on his way home, and we've come here on purpose to meet him at Harwich, and I can't meet him and have to explain that most of his family's gone off to sea."

"I wouldn't take them to sea," said Jim. "There's the Orwell and the Stour and Harwich harbour. If you'll let me have them for three days there's lots we could do without ever going outside the Beach End buoy."

"I say, Mother, couldn't we?" said John.

"He's got an engine," said Roger.

"You go right down into a real cabin," said Titty.

"I've four proper bunks," said Jim. "The only

trouble is I'm a bit short of bedding. I've only got blankets for two . . . But I'm sure I could borrow some . . ."

"Roger!"

But Roger was out of the room already, and the higher notes of eager talk could be heard from the other end of the passage. Almost at once he was back.

"Miss Powell says it's quite all right," he said. "We can take the blankets off our beds."

"Oh, Roger!" laughed Mother. "I never said you could ask her. I really can't take the risk. We may get a telegram from Daddy any day, and you don't want to miss being at Harwich to meet him."

"But you said you didn't think he could be here before Saturday?" said Titty.

"And what if Saturday comes and you are all floating about on the river?"

Jim Brading looked round the table at the eager faces of his would-be crew. He had made that first suggestion almost in fun, but now it did seem rather a pity if they couldn't come. He rather liked the idea of having for once a crew a little younger than himself.

"If you say when you want them to be back, I'll promise they shall be at Pin Mill in plenty of time," he said. And then, "We could report by telephone every day, from Ipswich, or Felixstowe Dock, or Shotley, wherever we happened to be . . ."

"Can't I go too?" said Bridget.

"You're not old enough," said Mother, "and there isn't room for you anyway."

John half jumped up from his chair.

"She's going to say 'Yes,'" he almost shouted.

"Well, I don't think it's fair," said Bridget. "I've been growing up as fast as I can."

"I'm not asked, either," said Mother. "And, Bridget, somebody's got to stay and take care of me."

"I could sleep in the cockpit all right," said Jim doubtfully, "but even if I did there wouldn't really be room for six."

"No. No. No," said Mrs Walker. "I didn't mean that. Bridget and I have a lot to do. But, mind you, I haven't said they can come . . ."

"But you're going to," said Roger.

"Daddy always says, 'Grab a chance and you won't be sorry for a might-have-been,'" said Titty.

"We'd learn an awful lot," said John.

"I'm going to sleep on it," said Mother. "And Mr Brading must sleep on it too. He may wake wiser in the morning and not want to clutter his boat up with a cargo of children."

"Mother!" said Susan who, so far, had not put in a word.

But Mother was not to be moved. "We'll sleep on it," she said, "and think about it again in the morning . . . if he hasn't sailed away in a hurry to be rid of you. And now, Bridget ought to be in bed, and so ought Mr Brading . . . Remember he was at sea all last night."

"We'll see him off," said Roger, as Jim Brading, who at the thought of sleep was once more feeling his eyes closing, got up and thanked Mrs Walker for his supper.

It was growing dark outside, very dark, and they used their pocket torches to find the *Imp*, and to help Jim Brading to launch her off the hard.

"Thank you very much for letting us come on board," said John.

"Thank *you*," said Jim Brading.

Not one of them, not even Roger, said a word about joining the *Goblin*. They felt, somehow, that it would not be fair. Mother had said that he was to sleep on it, and sleep on it he must.

"Good night!" they called as he pushed off.

"Good night!" he called back.

The four of them stood on the hard in the darkness as he rowed away. It was a still, quiet night, and they heard his oars long after they could no longer see him. Then they heard a slight bump and the noise of oars came to an end.

"He must be jolly sleepy or he wouldn't have bumped," said John.

A moment later a light shone out through the portholes of the *Goblin*. He had lit the lamp in the cabin. They lingered, watching. The light went out.

"I say," said Roger. "Do you think he had time to undress?"

CHAPTER III

"WE'VE ALL PROMISED"

"Where's Mother?"

Mother's bedroom door was open, but there was no one inside. John banged on the door of the room in which Susan, Titty and Bridget were finishing their dressing.

"We're just coming down," shouted Bridget. "Susan's nearly done my last plait."

"Mother's gone out," cried Roger, as John came down into the little parlour. "And her toast's getting cold."

They went to the door that opened into the garden and saw Mother coming across from the boatsheds. They ran down the steps to meet her.

"Hullo!" she said, and then, as she saw them look out beyond the hard to make sure that the *Goblin* was still lying there moored among the other yachts in the morning sunshine, she told them something that filled their hearts with hope. "I've been collecting testimonials for that young man."

"Good ones?" asked Roger.

"Everybody here seems to think a lot of him. Miss Powell says he's the best-heartedest young man she ever knew. Frank, the boatman, says, 'What he don't know about handling that boat of his won't help anyone.' The boatbuilder says he'd trust him anywhere, and that old man scraping spars says, 'They don't fare to come to no harm along of Jim Brading.'"

"You're going to let us go," said John.

"He may have thought better of it," said Mother.

"But if he still wants us . . ."

"It almost looks as if I shall have to," said Mother. "But I wish I could ask Daddy . . ."

"Daddy'd say, 'Go . . .'"

"I believe he would," said Mother.

"Mother's going to let us go," shouted Roger as they met the others at the door.

"Wait till he asks you," said Mother.

They looked far away at the trim white *Goblin* lying to her mooring with the little black *Imp* lying astern of her. Yes, Jim Brading was aboard, or the dinghy wouldn't be there. But there was no sign of anybody stirring.

"He's still asleep," said Mother. "Let's go in and have our breakfast."

They were eating bread and marmalade when something large darkened the window and they saw Jim Brading looking in.

Bridget was off her chair first and ran to the door.

"Come in, please," she said.

"Did you have a good sleep?" asked Roger as seriously as he knew how.

"Splendid, thank you, and a good swim round the ship this morning. I'm all right now. Mrs Walker, I am most awfully sorry about the way I went to sleep on the table last night."

"Rubbish," said Mother. "It was a charming sight and we all enjoyed it. Come in and sit down. Roger, get another cup out of the cupboard. There's plenty of coffee in the pot. Well, now you've seen these animals in the morning

light, you won't want four of them in your little
ship. I've told them you won't, so you needn't be
afraid they'll be disappointed."

Roger was on the point of protesting, but
did not. He waited, cup in hand.

"How soon can they come aboard?" said Jim.

*

Five hours later John, Susan and Jim Brading
were resting in the cockpit of the *Goblin* after a
hard morning's work and a luncheon of bread and
cheese and ginger beer. "No good starting with a
fresh lot of things to wash up," Jim had said, "just
when you've scoured the sink and got everything
spick and span." So they had flung their crumbs
to the gulls, washed their plates and swilled out
their mugs over the side, wiped them and put
the plates in the cupboard where they belonged
and hung the mugs once more on the hooks over
the sink. Mrs Walker and the others had gone
to Ipswich to get stores ... "The fo'c'sle feeds
itself, of course," Mrs Walker had said ... and
Jim, Susan and John were sitting in the cockpit
and keeping an eye on the shore where the tide,
as it was not long after high water, was lapping
against the walls of the Butt and Oyster.

Jim was smoking a pipe with a good deal
of care, not letting go of it with his fingers for
more than a minute at a time. The others were
watching him with respect.

"I only began it these holidays," Jim confessed.
"My uncle made me promise not to till after I left
school."

"Do you like it?" asked Susan.

"It's very nice after work," said Jim.

"It must use an awful lot of matches," said Susan, as yet another was thrown overboard to join the long trail of dead matches that was floating with the tide.

"Tobacco's a bit damp," said Jim. "Bother it. It's gone out again."

"I found a tin of brass polish when I was tidying the place where the lamps are," said Susan. "Do you think it would be all right if I had a go at that porthole." She was looking at the porthole through which the steersman could see the compass, which was hung inside the cabin, over the sink.

Jim puffed out some smoke and looked at the porthole as if he was seeing it for the first time.

"It has gone a bit green," he said. "You simply can't keep them bright. I don't think I've touched it this year. But, you know, Uncle Bob and I will never be able to live up to all this tidiness after you've gone."

John said nothing. He knew Susan. They had had a busy morning, ferrying all the blankets and pillows lent by Miss Powell, and four small knapsacks, each with night things and a bathing suit and a change of clothes. When all this had been dumped down the companion-way into the cabin, it had looked as if there would never be room to turn round. But they had given Susan a free hand down there, while they rowed ashore twice more to fill the water-carrier at the tap in the boat-builder's yard, and, when they had emptied the second lot of water into the tank under the cockpit floor, they had looked down into the cabin and found it strangely empty. All the blankets had been rolled up into neat bundles. There was one at the head of each bunk. And Susan was on her knees with a bucket and a swab, cleaning the cabin floor, and looking very much as if she did not want to be interrupted. So they had left her to it and gone to work on deck. "Better learn the ropes," Jim had said. Three times they had hoisted the mainsail and lowered it again, and the last time John had been allowed to do it by himself, Jim watching and saying nothing, except right at the end, when he reminded John to slacken away the topping lift so that the sail should take the weight of the boom. Then Jim had explained the reefing gear, and taken a little brass crank from a locker in the cockpit, and brought it forward and fitted it in its place, and shown John how to reef, by turning the crank and easing off the main halyard inch by inch at the same time, so that the boom turned slowly round and round, winding up the sail. Then John had learnt the trick of the rolling jib, and how to make the foot of the staysail fast, and how to clip its hanks on the forestay. By that time the warm August sun had taken the damp out of the flag halyards, so that they had gone slack and the burgee on its stick at the masthead was swinging about all cockeye, and Jim had told John to tighten it up, and had shown him how to lower it hand over hand so that it came down without jerks, how to hoist it in the same way, and how to make the halyards fast with a rolling hitch. And now, sitting in the cockpit, after all that pulling and hauling, John

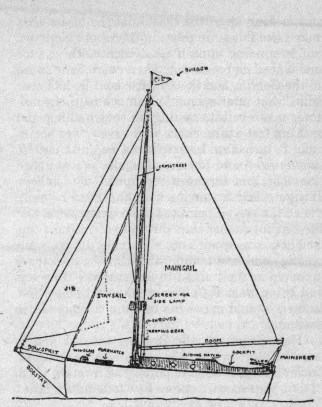

FIRST AID

was looking up at the mast, and the blocks that were hard to see up there in the bright sunlight, and reminding himself what each block was for and where its rope went. There were more ropes in the *Goblin* than in any little boat he had ever sailed, but after spending half the morning pulling, making fast, casting off, overhauling and making fast again, John, very happy, was beginning to hope that he might not be quite useless as a crew. As for Susan, when she had scrubbed the floor, and arranged the bunks, with pillow, blankets and a knapsack at the head of each, tidied the shelves, cleaned the cooking stove, and cleared out quantities of dirt from odd corners, she had got, so to speak, into her stride, did not want to stop, and, even while watching for the others from the cockpit, liked to feel that the time was not being wasted. A proper go with brass polish and rag would make the compass porthole fit to look at.

"Here they are!" Jim Brading was the first to see the borrowed dinghy, with Mother, Bridget, Roger and Titty aboard, putting off from the hard. "I say, your mother knows how to handle a boat."

"She's jolly good at it," said John.

Mrs Walker was rowing, working the boat neatly through a crowd of other dinghies anchored off the hard. Roger was in the bows. Titty and Bridget were in the stern sheets.

"They've got a lot of parcels," said Susan. "I'll have to finish that porthole another time." She slipped down into the cabin and put the brass polish back in its place in the forepeak. She came up again. It seemed a pity that her tidy cabin was going to be upset almost at once, but she supposed all that stuff would stow away somewhere.

Jim stowed his half-smoked pipe, that had gone out again, carefully away in one of the cockpit lockers.

Mother shipped her oars as the loaded dinghy slipped up alongside.

"Let's have that painter, Roger," said Jim. "Hullo! What's that you've got in your hand?"

"Penny whistle," said Roger. "At least it cost more than a penny."

"He *would* buy it," said Bridget.

"Well, Captain Flint's got an accordion in the houseboat," said Roger.

"Can you play it?" said Jim.

"Just a bit," said Roger. "I left mine behind at school."

"Luckily," said John.

"Unluckily," said Roger. "I can play it, really. A boy at school taught me." He looked round a little doubtfully. Nobody said he couldn't, but Mother laughed and said, "Mr Brading'll always be able to throw him overboard if he makes too much noise. May Bridget and I come aboard to say goodbye to the crew? We'd like to see the ship they're going to sail in."

"Please do," said Jim. "Come on, Bridget."

"I'll come next," said Mother, "and then Titty can hand up the parcels. Don't squash that bag with the sausage rolls. Or the one with the doughnuts, and do take care of the pork pie."

"We'll never get all this eaten," said Jim. "I mean, it's very good of you, but . . ."

"You don't know what these people can do

till you've seen them try," said Mother. "There's this evening, and all tomorrow, and most of the next day."

"Come down and look at the cabin," said Susan, who wanted Mother to see it while it was still tidy. "Look at the stove, two burners, and a real sink on the other side."

"She's a most comfortable little ship," said Mother, going down the companion-steps and looking round her.

"Titty and I are going to sleep here," said Susan, showing her the fore-cabin. "And Roger's going to be there, and John here."

"And poor Mr Brading?" said Mother. "It looks quite a hard floor."

"I can sleep like a log anywhere," said Jim, looking down from the cockpit, adding with a grin, "even with my head on somebody else's supper-table."

"And look how the backs of the bunks open," said Susan. "Huge cupboards behind."

"What," said Mother. "Stewed pears, and peaches, spaghetti and tomato, pea soup . . ."

"Uncle Bob and I mostly live out of tins," said Jim.

"It's wonderful what good things you can get in tins nowadays," said Mother. "What's this . . . a whole shelf of steak and kidney puddings?"

"They're very easy to hot up," said Jim.

"The things I've brought you are much tamer," said Mother.

"Doughnuts," said Roger, "and sausage rolls, and rock buns, and a lot of ham all ready for eating."

"Here's the pork pie," said Bridget, who had climbed down into the cabin, using only one hand while she clasped the pork pie to herself with the other.

"Lots of apples," said Roger, "and the right sort of chocolate, in squares. And two dozen eggs and a whole pound of butter."

"And two loaves of bread . . ." said Titty.

"I ought to have thought of that," said Jim. "But I mostly eat biscuits and so I forget. Uncle Bob always brings a loaf."

"Cherry cake," said Roger.

Susan had cleared a shelf in one of the cupboards, and was packing the parcels away as they came down.

"Better keep the ham outside the cabin," said Mother.

"I'll put it in one of the cockpit lockers," said Jim.

"And what about the bread and the cake?"

"There's a bread-tin specially for them in the cupboard under the sink," said Susan.

"And now," said Mother, when she had seen everything, and all the provisions had been put away and the cupboard doors closed, and the cabin was once more the tidy place that Susan had made it, "have you got a chart? Do show me just what you're going to do."

Jim pulled his chart of Harwich harbour from under one of the mattresses. "Keeps them flat," he explained as he let the mattress fall back into its place. He spread the chart on the table and explained.

"Where are we now?" said Mother.

"Here," said Jim, pointing with a finger.
"There's Pin Mill, and this is the river going
up to Ipswich. We might go up there tomorrow and look at the docks. Then going the
other way it comes down to meet the Stour
at Shotley."

"They'll like to see Shotley," said Mother.

"The two rivers together make Harwich harbour," said Jim, "and those buoys . . . Beach End
and Cliff Foot . . . show where the harbour ends
and the sea begins."

"And you won't go out beyond them?" said
Mother.

"No," said Jim.

Time passed very quickly while they were
looking at the chart and talking of what they
were to do, and how, in the *Goblin*, John and
Susan were to be first and second mate and Titty
and Roger were to be able-seamen.

"I hope they'll do what they're told," said
Mother.

"We'll have to," said Titty cheerfully, "or he'll
stiffen us out rusty corps and dump us to the fish
like the man in the poem."

"He has my full permission," said Mother.

"Oh I say," said Roger, and then, "But perhaps
he hasn't got an iron belaying pin."

"I expect he has," said Mother, and then,
seeing Jim glance up at the clock, she went on,
"How time does fly in a boat. Come on, Bridget.
Why, where is she?"

A faint grunt came from the fore-cabin, where
Bridget had curled herself up in Titty's bunk and
was pretending to be asleep.

"No, no, no," said Mother. "No stowaways . . . though I must say I almost wish I were coming too."

"Let's," said Bridget.

Mother looked at Jim Brading's face and laughed. He had said nothing, but she knew what he was thinking. The *Goblin* was going to be a pretty tight fit for five, and as for cramming in another two, the thing simply could not be done.

"They don't want us," said Mother.

"We do really," said Jim, "only . . ."

"I know," said Mother. "The extra sardine bursts the tin. And you ought to be off. Bridget and I will leave you a clear deck."

Jim glanced at the clock again, and out through a porthole at the hard, half of which had already been left dry by the tide.

"It's all right," he said, "so long as we have the ebb down to Shotley Spit."

"Anybody for the shore?" called Roger from the cockpit.

"Coming, coming," said Mother.

Mother climbed down into the borrowed dinghy and the stowaway was helped down by the skipper. Mother had already kissed goodbye to mates and able-seamen alike.

"Now Susan," she said, "and you too, John. No night sailing . . . No going outside the harbour . . . And back the day after tomorrow . . . You don't want to risk not being here to meet Daddy . . . Promise."

"We promise . . ."

"I promise too," said Jim. "It's high water at

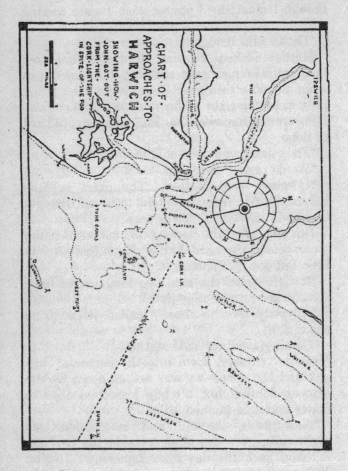

CHART·OF·
APPROACHES·TO·
HARWICH

SHOWING·HOW·
JOHN·GOT·OUT·
FROM·THE·
CORK·LIGHTSHIP·
IN·SPITE·OF·THE·FOG

SEA·MILES

HISVICH

PIN·MILL

STOUR·R.

ORWELL·R.

FELIXSTOWE

LANDGUARD

WALTON

STONE·BANKS

ANDREWS

PLATTERS

CORK·SAND

CORK·L.V.

WEST·ROCKS

CUTLER

DEBEN·R.

300 SCALE YARDS

BAWDSEY

WHITING

SHIPWASH

SUNK·L.V.

four on Friday. I'll have them here at Pin Mill
in time for tea."

"We've all promised," said Susan.

"That's all right," said Mother. "Have a good
time. And if you land at Harwich or Shotley
or Ipswich or other outlandish ports, you might
telephone to Miss Powell's . . ."

"And send picture postcards," said Bridget.

"I say," said Titty, "do let's send a postcard
to Nancy and Peggy and the D's."

"I'll send one for one tonight . . ."

"I've got some postcards," said Jim. "But only
plain ones."

Mother and Bridget waited alongside while Jim
dug out a postcard. Titty drew a picture on it of
the *Goblin* under full sail in enormous waves. She
wrote the address, "Aboard the Yacht *Goblin,* Pin
Mill. Master . . ." "You sign your name here." Jim
signed. "Mates and crew . . ." "And now we'll all
sign." The pencil was passed from hand to hand.
Titty added, "We're afloat now and just going to
SAIL." She addressed the postcard to Captain Nancy Blackett, at Beckfoot, and handed it down to
Mother. "It'll cheer them up a lot," she said. "They
never thought we'd get any sailing so soon. And
anyhow not sleeping in a boat."

Roger dropped the coiled painter into the bows
of the borrowed dinghy, and Mother pulled clear
and watched while skipper and crew set to work,
hoisting the mainsail, unrolling the jib, getting the
staysail all ready to hoist as soon as they should be
under way. Mother grew happier every moment as
she saw how easily everything went and what a
good capable skipper Jim was . . . There was no

hurrying. Nothing had to be done twice . . .

There was a pause. Skipper Jim came aft to the tiller. He was looking aloft and around. Yes. Everything was ready. The mainsail was set, and the boom slowly swinging to and fro. The jib was flapping. They were ready.

"John!"

"Sir!"

"Will you be ready to cast off the mooring. Take the buoy clear of the bowsprit shrouds. Drop it clear of the side when I sing out. We'll go off on starboard tack, and round under the blue boat's stern."

"Aye, aye, Sir!"

"Isn't it funny to hear John saying, 'Aye, aye, Sir!'" said Bridget.

"He's quite right," said Mother. "He's mate in this ship, not skipper."

The wind was filling the mainsail and the *Goblin* began to creep up. Her head was being pulled round. The sail flapped. The boom swung slowly across and the mainsail filled again.

"Now," sang out Jim, "cast off!"

There was a splash as the mooring buoy dropped into the water.

"All gone, Sir!" shouted John.

"Up with the staysail," called Jim. "Haul in the port jib sheet, Susan. That's right. She's sailing."

The *Goblin* swung round, gathered speed, cleared the stern of the blue *Coronilla* and headed out through the fleet as John sent the staysail up hand over hand. Two heads bobbed up out of *Coronilla*'s cabin as the tall red sail of the *Goblin* swept by.

"Going for a sail? Lovely day for it."

"Only in the harbour," called Jim.

"Goodbye," called Mother and Bridget, waving from the dinghy. "Goodbye."

"Goodbye, fare thee well," called Titty.

"Goodbye, goodbye," shouted the others.

They were fairly off. John hurried aft along the side deck, and waved as soon as he was safely in the cockpit. In another moment the Butt and Oyster disappeared behind an anchored barge. They were clearing the last of the yachts. Titty, Susan and Roger looked back to see Mother and Bridget in the dinghy making for the hard.

"Hullo!" cried Roger. "There's Miss Powell come down to see us off."

Miss Powell was standing on the hard, waving. The skipper and crew of the *Goblin*, slipping away down river in the afternoon sunshine, waved back.

*

Mother and Bridget joined Miss Powell on the hard and tied up their dinghy.

"Don't you wish you were going too?" said Miss Powell to Bridget.

"Somebody had to stay to look after Mother," said Bridget.

"I do hope I've done right," said Mother. "It seemed a pity not to let them take a chance like that. I know their father would have wanted them to go."

"They'll take no harm with Jim Brading," said Miss Powell.

"Anyway, they're not going outside the harbour," said Mrs Walker.

Far away down the river the little red-sailed *Goblin*, with the small black *Imp* dancing astern of her, disappeared behind a moored steamer.

CHAPTER IV

DOWN THE RIVER

THEY were off. After one frantic moment when Jim was letting out the mainsheet and Susan was doing her best with the jib sheet and the cockpit seemed to have almost more ropes and people in it than it could hold, things had settled down. The *Goblin* was slipping away down the river so quietly that they had to look astern at the ripple under the bows of the *Imp*, or close down at the water, or at the trees on the banks, to feel they were moving at all.

"Two days ago," said Titty quietly.

"We were in the train," said Roger.

"I was in the Downs wishing for wind," laughed Jim.

"And now we're all here," said Titty.

"You take her, John," said Jim, "while I go forrard and tidy up."

"Do you think I can?" said John, looking anxiously ahead at the big steamer moored in the middle of the river, unloading grain into barges tied alongside her.

"Of course you can. Keep her as she's going. Close by the steamer. This side of her, or we'll lose the wind."

The tiller was in John's hands, and Jim had run forward over the cabin roof and was busy with the halyards on the foredeck. John had done his best after hoisting up the staysail, but he had not really known how best to tuck the coil of rope out of the way. And now here he was, steering the *Goblin*. Titty and Susan were looking at him anxiously. Could he do it? It was not nearly as hard as he had feared. Just like steering old *Swallow*. He looked far down the river and chose a distant point on which to steer. The wind was light, and they were not moving fast through the water, but the ebb tide was carrying them along, and, in no time, it seemed, they were under the steep black side of the steamer. He would not look at her, but out of the corner of his eye saw that high black wall, that made the barges look small. The rattle of the derricks sounded close above him, and the shouts of the stevedores, as sack after sack of grain went down to be stowed in the holds of the barges. They had passed her.

"La Plata," read Roger, looking up at her stern.

"That's the River Plate," said Titty, and looked ahead again, like John, as if the little *Goblin* herself were bound for the Atlantic and the coasts of South America.

Jim Brading came back, and John made way for him at the tiller.

"You carry on," said Jim. "You're doing very well."

On they went. The trees on both banks of the river came to an end. Green fields sloped down to the water's edge on one side. On the other, further side, was a sea wall covered with long grass and green saltings and shining mud uncovered by the tide. Cormorants were on the edge of the mud, like black sentinels. A grey heron was wading. A flock of gulls swung up into the air and round to settle again in almost the same place. Now that they were clear of the trees, they had a rather better wind, and the *Goblin* heeled over, just a little, enough to make Titty take hold of the coaming that made a sort of wall round the edge of the cockpit, enough to make Roger think of doing the same, but stop with hand outstretched to find that with feet wide apart he could stand upright without holding on to anything.

"Can I go on the foredeck?" said Roger, after waiting a moment to make sure that the *Goblin* would not heel over any further.

"Better not," said Susan.

"He'll be all right while we're reaching like this," said Jim.

"Go along the windward side," said John. "Hang on to that rail while you're getting there, and then take a grip of the halliards."

"Do be careful, Roger," said Susan.

There was no need to say that. Roger climbed out of the cockpit, almost decided that he would go forward some other time, but then worked himself slowly along, sat down on the fore end of the cabin roof, and then, warily, pulled himself to his feet.

"I can hear the water creaming under her bows," he said, looking over his shoulder.

Jim was sitting on the cockpit coaming, relighting the tobacco that was left in that pipe of his, and giving a first lesson in pilotage.

"Red buoys and conical buoys to starboard," he was saying. "Black can buoys to port ... That's coming up with the flood," he explained. "So we leave the conical ones to port now, because we're going out, not coming in."

"That's a conical one?" said Titty.

"Yes. That's on the edge of the mud off Leving-
ton Creek, and that other one, just ahead, with a
cormorant on it, is conical, too. That's a can buoy,
over there, the black one off Collimer Point."

"So we leave it to starboard?" said John.

"Pass close to it. You can bring her head on
it now."

There was a shout from the foredeck. "Steamer
in sight," cried Roger. "We're going to meet her.
You can see her above that point where the river
turns to the right . . ."

"To starboard," murmured Titty.

"We'll give her plenty of room," said Jim, looking
at the smoking funnel and white-painted bridge
that were showing over the low green spit of
Collimer Point. "But her wash'll shake us up a
bit. Better come along aft, A.B. Roger. Wind's
going southerly, too. We'll be tacking down the
next reach. A long leg and a short . . ."

Roger worked his way back with a grave face,
but grinned happily when he was once more safe
with the others in the crowded cockpit.

"Close to the buoy," said Jim, "and then we'll
squeeze a bit closer to the wind."

HARWICH LOOKED LIKE AN ISLAND

The black, flat-topped buoy off the point was
coming quickly nearer.

"It's got a red light on the top of it," said Roger.

"Port-hand buoy," said Jim.

"But we're leaving it to starboard," said Roger.

"Because we're going down the river, not up," said John, and Jim grinned to hear his lesson passed on so very soon after it had been learnt.

Even before they had passed the buoy they could see down a new wide reach of the river, the last before it opened into Harwich harbour. Far away ahead of them they could see the little grey town, with its church spire and lighthouse tower, and steamers at anchor in waters wide enough to be almost like the sea. There were no woods now on either side, and the whole feel was different. It was as if the river were already saying goodbye to the land. Harwich, in the distance, looked like an island. Sailing down that last reach did not feel like sailing on a river any more. And now they were going to meet a steamer coming in from the sea.

She was a smallish, rusty-sided steamer, going up to Ipswich Docks, Jim said. He was keeping a wary eye on her. He had hauled in the mainsheet, and told John to keep his eye on the burgee and do the best he could. Nearer and nearer the steamer came. No. She was not going fast enough to let them pass under her stern, and the *Goblin* was not going fast enough to pass clear of her bows.

"We'll probably have to go about," said Jim.

"But steam gives way to sail," said Roger.

"Not when sail's got plenty of room and steam's got none to spare. We've got the whole river to play with, and she's got to keep in the deep water channel."

Titty, Susan, Roger and John all caught their breaths at once. A single short booming hoot startled the river.

"Gosh! What's that?" said Roger.

"One hoot," said Jim, putting down his pipe in a safe corner. "She's going to starboard. Come on. We've got to leave her to port." He slipped down from the coaming and made ready to deal with the ropes. "Here you are, Susan. Cast off this backstay when I sing out. Titty casts off the jib sheet. I'll do the rest. Bring her round, John, as soon as you like . . ."

"I say," said John, "hadn't you better . . ."

"Rot," said Jim. "Just think you're going about in a dinghy, but don't swing her round too fast. Now then . . ."

"Ready about," said John stoutly and put the helm down.

"Cast off jib sheet," said Jim, "backstay . . . That's right, Roger, cast off the staysail sheet."

The *Goblin* swung round under the steamer's rusty sides and headed back for the western shore. High above them, in the wheelhouse of the steamer, a man lifted his hand and let it drop forward again, the grave salute of East Coast sailors. The crew of the *Goblin* waved cheerfully back.

Presently they went about again.

"Good as clockwork," said the skipper, when all was done, and the *Goblin* was once more heading down river. "Now then, Mate Susan, give the first mate a rest and let's see how you can steer."

John handed over, glad to have steered so far without making any serious mistakes. Anyhow, if he had made mistakes they had not been serious enough for the skipper to say anything about them.

"Keep the sails just full," said Jim, as Susan

took the tiller. "Don't try to go too close to the wind. We'll have to go about again, anyhow, to clear Fagbury Point."

"No waggles in the wake, Susan," said Roger. "Titty and I'll tell you every time you make one."

"No talking to the man at the wheel," said Jim. "Don't you listen to them, Susan."

But Susan, with her eye on the burgee, hardly heard him and had not heard Roger at all. What was the rule? Don't let the sails flap, and don't let the burgee blow away from the mainsail. She had not sailed with Daddy as John had, going out of Falmouth in a fishing boat. But she could steer the little *Swallow* just as well as John, and she knew John was watching and as keen as she was that she should make no mistake in steering the *Goblin*.

Jim once more perched on the edge of the coaming, and Titty and Roger watched with awe blue puffs of smoke from his pipe blowing away with the wind.

"Hullo!" he said suddenly. "Somebody on the mud by Fagbury Point. Where are those glasses?"

"I know where they are," said Titty, and dived down into the cabin to fetch them. She was up again in a moment. "Here they are. I say, John, it feels simply lovely being inside her while she's going."

Jim was looking through the glasses. "Yes," he said. "She's on the mud all right. And there she'll sit till the tide comes up again to float her off."

"A wreck!" exclaimed Titty.

"She won't take any harm there," said Jim. "Not as if she were outside . . ."

But at this moment Able-seaman Roger suddenly jumped up on one of the seats in the cockpit and was pulled down again by John.

"Look! Look!" he cried.

"Where?"

"It's gone . . . There it is again . . ."

"But where?"

For a moment there was nothing to see and Titty and John thought it was just Roger stirring everybody up about nothing. Then, about thirty yards away the water was broken, a shining black lump heaved up, dived under, rolled up once more and disappeared.

"It's a black pig," said Roger. "Swimming."

"Porpoise," said Jim Brading, relighting his pipe. "There's another away to starboard."

"Close to us," shouted Roger.

"He's diving right under us," said John. "There he is . . . on the other side."

"Whales," said Titty. "Almost . . ."

"Altogether," said Jim. "They *are* a sort of whale . . . animals you know, not fish."

"It's as good as being at sea," cried Titty. "There they are again. They're racing us. One on each side . . . Oh, I do wish Nancy was here."

Porpoises were too much, even for Susan.

"There's a baby one," she cried. "There all by itself . . ."

"Look out for your steering," said John, putting out a hand but not actually touching the tiller.

Susan gulped, hearing the jib give an impatient flap. "Sorry," she said, and the sail filled once more. "There it is again. Is it a baby? All right, John, I won't look again."

"Oh," sighed Titty, "they're beating us."

The porpoises were already showing far ahead. Here and there a black fin cut the water, a black back rolled up into sight, hurrying, hurrying, and further and further away.

"Off to sea," said Jim.

"Lucky black pigs," said Roger. "Gosh! They'll be bobbing up to look at steamers in the middle of the night . . . I wish we were."

"What? Bobbing up from under water?" asked Jim.

"Going to sea," said Roger.

"Well we aren't," said Susan, almost impatiently. "We've promised. Isn't this good enough for anybody?"

Jim laughed. "I'd like to take you out myself. Perhaps, when your father comes and Uncle Bob and I get back . . . Look here, Mate Susan. We'll go about now, and then when we go about again, we'll be able to fetch the Fagbury buoy and have a look at Titty's wreck."

Susan looked at John, but John, Titty and Roger were all busy with the ropes they had to cast off or haul in. She bit her lip pretty hard. "Ready about," she called, and swung the *Goblin* steadily round. There was a moment of frantic business in the cockpit as she came head to wind and the headsails blew across and the boom swung over. Then the *Goblin*, with all sails drawing, was heading across the river. There was a general coiling up of ropes, and everything was at peace once more.

But not for very long. Once more it was "Ready about!" "Let fly jib . . . Backstay . . . Haul in jib

. . . And staysail." The *Goblin* never lost her way for a second as she swung round and headed for the red buoy off Fagbury Point, and that green boat that lay there, heeled over on one side with her boom down on the cabin top and her sails all anyhow.

"I wish we could go on for ever," said Titty.

"You'll have pretty sore hands," said Jim, "handling ropes for the first time."

Roger and Titty looked at their hands.

"Hot, but not sore yet," said Roger, rubbing his tenderly together.

Nearer and nearer they came to the green boat that had gone on the mud. Two men were balancing themselves on her sloping cabin top, looking miserably at the water that was ebbing away and would presently leave their vessel high and dry. As the *Goblin* came nearer, first one man and then the other slid down and wriggled sideways through the door into the cabin.

"They'll be awfully uncomfortable with the cabin all on one side," said Roger.

Jim grinned. "They don't want to talk about it," said he. "I wouldn't either. There's no excuse for going aground in a place like that. Lucky for them they're in the river."

"Why?" said Roger.

"Easily lose the boat going aground outside. Let alone the chance of being salvaged by a lot of pirates, like poor old Ellwright who had that boat before them . . ."

"Pirates?" said Titty.

"Longshore sharks," said Jim. "Same thing. That's right, Susan. Carry right on. Carry right on for Shotley Spit buoy. Yes, the big one right ahead now. A shallow runs right out to it from the point. See that ripple and the gulls on the mud?"

"Do tell us about the pirates," said Titty.

"Wait till we're at anchor and I can get at the chart and show you just what happened," said Jim.

"Where are we going to anchor?" asked John.

"Jolly good place," said Jim. "Off Shotley Pier in the Stour, so that we can nip ashore and let your mother know I haven't drowned you."

"Telephone?" said Susan.

"Yes. There's one close to the end of the pier. There's the pier. You can just see it now. But we've got to get round the Spit buoy before turning."

The *Goblin* had left the river now and was sailing out into the wide waters of Harwich harbour where the Stour and the Orwell meet before pouring out into the sea. Far away over blue rippled water they could see tall mills by Felixstowe Dock, and the green sheds which Jim told them were for seaplanes, and a huge gantry for lifting the planes out of the water, and a low fort of stone and earthwork on a sandy point. On the other side was another low point, and the houses of Harwich, and a white lighthouse on the water's edge, and dark wooden jetties, and barges at anchor. Three big vessels were lying quite near them, near enough for them to see the flags on the jackstaffs. Jim pointed out a Dutch motor vessel, a Norwegian timber-ship with a tremendous deck cargo of golden sawn planks, and a rusty-sided Greek with a tattered flag of blue and white stripes.

"But where are the boats that go to Holland?" asked Titty.

Jim pointed away up the Stour, where, on the Harwich side, they could see the masts and funnels of the mailboats along the Parkeston quays.

A small dumpy steamboat came hurrying out from the Harwich jetties. Its deck was crowded with people.

"That's the ferry," said Jim. "It runs between Shotley and Harwich and Felixstowe."

"We'll be going by it," said Roger. "We'll be going to Harwich to meet Daddy's steamer as soon as we know which day he's coming."

They sailed on as far as the first of the big anchored steamships, and then swung round to work their way up into the Stour.

"We're hardly moving," said Roger.

"Tide's against us," said Jim. "But it's all right. She's creeping over it."

Slowly, though the water was swirling past the *Goblin*'s sides, they drove up, past the Spit buoy, past Harwich town, past the Trinity House steamer, past a group of anchored barges.

"See those vessels?" said Jim. "The red ones, with lanterns half-way up the mast, lightships in for repairs. There's the *Galloper*. Her place is thirty miles out . . . There's the *Outer Gabbard*. Each one shows a light of its own, you know, flashes so that you can tell which it is, and each has its own fog signal."

"We've seen ones like them," said Titty, "in Falmouth. Daddy used to say they came in for cough lozenges when their throats got sore."

"I was forgetting you knew all about them," said Jim. "Have you heard the Cork yet? That's our local nightingale."

"Four moos a minute," said Roger. "John timed them, the evening we came. Miss Powell told us what it was."

"If there's any mist you'll hear it better tonight," said Jim. "It's a good deal nearer when you're down here. Close by those piers, Susan. We'll anchor just beyond the last of them. Well, what do you think of Shotley? If your father's going to be stationed here I expect you'll get some sailing in some of those boats. They all belong to the Navy."

SHOTLEY PIER

They looked up at the buildings on Shotley Point, houses, a water tower, and a flagstaff on the naval school as tall as the mast of a sailing ship. On one of the black, wooden piers were a lot of grey naval cutters and whalers and gigs. If Daddy's coming to Shotley meant sailing in those boats, and living somewhere up there, able to look down on Harwich harbour and on the ships coming in and out, things were going to be very good indeed. They looked at the place as people look at a stranger with whom they know they are going to have a lot to do.

Slowly the *Goblin* crept by the first of the piers.

"Only just enough wind," said Jim. "Can't take off sail till the last minute. Keep her going just as she is, close past the far pier. Bring her into the wind when I shout. I'm going forrard to get the anchor ready."

"Can I come too, to see how you do it?" said John.

"Come on."

Susan, Titty and Roger were alone in the cockpit. Susan was steering just as well as she knew how.

"They'll want those headsail sheets cast off at the last minute," she said, not taking her eyes off the pier ahead. "You take one, Titty, and Roger the other, and be ready when he shouts."

Up on the foredeck Jim was stocking the big anchor, and ranging a lot of chain on deck, while John sat on the cabin roof watching everything he did.

Jim was lowering the anchor over the bows. "You have to be careful the stock doesn't catch on the bobstay," he said, and John took a good grip of the forestay and looked over Jim's shoulder and saw how the anchor hung free at the *Goblin*'s forefoot, all ready to let go.

"Now for the staysail," said Jim.

From the cockpit the others watched, Susan doing her best not to think of anything but her steering. The staysail came rattling down. John was bundling it out of the way, while Skipper

Jim was standing up judging the distance they had gone beyond the pier.

"Straight into the wind," he called. "Cast off the jib sheet."

"That's yours," said Titty, and Roger cast it off. The jib was rolling up on itself. The boom swung slowly over the cockpit. Jim was stooping again. There was a sudden rattle and roar as the chain ran out, and the anchor went down.

"We've arrived," said Titty.

"Susan's still steering," said Roger.

Susan with a sigh of relief let go of the tiller.

"Who's for the shore?" called Jim Brading from the foredeck.

CHAPTER V

SLEEPING AFLOAT

"Who's for the shore?"

"I am," shouted Roger.

"Let's all go," said Titty.

But Susan looked through the cabin to the clock that was fixed on a bulkhead under the barometer.

"Hadn't they better have supper first?" she said. "It's after their time and Mother's sure to ask."

"Right, Mister Mate," said Jim. "If supper won't take too long to make, John and I'll be getting the sail stowed and the lamps filled. What are you going to give us?"

"There are all those sausage rolls," said Susan.

"What about hotting up tomato soup?" said Jim. "You'll find a row of tins in the starboard cupboard."

"Good," said Roger.

"I'll do the lamps right away," said Jim. "I've got to fill the cooking stove and it'll last for a couple of days. Let me just get the mainsail down."

The big red sail came down and the boom was lowered into its crutches. The sail was loosely stowed and tied. "No need to put the cover on," said Jim. "We'll be hoisting it again in the morning." Then from somewhere under one of the cockpit seats Jim pulled out a paraffin can and poured a lot of oil into the reservoir of the cooking stove.

Susan lit the burners and put a kettle on one to boil up some water for tea, and sitting on the companion-steps with a long spoon kept the tomato soup stirring slowly round a saucepan on the other. Meanwhile, Jim filled the cabin lamp and the riding light. He shook the big oilcan. "Enough to fill the riding light again tomorrow," he said.

"What about the red and green ones?" said Roger, who had been looking at them, roped in their places in the fo'c'sle. "Didn't you say they'd burnt out?"

"We shan't need them," said Jim. "It isn't as if we were going to sea. We shan't be sailing at night."

*

Though it was quite light outside, it seemed already dark in the cabin. Jim lit the cabin lamp and a mellow light shone on the faces of his crew. Supper was over. Everybody had thought well of the tomato soup and agreed with Roger that nobody who had not tried would believe how much nicer sausage rolls tasted in a ship's cabin than when eaten anywhere else. Susan had washed up, passing the wet things to be dried by Titty and Roger.

"Lucky they're Woolworth's unbreakables," Jim had laughed as one of the bright red plates had slipped out of Roger's fingers, bounced on the floor and rolled away to hide itself somewhere under the engine. He had gone down on hands and knees to look for it with a big electric torch. "What a torch!" Roger had said, and then as Jim scrambled to his feet again with the torch and the plate, he had exclaimed at the red light coming through the plate. "Good as a port light," Jim had said, and had held the plate in front of the torch and lit up everybody's face in turn with a warm red glow. "Grand torch," he said, flashing it on and off. "It makes as good a stern-light as anybody could want. I had to show it to a steamer two or three times the night before last."

"Do tell us about it."

"About what?"

"The voyage from Dover," said John.

"Nothing much to tell," said Jim, putting the plate away, dropping the last of the spoons into the spoon-box and showing Susan just where it had to go in the cupboard so that it shouldn't rattle. Earnestly watched by all of them, he filled and lit his pipe.

"Tell it, anyway," said Roger.

"You were all alone," said Titty.

"I know old *Goblin* pretty well," said Jim. "Nothing in being alone, except that I couldn't get any sleep. It wouldn't have been so bad if I hadn't had to hang about so long outside."

"Outside what?"

"The shoals," said Jim. "There was a bit of fog and I didn't want to come nosing in all blind. I don't like shoals when I can't see the buoys. Look here, you'd better have a squint at the chart. Heave up, John. You're sitting on them."

John got up, and Jim Brading rolled up the end of the mattress on the port bunk and pulled out a couple of charts.

"Have you got charts of everywhere?" asked Titty.

"No," said Jim. "Only Southampton to Harwich. Uncle Bob'll bring any others we're likely to want when he comes. He's got hundreds. Here you are. Here's the Downs. Oh. You know you were asking about Ellwright and the pirates. Here's where he got stuck. Just off Ramsgate. See those dotted lines. Shoals. He got on in a fog. He'd have been all right if he'd only kept clear of the coast. Jolly sight safer out at sea."

He spread the chart on the table and heads bumped together as they looked at it in the light of the cabin lamp. Jim Brading turned on his big torch and flashed a brilliant white circle on the chart to make the dotted lines of the shoals and the tiny drawings of the buoys show up better.

"But what about the pirates?" said Titty.

"Longshore sharks," said Jim grimly. "Well, poor old Ellwright was aground here, where my finger is. Calm weather, too. Pretty safe. He had only to put a kedge out and wait for the tide to rise. But some longshore sharks came off to him in a boat when the fog lifted, and offered to pull him off and tow him in. He had to get back to work next day, and he was jolly pleased, and they had him off in two minutes and towed him into the harbour, and he thanked them and was going to give them ten bob . . ."

"Gosh!" said Roger.

"And they wouldn't take it," said Jim. "They said they'd salvaged the boat, and that she would have broken up if they hadn't towed her off, which wasn't true, as he only went aground for lack of wind."

"You mean they wouldn't take anything?" said Titty.

"Jolly decent of them," said Roger.

"Wasn't it?" said Jim. "No. They wouldn't take his ten bob. They wouldn't take a pound. They put in a claim for salvage, a third of the whole value of the boat, and as the poor chap hadn't any money, he had to sell his ship to pay them. You see, he'd let one of them come aboard, to fasten a rope or something, and the man took the tiller and that was that . . . So if ever you get into trouble, never take a tow from anybody if you can help it, and never ever let anyone come aboard. Bang their hands with a boathook. Do anything you like, but keep them off. If they see a chance of claiming they've saved your ship, they'll take it."

"He had to sell his ship?" said Roger.

"Yes," said Jim, "and by the time he'd paid the sharks, and their lawyers and his lawyers, he'd next to nothing left. He hasn't got a ship any more."

"What beasts!" said Roger.

"One way of making a living," said Jim. "No. The only people to take aboard are pilots, and you don't want even to take a pilot if you can help it. I never do. Can't afford it."

"Where are the shoals off Harwich?" said John. He was almost more interested in that than in the sad tale of the loss of Jim's friend's boat. After all he was actually sitting in the cabin of the *Goblin*, and the *Goblin*, only two nights before, had been out at sea waiting to come in.

"Other chart," said Jim, and spread the second chart on the top of the first. "There's Harwich. Here's Shotley, where we are now . . . and that . . . and that . . . and that are the shoals outside . . . Shoals all over the place . . . West Rocks and the Gunfleet and the Cork Sand . . . this bit is uncovered at low water . . . Shoals all over the place. The big ships come in like this. They make for the Cork light-vessel . . . through this big opening between the shoals, and then slip along between the Cork Sand on one side and the Platters and Andrews on the other. Well, *Goblin* likes to do the same, specially in fog or dark . . . No fun for a little boat to crash into an unlighted buoy. Easily sink her, even if she didn't go aground. No. Only one motto for the *Goblin*. When in doubt keep clear of shoals . . . Get out to sea and stay there."

John listened, telling himself that he too would have that motto, when at last he should have a ship of his own. He too would do the same . . . He gripped an imaginary tiller . . . Shoals to the right . . . Shoals to the left . . . Out to sea . . .

"What did you do?" asked Roger.

"Just jilled about," said Jim, "outside everything, first on one tack and then on the other, till things cleared. Then I made the Sunk light-vessel, then the Cork, and so to Beach End buoy (you'll see that tomorrow) and into Harwich harbour and up the river to Pin Mill, where I made a bad shot at picking up my mooring and was glad of help from some jolly good sailors who were hanging about in a dinghy . . ."

"How did you know we weren't pirates?" said Titty.

"Or sharks?" said Roger.

"Just guessed," said Jim, laughing.

"Lucky for us," said Roger. "Or we wouldn't be here."

"And for me," said Jim. "Look here. It's getting dusk outside, and we'll put up the riding light. No good having a barge coming along to bring up and sending us to the bottom in the middle of the night."

"And then let's go and telephone," said Susan. "It's getting on for nine, and we ought to try to get some milk for breakfast."

A few minutes later, when the riding light, burning palely in the dusk, had been hung from the forestay, the *Imp* was pulled alongside. It was a close fit for five. John and Roger sat in the bows, Susan and Titty in the stern, while Jim paddled them off to the wooden steps of Shotley pier, which had seemed quite small when they had sailed past in the *Goblin*, but towered above them when they came close under it in the *Imp*.

"Can I tie her up?" asked Roger. "I always tie up *Swallow*."

"All right," said Jim, and watched while Roger made fast the end of the *Imp*'s painter.

They walked ashore along the uneven planking of the old pier. They had come only a few miles from Pin Mill, but it felt like landing in a different country.

"What's that bag for?" asked Roger, looking at a rolled-up green kitbag in Jim's hand.

"Pop," said Jim. "I'd forgotten the *Goblin*'s cellar's getting rather low."

"Grog," said Titty.

"They've a very good brand of grog in Shotley," said Jim. John looked at Susan.

"We ought to pay for it," said Susan. "I'm sure Mother'd want us to."

"I've got enough for that," laughed Jim. "Besides, Uncle Bob'll be here on Monday."

They went to the inn, and watched a dozen bottles of ginger pop being stowed away in Jim's green kitbag. The landlady took the milk-can from Susan and filled it. Then she took them to a little room where there was a telephone, and Jim rang up Miss Powell's at Pin Mill, and put two pennies in the box. They stood round him, listening to his half of the talk, guessing for themselves what was being said at the other end.

"Is that Miss Powell? How are you? Jim Brading. Can I speak to Mrs Walker . . . How do you do? . . . We've anchored for the night by Shotley pier . . . Yes, Shotley . . . Very well indeed . . . Yes, they've had supper . . . They're all here . . . going to bed as soon as we get back aboard."

"Let's all say Good night," said Titty.

"We'll have to be jolly quick," said Roger. "Or it'll be another twopence."

The telephone was passed from hand to hand. Each one of them said "Good night," and heard Mother's voice, oddly near, yet far away, saying "Good night" to these mariners who had come ashore from an anchored ship. Jim took the telephone again.

"We'll ring up again tomorrow if we have a chance," he said, "and we may come up to have a look at Ipswich with the flood tide. We'll

signal as we pass Pin Mill . . . I beg your pardon
. . . Who? Susan? . . ." He turned to Susan. "It's
Bridget, with something to say to you."

Susan took the telephone and listened for a
moment. "Take care of her," she said. "Good night,
Bridgie," and passed the telephone back. Jim was
saying "Good night" too. "I'll be as careful as ever
you could wish . . . Good night."

"They gave us quite a long time for two
minutes," said Roger.

"What did Bridget want?" asked Titty.

"Only to say that she was going to sleep in
Mother's room," said Susan.

They were silent as they left the inn and
started back to the pier. It was funny how
that single sentence made them feel almost like
deserters. Bridget was sleeping in Mother's room
because the expedition in the *Goblin* had left Alma
Cottage a rather lonely place for both of them.

*

It had been still dusk when they went into
the inn, but those few minutes had made a
difference. Lights had sprung up everywhere.
There was a string of blazing lamps over the
Parkeston quays at the other side of the river.
There were lights in Harwich town, and lights
far away across the harbour in Felixstowe. The
flashes from the buoys that had been hardly
visible by day kept sparkling out, now here,
now there, the white flash of Shotley Spit buoy,
the red one of the Guard buoy, and others of
which they did not know the names. There
were riding lights on all the anchored barges

and on the ships in the harbour. The wind had dropped to nothing, and long glittering lanes led from every light across the smooth water. And there, a little way above the pier, lay the *Goblin*, she too with a light on her forestay, and the glimmer of the cabin lamp showing through her portholes.

They climbed down the steps in the dusk, found the *Imp*, and pushed off.

"We're going to sleep in her," said Titty, almost under her breath, as they drifted silently towards the *Goblin* with her riding light, and her tall mast dimly showing against the darkening sky.

"Pretty soon, too," said Susan. "It's after your bed-time already."

They climbed aboard.

"Take the painter a moment, John, while I hang a bucket from the *Imp*'s bows."

"What for?"

"To catch the tide, so that she won't come nuzzling round, knocking us up in the middle of the night."

It was done, and the *Imp* went astern, to lie quietly, a black blot on the dark water.

Roger, as soon as he was aboard, had dodged down below and scrambled up again through the forehatch. The others were still in the cockpit when the penny whistle broke into the quiet night . . . "We won't go home till morning . . . We won't go home till mooooorning." The musician, sitting on the cabin top, was getting through it with expression, but as fast as he could before he should be stopped.

"Shut up, Roger," said John.

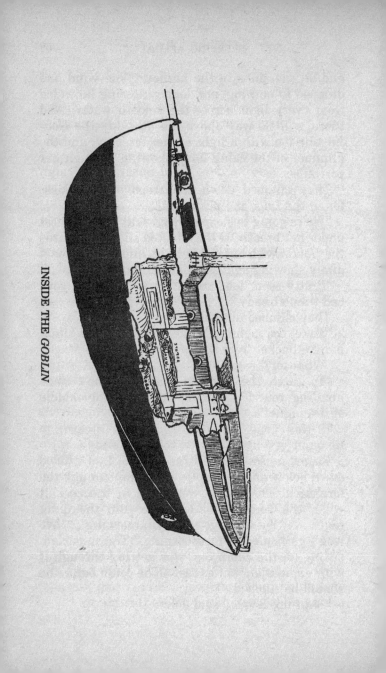

INSIDE THE GOBLIN

"Don't spoil it," said Titty, and she did not mean Roger's music.

"Oh well," said Roger, ending with a long-drawn note. "I'll never learn if you don't let me practise sometimes."

"All right," said Titty. "But not now."

"There's a lot of dew," said Susan. "The cabin top's quite wet. What are you sitting on, Roger?"

"The usual place," said Roger, feeling with a hand. "It *is* a bit damp."

"We'll get up early tomorrow," said Jim, "and go down to the harbour mouth with the last of the ebb and have a look at the sea."

"Come on to bed, you two," said Susan.

*

For a little while longer, Jim and John stayed on deck, Jim smoking his pipe in the cockpit, standing on a seat so that he could lean comfortably on the boom. Down below in the cabin they heard the small noises of people moving about, and one squeak on the penny whistle, which came to a sudden end. Presently Susan's voice called up, "We're all in bed. But I didn't know how to fold Captain Jim's rugs. He's going to be awfully uncomfortable."

"Coming," said Jim. "I'll deal with them." He shook out his pipe, and John heard the ashes hiss as they met the water.

For a few minutes John stood in the cockpit alone. Almost the *Goblin* might have been his own ship, and he at peace after a long voyage, taking a last look round before turning in.

"John," came the skipper's voice from the cabin, and John jerked back to real life. "Your watch below. Come on down. I'll be asleep the moment I put my head on the pillow, and it won't be much fun to be waked by you trampling about on the top of me while you're getting into your bunk."

John went down. Roger had been tucked up on the port bunk, but in the light of the cabin lamp John could see a bright and wakeful eye. Jim was sitting on the starboard bunk, where John's blankets were waiting for him. Looking through into the fore-cabin, John could see a lump under the blankets in each bunk . . . Titty and Susan ready for sleep.

"Sorry," he said, "I won't be a minute," and while the skipper went up on deck to make sure that all was well with the riding light, he tore off his clothes, got into his pyjamas, stuffed the clothes into a heap under his pillow, and wriggled into bed.

The skipper came down and took his shoes off.

"Aren't you going to undress?" said Roger.

"No," said Jim.

"Gosh!" said Roger.

"Somebody's got to be on hand," said Jim. "I'm anchor watch really. But I'm going to sleep just the same. Where's the big torch?" He found it, blew out the cabin lamp, lay down, and rolled the blankets about him on the cabin floor.

*

They slept. The night was so calm that it was hard to believe that the Goblin was afloat. It was an hour later before they were reminded that they were sleeping in a ship and that she was very near the open sea.

A drumming noise broke the stillness. Suddenly the *Goblin* seemed to be picked up, flung aside, and picked up again. Everybody was awake in a moment.

"What's happened?" said Roger.

The white light of the big torch shone upwards from the cabin floor.

"Steamer going out from Parkeston," said Jim. "Sorry. I forgot to warn you. There'll be another in a minute or two ... There she goes ... One for Holland and one for Denmark ... They go out every night."

Again the *Goblin* was violently rocked in the wash as the second steamer went by. Roger, kneeling in his bunk, holding on by the shelf behind it, caught just a glimpse of the steamer's blazing lights.

"I wonder if those porpoises'll be seeing them," he said, as he settled again under his blankets. No one answered him. A few minutes later the *Goblin* had stopped rolling, and the only sound to be heard in her cabin was the quiet breathing of her sleeping crew.

RIDING LIGHT

CHAPTER VI

"NOTHING CAN POSSIBLY HAPPEN"

Splash! Splash! Splash! Splash!

It was seven o'clock in the morning and they had been waked by a shout down the forehatch, "Rouse up there, the watch below. Anybody want a dip? No time to spare, if we're going down the harbour before the tide turns." Jim was already on the foredeck, in bathing things. There had been a hurried rush to join him.

"Now then," he said, and dived.

But there were four splashes only. John, Susan, Titty and their skipper came up with the taste of salt water in their mouths, shaking their heads and blowing like seals.

"Come on, Roger," said John.

"It's waste not to use the ladder," said Roger.

Jim had slung a rope ladder over the side, and fastened it to the shrouds to make it easy for people to climb aboard again. Roger meant to use it both ways.

"Go on, Roger! Head first!" said John.

But Roger was already on the lowest step of the ladder and was feeling the water with the toes of one foot.

"It isn't very cold, really," he said.

"It's boiling," said Titty. "Come on."

Roger lowered himself into the water, let go of the ladder, and swam to join her.

"Don't forget the ebb," said Jim, bobbing up

MORNING DIP

close beside them. "Keep close to the ship, and keep swimming. I don't want to have to come rowing after you in the *Imp* if you get swept away. Go on. Swim hard, against the tide. Just a dip and out again. We can have another later on ... There's no time now. We ought to be sailing."

Susan was already at the ship's side, hanging on to the ladder.

"Out you come, Roger," she said. She climbed up with the help of the shrouds, grabbed one of the towels she had left on the foredeck, and began a rub down.

One after another they joined her, and the foredeck ran with water.

"Come on, Titty," said Susan. "We'll get into our clothes in the cockpit. No good bringing half the North Sea into the cabin."

"It isn't the North Sea," said Titty. "It's only the river."

"Just as wet," said Susan cheerfully. She had been a bit bothered about that bathing from the anchored *Goblin*. Roger had been able to swim for some time now, but swimming in deep water, with the tide ready to carry you away if you gave it a chance, was very different from swimming in the lake. She was a good deal relieved to have everybody safe back aboard. Now she would get those burners lit and make them start the day properly with a solid breakfast.

But that was not to be. She was hardly dressed and down in the cabin filling the kettle before Roger, a pink savage with a towel round his middle, crawled aft along the cabin roof and looked down at her through the companion-hatch.

"I say, Susan," he said. "Please pass up my clothes and John's. Jim's got into his already and they're just going to hoist the mainsail."

"Oh, look here," said Susan. "They can't start with nothing to eat after bathing."

"I thought so too," said Roger. "But Jim says there isn't time to wait for it."

Susan put her head out, to see Jim, fully dressed, and John, a kilted savage like Roger, busy with the ropes at the foot of the mast.

"You must have breakfast first . . ." she began, but they were thinking of quite other things.

"Good," said John. "Susan's ready."

"Hang on to that crutch, Mate Susan," called Jim, "and slack away a little mainsheet."

In a ship, orders are orders, and Susan took hold of the crutch, and Titty, who had been squeezing bathing clothes over the side, let out some mainsheet, and they saw the boom cock up over their heads.

"Breakfast," began Susan again. "You must have something to eat before starting."

"Have it when we're under way," called Jim. "Here you are, John, hold on to that while I get the main up. Susan! Can you just cast off that tyer, just above your head?"

The mainsail, fold on fold, was lifting off the cabin top. Roger had scrambled out of the way. The sail was up. Susan heard Jim say, "Slacken away the topping lift. That's right . . ." and then, "Hullo, there, Mate Susan. Stand by the tiller, will you? A.B. Titty, will you be ready to harden in the port jib sheet . . .? No. No. Not until I've got the anchor off the bottom. Where's that mop,

A.B. Roger?"

The next moment she heard the rattle of
the chain coming in. It was no good talking to
them about breakfast. The chain was coming up,
fathom after fathom. Roger had untied the mop,
and John was dipping it over the side and washing
the Shotley mud off the cabin. "Now then, Roger,
let the jib unroll. Yes. That's it. Just cast it loose.
She's up and down now." Jim was looking over
the bows. He was hauling again. "Anchor's up,"
he shouted. "Back the jib, John." The chain was
coming easily now, hand over hand. There was a
sudden clank. "That's right. Hold the jib out to
starboard till she pays off. That'll do. Let draw.
Haul in your jib sheet, A.B. Titty."

They were off. The boom had swung across,
the mainsail had filled and the *Goblin* was sailing.
Susan, at the tiller, was steering out to clear the
Shotley piers, past which the tide was carrying
them. Jim, wiping the mud off his hands on the
wet mop, raced aft, cast off the mainsheet and
pushed the boom out by hand.

"Not enough wind," he said.

"But we're moving," said Titty.

"Mostly tide," said Jim. "Look at the mainsheet."

The boom was swinging in again, and the
mainsheet hung in loops, dragging in the water.
There was not wind enough to pull it straight.
Still, the *Goblin* had steerage way, and the tide
was helping her, sweeping down towards the harbour.

"Can't somebody else steer?" said Susan.
"They've simply got to have their breakfasts. It'll

be all right if they have just cornflakes and milk, to begin with . . ."

"Not down in the cabin," said Titty.

"You can have it in the cockpit," said Susan.

"I say, Jim," said Titty. "Do you think I might steer just for a bit."

"Go ahead," said Jim. "You can't do much harm with the wind like this."

But Susan had hardly slipped down the companion-steps, to get plates and spoons and cornflakes, before she remembered something else that ought to come before breakfast.

"Nobody's cleaned their teeth," she said. "Can they have fresh water for it?"

Jim laughed. "Half a glass each," he said. "But salt water to spit into. Aboard ship fresh water's liquid gold."

So a bucket was dipped overboard, and, while Susan was ladling cornflakes into the plates, the crew of the *Goblin* cleaned their teeth, John taking the tiller when it was Titty's turn.

"There's lots more to do, Mate John," said Jim. "We haven't half got the mud off the foredeck. Better not put your shoes on till we've done washing down."

No one could have guessed, looking at the *Goblin* sailing slowly past Harwich out of the mouth of the Stour, what a lot was being done aboard. There was hardly a ripple on the water. A misty sun was climbing over Felixstowe. Smoke was rising from the chimneys of Harwich, where people ashore were cooking their breakfasts. The smoke climbed almost straight up and then drifted idly away. The movement of the tide shook the reflections of the anchored barges and of the ships in the harbour and of the grey jetties and houses of the town.

"If you've done with that bucket," said Jim, "we'll have it forrard for sloshing water on the deck."

"There's a barge with its riding light still burning," said Roger.

"Sleeping late," laughed Jim. "They'd be up and moving if there was a bit of wind. But I dare say there'll be wind later. Or fog. Or both. You never know what's coming with a day that starts like this."

As he spoke a long wail sounded from out at sea.

"Beu . . . eueueueueueueu!"

"Cork lightship," said Jim. "They've got enough mist out there to give them their twopence an hour."

"Twopence an hour," said Roger.

"They get twopence an hour extra while that row's going on in their ears."

"First course. Cornflakes and milk," said Susan, passing up the filled plates one after another. "Who's ready?"

"I am," said Roger.

"Everybody," said Jim. "What about yourself?"

"I want to get the stove lit . . . Tea and eggs," said Susan.

"No hurry," said Jim. "We're not going to start our breakfast if the cook isn't tucking into hers."

So Susan came up too, and deck-washing came to an end, and the crew of the *Goblin* made themselves comfortable, sitting on the cabin top and in the cockpit, with deep plates full of milk and cornflakes.

"Beu . . . eueueueueueueu . . ."

Every fifteen seconds that long wail sounded from somewhere beyond Felixstowe, somewhere out at sea.

"But it isn't foggy here," said Roger.

"It may be outside," said Jim. "It's nothing like as clear as it was last night. You won't be able to see the lightship even when we get down to the Beach End buoy. On a clear day you'd see it easily. And we ought to be able to see the Naze from here."

They had passed the Guard buoy now, and were heading down as if for the sea. Now and again a gentle little puff filled the mainsail, and by watching floating weed they could see that they were moving through the water as well as past the land. A seaplane roared overhead and came down on the water in a long swoop, sending the spray flying. "Like a swan coming down in Rio Bay," said Titty. Far ahead of them they could see the two buoys, Beach End and Cliff Foot, that marked the way out for the steamships. Beyond those buoys the sea seemed gradually to lose itself in mist. It was hard to tell where sea ended and mist began, though here, in the harbour, they could see quite clearly the houses of Felixstowe on one side and Harwich on the other.

"It doesn't look as if it could ever turn into waves," said Titty, staring across the wide stretch of almost oily water.

"I've seen it just like glass," said Jim. "And then, an hour or two later, I've been taking in reefs and having a job to keep the sea where it belongs."

"Where's that?" said Roger.

"Not in the cockpit," said Jim with a grin.

Not in the cockpit. They looked at the cockpit, comfortable and deep, with its high coamings, with the deck outside them and the water so far below. It seemed impossible that ever the sea could come heaping up and throwing itself aboard.

"Has it ever come in here?" said Titty.

"Hasn't it?" said Jim.

"What do you do when it does?" asked John.

"Pump it out," said Jim, and he showed them the small square lid in the seat, and the pump handle just below it, and let Roger pump for a little, just to feel what it was like.

Light though the wind was, and fitful, the last of the ebb took them down the harbour at a good pace. Those outer buoys, at first dim black specks in the distance, were now clearly different. One, with a pointed top, was the Beach End buoy. The other, flat-topped, was called Cliff Foot. Roger was told he had earned full marks by remembering that Beach End must be the starboard hand buoy and Cliff Foot the port hand buoy for vessels coming in. Not even Susan wanted to go below deck just now when they were coming nearer and nearer to the place at which harbour ends and sea begins.

"Are we going right down to the buoys?" asked

John.

"I promised you shouldn't go further," said Jim, "and it really isn't worth while going so far on a day like this. There's nothing to see . . ."

"But sea," chuckled Roger.

"Not much of that with this mist," said Jim. "Never mind. We'll go up to Ipswich this morning, and it may be clearer when we come back."

"Did you mean it when you said we'd signal to them as we go by?" asked Titty.

"Why not?" said Jim. "We've got the flags . . . But Mrs Walker won't have a code book."

"She knows the flags," said John.

"Good," said Jim. "We'll hoist o and к to the cross-trees to show her that everything's all right."

"May we look at the flags?" asked Titty.

"They're in a roll in the shelf over your bunk," said Jim, and a minute later Titty had brought up the white canvas roll and opened it, and they were looking at the neatly folded flags, each in a labelled pocket of its own. She found the o, red and yellow, and the к, yellow and blue.

"Do you ever use them?" asked John.

"Only for fun," said Jim. "Uncle Bob likes to have them just in case he wants a pilot or something."

"What's the flag for a pilot?" asked Titty.

"S," said Jim.

Titty pulled out the s flag, a dark blue square with a wide white border.* She folded it and put it away. "We shan't want a pilot flag on this

---

* In the International Code of Signals the signal for a pilot is G, with upright stripes of blue and yellow.

voyage," she said regretfully.

"I never take a pilot anyhow if I don't have to," said Jim, thinking of something else. He stood up and looked round the sky.

"We'll have to get that staysail up without waiting for the deck to dry," he said. "And we'll have to turn back in a minute. There's hardly enough wind to beat the tide, and I don't want to drift out beyond the buoys . . ."

"Let's turn now," said Susan.

"Oh I say, let's go as far as the buoys," said John.

"Clang!"

"What's that?"

Susan, Roger and Titty all asked at once, in different tones.

"Somebody ringing at us?" said Titty.

"Breakfast gong," said Roger.

"It's the Beach End buoy," said Jim. "There isn't enough of a ripple to set it properly booming. Look here, John. I'll have that staysail up. Will you go through the cabin and pass it up through the forehatch?" He went forward along the side deck.

"Bring her round, Titty," he said.

"But nothing happens," said Titty, putting the tiller across first one way and then, desperately, the other. The mainsail hung idle and half the mainsheet was slowly sinking. The wind had dropped to a dead calm and the *Goblin* had not even steerage way.

A bundle of red staysail appeared through the forehatch.

"No. Stow it away again," said Jim. "There's no wind at all."

He hurried aft, looking over his shoulder at the buoys. The ebb was still running and the buoys were coming rapidly nearer.

"Feet out of the way everybody," he said. "Got to start up Billy. That's it. Feet out of the way."

"Can I be engineer?" said Roger.

"All right. Get the spanner out of that starboard locker. Got to give a turn to the grease cap on the stern tube. Always have to do that before starting."

He lifted a board in the floor of the cockpit, reached down with Roger trying to look over his shoulder, came up again, wiped his hands on a lump of cotton waste, and put the board back into place.

"Hope to goodness Billy has the sense to start when he's wanted," he said, as he dropped down the companion, into the cabin.

"Clang!"

"We're nearly out of the harbour already," said Susan.

"You try to steer," said Titty, and John took the useless tiller.

From below in the cabin came talk of grease and oil, Roger's voice, "Oh let me pour it in," and Jim's, "Buck up, then," and "Keep clear while I swing her." They had almost reached the Cliff Foot buoy when there was the noise of the engine being turned over, and suddenly the quiet of the windless morning was broken by a slow chug, chug, that quickened, chug, chug, cough, chug, and steadied again.

Jim, followed by Roger, shot up from below.

"Good old Billy," he said. "Just in time to keep

our promises." He leaned out over the transom, to see that the water was coming out of the exhaust as it should, hauled in the *Imp*'s painter, for fear it should get wound up by the propeller, and turned to Roger. "Now then, engineer. Put her ahead. Shove that lever right forward."

"Look out for your leg, Titty," said Roger, and as Titty took her leg out of the way he pushed forward the lever that stuck up out of the cockpit floor. The engine took up the work, and Jim let go the *Imp*'s painter and fiddled with the throttle. The chug, chug quickened.

"She's moving," said Roger, looking over the side.

"That's right, John. Swing her round. We'll go close up the Felixstowe side." He was rattling in the mainsheet, and made it fast with the boom well in. They could hear the relief in his voice.

"What would have happened if the engine hadn't started?" said Titty.

"We'd have drifted out to sea," said Jim.

"Which way?"

"Out by the Cork lightship," said Jim. "The ebb runs about north-east. We shouldn't have gone very far because it's practically low water and the flood would have brought us back. But I promised your mother we shouldn't go outside the buoys."

"We all promised," said Susan, looking astern at the Cliff Foot buoy.

"Beu . . . eueueueueueu," sounded the foghorn from the lightship.

"Thank goodness the engine did start," said Susan, and then, in an altogether happier voice, she said, "I'm going to light the stove now, and we'll have the rest of breakfast. Boiled eggs, I think, and tea."

"Good," said Jim. "We'll lower the mainsail and roll up the jib. No good pretending to be sailing. We'll run up to Ipswich with the motor."

"Can I try steering her?" said Roger.

"Go ahead," said Jim. "Keep her straight for the mills by Felixstowe Dock. Yes. Those high buildings."

"I can't see while everybody's just in front of me," said Roger, feeling that for the first time he was in command.

Except, perhaps, Roger, not one of them would in the ordinary way have been glad to feel that the *Goblin* had her motor running. But today, even John, who cared for nothing but sail, was grateful to the little engine chug-chugging away under the companion-steps. It had saved them at the very last minute and was taking them quickly further and further away from the danger of a broken promise.

John and Jim quite cheerfully rolled up the jib, took the weight of the boom on the topping lift, and let the useless mainsail down on the cabin top. Jim put a couple of tyers round it, for neatness' sake, leaving it all ready to hoist again as soon as there should be some wind.

The stove in the galley at the side of the companion broke into a cheerful roar. Susan passed up a saucepan for salt water in which to boil the eggs.

"Will she go any faster?" said Roger, talking very loudly, because of the noise of the engine.

Jim grinned and bent down and opened the throttle. The *Goblin* shot forward, the water foamed past her sides, and the *Imp*, towing astern, had a good bow wash of her own.

"Gosh," said Roger. "We'll be at Pin Mill in two minutes."

"About an hour," said Jim.

Already the *Goblin* was pushing up the channel close to the pierheads of the dock at Felixstowe. They could read the name of the Pier Hotel, and could see a red motor-bus by the dock gates.

"Water's boiling," said Susan. "How many eggs shall I put in?"

Down there, at the foot of the companion-way, she was close to the engine, and, in the cockpit, they could not hear a word that she was saying. They leaned forward to listen.

"How many eggs for the skipper?" she shouted.

"TWO!" shouted Jim.

"SOFT OR HARD?"

"HARDISH."

Looking down, they could see her putting the eggs, one by one, into the saucepan of bubbling water. She was just putting the saucepan back on the stove when they looked suddenly at each other. The noise of the engine was changing. That quick, whirring, chug, chug, chug slackened, faded out, stopped, went on once more, and finally, after a few half-hearted chugs, died altogether. For a moment there was silence. It was broken by Roger.

"Oh I say, Susan, you've gone and stopped the engine."

"I haven't touched it," said Susan from below.

Jim jumped down and gave a few turns to the starting handle. The engine coughed, chugged twice, and stopped once more. He climbed out into the cockpit, swept Titty off the starboard seat, lifted a little lid, like the lid over the pump, unscrewed a cap beneath it, and peered down into the petrol tank.

"Bone dry," he said. "What an idiot. I must have used more than I thought the night before last. I ought to have filled up before starting. Hi, Roger, look out . . ." He glanced round at the Felixstowe pierheads and then the other way. The *Goblin* was still moving. He swung her round slowly and let Roger have the tiller again.

"Keep her heading like that, on Harwich Church spire. She'll carry her way till she's out of the channel. We'll anchor on the shelf . . ."

Susan had come up from below. All four of them stood in the cockpit, while the *Goblin*, steered by Roger, slipped silently, more and more slowly, past a large flat-topped buoy on which they could read "NORTH SHELF." Jim had run forward, and they could hear chain being hauled up on deck.

"She's hardly moving," called John.

There was a great splash and then a rattle of chain as the anchor went down. Jim made fast and came aft.

"What are we going to do?" asked Roger.

"Wait for wind," said John.

"Get some petrol," said Jim. "There's a garage between here and Felixstowe, and if I can catch that bus it won't take ten minutes." He was rummaging under the cockpit seat and presently pulled out an empty petrol tin. "Couldn't have run out of petrol at a better place," he was saying. "I never use old Billy if I can help it, but I hate to feel he isn't on duty and ready if he's wanted. Next time I miss my moorings, there may not be a boatload of sailors to take a rope for me. I'll just get a couple of gallons and then we'll be all right. Blooming donkey I was, not to have looked in the tank yesterday."

"What about getting more paraffin at the same time?" said Susan.

Jim emptied his trouser pockets. Half a crown, a shilling and a few coppers. "Jove," he said. "It's a good thing I didn't get two dozen of pop instead of one last night. No, I won't bother about paraffin. Plenty in the cabin lamp, plenty in the cooker. I filled the riding light when I took it down, and we shan't be using the others."

"I've got some money," said John, feeling for a half-crown that he knew was somewhere mixed up with the string in a trouser pocket.

"Never mind," said Jim. "We shan't want paraffin before we get back to Pin Mill."

"Can I come with you?" said Roger.

"No," said Jim. "I'll be quicker by myself."

He pulled the *Imp* alongside and slithered down into her, while John passed down the red petrol tin.

"Cast off," said Jim. "You're in charge, John. Don't let anybody fall o.b. If anybody does, bat them on the head. Tide's just turning now. Dead low water. She'll be all right here, out of the channel. I'll be back in half a jiffy. Nothing can possibly happen . . ."

John dropped the coiled painter into the *Imp*'s bows. Jim spun the *Imp* round and pulled for Felixstowe Dock. The water spirted from under her bows at every stroke, and the sharp ripple of her wash spread across the oily water.

"Can't he row?" said Roger.

CHAPTER VII

"HE'S BEEN AN AWFUL LONG TIME..."

THEY watched the little black dinghy disappear
between the pierheads into Felixstowe Dock.
Susan suddenly remembered the eggs.

"They'll be as hard as stones," she cried. "It's
ten minutes past eight and I put them in at ...
Bother it. When did the engine stop?" She took
the heavy saucepan off the stove and fished for
the eggs with a tablespoon. One good thing about
being anchored. No deafening, throbbing engine,
and those two would at least be able to finish their
breakfasts properly. She set up the folding flap of
the cabin table, and took the roll of American cloth
from the shelf.

On deck, now that Jim and the dinghy were
out of sight, John was enjoying the thought that
they had the ship to themselves. It did not really
matter, her being anchored. For the moment she
was theirs. He hung the coils of the mainsheet on
the tiller, and told himself secretly that he had just
sailed the *Goblin* from Dover and was waiting to
take the tide up the river.

"John," said Titty. "Where've we come from?"

John started. It was as if she had heard him
speak his thought out loud.

"River Plate," he said. Dover seemed too near,
if Titty also was thinking they had come in from
the sea.

"Months on the voyage," said Titty. "Isn't it

90

lovely to be in home waters at last?" She looked across to the old grey town of Harwich and the anchored steamers and barges, and then back at the tall mills, and the pierheads behind which the skipper and the dinghy had just disappeared. Yes, the red motor-bus was still there. He was going to be in time to catch it. She went on, "To think that last time we anchored there were palm trees on the banks, and crocodiles. I say, it's an awful pity we haven't got the ship's parrot with us, to sing out 'Pieces of Eight!' and make things seem more real."

"Gibber, too," said Roger. "He'd be simply fine sitting on the cross-trees and much happier than in the Zoo."

Titty, looking up at the cross-trees, found it easy to see the monkey and the parrot perched up there side by side.

"They were jolly glad to get into harbour out of the fog," she said, listening to the long "Beu ... eueueueueu" from the Cork lightship out at sea.

"The Goblin's turning round," said Roger.

Not only the Goblin but all the anchored vessels, the big steamers and the barges, were swinging with the tide, and instead of pointing inland were one by one turning their bows towards the sea.

"What's the time, Susan?" said John. "Tide's changed. The flood's just begun to make."

"Sixteen minutes past eight," said Susan. "Is he in sight? Breakfast's all ready."

"There goes the bus," said Titty. "He's had plenty of time to catch it."

"If it's only just gone, his eggs'll be cold by the time he gets back. Come on down and eat yours."

*

It was only the second half of breakfast, but Susan had done her best with it and was a little disappointed that Jim was not there to see his cabin table. She had laid for five, Titty, Roger and herself on one side, Jim and John on the other . . . five red Woolworth plates, five blue egg-cups each with a hard-boiled egg in it, with an extra egg on the plate that was meant for Jim, five spoons, five mugs, five slices of bread and butter, and five apples. It was a pity that he was not here to see the table in its beauty before people had begun eating and pushing things about. Still, it could not be helped. Roger and Titty ought to have had something hot inside them as soon as they came out of the water. Susan did not think of waiting, even to let Jim see the breakfast table at its best. All she said was, "Look here. We'll try to keep his place nice and tidy." So, while the others ate their bread and butter, and took the shells off their eggs (Roger bounced his on the table to prove that it was really hard) and pushed their mugs along for more tea, Jim's corner of the table, in front of his empty seat, remained an example of what a laid place should be.

Two or three times Susan looked out of a port-hole to see if he was on his way back. She was a little bothered about those eggs. "Hardish," he had said. There had not been much "ish" about the hardness of the others, and his would not get

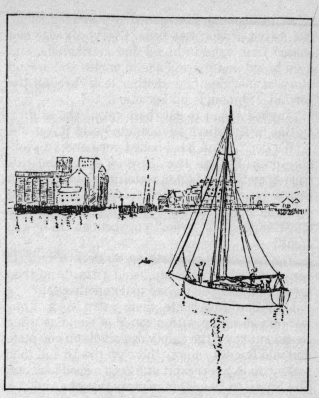

JIM ROWED AWAY

softer by keeping. She leaned over and felt them.
Not as hot as they had been. Everybody else had
passed from eggs to bread and marmalade, and
from bread and marmalade to apples and second
mugs of tea. She had another look through the
porthole. She made up her mind.

"Anybody want to eat those eggs?" she said.

"But he'll be here any minute," said Roger.

"We don't mind hard-boiled ones and he probably does. I'll boil two more for him. And this
time somebody'd better watch the clock. Go on
Roger, you like them hard . . . You have one and
John had better eat the other. I'll do the new ones
four minutes, and I won't put them on till he's in
sight."

"We can keep him talking on deck if he gets
back before they're ready," said Titty. "And then
he won't know you've had to do another lot."

John and Roger ate their extra eggs. They
were finishing up with a round of bananas when
Susan swept all the empty egg-shells on one plate
and told Roger to empty them overboard and then
to stay up in the cockpit and keep a good look out.
She began to clear things away into the sink.

"It's a lot mistier than it was," said Roger,
passing down the empty plate. "But he isn't in
sight anyhow . . . Hullo! There he is."

"Quick!" said Susan. She put Jim's two eggs into
the saucepan. "You keep an eye on the clock, Titty,
in case I forget, and sing out when it's twenty-one
minutes to nine."

"It isn't him," said Roger presently. "It's a bigger boat than the *Imp*, and it's gone away towards
that steamer."

"Oh, Roger," said Susan. "And the eggs are in . . ."

"I bet he'll be in sight before they're ready," said Roger.

"Oh well," said Susan. "He's been such an age, he can't be long now. They won't have time to get cold."

"Time, Susan," said Titty, who had never taken her eyes off the clock.

A minute later, if Jim had come back, he would have found breakfast laid for one on the cabin table, and two eggs, neither too hard nor too soft, still steaming from the saucepan, one in his egg-cup and the other lying ready beside it.

But there was no sign of him, and Susan tapped each egg on the thin end with a spoon, because she had heard that doing so stopped them from getting harder.

*

An hour passed and Jim's breakfast still waited for him in the cabin. The crew were all on deck. Susan had brought up the brass polish and was having another go at the porthole through which the steersman had to look at the compass. There was no point in sitting about doing nothing. John was by the mast, taking the halyards off their pins and putting them carefully back again, learning his ropes, ready for the moment when Jim should come back and they should be hoisting sail once more. A little wind was coming across the water from Harwich, and he knew that if there was any wind Jim would not be using the motor, even if he had a couple of gallons of petrol in the tank. Roger

and Titty, inspired by Susan, were also polishing
brass work and getting quite a shine on the cleats
for the headsail sheets. But all four of them kept
looking across the rippled water to the pierheads
of the dock.

"The bus is there again," said Titty. "That's
the second time."

"What's happened to him?" said Susan almost
crossly.

"If he'd only known the wind was coming he
wouldn't have gone for the petrol," said John.

"He said he wanted to have some anyhow,"
said Roger.

"Well, why doesn't he come back?" said Susan.
"He must have got it by now."

"He's probably met an ancient mariner," said
Titty. "You know, with skinny hand and glittering eye, and they got talking about boats, and
Jim couldn't get away. And when he heard the
lightship howling, he thought it was the loud
bassoon."

"They're earning their twopences," said Roger.
"And it really is foggy now. It's getting foggy even
here."

There was no doubt about it. The long wail
of the lightship that had seemed ridiculous when
they had been sailing down the harbour in the early morning seemed ridiculous no longer. Fog was
coming in from the sea with the tide, and already
things that they had seen clearly had turned into
faint shadows. The North Shelf buoy, quite near
them, was clear enough, but the outer buoys had
disappeared, and they could hardly tell where the
land ended and the sea began at the mouth of the

harbour. That red morning sun was now no more
than a pale spot in the mist.

"Perhaps he isn't coming back at all," said
Roger.

"Rubbish!" said Susan.

"Don't be a little idiot," said John.

Jim had been away so long that the pleasure
of having the ship to themselves had come to an
end. Roger changed the subject.

"Here's the ferryboat again. Gosh, won't it be
fun when we all go to meet Daddy?"

The little ferryboat, crowded with passengers,
had come into sight out of the mist that hung over
the water between Harwich and Shotley. They
watched it hurrying across. They saw it disappear
between the Felixstowe pierheads, where Jim and
the *Imp* had disappeared so long before.

"It'll be coming back in a minute," said Roger.
"Which'll come out first, the ferryboat or the *Imp*?"

Brass polishing slackened. There were long
pauses even in Susan's rubbing of the compass
porthole. John came aft and sat on the cabin top.
All four were watching those pierheads. What
would come out first, the noisy little ferryboat,
or the skipper of the *Goblin* rowing for all he was
worth to tell them how it was he had been kept
so long?

Four times every minute, the long "Beu ...
eueueueu ..." from the Cork lightship, out at
sea, wailed through the mist.

The ferryboat came out, passed to the north
of them, dark against a pale background of
mist, and vanished beyond an anchored
steamer.

And then, suddenly, the fog that had been coming in with the tide closed over them.

"Harwich has gone," said Roger.

"The steamers are fading away," said Titty.

"Felixstowe's going," said Roger. "I can't see the mills. I can't see even the crane."

"Oh John!" gasped Susan.

"If he isn't jolly quick, he'll have to wait till it clears," said John.

"I can't see the pierheads any more," said Roger.

The pierheads, dim and shadowy, were swallowed up in the fog. Titty and Roger, pointing at them, found they were pointing at different places, in a grey wall of fog. For a few minutes they could still see the North Shelf buoy. Then that too disappeared. They could see nothing at all. Whichever way they looked was grey fog.

"Doesn't it taste funny?" said Roger.

"It's half-past eleven," said Susan, after looking at the clock and at the cabin table, where Jim's breakfast still waited and his second pair of eggs had gone cold. "What *can* have happened to him?"

Suddenly the fog was alive with noises. The "Beu ... eueueueueueu" of the Cork lightship out at sea, hooting four times a minute, had been going on all the time. They were accustomed to that and to the noise of the crane in Felixstowe Dock. These were new noises. Somewhere up the Stour there was a sharp howl from the siren of a tug. Then, now here, now there, ship's bells were being hurriedly banged. Again came that distant howl, and again a chorus of ship's bells, of all notes and sizes.

"They don't want to be run into," said John.

"Ought we to hoot, too?" said Roger. "He's got a whacking big foghorn."

"We're at anchor," said John. "We ought to be sounding a bell ... Is there a bell, Susan? I haven't seen one."

"I don't know," said Susan.

"What about banging a saucepan?" said Titty.

"We can't," said Susan. "We'd only crack the enamel. But the frying-pan would be all right. It's an iron one. You can bang on it with a ladle."

"How would it be if I played my penny whistle?" said Roger.

"Oh, anything you like," said Susan, bringing up the big frying-pan and banging it hard and fast. "Yes, you'd better play the whistle. That way he'll know it's us if he's rowing about looking for the *Goblin*."

Roger dived into the cabin and came up again, and a moment later, at uncertain speed, the notes of "Home, Sweet Home" were dropping into the fog.

Everybody felt happier. When you are lying anchored in a fog, even "Home, Sweet Home" on a penny whistle and the clatter of a spoon on a frying-pan make you feel that other boats will have less excuse for running into you.

John went down into the cabin and took Knight's *Sailing* from the bookshelf. He looked up the page about signals in fog.

"Hi, Susan!" he called, when he had found it. "Don't keep banging it all the time. It says, 'a ship, in fog, mist or falling snow, when not under way, shall, at intervals of not more than two minutes, ring the bell.'"

"It doesn't say anything about whistles?" asked Roger.

*

No big steamers seemed to be moving, and they knew they were anchored in the shallow water well outside the channel for big ships. An hour had passed, and they had almost come to think that there was no need to make a noise at all, when they heard a long hoot of a foghorn somewhere ahead of them. Presently it came again.

"That's somebody moving," said John.

"It can't be Jim, looking for us, can it?" said Susan.

"He hasn't got a foghorn in the dinghy," said John. "No. It's someone coming in from the sea. Look here. Shall I have a go at the frying-pan?"

"I'll do it just as loud," said Titty, whose turn it was, and Roger, blowing for all he was worth into his penny whistle, lifted several notes by an octave.

They heard the foghorn again, close to them, and then the very slow drumming of a small engine.

"They're jolly near," said John, trying his hardest to see through the thick grey curtain of fog that hid everything more than a yard or two away.

They never saw the other boat, though it came so near that the drumming of its engine sounded almost as if it had been their own . . . Voices aboard that other boat sounded as if they were in the *Goblin*'s cockpit.

"Keep her just ticking over . . ."

"Can't see a blessed thing . . ."

"No bottom at three fathoms ..."

And then: "Hullo! What's that row over there? And somebody's whistling. Ahoy there! Who are you?"

John hesitated only for a moment, and then remembered he was in charge.

"*Goblin!*" he shouted back.

"That's young Brading's boat ... Ahoy! Are you under way?"

"Anchored!"

"Where are we?"

"Just across the channel from Felixstowe Dock." John gave the position with some pride. "Close to the North Shelf buoy."

"Thank you. Pretty thick, isn't it? ... All right, Tom. Open the throttle a bit. Know where we are now. Deep enough right across with the tide so far up."

"Who are they?" whispered Titty.

"Ahoy!" shouted John. "Who are you?"

"*Emily!*" a shout came back out of the fog. "Been fishing outside. Had a bit of a job getting in again." The drumming of the engine quickened slightly. The next long hoot of the foghorn was further away. Presently they could hear it no longer. They were alone once more with the regular bleat from the Cork lightship and the occasional clanging of bells on the vessels anchored in the harbour.

*

Another hour had gone by. Not even Roger hoped any longer that Jim was rowing about in the fog, and that "Home, Sweet Home" would help him to find his way to the *Goblin*. He had

stopped playing the penny whistle. The banging
of the frying-pan no longer seemed as interesting
as it had. Nobody now disputed as to whose turn it
was to bang it. They had made up their minds that
Jim would have to stay ashore till the fog cleared.
John was alone in the cockpit, looking at Knight
on *Sailing* and banging the frying-pan every now
and then. The other three were down in the cabin
considering what was to be done about dinner.

They had opened the cupboards behind the
bunks in the main cabin and were looking at
the stores.

"Four kinds of soup," said Roger.

"And five kinds of tinned fruit," said Titty.

"Yes, I know," said Susan, "but it's all for
his cruise with his uncle."

"He said his uncle would be bringing lots
more," said Roger.

"Mother said the fo'c'sle feeds itself," said Susan.
"And we've got half those sausage rolls . . ."

"Sausage rolls still unhogged," said Roger, "but
we'd better leave some for him. He liked them last
night. And I bet he'd want us to have some of his
soup."

"And there's the pork pie," said Susan. "That's
ours."

"Let's keep that for supper when he'll be here
too," said Titty. "It's all right having a sausage
roll or two left over, but if we eat the pork pie,
it'll mean only leaving him a slice. He ought to
be here for the carving."

"What's medicinal purposes?" asked Roger.

"Put that bottle away," said Susan. "That's
rum for Jim's uncle. Jim says his aunt always

writes 'Medicinal purposes only' on the label. It's in case one of them tumbles overboard or gets a chill or something, not for general swilling."

"We won't drink it," said Roger. "But, I say, Susan, I'm sure he'd want us to have hot soup in a fog."

Susan was looking at the labels on the tins. She had a tin of mushroom soup in one hand and a tin of tomato soup in the other. She looked up out of the companion-way at the thick fog and made up her mind that Roger was right.

"We'll have soup," she said. "The fog is a bit cold."

"Mushroom," said Roger.

"And there are those two eggs," said Susan, looking at Jim's uneaten breakfast. "You get the shells off them, Titty. He won't want them cold anyway, and they'll go quite well with the soup. And then sausage rolls, and after that bananas."

*

Dinner was a solider meal than breakfast, but less formal. Somebody had to be on deck banging the frying-pan every two minutes. And if they couldn't all sit down at once, there did not seem to be much point in laying the table. Besides, Susan did not want to be reminded of that place laid for Jim at breakfast, that had waited for him in vain, and had only now been cleared away. So people came down into the cabin for their soup, and the sausage rolls and bananas were taken up into the cockpit and eaten in the fog.

"The ferry never came back," said John. "We'd have heard it. And if it's too foggy for them, it's too foggy for anybody paddling about without a compass."

All the same there were two false alarms, when first Susan and then Roger heard the sound of oars. You could have told by the way everybody listened that all of them were really wondering about Jim, even when they were cheerfully talking of soups and other things.

But Jim never came.

"He's been gone nearly six hours," said Susan to John during the washing up. Titty and Roger were in the cockpit, keeping anchor watch, banging the frying-pan every two minutes, and practising on the penny whistle, just in case. Susan was washing, and John, quite glad to have come down into the cabin out of the fog, was drying the plates and spoons as Susan passed them on to him.

"We've only got to wait," said John. He looked at the barometer. "Hullo!" he said. "Did Jim set the barometer this morning? It's gone down three-tenths if he did."

"Rain coming?" said Susan.

"Wind more likely," said John. "Specially after that calm."

Susan went suddenly up the companion-steps to look out into the fog. "There isn't a sign of him," she said as she came back.

"There couldn't be," said John. "Not till the fog blows away. He'll come the moment it does. He's got the *Imp*. We can't go swimming ashore to look for him. He'll be counting on our sitting still."

Just then there was a pause in penny whistling and beating the frying-pan, and John and Susan in the cabin heard talking in the cockpit.

"Not being able to see things makes it almost better." That was Titty, of course. "If we were in a fog in the middle of the Atlantic Ocean we wouldn't be able to see any less. I say, Roger, let's be there. When did we leave our last port?"

"This morning."

"Don't be a donk. We couldn't have or we wouldn't be in the middle of the Atlantic."

"Oh well, months ago," said Roger.

"A week anyhow. And we're rushing along, keeping a look out for icebergs."

"You can see how we're sluicing through the water."

And then, while John and Susan listened in the cabin, there was more banging of the frying-pan on deck and the first part of the chorus of "The Old Folks at Home," played doubtfully, note by note, and then repeated a little faster, on the penny whistle.

"They're all right so far," said Susan. "But I can't help thinking something must have happened to Jim. It's two o'clock already."

"High tide," said John. "The fog's almost sure to go out with the ebb. Jim's probably sitting on a bollard on the pierhead, smoking his pipe and watching for the fog to go."

"He didn't take his pipe with him," said Susan. "He left it, half full of tobacco, and I've propped it up at the side of the sink."

Somehow, Jim's having left his pipe behind made things seem worse. He really had meant to be only a few minutes away. And that was six whole hours ago.

"The wind'll blow the fog away," said John.

"What's that tapping?" said Susan.

"Halyard against the mast," said John.

"I do wish he'd never gone ashore," said Susan.

"Look here, Susan," said John. "We're perfectly all right. We're anchored in a safe place. And he knows we are. Nothing can possibly go wrong. He said so himself."

And then Susan saw John's eyes suddenly widen. She too had heard the noise that had startled him, the sudden metallic scrawk of the anchor chain against the chain of the bobstay.

"Oh, it's all right," said John. He had half got up, but now sat down again. Whatever happened he must not show Susan that he was getting worried too. "It's the turn of the tide, and she's swung round to ride to the ebb. She made the same noise when the tide turned last night."

But a few moments later the noise came again, and with it another noise, and a sudden jerk of the whole ship. Susan looked at John, but did not say a word. He sat still, listening. The look-outs, in the cockpit, had heard something too, and were looking down the companion-way to make sure John and Susan thought it was all right. Susan signalled to them to be quiet. The next moment the jerk came again, followed by a scraping that they seemed to feel rather than hear, and then another jerk.

"She's dragging her anchor!" cried John. "Look out of the way." With one jump he was half-way up the companion-steps.

CHAPTER VIII

THE BEACH END BUOY

"What's happened"

"What's the matter?"

Titty and Roger dodged out of the way as John came tumbling up out of the cabin. John did not really know himself, not for certain. But that jerk and then the queer feel of something scraping and then the jerk again had reminded him of a day out fishing long ago when the anchor had dragged because the rope had not been long enough. Then it had not mattered. But now, if the *Goblin* was dragging her anchor in a fog, with a tide under her ... It didn't really matter Jim Brading being ashore while the *Goblin* was safely anchored where he had left her. But if she dragged ...? John hurried along the side deck, holding on to a rail on the cabin top that was dripping wet in the fog. That was the worst of it. You couldn't see the shore. You couldn't see anything. Perhaps nothing had happened and she was still in the same place.

"Beu ... eueueueueueueu ... "

That was the lightship, somewhere away over the starboard quarter, and it had been somewhere on the port bow. He remembered that the tide had turned, so that now the *Goblin*'s bow would be heading up the harbour. The ebb was racing past her out to sea.

Just as John got to the foredeck, that strange

shiver ran through the boat again. He steadied
himself with a hand on the winch, half covered
with rusty chain. He grabbed the forestay and
looked down over the stemhead. The chain was
hanging straight up and down. Last time he had
seen it it had been leading well away from the
stem as the *Goblin* was pulling at her anchor.
Something had happened. He knelt as near the
stemhead as he could get and leaning over pulled
at the chain. It was as if something under water
was gently tapping at it. Yes, the anchor was
dragging. But surely the anchor had gone down
all right, not tangled in the chain or anything
like that. Why, Jim Brading had anchored the
Goblin himself . . . and then Jim Brading's last
words flashed into John's mind . . . "Tide's just
turning . . . dead low water . . ." But that was six
hours ago. Six hours the tide had been pouring in.
The chain that had been long enough to hold the
Goblin at dead low water was far too short to hold
her at high water, at the top of the tide, when the
water was more than twice as deep. The anchor
must be hardly touching the bottom.

John scrambled to his feet, almost more
ashamed than he could bear. Call himself a
mate, indeed. He ought to have thought of that
ages ago and let out more chain as soon as the
fog had come, or even sooner. Jim had said himself he was anchoring only for ten minutes and he
had left John in charge. He ought to have been
thinking about that chain and the rising tide as
soon as those ten minutes were up and Jim had
not come back. Jim must have counted on him.

He scrambled to his feet and looked at the

chain, which ran from a fairlead at the stemhead
to a small windlass. A lot of the chain was coiled
this way and that round first one and then the
other drum of the windlass, like rope belayed on a
cleat. The rest of the chain was in the chain-locker
below. John could see where it came up through a
chain-pipe in the deck. Well, the first thing to do
was to cast off those turns and let out more chain
. . . quick. Though there was nothing to be seen
but fog, John knew the *Goblin* must be moving.
He tugged at the rusty links.

"Is it all right?"

He looked over his shoulder, and saw that
there were three faces, dim and white in the
fog, looking at him from the cockpit.

"It will be in a minute," he said. "I've been an
awful idiot. I ought to have let out more chain
ages ago."

"Are you sure you know how?"

"As soon as I've got it loose," said John.

He spoke cheerfully, while his hands pulled this
way and that at the coils of chain that seemed to
grip each other and the windlass as if they had
been made in one solid piece.

"Can't I help?"

"No," he panted. "It's coming now."

He had freed one coil. The next came unwound
quite easily. He slipped another from under the
drum on the opposite side. Now it ought to go.
There were just two turns round the drum. Surely
that drum ought to go round so that he could pay
out as much chain as he wanted. How on earth
did the thing work?

"Is it all right now?"

"It won't go out."

"What won't?"

"The chain."

He hauled some chain up out of the chain-pipe and tried working it round the drum. A foot or so of chain pulled round and went out with a jerk. But he wanted yards and yards out before the anchor could hold again, and they were moving . . . moving . . .

He pulled up more chain out of the chain-pipe, hand over hand as fast as he could get it on deck. Horribly heavy it was. And what was the good of getting it up if it would not pay out? He must get it clear of that winch in order to be able to pay it out at all. He got one turn off the drum and as nearly as possible got his finger nipped in getting off the other. And just at the very worst moment there came a jerk. John slipped and grabbed with one hand at the forestay. He never knew exactly what happened to the other hand. He had been holding the chain with both of them. There was a rattle and roar as the loose chain he had hauled up on deck went flying out over the fairlead close by the bowsprit. More chain came pouring up out of the chain-pipe in the deck and went flying overboard to join the rest. There was nothing to stop it. It raced out through the fairlead rattling and roaring, fathom after fathom of heavy iron chain.

Stop it. He must stop it. Questions darted through his mind. How was the end of the chain fastened in the chain-locker down below? Was it fastened at all? How long was the chain? But there was no time to get answers. Somehow or other, now, at once, he must stop the chain roaring out

over the bows. He jammed his right foot hard
down on the leaping chain. On the instant his
foot was torn from under him and he was flung
heavily on his back.

There was a shriek from the cockpit. Desperately he scrambled up again. The chain was still
pouring up and overboard. He had no time to do
another thing before he saw the end of the chain
come up out of the chain-pipe and fly out over the
bows with a bit of frayed rope flying after it. The
rattle and roar ended in a sudden silence.

"Beu . . . eueueueueueu . . ." The Cork lightship
far away outside the harbour was still sending its
long, melancholy bleats into the fog. But aboard
the *Goblin* Titty was not banging the frying-pan,
and Roger was not playing the penny whistle.
They knew that something awful had happened,
though they did not know exactly what. Susan
was hurrying forward along the side deck, holding
on to a rail on the cabin top. She had seen John go
flying backwards.

"Have you hurt yourself?" she asked.

But John in his horror at what had happened
had hardly felt the ringbolt in the deck on which
he had come down.

"It's all gone," he panted. "All his chain and
his anchor. I've let it all go overboard . . ."

"But are you all right?"

"Chain and anchor and everything," said John.
"Miles of it . . . It's all gone . . ."

"John," cried Susan. "We're adrift." And then,
at the top of her voice, she shouted, "Jim! Ahoy!
Jim! Ahoy!"

"Shut up," said John furiously. "He can't hear

you, but someone else might. And if they found us adrift they'd grab his boat. Quick. We've got to get the other anchor over . . ." He looked at the spare anchor, the kedge, which was stowed flat on the foredeck and held in its place with rope tyers. "There must be a rope for it somewhere. See if there isn't one in the cockpit, while I get the anchor ready. But whatever you do don't start yelling to make people think something's wrong. We don't want to lose his boat for him as well as his anchor and chain . . ."

If only he knew how fast they were moving and which way? The noise of the cranes unloading coal from a steamer in Felixstowe Dock sounded much further away than they had been. He flung himself on the kedge anchor and fumbled at one of its tyers with fingers that were in too much of a hurry to be much good.

"Rope . . . Rope . . ." he heard Susan, now back in the cockpit. "*Not* that one . . . That's the mainsheet . . . Quick . . . Quick . . . We're drifting away."

That knot in the tyer must have been made a long time ago. It had got jammed. There was a rule in the family against cutting knots, even on parcels. But this was no moment for rules. John had his knife out in a flash and cut the knot. He did not even try to untie the second tyer, but cut that also. He had the kedge anchor free. It was smaller than the other, but quite heavy enough for John.

"Will this do?" That was Titty's voice. They were still hunting for a rope to use as an anchor warp.

GOODBYE TO ANCHOR AND CHAIN!

"What about this?" That was Roger.

"Haul all the lot out." That was Susan again. "No. No. We must get one that isn't made fast somewhere."

They were being as quick as they could. It was no good going to help them till he had the anchor itself ready for use. Now anchors are made in two parts. There is the crown with the two flukes and the long shank. All that is in one piece. Then there is the stock. This is a bar which goes through a hole in the shank, and has a short bend at one end of it, so that when it is not in use it can lie flat along the shank. When the anchor is to be used, the stock is pushed through the hole in the shank, so that half of it sticks out on one side and half on the other, at right angles to the flukes. This

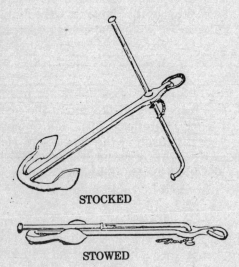

STOCKED

STOWED

stock turns the anchor on its side when it is on the bottom, so that one or other of the flukes gets a chance of digging in. If it were not for the stock, the anchor would just drag along the bottom and get no grip at all. A little iron fid drops into a slot in the stock to keep it in place.

John had to lift the anchor on end, push the stock into place, put in the fid, make fast an anchor rope, and then get the heavy anchor overboard so that he could lower it between the bowsprit shrouds and the bowsprit.

He had a hard time getting the stock into place. The fid was hanging on a bit of chain. He slid it along and dropped it into the slot. That looked all right, but was it? With the anchor of *Swallow*, the little boat on the lake, one just batted the fid in with a stone or one of the rowlocks. There was nothing to bat this with. Moments were flying. He gave it a desperate whack with his pocket knife.

"Here's some rope," panted Susan at his elbow. "It's not awfully long, but it's the thickest bit we could find."

"Let's have an end," said John. He pushed it twice through the ring at the end of the anchor's shank, then through both turns and finished off with a clove hitch round the rope itself. He was not quite sure if that was the proper anchor knot, but anyway it was safe, and he was not going to lose two anchors if he could help it.

"Do be quick," said Susan.

"Take a turn with the rope round the drum of the windlass," said John, "and hang on. I've got to get the rope through the fairlead and lower. I daren't just shove it over."

"Don't go over yourself," said Susan. "Look out!
John!"

"All right," he panted. "We can lower away
now. Go on. A bit more. Ow! It's scraping the
paint most dreadfully. It can't be helped. Look
here, Susan, get hold of the very end and make
it fast to that bollard. We don't want to lose it
too."

"I've done it."

"Come on then. Lower away . . ."

They lowered away. The weight of the anchor
was almost as much as they could manage even
with the rope going round the drum of the winch.
Suddenly the rope was slack and they felt no
weight at all. John looked down over the stem.

"Hang on, just for a minute. Where's the boathook. The wretched stock's gone and caught on
the bobstay."

He grabbed the boathook from the cabin roof
and poked with it at the stock of the anchor. It
slipped free at last and if Susan had not had the
sense to take an extra turn with the rope round
the drum it might have jerked it from her hands.
All went well now, and together they paid out rope
as fast as they could. They felt the anchor reach
the bottom, but went on paying out rope till they
had no more.

John looked over the stem again.

"It's holding all right," he said. "Lucky it is.
The rope's awfully short. He must have a proper
one somewhere."

"It's the only one we could find," said Susan.
"How far do you think we've moved?"

"Don't know," said John. "Not awfully far. At

least I shouldn't think so. You simply can't tell in the fog."

"I say, John," said Susan. "I'm sorry I yelled for Jim. I never thought of someone else hearing instead."

"It's all right," said John. "Nobody did. I'm sorry I was a bit ratty. I wasn't really ratty with you. It was me I was ratty with really, because of losing his chain and anchor."

"We've moved a good long way," said Susan. "The steamers are a lot further off than they were, and the noise of those cranes. I do wish the fog would go. Jim'll never be able to find us if he does try to come out in the *Imp*."

"He won't try," said John. "He doesn't know I've gone and lost his anchor. He thinks we're all right, exactly where he left us."

"You're sure we're all right this time?"

"Yes," said John. "That other anchor's got a beautiful hold." He looked over the side. "You can see the tide pouring past."

They went aft to the cockpit, Susan along one side deck and John along the other.

"Why have you stopped banging the frying-pan?" said Susan.

"Sorry. I forgot," said Titty, and for a few moments rattled away with the spoon.

"Do anchors cost an awful lot?" asked Roger.

"Pounds," said John. "Pounds and pounds. And chain costs a lot too."

"Will he be able to get it by diving?" asked Titty. "Like when *Swallow* was wrecked, last summer."

"If only it hasn't sunk in the mud," said John.

"They'll have to drag for it with a grapple. He'll know just where it is. But he'll have to borrow a grapple from somewhere. And someone else may get it first . . ."

"Oh I do wish he'd never gone ashore," said Susan. "And then none of this would have happened."

"Let's get everything straight," said John. "The cockpit's like a cat's cradle with ropes. Let's get it straight before he comes back. He'll come off the moment the fog clears. Let's have everything as he left it, even if I have gone and lost the anchor and chain."

"The mess," said Roger, "is because we were trying to get a rope in a hurry."

"Come on," said John, "and let's get them all coiled away again. And bang the frying-pan, Ableseaman, to let anybody know we're a ship at anchor."

One by one they coiled the ropes again, jib sheets and staysail sheets and backstay falls and the big coil of the mainsheet that Roger had pulled off the tiller. Presently the cockpit was tidy once more, and they settled down again, to wait for the fog to blow away, to listen to the distant tinkling of the bells of anchored steamers, and the bleating of the lightship out at sea. Roger did a little penny-whistling. Susan was thankful that they were again at anchor. Titty was remembering the wreck of the *Swallow*, and John was miserably thinking how he could explain to his skipper about the loss of the anchor and chain. If only he had thought of letting some chain out earlier before they had begun to drift. If only he

hadn't slipped. Once the chain had started roaring
out like that he didn't see what he could have done
to stop it. Anyhow, he had done the best that could
be done now, by getting the kedge over, even if it
wasn't much of a rope. Nothing more to be done
except sit tight and wait for the fog to clear and
Jim to come back and hear the bad news.

"Clang!"

The noise of a deep-toned bell startled them
by coming out of the fog astern of them. All
the bells that kept jangling aboard the anchored
steamships were ahead of them, further up the
harbour.

"What's that?"

"Another boat probably," said Susan. "Bang
that frying-pan, Titty, or let me have it."

"She must be at anchor if they're ringing a
bell," said John.

"Clang! . . . Clang!"

John stood up and peered into the fog.

"Listen! Listen! We may hear them talking."

"Clang!"

"Clang! . . . Clang!"

"It's like the bell we heard this morning," said
Roger, "on that buoy. You know, when Jim said
there wasn't enough of a ripple to set it properly
ringing."

"It can't be anchored," said Titty. "It's ever
so much nearer."

"Clang! . . . Clang!"

Roger was leaning out of the cockpit, listening
and looking down at the grey water close to the
side of the *Goblin*, the only thing there was to see
in the fog.

"The tide's not moving as fast as it was," he said. "It was swirling past a minute ago."

"Do be quiet a moment."

"Clang!"

"The tide's not moving at all," said Roger.

"What?" shouted John. At first he had hardly heard what Roger was saying. Then, for a moment, he had not realised what it meant. He too looked down at the water. He climbed out of the cockpit and hurried to the foredeck. What on earth was happening now? He watched the anchor rope leading away from the stem. It tautened till it looked like wire. The tide was pouring past, rippling against the *Goblin*'s bows. Suddenly the rope slackened, then tautened, then slackened again. The rippling stopped. It was as if the *Goblin* were anchored in still water.

"Clang!"

"It must be a boat," said Titty. She beat a hard tattoo on the frying-pan.

"Shall I play my whistle?" said Roger. "We don't want them running into us."

John hardly heard them. What *had* gone wrong with that anchor? The rippling against the *Goblin*'s bows had stopped altogether. Yet the tide must be still pouring out of the harbour. That meant that the *Goblin* must be moving with it. Yes. The anchor rope was now hanging straight up and down as the chain had hung before. Desperately he began hauling it in.

"Hi! Susan! Come and lend a hand. Quick!"

"What's happened?" Susan was at his elbow.

"Get a hold of the rope and haul when I do? Now then. Now . . . Now . . . Up she comes."

"But why?" panted Susan. "You're not getting up the anchor?"

"Got to," said John. "It's not got hold of anything. Something's wrong with it."

"Clang!"

The noise of the bell was nearer than ever. There was a frenzy of banging on the frying-pan in the cockpit and the first verse of "God Save the King!" on the whistle. The kedge anchor, not so heavy as the big one that had been lost, came up against the bobstay with a sudden jar.

"Hang on, Susan, while I have a look," said John. "It's gone and come unstocked. It's my fault again. The fid's come out. I didn't know how to make it fast. At least I thought I had . . ."

"Clang!"

"Pull now. We've got to get it on deck."

With an awful struggle they hauled the anchor aboard. Anybody could see why it had not been holding. The fid had come out, the stock had slipped and was swinging loose beside the shank.

"Clang!"

The noise was so near that John and Susan on the foredeck turned to look into the fog even while Susan was holding the anchor and John was working the stock back into place.

"Clang!"

There was a yell from the cockpit. "God Save the King" came to an end in the middle of a bar.

"John! John! It's here . . ."

Something large loomed out of the fog astern. It was a big red-painted cage, like an enormous parrot cage with a pointed top, built on a round raft. On the top of the cage was a lantern, and, as

THE BEACH END BUOY

they watched, they saw a thin line of white light
leap up in the lantern, vanish and leap again. It
was a buoy. In the cage was something big and
black . . . the bell.

"Clang!"

"It's coming jolly fast," shouted Roger. "Look
at the wash round its bows."

"It's going to bunt into us," cried Titty.

"It isn't the buoy that's moving," said John.
"It's us."

They swept past it, missing it by only a yard.
The heavy hammer in the cage swung against
the bell when they were near enough almost to
touch the buoy. The melancholy "Clang!" boomed
in their ears. They read the big white letters
painted on the side of the cage . . . "BEACH END."
A moment later the buoy had faded away into the
fog, and the next "Clang!" sounded out of nothingness.

"Oh, John!" gasped Susan. "That was the Beach
End buoy. We're out at sea."

CHAPTER IX

DRIFTING BLIND

"Out at sea . . . The Beach End buoy . . ."

Titty and Roger stared at each other in the cockpit. They had heard Susan say it. They had seen the great buoy with its iron cage and its clanging bell. They had read the words "BEACH END" themselves. But, now that the buoy had vanished in the fog, there was no more to be seen and no less than when they had been anchored in the harbour close to the North Shelf buoy, listening to the noises of Felixstowe Dock and the bells of the steamers.

"We can't be really," said Roger.

"We probably are," said Titty.

They stared forward into the fog to see what John and Susan were doing. They heard a bump of the anchor on the deck. They could see John working it over the bows, and then both John and Susan, one behind the other, paying out rope. The "Clang! . . . Clang!" of the buoy was sounding more and more faintly, and the queer thing was that it kept on sounding in a different place. Now it was over the bows, now broad on the starboard beam, now over the port quarter, now on the bows again. "It's no good," they heard John say. "Deep water . . . Not long enough . . ." "Perhaps it's come to pieces again," said Susan. And there they were, the two of them, hauling as if in a tug-of-war, till they had the anchor once more at the stemhead.

"They're in an awful hurry," said Titty.

"Susan's in a stew," said Roger.

"They both are rather," said Titty.

"They're putting the anchor down again," said Roger.

"Which way is the sea?" said Titty.

"Over there . . ."

"It can't be . . . I can hear the noise of a train . . . The sea must be the other way . . ."

"But the train's this side now . . ."

The "Beu . . . eueueueueueu" of the lightship settled the question for a moment, but its very next bleat sounded somewhere else.

"John," called Roger. "Why are all the noises moving round?"

"She's twirling about in the tide," came the answer. "Look here, Susan . . . We'd better have one more shot . . ."

"She's quite bobby about," said Roger.

"Yes," said Titty. She had noticed that already. The coming of the wind had made a little difference even in the harbour, but now small smooth-topped waves seemed to come sliding along out of the fog first from one direction and then from another, and the *Goblin*'s mast swung this way and that, and Titty found herself trying to breathe in time with the lurching of the boat. Very strange and rather bothering it was.

"Jim'll have a long way to row when he comes after us," said Roger.

"Yes," said Titty again. It wasn't exactly that her head was aching, but the skin across her forehead was somehow tight. Was it the fog, or was she really not seeing things very clearly? What

were they doing on the foredeck? Still hauling
in. No, they had let the anchor down twice. They
must be hauling in again. And Susan was trying
to hold on to things. The *Goblin* really must be
lurching a bit. Well, Roger had said so too. It
couldn't be only in her head. Suddenly she heard
John saying very clearly, "I can't help it. It's no
good leaving it dangling. I've lost him one anchor
already. I'll have it on deck all ready to let go."
And then Susan, "We promised we wouldn't go
outside the harbour." And then John again, "We
didn't mean to. Come on, Susan. Do help. I must
go and look at that chart and try to see where
we are . . ." And then they were hauling in the
rope, and the anchor bumped on the deck, and
she could see John bending over it, making it fast
and coiling a rope. Susan was working her way aft
again, with both hands on the rail on the roof of
the cabin. Roger pulled at Titty's elbow.

"Susan's going to cry," he whispered.

"Look the other way," said Titty.

But there was no need for that. Susan was
not going to give in without a struggle. Talking
to John was one thing. Talking to Titty and
Roger was something altogether different. Susan
gave her head a shake, and as soon as she was
safely back in the cockpit asked Titty why she
had stopped banging the frying-pan. Titty gave
the frying-pan a beating and felt better.

Then she heard John's voice calling from inside
the cabin. Funny she had never noticed that he
had slipped down through the forehatch.

"Susan. Where's that chart showing Harwich?
The one we were looking at with him last night."

Susan took a deep breath and went down the companionsteps to join him.

Titty and Roger were once more alone in the cockpit.

"Do you think I ought to play the whistle or not?" said Roger. "I say, Titty, what do you think they'll do?"

*

Down in the cabin John had lifted the mattress on the port bunk, and, keeping it out of the way with his head, was turning over one chart after another ... Spithead Approaches ... Selsea Bill ... Owers to Beachy Head ... Beachy Head to Dungeness ... Plans of Newhaven and Shoreham ... Langston and Chichester Harbours ... Dover to Dungeness ... He seemed to get his fingers on every chart except the one he wanted.

"Susan," he called. "I can't find it ..."

"He put it under the mattress on the other side," said Susan. "He was going to use it today going up to Ipswich ..."

John banged down the mattress he had been holding up. Susan was lifting the other and he had the chart out in a moment. He laid it flat on the cabin table and stared at it for a full half minute before he saw that he had it upside down. His cheeks burned. But it was all right. Susan had not noticed. It would never do for her to think that he was worried too.

A tremendous tattoo on the frying-pan sounded from the cockpit and Roger put his head in and called down:

"Ought I to whistle? Titty says I'd better ask."

John looked up. He answered Titty's tattoo instead of Roger's question.

"We're not at anchor," he said grimly. "We ought to be sounding a foghorn, not a bell."

"I know where it is," said Roger. He came scrambling down into the cabin, pushed his way through, and hauled a long, green-painted foghorn out from its place behind a spare pair of sea-boots. "How does it work?" He found the brass knob on the end of the long piston rod. He pulled it out and pushed it in again.

"It won't hoot," he said.

"Of course it will," said John. "Pull it right out and try pushing steadily."

The cabin was suddenly filled with a deafening blast of noise.

"Nobody'll be able to help hearing that," said Roger.

"Take it on deck," said John. "Hi! Titty! Stop banging the frying-pan. Take turns with the foghorn, and hoot for all you're worth if you hear anybody else hooting."

He went half way up the companion and looked round into the fog. Nothing to be seen. He came down again and found Susan staring at the chart.

"I can't see which is land and which is water,"

said Susan. "And, anyway, what can we *do*?"

"There's where we were anchored," said John, pointing with a finger. "There's the dock where he went in, and there's that flat-topped buoy. And we must have drifted right down here . . . unless there's another buoy called Beach End somewhere else. There can't be. That must be the one we saw. And he said the ebb tide goes north-east . . . We must be about here . . ."

"Beu . . . eueueueueu" came the bleat from the lightship as if to remind him.

"We must be drifting towards the lightship . . . Look. It's marked here . . . I say, what's the matter, Susan?"

"Let me get past," said Susan. "I've got to go on deck."

He made way for her, and almost as if she were blind she groped for the companion-steps and climbed hurriedly up to the cockpit.

John stared after her. No. It couldn't be that Susan was going to be sea-sick. There wasn't really much motion . . . not as much as they had had in *Swallow* scores of times. And then, he suddenly found himself grabbing at the table. Perhaps, after all, there was a bit of a swell.

"I say, Susan," he called. "Are you all right?"

"Yes . . . But don't stay down there. Do hurry up and come out."

It was no good talking about hurrying up. It was not as if he had had charts to look at every day. Maps are easy, with the roads marked in red and the rivers marked in blue. Charts are different altogether. Land and sea are so much alike. He was glad Jim had let him have a look at this

one last night. The plain part was land, though
you would not think so, because there were no
roads marked on it. That thick line marked the
edge of high water . . . or was it low water? And
those dotted lines marked the shoals, and Jim had
said that the shaded bits out at sea in the middle
of the dotted lines meant shoals that were dry at
low water. And the others might be even worse,
lurking just below the surface. And what a lot of
them there were. And buoys, too. There were little
pictures of buoys on the chart, with letters beside
them, "R" or "B" or "B.W. Cheq." That last he
guessed must mean Black and White chequered.
The little picture, that made the buoy look like
a leprosy flag, and was marked "B.W. Cheq,"
showed that clearly enough.

All the time, the bleat of the Cork lightship,
four times every minute, reminded him that the
Goblin was not still but moving. And there seemed
to be shoals everywhere. With names to them.
There was the Andrews and the Platters and
the Cutler and the Cork. There were others, too,
without names. "Get out to sea and stay there"
Jim had said last night. If only Jim was aboard
and in command. But if he had been, everything
would have been all right. Where had he said was
the safe way? . . . By the Cork light-vessel. It must
be here, and John put his finger on what looked
like a broad, clear road leading out to deep water
between the threatening shoals.

Just at that moment a lot of noises came
together. There was the "Beu-eueueueueu" of the
lightship, a sudden blast on the foghorn up in the
cockpit, and then a shout from Titty.

"There's another buoy."

"Where? Where?" That was Susan.

"Over there. It's gone now. A speckled one."

John jumped for the companion-steps and with his head out above the cabin roof stared round into the grey nothingness of the fog.

"What shape was it?" he asked.

"Square, I think," said Titty.

"I never saw it at all," said Susan.

Roger was pulling out the handle of the fog-horn as far as it would go. He let drive. The foghorn blared so loud that it seemed impossible that nobody should answer it. But the only reply that came out of the fog was the regular bleat from the lightship.

"It's a lot nearer than it was," said Susan.

John had dropped down again into the cabin. A square buoy, speckled, Titty had said. He hunted frantically on the chart for a picture of a square buoy. He found one, then another, then a third. And buoys meant shoals. And shoals were everywhere. What was the right thing to do? What would Jim do? What would Jim think he ought to do? Drifting like this with the tide, waiting for the awful scrunch under the keel that would mean she was aground. He thought of wrecks on the Goodwins. He thought of the *Goblin* heeling over, lifting and bumping. He almost saw her planks stove in and sand and brown water swirling into her.

There was a yell from on deck, almost a shriek.

"There's another buoy! A big one!"

"It's going to hit us!"

"John! John!"

He was up in the cockpit in a moment, bumping his head on the way but hardly feeling it. He saw this buoy all right. A huge cage buoy, with a flat top and a lantern on it, had loomed out of the fog and was coming at them amidships. It was twenty yards off . . . fifteen . . . ten . . .

John grabbed the useless tiller and waggled it, as long ago he had waggled the tiller of the tiny *Swallow*, trying to move her in a flat calm.

"Grab the lifebelt, Susan," he shouted. "It's going to bust her like an egg-shell." He flung himself forward, tore the lifebelt free and dropped it in the cockpit, while he tried to get at the boathook. Titty grabbed the mop. But there was no time for fending off. There was no time for anything, and all four of them held their breaths, waiting for the crash of the huge iron buoy into the slim wooden side of the *Goblin*.

The crash never came.

The *Goblin*, slowly turning in the tide, came end on just in time. The monstrous buoy slid past with hardly a foot to spare, while Titty frantically poked at it with the mop. It was ten yards off . . . fifteen . . . twenty . . . It faded into the fog.

"Gosh!" said Roger.

"Oh, John!" cried Susan.

John made up his mind.

"We can't go on like this," he said. "If we can't steer, we haven't a chance of dodging, and we may come full wang into the next one."

"But what are we going to do?"

"I've got to get some sail on her."

"Would he want you to?"

"It's the only thing to do. We're helpless, drifting

FENDING OFF WITH THE MOP

like this. And it isn't only buoys. We might have
to dodge a steamer any minute. And if we aren't
sailing we can't get out of the way."

"But do you know how?"

"I think so," said John. "I did it all right yesterday when he was watching, and he's left everything all ready for hoisting. I'm sure I can get the
mainsail up somehow. Well enough to get her
moving so that we can steer. And the jib's only
rolled up. It's easy to let it unroll."

"Can I come and help?" said Roger.

"Sit still," said Susan.

*

From the cockpit they watched John slither
along the cabin roof to the foredeck. They saw
him pull first at one and then at another of the
ropes until he had made sure of having found the
right one. They saw him pulling on it hand over
hand. The head of the mainsail shook itself free
of the mass of red canvas and began to climb the
mast. It stuck. John was scrambling aft to cast
off a tyer half way along the boom. Susan and
Titty, ill as they were feeling, jumped to cast off
other tyers close above their heads. The sail was
all loose now, and a great fold of it suddenly filled
with wind, billowed up, and flopped down again.
John was hauling away again. Up went the big
sail, foot after foot up the mast, bellying as it rose.
Again it stuck.

"It's that backstay stopping it. Let it go
loose . . ."

"Backstay? Backstay? Which one?"

"That's the one. Starboard side."

John was hauling again. For a moment the flapping sail hid him. It climbed to the top of the mast. They saw him again, now swinging his weight against the halyard, just as they had seen Jim Brading do ... Swigging ... That was the word ... Nothing to do with grog, Jim Brading had told Roger who, of course, had asked. Now John was making that rope fast. He was busy with another. The boom dropped a little. The sail smoothed out. The *Goblin* heeled over.

"What do I do, John?" shouted Susan. "She's pulling."

"Slack away some mainsheet."

He was stooping now to loose the furling rope of the jib. The jib suddenly unrolled and began to flap.

"Haul in the sheet. This side. Stop it flapping."

"This one, Titty," said Roger.

"I know! Come on! Help! It's pulling like I don't know what."

The two of them hauled in the jib sheet as well as they could. The sail quietened. The *Goblin* was sailing once more. John, getting his breath again, was coiling away the halyard on the foredeck and stowing it at the foot of the mast.

"Come and take her," called Susan. "I don't know which way to go."

"How's she heading now?" asked John, hurrying aft along the side deck.

"I can't see anything," said Susan.

"Look out of the way, Roger," said John, jumping down into the cockpit, and Roger slid across to the lee side of the cockpit while John peered through the porthole that Susan had polished so carefully to see the compass just inside. The card was swinging ... north-west ... north-west by north ... north-west again ... But hadn't Jim said the tide would take them north-east to the Cork lightship? And they were heading north-west ...

John jumped for the mainsheet and began slacking it out hand over hand as fast as he could.

"Let her pay off, Susan. Let her pay off. Right off ... More. Quick. We're heading straight for the shoals along the shore."

He made the sheet fast and took the tiller. The regular bleats of the lightship were ahead of them now and no longer broad on the beam. He watched the compass card ... North-west ... north by west ... north ... north by east ... north-east ... north-east by east. He looked up at the fluttering burgee, dim in the fog at the masthead. It was blowing straight out before the mast.

"John," said Susan. "If you're sure the land's over there, why not go straight for it and get ashore somehow or other?"

All three of them looked at him.

"We can't," said John. "We'd only wreck the *Goblin*. And already I've lost his anchor."

"I believe we ought," said Susan.

"We can't," said John, almost angrily. "Go and look at that chart. We might easily hit rocks ever so far out from the shore, and in the fog we wouldn't know which way to swim."

"Mother'd be wanting us to try ..."

"I don't believe she would ... And Daddy

wouldn't, anyway. Look here, Susan. So long as
the *Goblin*'s all right, we're all right. But if we go
and smash her on a rock or something, anything
might happen. We've only got to keep clear of
things. The fog can't last for ever . . . Keep a look
out for anything you can see. Anything . . ."

The *Goblin* was sailing steadily now, with
a gentle, swishing noise, as she drove through
the water. John steered, glancing up and down,
between the compass and the ghost of the burgee
fluttering high overhead. Susan, Titty and Roger
tried their best to see into the fog. Every quarter
of a minute the Cork lightship moaned its "Beu-
eueueueueueu . . ." And each melancholy bleat
sounded a little nearer than the last.

CHAPTER X

OUT TO SEA

IT was worse for Susan than for any of the others. John was having a tricky time steering with the wind dead aft, afraid every moment that there would be a jibe, and that the boom would come swinging across. Titty and Roger were peering into the fog keeping a look out for another of those huge iron buoys that were as dangerous as rocks. But Susan was thinking of Jim Brading desperately rowing to and fro over the place where he had left the *Goblin*. What would he do when he found that the *Goblin* had gone? Telephone to Mother at Pin Mill? . . . The thought of Mother answering the telephone and hearing that Jim Brading, in whose charge they were, did not know what had become of them, came at her like a blow. They had been allowed to sail with Jim Brading only because everybody had promised that they would not go outside the harbour. And here they were sailing blindly a bigger boat than they had ever sailed before. Mother would never have trusted them alone in a boat like the *Goblin*, even inside the harbour on a calm day of sunshine and clear weather. And here they were outside the harbour, sailing faster every minute, in a thick, choking fog and rising wind. They could not have broken that promise into smaller bits.

"Beu . . . eueueueueueu . . ." Nearer and nearer

sounded that melancholy bleat from the lightship ahead of them.

Suddenly Roger slid down from his seat and pulled out the long handle of the foghorn. What with the hoisting of the sails, and the *Goblin* really moving, and his eagerness to see the next buoy in time to give John a chance of not hitting it, he had forgotten the foghorn altogether.

"How many hoots do I give?" he asked, looking at John.

John did not hear him. That lightship was getting dreadfully near, and he was thinking about what he ought to do next. He would have to make up his mind pretty quick.

Titty answered. Her head was throbbing and she was afraid she was going to be sick, but she did know something about fog signals. "Three hoots," she said. "Sailing vessel with the wind aft. Remember *Peter Duck*."

Roger drove in the handle and startled Susan with the long blast of the horn. "It's a real bull roarer," he said. He hauled out the handle and drove it in again. Then once more. Then he stopped and listened.

"Somebody may be answering," he said.

But no answer came out of the fog ... no answer but the long-drawn-out wail from the invisible lightship.

The wind was much stronger than it had been. Ripples had turned to waves, and every now and then the top of a wave turned to a splash of white foam as it came into sight out of the fog, lifted the stern of the *Goblin* and passed on.

"Look here, Susan, " said John. "We can't go

on like this. We must be close to the lightship and
there's another lot of shoals beyond it. You take
the tiller while I go down and have another look
at that chart. But whatever you do, don't have a
jibe. The wind's pretty well dead aft, and it's jolly
hard not to. Come this side so that you can see the
compass."

Susan took the tiller. John pointed through
the porthole at the compass card. "Practically
north-east ... Keep it as near that as you can
... But do look out for a jibe ..."

Susan watched the card. If only it would keep
still with the point marked N.E. against the thin
black lubberline in the compass bowl. Too far one
way ... Now too far the other.

The mainsheet suddenly slackened. The sail
flapped. The boom began to swing inboard. John
put a quick hand on the tiller. The boom swung
out once more and the sheet tautened with a jerk.

"Only just in time," said John. "You have
to be awfully careful."

"You keep the tiller," said Susan with a gulp.
"I'll go down and get the chart."

She climbed down the steep steps into the
cabin. She had hardly got both feet on the cabin
floor and a hand on the table to steady herself,
when she found herself swallowing hard though
she had had nothing to drink. There seemed to be
no air down here ... none at all. It could not be
that she was going to be sea-sick ... yet ... she
found her mouth open ... Air ... That was what
she wanted ... She looked up at the fog through
the companion-way ... She saw John's head and
shoulders, leaning forward, swinging this way and

that against the dim grey background . . . If only the cabin floor was not jerking about under her feet . . . She slipped and sat down on a bunk . . . Worse than ever . . . She clawed herself upright with the help of the table that was fixed to the floor but seemed to be trying to escape. Quick. Quick. Another minute down here and anything might happen. Where was that chart? It had slipped off the table and under it. She grovelled for it, grabbed it, flung herself at the steps and climbed out . . .

"I say, you haven't hurt yourself?" said Titty.

"I'm all right," said Susan, swallowing fast and taking deep breaths of fog. Already she felt better. Perhaps it had been another false alarm. But even to look down those steps into the deep little cabin made her feel funny again. She must not look down there. She must look ahead, out into the fog . . . Buoys . . . lightship . . . Who would look after the others if anything were to go wrong with her?

She heard John talking. It was as if he were talking from far away. Perhaps he had already been talking for some time. What was he saying? No . . . No . . . He couldn't mean it . . .

"Shoals the other side of the lightship . . . Lots of them . . . And shoals inshore . . . And that big lot where Jim said all those yachts had been wrecked must be somewhere over there." He was pointing into the fog. "But there's a clear way out between them. It's wide enough for anything, so long as we don't get too far north first . . ."

"But we can't . . . We can't." Susan was again very near to tears.

"We've got to get outside the shoals," said John. "It isn't safe not to. Just look at the chart for yourself . . ."

Susan stared at the chart. It flapped in the wind as she held it. She stared at it, but it was as if she were looking at a blank sheet of paper. Her eyes simply would not work. What was it John wanted to do? Where did he say they were? John was talking still, almost as if he were arguing with himself, not with her. And then that foghorn blared again, close beside her.

"Oh, shut up, Roger!" she cried.

"I must do it twice more," said Roger, "or they'll think we're close-hauled."

"Who'll think?"

"Anybody who hears it," shouted Roger, as he pressed down the handle and the foghorn blared again.

"Only once more," he said apologetically, hauling out the handle. "This is the last of the three."

Susan pushed the chart at John and put her hands to her ears.

John was still talking when she was able to listen to him again. "We can't stop," he was saying. "Even if we had no sails, the tide would be taking us somewhere. You saw how it rushed us past those buoys. If it took us on a shoal, we'd be wrecked before we could do anything at all. And if we go on past the lightship we'll be charging into shoals on the other side of it. Remember what Jim said about that man who lost his boat. When in doubt keep clear of shoals. Get out to sea and stay there. If he were on board he'd be doing it now. He'd get outside as soon as he could and wait till

he could see before trying to come back. And if we
steer a bit south of east . . . Do look at the chart
and you'll see . . ."

"But you don't know where we are now . . ."

"Yes I do. We must be getting near the lightship.
Listen to it."

"Beu . . . eueueueueueu . . ."

"But we can't . . ."

"It's the only thing we can do," said John.

"But we promised not to go to sea at all . . ."
Susan moaned and turned her head away. Titty
and Roger were both looking at her, and she could
not bear to see their questioning faces.

"We didn't do it on purpose," said John. "We're
at sea now, and we can't get back in the fog. If
we tried we'd be bound to wreck the *Goblin* on
something. Like trying to get through a narrow
door in pitch dark. The door's wide open if we
go the other way. You can see it yourself. If
we go a bit east of south-east we'll get through.
There's nothing for us to hit for miles. It's no
good thinking of doing anything else. We've got
to do it. South-east and a little bit east . . .
and we'll be all right. But we've got to do it
now or it'll be too late. That lightship's awfully
near . . ."

"Beu . . . eueueueueueu . . ."

The Cork lightship, sending its bleat out into
the fog once every fifteen seconds, was like the
ticking of an enormous clock telling them they
could not put things off for ever.

"We can't keep a promise when it's already
broken," said Titty.

"Is that another buoy?" said John. "Over there.

Do keep a look out. I've got to watch the compass and the sail . . ."

"Can I sound the foghorn again?" said Roger.

"No . . . Wait half a minute. We've got to make up our minds."

"Let's do what John says," said Titty. "Daddy'd say the same . . . You know . . . When it's Life and Death all rules go by the board. Of course, it isn't Life and Death yet, but it easily might be if we bumped the *Goblin* on a shoal."

"How shall we ever get back?" said Susan.

"If we keep her going about south-east till the fog clears, we'll be able to get her back by turning round and coming north-west . . . And anyway, when it clears we'll be able to see things . . ."

"Beu . . . eueueueueueueu."

The lightship bleated again and John's decision was made. There was not a moment to lose.

"I'm going to take her right out," he said. "Come on, Susan. We'll have to jibe. It'll be easier steering too. Come on. Will you take the tiller or shall I? You'd better. Bring her round when I say. Got to get the mainsheet in first. And there'll be the backstay to set up and the other one to cast off before the boom comes over. Titty . . . You be ready to let it go . . . Come on, Susan . . ."

"What about the jib?" said Roger. "Shall I? . . ."

"Never mind about the jib till afterwards . . . So long as we get the boom over all right . . . Ready, Susan?"

Susan found herself at the tiller . . . found herself watching the burgee away up there in the fog as she had often watched the flag at the

masthead of the tiny *Swallow* away on the lake
in the north. John was hauling in the mainsheet,
hand over hand, as fast as he could.

"Not yet, Susan ... Not yet ... Don't let
her come yet ... Help her, Roger ... Just while
I make fast." He took a turn with the sheet and
made ready to set up the backstay. The cockpit
seemed full of ropes.

"Now then. Let go, Titty. Go on, Susan. Bring
her round. Put your weight on the tiller, Roger.
Good. She's coming ... Now ..."

The boom swung suddenly over their heads,
but John had hauled it so far in that it had not
far to go. It brought up with a jerk not half as
bad as he had expected. The *Goblin* heeled over
to port. John had his backstay fast and was letting
out the mainsheet a good deal quicker than he had
been able to haul it in.

"Steady her," he shouted. "Don't let her come
right round."

Susan and Roger wrestled with the tiller.

"Oh look out ... Don't let her jibe back again."

"You take her," begged Susan.

John, out of breath, took the tiller once more.

"We can let the jib come across now. Yes.
Let go the sheet."

The jib blew across the moment it was free. It
hardly had time to flap before Susan had hauled
in the port jibsheet and tamed it to quiet.

John, with two hands on the tiller, peered
through the porthole at the swinging compass
card. South, south-east ... south-east ... south-
east by east ... He must keep her heading like
that. Easier now, with the wind on her quarter.

No need to be afraid of a jibe, with all its dangers of breaking boom or backstay or even bringing down the mast in ruin. And even if the sails were not set as well as Jim would have set them, the *Goblin* was going beautifully. The chart, in the turmoil of jibing and changing course, had slipped to the floor of the cockpit. He picked it up from under his feet and looked at it, and then at the compass again. Gosh! Already pointing too far south. He pressed on the tiller and the compass card swung back to its old position and a little beyond it. Back again. He leaned on the tiller and tried to see both chart and compass at once. Yes, it must be all right. Clear water all the way till you came to the Sunk lightship right on the edge of the chart. Out there they would be all right. Jim had waited out there himself. This was what Jim would do. This was what Daddy would do. John, in spite of being able to see nothing but fog, in spite of the broken promise, in spite of the awful mess they were in, was surprised to find that a lot of his worry had left him. The decision had been made. He was dead sure it was the right decision. Sooner or later the fog would clear and he would have to think about getting back. Now the only thing to do was to steer a straight course, not to hit anything, to go on and on till he was clear of those awful shoals that were waiting to catch his blindfold little ship. John, in spite of his troubles, was for the moment almost happy.

He nodded to Roger, who was waiting with the foghorn handle pulled out.

"All right. Three blasts. Wind's still aft. But keep a look out at the same time. Keep a look

out for all you're worth. We mustn't run into a
buoy ... You, too, Titty ... I say, what's the
matter?"

Titty was holding her forehead with both hands.

"I'm awfully sorry," she whispered. "I ... I
think I'm going to be sick."

"Nobody's going to be sick," said John, and
tried to say it as if he thought it, though he found
that difficult when he saw the greenness of Titty's
face. There certainly was much more wind and the
Goblin was bucketing along. He looked from Titty
to Susan. Susan was hunched up in a corner of
the cockpit, with her head in her arms, leaning
against the cabin top. Her shoulders heaved.

"Susan," said John. "Susan. I know it's all right."

There was no answer. Susan had helped in
bringing the *Goblin* on her new course. She had
been the mate, as of old in the little *Swallow*,
taking the Captain's orders and doing what she
was told. But now that all that hurried business
was over and she had time to think again, all her
doubts had come back. It was all very well for Titty
and Roger. They could not help themselves. They
were in her charge and John's. "Not to go outside
the harbour." .... And where were they? Outside
the harbour, and sailing, and going faster every
minute with the rising wind. With every minute
they were further out at sea, further from Pin
Mill where Mother and Bridget were waiting
to see them come sailing up the river, further
from Felixstowe Dock where Jim Brading must
be straining his eyes to get a glimpse of his ship in
the fog. The wind was getting up. The night would
be coming down on them. And there they were in

this thick blanket of fog, sailing, sailing. And on the top of all that, there was this horrible feeling in her inside, and she had to keep swallowing, and no matter how deep she breathed she did not seem able to get enough air.

"Susan," said John again.

She turned, and he saw that tears were streaming down her face.

"It's all wrong," she cried. "We must go back. We oughtn't to do it. I didn't want to, and I can't bear it."

"We can't go back," said John. "It isn't safe to try."

"We must," said Susan.

Roger, who had just been going to give another three hoots on the foghorn, stared at her. This was a Susan he had never seen.

And then Titty suddenly clutched the coaming of the cockpit and leant over it.

"She's being sick," said Roger.

John stretched out a hand to hold her shoulder.

"Leave me alone," said Titty. "I'm not. I can't be. It's only one of my heads. I'll be all right if I lie down just for a bit."

She scrambled to the companion-way, got down one step, slipped on the next, and fell in a heap on the cabin floor.

"Titty, are you all right?" cried John. "Look here, Roger. You go and help her. I can't let go of the tiller."

This was too much.

"I'm going," said Susan furiously. She took a long breath and struggled down into the cabin, leaving John and Roger looking at each other with horrified eyes. Neither of them said a word. John attended to his steering. Roger waited a moment and then went on staring into the fog.

Down in the fore-cabin Titty scrambled into her bunk. Something was hammering in her head as if to burst it. Susan, once more the mate, with a job to do, wedged her in with rugs. It was all she could do to keep her footing. One moment she was leaning over Titty, and the next moment had to grab at the side of her bunk so as not to fall. Somehow or other she managed to spread a blanket over her.

"Try to go to sleep," she said.

"It's all right now I'm lying down," said Titty.

And then the thing Susan had dreaded happened. Could she get out of the cabin in time? Spots danced before her eyes. She swallowed, though there was nothing in her mouth. She flung herself at the companion-steps. She scrambled up them, fell into the cockpit, grabbed the coaming, just as Titty had done. "Oh . . . Oh . . . Oh . . ." she groaned, and was sick over the side. She was sick again and again. When it was over she remembered that she was in the way so that John could not see the compass. She dragged herself across the cockpit and sat in the opposite corner, holding the coaming, ready to be sick once more.

"Susan," said John at last. "Poor old chap."

There was no answer.

"Susan," said John again. "We've simply got to sound the foghorn."

Susan leaned her head against the cabin and sobbed.

John's lip trembled. He bit it. There was a hotness behind his eyes. For one moment he thought
of giving in and going back. He looked astern into
the grey fog. No. He must go on. The only hope
of safety was outside. He wedged himself firmly
with a foot against the opposite seat. He had the
tiller with both hands. He peered at the compass
card with eyes that were somehow not as good
as usual. South-east ... East-south-east ... East
by south ... South-east by east ... He nodded to
Roger.

Roger drove in the handle of the foghorn, once,
twice and again. If John said it was all right, it
must be. He patted Susan's cold hand.

The bleat of the Cork lightship sounded already
far astern.

Before them was the grey curtain of the fog.
And beyond it was the open sea.

POINTS OF THE COMPASS

CHAPTER XI

WHOSE FAULT NOW?

"But what is it?"

For a long time they had been hearing a new noise in the fog ... a long hoot that seemed as if it were never going to stop, then a moment's pause, and then another hoot as long as the first, then silence for nearly a minute, and then those two long hoots again.

"It's the lightship on the edge of the chart," said John. "It's the Sunk, where Jim waited about when he was coming from Dover. It can't be anything else ... We've done it. We're safe outside and we haven't hit anything. Susan, don't you see we were right?"

"But we oughtn't to be here at all," groaned Susan. "Oh. ... Ough ... Oh." It was as if she had swallowed an apple whole and the apple was trying to get back and finding her throat too narrow for it.

It was blowing harder now, and the *Goblin* was racing through the fog, heaving high on the top of a sea and dropping down into the trough, only to be heaved high again as another rose under her. John had found out how to make things easier for steering by using a tiller line. At first he had not known what they were for, but for some time now he had hitched a line round a cleat and was letting it take some of the tremendous pull of the tiller. Roger was sounding the foghorn every now and then. He had been a good deal frightened but was already much less so. He could feel that John was less worried than he had been, now that they were outside the shoals. And with Titty stretched on her bunk below, and Susan being sick, he felt that he and John had charge of the ship. And anyhow, he was going to be a sailor some day, like Daddy, and being frightened was not going to do any good. Besides, time was passing and nobody could go on being frightened for ever.

"I say, John," he said. "She's sailing faster than her fastest."

"Not bad," said John.

*

Those two long hoots had sounded nearer and nearer, and then had been left astern and had sounded further and further away. They never saw that lightship at all, though they must have passed it fairly close.

*

Two hours later there was a change. For a moment it was as if there was suddenly more light.

"I can see a lot further than I could," said Roger.

"Fog's lifting at last," said John. "With this wind I thought it was bound to blow away."

"It's going," said Roger, looking at wisps of mist that were blowing across grey white-capped waves.

"There's something else coming," said John, glancing over his shoulder.

"What is it?" said Roger. He, too, looked astern.

The fog was certainly lightening all round them, but astern it was as if a dark cloud was pressing down into the sea.

"Rain," said John.

"The wind came first," said Roger cheerfully, remembering the old rhyme he had often heard from Daddy ... "When the wind's before the rain, Soon you may make sail again ..." "Will we put the staysail up?"

"Of course not," said John. "We don't want to go any further than we need, because of getting back. Anyway, she's got all she can carry. She's jolly hard to hold even now. Hullo! Listen! Can you hear anything?"

They listened. The wind thrummed in the rigging. The seas rushed noisily by. Every now and then the top of a wave broke and crashed into white foam.

"There it is ..."

Faintly ahead of them they heard it ... Two long blasts and then a short one.

"That's another lightship," said John. "It's a long way off."

Susan lifted a weary head and looked round.

"It's clearing, John. It really is. I can see quite a long way. Aren't we going to turn back?"

John looked astern again.

"Not clear enough to see anything yet," he said. "And look what's coming up ... It's no good turning just now ..."

As he spoke the first raindrops hit them. Ping ... Ping ... they sounded on the taut sail.

"Oilskins," said John. "Quick."

"I can't go down," said Susan.

"Take the tiller," said John. "No, look out. This
is a tough one . . ." He forced the tiller up with
all his strength as wind and rain leapt at him
together. "Good man, Roger."

*

Roger was already tumbling down the companion-steps into the cabin. He struggled forward.
Titty's white face looked at him from her bunk.

"What is it?" she asked.

"They want oilies," said Roger. "It's rain . . ."

"Have we turned back yet?"

"No . . . But I think we're going to, soon . . .
Susan wants to, but John says it's no good till
the rain's passed. It's coming up inky."

Roger struggled on, squeezing between mast
and bunk, and pulled an armful of oilskins out of
a cupboard. He slipped and sat on the floor, and
stayed there to sort them out.

"I've got John's and mine," he said. "And here's
Jim's . . ."

"Oh, I say," said Titty. "He'll get awfully wet
without it." For a moment she saw the skipper of
the *Goblin* sitting on a bollard on the pierhead in
the pouring rain.

"Is this Susan's?"

"No. It's mine," said Titty. "It's got a green
tab. Hers is brown."

"Got it. I say, Titty, how's your head?"

"Better. Don't shove my oilie away. I'm coming
too."

Roger staggered to his feet and worked his
way back through the leaping cabin. Overhead,
the rain was already spattering on the cabin roof.

He lurched against the table, tripped, and fell with the oilskins in his arms. He picked himself up. Rain was dripping from the companion-steps. He must hurry. He pushed the oilskins up through the companion. Someone took them from him. He scrambled after them.

"Titty's better," he said. "She's coming up . . ."

"No she isn't," said Susan. "No good everybody getting wet. Titty! You stay where you are, lying down."

Titty heard her, just as her feet were on the floor. For a moment she hesitated. A lurch of the ship and a sudden throb behind her eyes decided her. It was no good going up there to be ill and make things worse for everybody. She lay down again in her bunk, listening to rain overhead, and the swish and swirl of the water on the other side of the *Goblin*'s thin planking . . . Jim on the pierhead . . . Mother and Bridgie . . . Awful . . . But a real voyage at last . . . If only Captain Nancy knew . . .

*

"You too, Roger," said Susan. "You'd better keep dry."

"Who's going to keep a look out?" said Roger. "Who's going to sound the foghorn? And my oilskin's a new one. No leaks at all."

"Oh let him stay," said John. "Look here, Rogie. Hang on to this tiller rope for all you're worth, just while I get my arms in. No. Finish getting into your own oilies first."

It was no easy job getting into oilskins while the *Goblin*, leaping along, threw him first to one

side of the cockpit and then to the other. Roger
managed it, and then, for one moment of mixed
joy and terror, hung on to tiller and tiller rope
and felt he was steering the ship. Susan had
not bothered to put her oilskins on. She had
wrapped them round her shoulders like a cloak,
without trying to push her arms into the sleeves,
as she sat miserably in a corner and felt the rain
trickling down her neck. John, leaning with his
back against the tiller to help Roger, struggled
into his, pulled his sou'wester from the pocket
and crammed it firmly on his head.

"Put your sou'wester on, Susan," he said. "No
good getting your hair wet for nothing. Tie yours
under your chin, Roj, or you'll be losing it. All right
now. Here it comes properly. Just listen to it on the
water . . ."

It came, a white wall of rain beating down
into the sea.

In one moment the red mainsail had darkened, soaked through from head to foot. The
water poured from it, running along the boom,
dripping on the cabin top. The rain seemed to
come in bucketfuls, splashing noisily on the decks,
sluicing through the scuppers of the lee rail. The
ropes darkened and stiffened. Waterfalls spurted
down from the cabin roof into the cockpit. Susan
roused herself to pull to the sliding hatch in the
cabin roof and to close the doors, but already there
was a pool at the foot of the steps.

"It's a pity the water tank's full," said Roger,
turning to face wind and rain, and opening his
mouth as if he were a shipwrecked sailor on a
raft, seeking to wet his parched throat.

John gave him half a grin, no more, for the wind
that had come with the rain had made it a good
deal harder to keep the *Goblin* on her course. He
wriggled his shoulders as, in spite of his sou'wester, the cold rain found its way somehow down the
back of his neck. He peered through the porthole
at the compass, but could hardly see it because of
the water streaming down the glass.

Roger undid the thumbscrew and swung the
porthole open, the porthole that Susan had polished so carefully not a thousand years ago,
though it seemed as long, but only this morning, while anchored in the shelter of Harwich
harbour. John felt easier again. At least he
could see the compass card, though not very
well, now that the slide in the roof was shut
and both doors at the top of the companion.
He had to get his head close to it to make
sure.

"The rain's as bad as the fog," he said. "Better
sound that horn again."

"Aye, aye, sir," said Roger.

Susan shuddered as those three long deafening
roars came from close beside her.

They heard the siren of a steamship far away,
and the regular fog signal from a lightship, two
long hoots and a short one, that had been
bothering John for some time.

One rain-squall followed another. One would
pass, and for a few minutes the sea seemed
to widen out around them. Then another came
sweeping after them, and the sea narrowed till
they were sailing in a little circle of water walled
in by pouring rain.

"I say, Susan," said John. "You can see it's no good turning back while it's like this."

"You'll turn back as soon as it stops, won't you?" said Susan. "It'll be dark before we know where we are."

"We'll turn back the moment it clears enough to see things," said John. "You don't want to turn back before . . ."

"So long as we turn back at the very first chance," said Susan.

"We will," said John.

Susan, holding firmly to the cockpit coaming and the cabin roof, got to her feet. Lakes of water splashed from her oilskin to the cockpit floor. She got first one arm into a sleeve and then the other. John, for all his careful steering, watched her hopefully.

"Better now?" he said at last. "Good old Susan."

"Daddy says lots of sailors are sick every time they go to sea," said Roger.

"It was partly because we oughtn't to be at sea at all," said Susan. "How many hours have we been sailing?"

"Hours and hours," said Roger.

"My watch is in the cabin," said John. "Have a look at the clock, Roger."

Roger opened one half of the door to the companion and craned in. "Gosh," he said. "It's nearly seven . . ."

"It'll take us just as long to get back," said Susan.

"Longer," said John. "Going against the wind . . . It'll be dark long before we get back . . ."

"Will it be tacking?" said Susan.

"It'll be like that night on the lake in the *Swallow*, when we counted a hundred first on one tack and then on the other."

"The night we nearly ran into an island," said Roger.

John was silent. There was no need to remind him of that. He remembered it very well indeed, and how Mother had said that he had very nearly been a duffer, and how all-night sailing had been forbidden. For some time he had been worrying about how he would have to steer to get back on the same course if they had the wind against them. It was going to be a good deal worse if it was dark. He told himself that the wild night in the dark on the lake had been two whole years ago, so that he was now a great deal older. But this was the sea and not a lake. There would be no friendly landing-stage to which they could tie up while they had a sleep.

"Perhaps the wind'll change," he said at last.

But the rain-squalls came one after another from the same direction, and they drove on and on, with the rain beating on the sails, the deck, the cabin roof and their oilskinned backs. The noises from the lightship that had been ahead of them, came from somewhere to the north, and then grew fainter and fainter astern.

*

By the time the last of the rain-squalls had blown away over a grey tossing sea the sky ahead of them was already darkening.

"It's stopped raining," said Roger.

They looked astern, and could see grey water,

white tops of waves, and a strip of pale sky under grey clouds. Of the land there was nothing to be seen at all. The *Goblin* was utterly alone, racing along, up and down, up and down. Fast as she was sailing, the seas moved faster still. Wave after wave swept up on her quarter, lifted her, and passed on. Wave after wave came rolling up, broke with the loud noise of churning water, and left a long mane of foam.

"Let's turn back now," said Susan.

John took a deep breath and looked at the compass for help. Somewhere near south-east they had been sailing all this time. To get back they must go somewhere near north-west. He turned for a moment and stood facing the wind, getting it to feel the same on both cheeks at once, so that he knew he was facing directly into it. Worse than he had thought. The wind had veered a little. It was going to be nearly in their teeth on the return voyage. They would have to tack all the way, zigzagging to and fro along their course. And he could not be really sure even of what their course ought to be. The tide must have made that course quite different from the one shown by the compass. The ebb-tide must have swept them one way and the flood would be sweeping them the other, and then the ebb would come again. And the dark was close upon them. Well, in the open sea the dark would be no worse than the fog. But what about closing with the coast and all its shoals in the middle of the night? And there was Roger looking at him, and Susan trusting in him to bring them back as he had brought them out. He had to keep his doubts to himself. Anyway, he

would try to get back to the lightships. What had
Jim done? Hung about till he could see his way in.
If they could find the Sunk lightship as Jim had
done and keep in sight of it till dawn . . .

"All right," he said. "I'll bring her round now.
We'll have to haul in the mainsheet as she comes
round. Sing out as soon as you're ready."

"Ready now," said Susan. "The sooner the
better . . ."

"Now," said John, glancing over his shoulder
at the white-capped seas. He cast off the tiller
rope, let the tiller swing down, and, with Susan
helping, hauled in the mainsheet hand over hand.

The next moment things began to happen.

It was as if, suddenly, the strong wind had risen
to a hurricane. You never know quite how hard
the wind is blowing when you are sailing with it.
It is a very different thing when you come to turn
against it.

As the *Goblin* came round, broadside on to
the waves, she was flung over on her side.
Water poured along the lee deck. John and
Susan together were flung against the coaming
of the cockpit. John, who was trying to make
the mainsheet fast, found his hands under water
fumbling at the cleat. Susan lost her grip of the
sheet. John hung on, making the sheet fast while
the water sluiced over his elbows.

"Push the tiller down," he shouted, but Susan
had slipped and could not get hold of it. Roger,
luckily, had been thrown from his seat into the
bottom of the cockpit, and stayed there. "I might
easily have been thrown right overboard," he said
afterwards. At the time he said nothing at all.

John pulled the tiller down himself, as the *Goblin* picked herself up and rushed along the deep furrows of the sea. Round she came.

Crash!

Her bowsprit plunged into a wave. A lump of water hurled itself into the jib. Up she came again, her bowsprit pointing high in the air. Down she dived once more.

Crash!

A sea broke over her bows, and sheets of water flew up over the cabin roof, into the mainsail, and splashed down over the struggling figures in the cockpit.

They came too near the wind and the jib flogged as if it would tear to pieces or pull the mast out of the ship. Another sea burst over the bows and came sluicing aft over the cabin roof. They were knee deep in water. John wrestled with the tiller. The thunder of the jib stopped, and the *Goblin* again darted forward, met a sea as if it had been a rock, dived, and rose heavily, only to meet the onrush of another breaking crest.

Roger, in the bottom of the cockpit, with water sloshing round him, did not try to get up. John, white-faced and desperate but still thinking of how they were to get back, tried to see the swinging compass, to ease the mainsheet, and to steer against a force that was too much for him.

"Stop it, John! Stop it! I can't ... I can't ... Ough! ... Oughgulloch! ... Ough! ... Oh! ... Oh! ..." And Susan, shaken almost to pieces with this new violent motion of the battling ship, lay half across the cockpit, with her head over the coaming, and was sick. A wave broke across the cabin roof and a lump of green water hit her on the side of the head.

"John! John!" she cried. "I can't bear it. Stop it! . . . Stop it just for a minute!"

And John, frantically feeling under water for the cleat to which the mainsheet was fast, cast it off, lost hold of it, caught it again, paid it out, and leaned back with all the weight of his body against the tiller, bracing himself against the side of the cockpit. Would she answer, or wouldn't she? Slowly, wallowing in the trough of the sea, the *Goblin* turned away from the wind and back on her old course. She gathered speed once more. The wind seemed suddenly to have dropped to half its strength. Once more, running before wind and sea instead of punching into them, she was making easy weather of it, swinging on her way. It was a return to peace after a raging, desperate struggle.

"Oh . . . Oh . . . Oh." Susan's spasms of sea-sickness were subsiding.

Roger pulled himself up from the cockpit floor and looked back at the following seas. "Gosh!" he said. "That was pretty awful."

A wail for help sounded from inside the cabin. Titty had been calling before, but in the turmoil of those last few minutes nobody had heard her. Now she was beating at the cabin door from inside. Roger opened a flap of the door and Titty's frightened face looked out from below.

"Are we sinking?" she said. "There's some water on the floor of the cabin. I was thrown right out of my bunk."

"It's all right," said John. "We got some water over when we tried to go the other way."

Roger looked down the companion.

"There's a book floating about," he said. "Everything's all over the place."

"Somebody's got to pump," said John. "We took a lot of water over and we've got to get it out again."

"Oh . . . Oh . . . Oh . . ." moaned Susan.

"Try pumping," said John. "You'll feel better with something to do. And we've got to get all that water out before we have another shot at turning back . . ."

"Oh not again," Susan groaned. "I can bear it all right like this, but it's too awful going the other way."

"We could go right on till the wind drops a bit," said John doubtfully. "And the wind may change. It can't blow like this for ever . . ."

"Oh, what are we to do?" said Susan. "And it's going to be night."

"It'll be night anyway," said John. "It won't be worse than the fog."

"I've got the lid of the pump off," said Roger. "If Susan's going to pump, I'd better go down and help Titty in the cabin."

"Don't you feel sea-sick at all?" said Susan almost angrily.

"Not a bit," said Roger.

"Oh . . . Oh . . . Oh . . . Oh . . . Where's the handle?" She got hold of the handle of the pump and began pumping. Up and down. Up and down. "John," she said, "I can't help it. We've got to go on like this till it gets better. If we turn round and

start jumping and banging again I shall simply
die . . ."

"All right," said John. "Count your strokes . . ."

"One . . . Two . . . Oh . . . Four . . . Oh . . .
Ough . . . Oh . . . Sorry, John. I really am better
. . . Six . . . Seven . . ."

"Just shout if I'm wanted on deck," said Roger,
and John, for the first time for many hours, felt
like laughing.

Roger went carefully backwards down the companion-steps, finding water over his ankles when
he got to the bottom. Titty was down there, picking one thing after another out of the wet.

"Are you all right now?" he said.

"Yes," said Titty. "At least I think so. My
head's stopped aching long ago. I was asleep
for a bit until I got flung out. What happened?"

"We tried turning round but it didn't work,"
said Roger. "So we're going on . . . But it's Susan
herself who wants to go on now."

CHAPTER XII

A CURE FOR SEA-SICKNESS

TITTY, who had been asleep, coming down with
a bump on the cabin floor, thrown this way and
that as she crawled on all fours towards the
companion-steps, and seeing water pouring down
over the engine, had been more frightened than
she liked to admit. And then things had suddenly
quieted, and the door had opened, and John had
said it was all right, and Roger had come down, as
cheerful as could be. Titty, now that it was over,
was very much ashamed. She, an able-seaman, to
get into a panic like that! How much had Roger
guessed?

"Get your feet out of it," she said. "Up on that
bunk. I've got no shoes on, so it doesn't matter."

"I'm pretty wet anyway," said Roger.

"Don't get wetter," said Titty. "Let's get the
things all that side. Lucky John's blankets didn't
go. What's that noise?"

"Susan's working the pump."

"Did we run into something?"

"I don't think so."

"Where did the water come from?"

"It just came . . . Dollops and dollops of it."

"Were you frightened?"

"Just a bit," said Roger, "but it's all right again
now."

"Grab that book . . . No . . . Don't put it in
the shelf."

166

Roger caught Knight on *Sailing*, that John had not put away. He grabbed it out of the water, and, just in time, was stopped from pushing it in among the dry books.

"Put it in the sink," said Titty, "to let it drain."

Not even Susan at her best could have hoped to make the *Goblin*'s cabin properly tidy. But Titty and Roger did what they could by piling all loose things on the lee bunk from which they were not so likely to fall off. It took them a long time.

"How's the water?" John called down to them.

"Gone," shouted Roger. "The floor's nearly dry."

"This box of matches is soaked," said Titty.

"Shall I put it in the sink too?" said Roger.

"Aren't there some matches in that shelf?"

Roger scrambled across the cabin and felt along the shelf over the bunk. There was a low coaming along the shelf to keep things from falling off, and he found a box of matches lying snug against it. Titty, wedging herself between bunk and table, was trying to lift the chimney from the cabin lamp.

"I say," said Roger. "Would she want you to?"

"Of course," said Titty. "She'd be doing it herself if she wasn't ill."

Four matches were spent in lighting that lamp, but the result was certainly worth it. The little lamp, swinging wildly in its gimbals, sent shadows chasing all ways about the cabin, but gave a feeling of triumph to both the able-seamen, who, for a moment, sat holding on by the table, watching it. Having that little lamp properly lit in the cabin was almost like snapping their fingers at the storm.

"I'm going to light the lamp for the compass,"

said Roger. "It's just a candle, but it's in gimbals too."

"We ought to have thought of it first," said Titty. "Here are the matches . . ."

"Gosh!" said Roger suddenly. "What's happening now? Susan's steering. Where's John?"

Something queer was going on. From down below in the cabin they could see Susan, her sou'wester all awry, her face white and worried, wisps of hair blown across it, hanging on to tiller and tiller rope, steering with her eyes not on the compass but on something over their heads. What was that banging on the cabin roof? John couldn't have gone forward . . . Or could he? . . . How long had Susan been at the tiller? She was calling out something . . . not to them in the cabin. John must be on the foredeck.

"I expect they'll want me," said Roger and made for the companion-steps.

And just then they heard Susan shriek, and saw her let go of the tiller altogether.

*

Even before they had made up their minds to go on, John had been finding it harder and harder to keep the *Goblin* from charging round into the wind. Those few moments when they had tried to turn back had shown him how strong the wind really was. And it might get stronger. Night was coming. Something had to be done about it. He knew he ought to reef. He had put it off as long as he could, hoping the wind would slacken. But he was getting tired, and it was blowing as hard as ever, and reefing would be much worse if

he had to do it in the dark. He looked at Susan.
She was huddled up over the pump in the corner
of the cockpit, leaning her head against the cabin.
She had stopped pumping. The pump had sucked
dry at last . . . four hundred and seventy strokes
. . . or was it five hundred and seventy? . . . Twice
she had had to break off to hang miserable and
groaning over the coaming.

"Susan," said John.

She did not hear him in the noise of wind
and water.

"Susan!" he shouted.

She lifted her head. He saw something that
was hardly Susan's face, blotched and white, with
wisps of bedraggled hair across her eyes, a face
wet with rain and tears.

"Not yet," she gasped. "Not again . . . I can't
. . . I can't bear it." For one awful moment she
had thought he meant to try once more to turn
back, to bring the *Goblin* round and head her into
that raging wind and battering, leaping sea.

"It's going to be dark," he shouted. "I can't
go on holding her like this . . . Too much sail
. . . Reef . . . I've got to reef . . ."

"You can't," groaned Susan.

"I've got to!" yelled John. "He showed me
how . . ."

"You'll be thrown overboard . . ."

"Rope," shouted John. "I can't let go the tiller
. . . Rope . . . Starboard locker . . . That one . . ."

Susan slid herself along the seat and hauled
a bundle of ropes out of the locker. She tried to
disentangle one rope from all the others that had
fallen in a heap on the cockpit floor. Bending to do

this was too much for her. She flung herself across
the cockpit, collided with John, hit the tiller with
her elbow, grabbed the coaming, and was sick once
more.

When she looked again at John, she saw that
he had one end of a rope and was kicking at the
tangle, trying to free the rest of it. He could not
do it. She dropped on the cockpit floor, and there,
grovelling at his feet, cleared the rope. She struggled up again. What was he doing? Pushing with
his body against the tiller and making the end of
the rope fast round his middle.

"Oh, John," she groaned. "What *are* you going
to do?"

"Life-line," shouted John. "Look here. You'll
have to steer her . . . Just for a minute . . .
No time to spare . . . I ought to have done it
before . . ."

"I can't . . ."

"You must," said John. "Buck up, Susan . . . It'll
be easier the moment she's reefed. Look here. Get
your foot like that. Hang on to the tiller rope and
push against the tiller for all you're worth. Don't
let her come round whatever you do . . ."

Susan found herself in John's place. He was
rummaging in a locker . . . What was that brass
handle that he was forcing into the pocket of his
oilskins? He was making the other end of the rope
he had tied round his middle fast to a bollard on
the side deck. He was shouting . . . She caught the
words . . . "If I do go overboard I'll still be tied on
. . . and you'll have to let her come into the wind
while I get back . . . It'll be all right . . ."

"Oh, John! . . . No! . . . NO!"

But already he had climbed out of the cockpit. He was sitting on the cabin roof, clinging to the hand rail, wriggling himself forward. A sea leapt up on the quarter and splashed aboard. She saw him look back at her . . . Not to let her come to . . . Keep her steady . . . She must . . . She must . . . She pushed at the tiller with all the strength she had. Again she saw John's face. He said something, she could not hear what, but she could see from his face that she was doing right. He was going on, inch by inch, along that dancing, swaying, dripping cabin roof. And no matter how she fought the tiller, the *Goblin* leapt and pitched as if she were *trying* to jerk him off.

*

John had never felt so lonely in his life. In the cockpit, with its high coamings, he had been flung about and bumped here, there, and everywhere in his desperate struggle with the tiller, keeping the *Goblin* before the wind and stopping her from broaching to. But he had felt that he was inside something, in the boat, together with Susan, Titty and Roger. The moment he had climbed out of the cockpit that feeling was gone. He was not *in* something but *on* something, and on something that was doing its best to be rid of him. Wild water churned close past his feet. The *Goblin* leapt and dived and leapt again as the seas swept by.

Crash! That sea coming up on the quarter burst over the coamings. A biggish dollop must have come aboard. A hard bucketful of spray landed on his back as he clung there on the roof of the cabin. He looked over his shoulder, blinking with the wind and spray in his eyes. Susan seemed very far away. What was she doing? Perhaps she wasn't strong enough to hold the *Goblin* on her course. Another sea like that and he would have to go to help her. But he must get some of the sail off first. The thought of Susan's misery when they had come head to wind came again into his mind. The wind was stronger now. Reefing was the only way. Hadn't Jim said that with roller reefing, just winding the sail down on the boom, you could reef with one hand no matter what the ship was doing? He looked forward. The water from that last splash was pouring down the sail and dripping from the boom. The cockpit seemed a hundred miles away. But so did the foredeck. Somehow or other he must get there. High on the leaping cabin top, hanging on with both hands, he hardened his heart. The thing simply must be done. The *Goblin* was going steadier now. Susan had got the hang of it. He shouted to tell her so, but the wind blew the words back down his throat with a lot of salt spray, and he gulped and gave her a wet encouraging grin.

Now for it. Once more he measured the distance to shrouds and mast. The rail on the cabin top seemed a flimsy little thing to hold. But till he reached the mast there would be nothing else. He pulled at his life-line to make sure it was coming free out of the cockpit. Never do if it got hitched up on something and he had to go back to loose it. All right. He reached forward and slid himself along the roof. Gosh! How did she manage to leap like that just at the wrong moment But he was

still on board and had gained a good six inches.
He did it again and yet again. Lonely? It was as
if he was outside life altogether and wouldn't be
alive again till he got back. He remembered a
man he had once seen putting in a loose slate
on the steep roof of a house. But at least the roof
had kept still and had not tried to throw the man
about.

Come on! He had got half way, and things were
no worse than when he had first left the shelter
of the cockpit. He was still on the cabin roof and
the rail wasn't so flimsy after all, and he would
soon get a grip on the shrouds, the halyards, and
the mast itself. He could take a rest then. Oh, no,
he couldn't. Susan wouldn't be able to hang on to
that tiller for long. Buck up! In quick, short jerks,
he slid along the roof. Ah! The halyards were in
his left hand, a shroud in his right. He was there
and it would take something pretty bad to throw
him off now.

Loose ends of rope were sloshing about on
the foredeck. Lucky he had lashed the anchor,
as Jim had shown him how to do it. What would
have happened if that had come adrift? And the
rope that they had used for an anchor warp, a
rope neither thick enough nor long enough, was
coiled round the winch. That was all right. All
this mess must be the falls of the jib halyards
and the main. Well, he couldn't tidy it up now.
Hanging on by the shroud, he felt in his pocket
for the little brass crank handle for the reefing
gear, got it out and, after a struggle, fitted it in
its place. Now for reefing. He had to ease off the
main halyard while he turned the little crank and

wound the sail down on the revolving boom. One hand for the crank. One hand for easing off the halyard, though it would want two, really. That made three. And at least two hands for holding on. That made five, and he had only two altogether. "One hand for yourself and one for the ship." His father had told him that years ago, when he was a little boy and had tumbled down in the bottom of a fishing-boat while using both hands to pass Daddy a rope. Well, he hadn't got a hand to spare. Far from it. Perhaps he could ease off the halyard and hang on to it at the same time. He worked himself down on the foredeck with one arm round the ropes that stretched taut up and down the mast. Main halyard? This was it. Sopping wet and jammed on the pin. His own fault, making a tight hitch for fear it would slip when he had been hoisting the sail. The struggle to free it was the worst bit yet. "Beast! Beast! Come on, will you!" He got it loose at last. Now then. He gave a jerk at his life-line which was getting in his way. Then, cautiously he slackened the halyard. If only that had been all. But he had that crank to wind as well. He reached up round the mast, found the crank, and, thanks to a sudden lurch of the *Goblin*, pulled it off. He was rather out of breath. But he had not gone overboard and neither had the crank. It was still in his hand. He fitted it on again and turned. Pretty stiff. He went on turning. Yes. The thing was working. The boom was twisting just as it should. Brown sail, rolled on it, showed on the nearer side. Hullo! Stuck? Of course he had to slack away the halyard a bit more because of the sail already wound down on the boom. He did it, and went on, forcing that crank round and round, winding, slacking the halyard, and then winding again. The first cringle in the luff of the sail was down on the boom. That meant one reef. But she needed much more off her than that. Then he noticed a girt in the sail, and remembered that he had to cast off the lower mast-hoops. That meant standing up.

Anyway, one reef was rolled down. The sail was that much smaller. Already she must be not quite so hard to steer. He pulled himself to his feet and knelt on the cabin roof. How were those mast-hoops fastened to the sail? Key-shackles. You had to give the key half a turn and then it would slip out of its slot. Easy. Yes, with dry hands, but his were wet. The key would not turn. He needed the spike of his scout knife. That meant getting a wet hand inside his oilskins, which were held tight round his middle by the rope he had knotted round himself, and then getting that wet hand into his hip pocket. An awful job with everything bucketing about. He did it, and the key slipped round and out of its shackle so easily that he thought he could after all have done it without the spike. He could only just reach the second mast-hoop. With both hands above his head, holding on by the mast-hoop only, his feet felt as if they were going to slip from under him. He thought of himself clinging on, and flapping out from the mast as if he were a flag.

Far away in the cockpit he saw Susan's face, white and frightened.

Gosh! He had been frightened too, but the worst was over now. He was down on the foredeck again, winding steadily. There was that second cringle . . . Two reefs . . . He went on winding . . . Better have all three down while he was about it. What was it Daddy had said? "Never be ashamed to reef in the dark." And it was going to be dark almost at once. He glanced about him. Darkness ahead. Dark clouds everywhere and under them nothing to be seen but white-capped waves, and spray blown from their crests.

There. The thing was done. The crank that had once come off too easily, stuck for a moment. He jerked at it and freed it and then nearly lost it, through missing the way to the pocket of his streaming oilskin. The main halyard was fast. He looked aft at Susan and could see that the steering was no longer the fight that it had been. With her mainsail only half its proper size, the *Goblin* no longer tried so hard to turn into the wind.

He felt suddenly confident. He raised himself to his feet and stood on the foredeck, holding on by shrouds and halyards, while the deck lifted beneath him, dropped away, and lifted again. The *Goblin* was safe now. They could run on all night like this. They could run on for ever. Hullo! Was that Susan calling? He turned, stepped on a rope, took his foot off it, found he had a bight of it round his ankle, kicked, let go with one hand to get rid of it, and, as he slipped and fell, heard Susan's piercing shriek . . .

*

It had been worse for Susan watching him than for John working his way along the cabin roof. It would have been worse still if she had not been steering and finding it as much as she could do. But he had reached the foredeck safe and she had felt very much happier. Then she had seen his hand turning the crank by the mast. She had seen the sail growing smaller. She had felt the steering easier with the shrinking of the sail. And then, suddenly, there was John on the cabin roof again, reaching up at mast-hoops. What for? What for? Why couldn't he just wind up the sail and come back, quick, to the safety of the cockpit? He was down on the foredeck again. The winding was going on once more. It stopped. She saw him jerk the brass crank off and feel for his pocket with it. And then she saw him get to his feet and stand there, swaying with the leaping boat, with his hands on shrouds and halyards.

"John!" Her call was indignant. What on earth was he doing that for?

"John!" Her angry call turned unexpectedly into a call for help. She was going to be sick again. She choked. Something buzzed in her head. Spots dithered before her eyes. Yes. She was going to be sick now, at once . . . He must come, quick, to take the tiller for her.

"John! . . . oh!" Her call for help turned to a shriek of terror. John was gone. One moment he had been standing on the foredeck, swaying with the motion of the *Goblin*. The next moment he was gone. A clutching hand, missing the shrouds . . . the life-line jerking taut. He was gone. Without knowing what she did she threw up both hands, loosing the tiller. She looked at the seas racing past the *Goblin*'s side. And then, when she thought he had gone for ever, she saw a black

ALL BUT O.B.

sou'wester beyond the cabin top, a hand at the ropes by the mast. He was still aboard. In awful shame at having let it go, she grabbed the tiller once more. She never saw John's struggle when, after he had slipped and all but gone over the side, held by his life-line that had caught against the shrouds, he had fought for a grip, got a hand to the end of a halyard and somehow (he himself never knew how he did it) scrambled back to his old place beside the mast. Susan never knew the effort it cost him to stand up once more, just for a moment, so as not to feel himself beaten, before sitting again on the cabin roof and working aft, carefully but wasting no time at all, towards the safety of the cockpit.

*

"Where's John?" said Roger, scrambling out on all fours, and tumbling head first into the cockpit.

By the time he had picked himself up, John had swung his legs over the coaming.

"Sorry, Susan," he said. "It's all right. You steered awfully well. Look here. It's all right now. Nothing's happened . . ."

"John! Oh, John!" said Susan.

"What happened?" said Roger.

"Nothing happened," said John. "I slipped. The life-line works beautifully. I'd have been all right even if I had gone overboard." With hands that shook a little in spite of nothing having happened, he untied the rope he had knotted round his middle, coiled it carefully and put it away in the rope locker.

Titty, climbing out, looked from John to Susan and from Susan to John. She was just going to ask a question, but did not ask it. She felt that the ship was suddenly full of happiness. John was grinning to himself. Susan was smiling through tears that did not seem to matter.

"Let's have the tiller," said John. "How's she steering? Gosh, that reefing's made a difference. I can hold her with one hand, almost. I ought to have reefed long before."

"Let me go on for a bit," said Susan. "I can manage it easily now."

"You did jolly well. It was pretty beastly with the full sail. But I say, didn't you shout? Just before I went and slipped. I thought I heard you."

"I was going to be sick," said Susan. "I knew I was going to be sick . . . and John . . . It's very strange. I don't feel seasick any more."

"Good," said John. "Once it's over, you'll probably never be sea-sick again. How's Titty?"

"All right," said Titty.

"She lit the cabin lamp," said Roger. "I was just going to light the candle lamp for the compass. May I?"

"Go ahead," said John. "I can't see the compass even with the hatch open. And look here. Dig out the big torch. We'd better have it up here for the night . . ."

"What about our red and green lights in the dark?" asked Titty.

"No oil in them," said John.

"How long does the night last?" said Susan. "How long will it be till dawn?"

"Don't know," said John. "A good long time. But it doesn't matter. You can feel she's all right now."

CHAPTER XIII

WOOLWORTH PLATE

THE night closed down on them, making the little
world of the *Goblin* smaller than it had been even
in the fog. They grew accustomed to the dark. It
was still blowing very hard. The seas lifting them
along were no less big. But now that the mainsail
was only half its proper size steering was no
longer such a battle. It was dreadful to think
of Mother and Bridget at Pin Mill not knowing
what had become of them. It was dreadful not
knowing what had happened to Jim, and dreadful
to think of him not knowing what had happened
to his ship. But even Susan, who could not forget
these things for a moment, began to share John's
confidence. As he had said, you could feel the
Goblin was all right. Best of all, John had not
fallen overboard. All four of them were together.
And sooner or later the night would end, the sun
would rise, the wind would ease, and they would
get back to Harwich. Titty was herself again, her
headache gone, enjoying the swoop and rush of the
Goblin in the darkness. Roger, except that for a
long time he had been wondering if nothing was
going to be done about supper, was sitting in the
top of the companion, watching the candlelight on
the compass, and seeing the card swing slowly this
way and that, so that the lubberline was first one
side of south-east and then the other. John, whose
arms were stiff with steering, knew now that so

long as things got no worse he was going to be
able to stick it out.

"Whoa, old lady," he muttered to himself, as
an extra hard puff asked for an extra bit of beef
on the tiller.

"Steady," he muttered. "Now then . . . not too
far . . ." as a curling white wave rolled up out of
the darkness, and he brought the *Goblin* almost
straight before it till its crest had gone creaming
past.

Roger looked through into the lamplit cabin to
see the clock. He turned and spoke over his shoulder to the huddle of dark figures in the cockpit.

"Susan," he said. "It's ten o'clock. Don't you
think I might dig out a bit of chocolate. I know
just where it is."

"Ten o'clock," exclaimed Susan. "Look out of the
way, Rogie. It's time everybody had something to
eat . . ."

"I'll get it," said Titty.

"Sit still," said Susan. "Let me come past."

"I say, Susan," said Roger. "Are you sure you
won't be sick if you go down?"

"I'm all right," said Susan. "I ought to have
gone down ages ago. John can't steer all night
without something to eat."

Roger made himself small to let her get by,
and then, looking down into the cabin watched
her struggle with the locker door, saw her flung
sideways into the lee bunk, saw her sit there a
moment, and then pull herself together and reach
once more into the locker. She had a handful of
those red Woolworth plates. The *Goblin* rolled,
and she fell back into the lee bunk. The locker door

slammed. She was up again now and reaching into
the locker on the other side. Then he saw that she
had got hold of the pork pie . . . and a knife. She
was cutting the pork pie in four . . . Gosh! That
made good slices. Roger knew that he was hun-
grier even than he had thought. Suddenly there
was Susan pushing one of the red plates at him
with a slice of pork pie ready on it.

"Take it," she said. "Quick. That's John's."

"Pork pie," said Roger, handing it on.

"Right," said John. "Shove it on the seat so
that I can get at it."

Roger watched Susan again. The *Goblin* lurched
sharply, and in saving herself she almost dropped
the paper with the other three helpings of pork
pie. The three plates on which she had meant to
put them slipped to the floor of the cabin. She let
them lie.

"Look here," she said. "I'm putting yours in
the sink. You'd better do without plates."

"Can we start?" said Roger.

"Yes," said Susan, half tumbling back in the
cabin, after reaching up to put the paper full of
pork pie in the sink, where it was lit up by the
compass lamp. She seemed in rather a hurry, as
she lifted a mattress, and a board beneath it, and
began pulling bottles of ginger pop from the store
under the bunk.

"You'll have to drink out of the bottles," she
panted, as she put them in the sink with the
bits of pork pie. "No good having mugs flying
about as well as everything else." Then she came
up the companion-steps, and stood on the top one,
with her head above the sliding hatch, holding on

to both sides and taking great gulps of air.

"Aren't you going to have any?" asked Roger, with his mouth full.

"Not just yet," said Susan.

"Ow!" said Roger.

"What's the matter?"

"Only the bottle trying to knock out my best teeth," said Roger.

"Keep your lips over your teeth," said Titty, "and let the grog just trickle in."

*

No. Susan was not going to be sea-sick, but trying to get things out of those cupboards and from under the bunks when you were being flung about and had to hold on where and how you could was enough to make anybody feel peculiar. But she was not going to be sea-sick. She faced into the wind and felt better almost at once. It was blowing so hard that she soon felt she had all the air she wanted. She turned round and looked forward over the cabin roof, when the wind picked up her sou'wester from behind and tried to blow it past her ears.

At first, on coming up out of the lighted cabin, she had been almost blind in the darkness. Presently she was able to see a little more, but not much, just wave-crests, pale splashes rolling up beside the *Goblin* and racing ahead. She stared forward, holding on firmly to the sides of the hatch, and letting her body swing with the motion of the ship. One moment it seemed that she must be looking down a steep slope as the *Goblin* lunged into the trough between two seas.

The next moment she was looking up, as a sea passed under the *Goblin* and tossed her bowsprit skywards. Suddenly, when the *Goblin* was on the top of a sea, she thought she saw the sparkle of a light. It was gone on the instant as if someone had struck a match and blown it out in a single movement. Again the *Goblin* lifted. Again in the darkness ahead came the glimmer of a light, no, two lights, close together.

"John," she cried. "Lights ahead."

"Is it land?" said Titty.

"It can't be," said John. "We must be clear of everything now."

"There they are again ... Gone ... No, there they are ..."

"Where?" said Roger, with a mouth full of pork pie slightly salted with spray.

"Which side?" said Titty.

"Right ahead," said Susan. "There they are again. Two of them. Close together."

"I can't see anything," said John, who for hours had been keeping his eyes fixed steadily on the glowing card of the compass.

"Keep on looking," said Susan ... "There they are ..."

"Got them," said John a moment later. "Fishing boats probably. Keep an eye on them as well as you can."

On and on the *Goblin* raced through the dark. Roger and Titty were steadily munching their pork pie, and now and then getting a few drops of ginger beer into their mouths as well as a lot on their chins. Even Susan had begun her supper. John, with his plate wedged beside him, was

tearing off a bit with his fingers and cramming it
into his mouth whenever he could spare a hand
from the tiller. He tried to see ahead under the
mainsail, but it was not much good. Meanwhile,
lights or no lights, he had to ease the *Goblin* along
on her way through these tumbling seas.

"They're much nearer," said Susan. "I can see
them all the time."

"There's a red light," said Roger. "Lower down."

"And a green," said Titty.

"Steamer," said John. "Those first two must
be her masthead lights. Coming this way."

"Perhaps she's going to Harwich," said Titty.

"Perhaps Daddy's on board her," said Roger.

"Mother said she didn't think he could come
till Saturday," said Titty.

"It's very nearly Friday now," said Roger, peep-
ing in past Susan to see the clock in the lighted
cabin.

Susan groaned. Very nearly Friday, and Mother had heard nothing from them since they had
telephoned on Wednesday evening from Shotley.
And they had promised to be back by tea-time on
Friday. And Jim . . . And there they were, further
and further from home.

"I can see lights on her decks," said Roger.
"And portholes."

And with the sight of those lighted decks and
glowing portholes a new idea came into Susan's
mind. She had agreed that they should keep on
as they were going and turn back only when
things cleared up. The mere thought of turning
back head to wind and sea was enough to let her
know that it would be more than she could bear,

even though she had not been sea-sick since that
awful moment when John had so nearly gone over
the side. But now, the sight of that steamer, full of
people, stewards, stewardesses, officers who knew
exactly where they were going, changed everything once more. Before, they had been alone
and it had been enough to keep the *Goblin* afloat,
waiting for daylight and better weather ... it had
been enough that they were still all four of them
together, and that John was still there as he so
easily might not have been ... But now, there was
that steamer, with rescue at hand, and people to
help ...

"John," said Susan. "Let's sound the foghorn
at them to show we're in distress."

"But we aren't," said John. "Not now ... It's
ever so much better than it was."

"Couldn't they tow us back?"

"No," said John. "Just remember what it was
like when old *Swallow* was towed behind the
Beckfoot motor launch and Nancy went too fast
by mistake ... And, anyway, Jim said, 'Never
take help.'"

"But they wouldn't have to come on board,"
said Susan.

"We simply can't," said John.

"All right," said Susan. "Let them just take
Titty and Roger, and they could tell Mother what's
happened ... and Jim. Yes. Look here, John, we
simply must. How do we stop them?"

"She's coming straight for us," said Roger. "Perhaps she's seen us and knows. Oh, I say, there goes
your pork pie ..."

John's voice rose to a shout.

"But she can't see us. We've got no lights. We've got to get out of the way. Where's the big torch? It's slipped down somewhere. Oh never MIND the pork pie . . ."

He let the tiller swing down. The *Goblin* turned towards the wind. A sea took its chance and slopped up over the quarter, splashing down into the cockpit on Roger and Titty who were fumbling round on the floor for the torch and John's plate and finding only bits of pork pie he had not eaten.

The steamer was coming straight at them, as Roger had said. There were the masthead lights high in the darkness. Below them were other lights, the shaded lights of the upper decks, the glow of portholes, and the two lights that really mattered, a round green eye and a round red one . . . coming nearer and nearer.

"She'll be right on the top of us if we don't look out," said John. "Where *is* that torch?"

"I've got the torch," cried Roger, and a sudden bright glow lit John's feet in the cockpit.

"Here's the plate," said Titty. "I've put it on the seat."

"Give me the torch," said Susan, and grabbed it and pointed it towards the steamer.

Red and green the two blazing eyes of the steamer came on.

"Foghorn!" said John.

"I've got it," said Roger.

"White is for a sternlight," said John. "We ought to be showing a red light to port."

"But we can't," said Susan, frantically waving the torch.

"We can ... We can ..." cried Titty. "Where's the Woolworth plate? Here you are, Susan. Susan! Put it in front of the torch like Jim did last night ... Let the light go through it ..."

"Quick, Roger," said John. "Go on! ... Beef!"

The white, narrow beam of the big torch turned suddenly to a bright red glow as it poured through the half-transparent scarlet plate that Susan held before it. At the same moment a blare of noise came from the foghorn as Roger drove home the plunger. Titty, to this day, thinks that aboard the steamship they could hardly have heard the foghorn, loud as it sounded beside her in the cockpit. Roger, to this day, doubts if, without the foghorn, the steamer's look-out would have noticed the fiery glowing of the Woolworth plate. However it was, over all the noise of wind and water they heard a shrill whistle and a single short hoot of the steamer's siren.

"She's seen us," said John, with a gasp of relief. "The green's gone."

The green starboard light of the big steamship had vanished. The red port light glowed nearer and nearer. A huge wall, blacker than the blackness of the night, towered above them. The steamer's bow wave lifted them and dropped them. Rows of shining portholes raced past. The darkness throbbed with the noise of engines. Just in time, the red glowing plate had been seen, or the foghorn heard, and the steamer had altered course.

A tremendous voice boomed down at them out of the sky, an officer on the bridge roaring into the darkness through a megaphone.

"Yah! You blooming fishmongers! Why don't you show yer lights in proper time?"

"We tried to," shouted John, but he had no megaphone to shout through and nobody aboard the steamer could have heard him.

Already the second masthead light of the steamer was towering past, and the next moment the *Goblin* was caught by the steamer's wash, smashing across the regular seas. The *Goblin* was tossed about like a cork in boiling water. Susan slipped on the companion-steps and all but lost torch and plate in saving herself from tumbling down into the cabin. Roger, Titty and foghorn were flung about in the bottom of the cockpit. John, thrown first one way and then the other, had the breath nearly knocked out of him by the tiller and bruised an elbow and grazed a wrist on the cockpit coaming. Two crests of waves, one after another, sloshed aboard. John, unable to speak, pushed desperately at the tiller. By the time he had managed to get the *Goblin* back on her course, with the wind on her quarter once more, the steamer was already far away. There could be no thought now of asking for a tow or of trying to put anybody aboard.

"Gosh!" panted John, recovering his breath and looking over his shoulder at the steamer's sternlight. "We might have had her mast shaken out of her in a wash like that."

"John," said Roger, picking himself up off the floor. "I've got a good big bit of your pork pie. It was under your foot."

"Good," said John. "Let's have it." His jaw was a little inclined to tremble, and he was glad to wedge a damp lump of pork pie into his mouth.

"Why did they call us fishmongers?" said Titty.

"Probably thought we were fishermen," said John.

"But fish*mongers*," said Roger. "Jolly cheek!"

"I suppose they wouldn't have stopped anyway," said Susan.

"They jolly nearly sent us to the bottom," said John.

"If only we had some green plates too," said Titty. "We could show a starboard light as well."

"If we meet any more steamers," said John, "I'm going to get out of the way before they come anywhere near us. Do look out with that torch, Susan. If you go flashing it about I can't see the compass or anything else."

"I was looking for your supper," said Susan, who was shining the torch here and there about the floor of the cockpit. "Here are two more bits . . . Oh, I say. Where's that blood coming from?" She turned the torch on John's wrist.

"It's only a scrape," said John. "Do put that torch out."

"I know where he keeps the iodine," said Susan. "I'm sure Mother'd say you ought to put some on."

She scrambled down into the cabin, and found it a most comforting place. "Sent us to the bottom." She thought of the great bows of the steamer crashing through the little *Goblin* . . . the steamer on the top of them . . . Titty . . . Roger . . . And instead, there was the cabin lamp swinging easily in its gimbals . . . shadows dancing along the row of Jim Brading's books. The *Goblin* was all right, though a little water was again showing

NIGHT ENCOUNTER

on the cabin floor. And surely she could not be mistaken. The motion was nothing like so bad as when she had last come down. She picked up the plates that were sliding about on the floor, and put them back into the cupboard. She found Jim Brading's medicine chest, got out the iodine, and wedged the chest behind a pillow. She worked her way forward and pulled a clean handkerchief out of the knapsack on her bunk. On the way back, remembering Roger, she took a slab of chocolate.

Up in the cockpit John, holding the tiller with one hand, held out the damaged wrist. Titty, just for a moment, flashed the torch on it. Susan slopped iodine on it out of the bottle.

"Yow," said John. "I wish you hadn't spotted it."

She bound up the wrist with the handkerchief.

"There's water on the floor again, but not much," she said. "I'm going to do some pumping. And we're going to have a ration of chocolate. And aren't there a few bananas left in the bag in the starboard locker?"

"Have a rest, Susan," said John, after a bit.

"Let me pump," said Roger. "I've finished my supper. There can't be much water left anyhow. There's none showing in the cabin."

Roger was quietly counting his strokes at the pump. "Thirty-six . . . thirty-seven . . . thirty-eight . . ." "Thirty-nine" never came. That was a comfortable corner by the pump, and after the excitement of the steamer, counting pump strokes had been very like counting sheep.

"Pump sucking dry?" asked John.

There was no answer.

"Look here," said Susan. "We're going to be

sailing all night. Roger and Titty had better get
into their bunks and go to sleep properly."

Titty started and looked round in the darkness.

"Let's stay awake just for a little," she said.
"It's clearing up. Bits of the sky are quite prickly
with stars."

CHAPTER XIV

AT PIN MILL

(Thursday night and Friday morning)

Upstairs in Alma Cottage, Bridget stirred in bed.
Slap, slap, slap . . . slap, slap, slap . . . Something
was beating on the bedroom window. Bridget
opened her eyes. It was black dark. She lay there
listening. Slap, slap, slap . . . She turned over,
pushed an elbow into her pillow and lifted her
head.

"Bridget."

A quiet voice in the darkness made the room
seem comfortable and Bridget's breath came less
jerkily. Mother was awake too.

"What's that noise?" said Bridget.

"Only the rose tree on the wall," said Mother.
"You know, that branch that hangs down across
the top of the window."

"Did you hear the rain beating on the roof?"
said Bridget. "Before I went to sleep."

"It's stopped raining a long time ago," said
Mother. "But it's blowing rather hard."

"Have you been awake all night?"

"Oh, no. I expect I've been to sleep quite a
lot really."

There was a long silence. At least, for a long
time no one spoke in the little bedroom, but every
now and then the rose branch beat, slap, slap, slap
on the window, and the wind, rising in a sudden

196

gust, made a hollow, blowing noise in the chimney.

"Mother," said Bridget at last.

"Haven't you gone to sleep again?"

"No," said Bridget. "I was wondering what noises they'll be hearing in the *Goblin* . . . No chimney or roses or anything like that."

"They'll be asleep," said Mother. "And you ought to be asleep too."

"But if they aren't?"

"They'll be at anchor in some sheltered place. If there are trees near they might be hearing the wind in the trees. And they'll be hearing the lap, lap of the water against the dinghy, and there'll probably be a rope tapping against the mast, and when it blows really hard . . . like that . . . they'll hear the rigging thrum, and they'll snuggle down in their blankets. But John and Susan'll sleep through anything, and so will Roger."

"Titty won't, will she?" said Bridget.

"Titty'll be enjoying herself," said Mother. "She'll be listening to the noises on deck, and the lapping of the water, and she'll be imagining she's really out at sea."

"It's a pity the *Goblin* isn't a little bigger," said Bridget. "I wish we could have gone with them too."

"So do I. But I expect they're better off without us. Quite all right anyway . . . with Jim Brading looking after them . . . He's sure to have found a snug place for the night . . . And now, you just pretend you're in the *Goblin*, curled up in a bunk, and you've heard Jim go on deck to see that the riding light is burning, and you've heard him come down again and lie down quietly so as not to wake

anyone, because he wants his crew to have a good
sleep. So naturally you mustn't keep awake."

"I'm very nearly asleep," said Bridget.

"Good," said Mother. "Sleep well."

And Bridget dozed off, and half-waked and
remembered she was pretending to be in the
Goblin, and dozed off again. It was already much
later when a rattle of the rose branch on the window pane and an extra loud whistle in the chimney
woke her once more. Dimly now she could see the
shape of the window. The night was not so black.
Morning was on its way. Something was moving
in the room. Yes, Mother in her white nightgown
was out of bed and had gone to the window and
was looking out into the night, listening to the
wind.

"I can see where the window is now," said
Bridget.

"Oh, Bridgie," said Mother. "And I thought
you were asleep. Do go to sleep again. I'll tell
you when it's time to wake."

*

It was a long August night, but it came
to an end at last, and though the wind was
still whistling in the chimney and rattling the
rose against the window, the sun kept breaking
through the clouds, shining on the damp roofs of
the boatsheds and the crowds of little yachts at
anchor at the end of the hard.

"Ready for your breakfast?" said Mother, as
they came downstairs, "or how would you like to
come along the hard and back to make sure of an
appetite?"

Bridget wondered a moment, because one of the rules of ordinary days was, "Breakfast before everything." If people once got loose out of doors, Mother used to say, you never knew how much time you would have to waste before you could catch them again. Today, Mother herself was suggesting going out. Porridge was steaming on the round table in the little sitting-room. Mother glanced at it, and looked away.

"Good morning, Miss Powell. Good morning . . . Do you think we've time to run out and look at the hard before the kettle boils?"

"That's on the edge of boiling now," said Miss Powell. "But it'll do the tea no harm to stew a minute or two. So run along together. The wind blew the fog away last night and it's nice to see the sun again. Well, child, and did you sleep through it all?"

"Part of it," said Bridget.

"Most of it," said Mother.

"Mother kept awake," said Bridget.

"A lot you know about it," said Mother with a laugh, and went out of doors, taking Bridget with her, while Miss Powell came to the doorway and stood looking after them, with a slice of bread in one hand and the toasting-fork waiting for it in the other.

"Worrying about those children," she said to herself. "I must tell the men not to . . ."

But it was already too late.

"Good morning, ma'am," said one of the young carpenters from the boatsheds, as Mrs Walker and Bridget came down the steps from Alma Cottage. "That was a wild night and no mistake."

"You think it was really bad," said Mother anxiously.

"Cruel bad," said the man. "Why, more'n once I thought we'd be having the chimney pots about our heads and the roof lifted off us. When that blow like that blow last night, dry land and a snug house is the best place for anybody . . ." He looked at the crowded anchorage. "Funny to think some people go to sea for pleasure." And then, perhaps because he saw Miss Powell signalling to him from the door of the cottage, or perhaps because he saw something in Mrs Walker's face, and remembered that last night four of her family had been neither on dry land nor in a snug house, he broke off suddenly . . . "Not but what they'll have been all right with Mr Brading to look after them. Having the time of their lives, I reckon. Coming back today, I hear Mr Brading tell Frank."

"Hurry up, Bridget," said Mrs Walker. "Let's run along and see if they're in sight."

The tide was at half ebb, and the mudflats were mostly uncovered. The sun shone on the wet mud, and the patches of green weed, and the little boats lying here and there on the mud waiting to float when the tide should rise again. It shone on the big steamer moored between the buoys, and on the forest of masts about her, belonging to the barges tied alongside and loading grain out of the steamer. Nearer, the sun lit up the yachts that were tossing in the anchorage, the ruddy brown sails of three barges sailing down with the ebb to join the others by the moored steamer, the glistening new tar on the sides of a barge that was high and dry on the hard and the gleaming gold of her new-scraped sprit and mast.

Mother and Bridget picked their way along the wet gravel of the hard under the black shining sides of the barge. The farther they went the wetter it was, and they stopped at last at the edge of the water. The stern of the barge was just above their heads, and a man was sitting on a plank slung out with ropes over the taffrail, busy with bright blue and yellow paints picking out the carved scroll work about her name, "ROSEMARY of HARWICH." Bridget looked up at him and down at a small puddle of blue paint in the wet gravel. On any ordinary day Mother would have been interested in that painting too, but today she did not seem to notice it. She was looking far away down the river, past anchored yachts and unloading steamers, hoping to see the red sails of the *Goblin* coming home.

There was a crunch in the gravel beside them and they turned round to see Frank, the boatman.

"Oh, good morning," said Mother.

"Good morning, ma'am," said Frank, and paused before going off in his boat to fill up the water tank in one of the moored yachts. "You won't be looking for them yet," he said kindly. "Tide's still ebbing, and they'll wait for the flood before coming up the river."

"I ought to have thought of that," said Mother gratefully. "But I really was a little worried about them in that fog yesterday, and then when it came on to blow . . ."

"They'll have come to no harm with Jim

Brading," said Frank. "He could find his way about the river blindfold, if he needed."

"When does the tide turn?"

"Not till close on ten," said Frank. "You may look for them any time after eleven, but not before."

"Come along, Bridgie," said Mother. "Let's go and have our breakfast."

"What are they doing now?" asked Bridget, and Mother, who felt a little more cheerful after talking to Frank, told her just what was happening. "They've anchored in a nice snug place at the mouth of the river," she said, "waiting for the tide to turn. And Susan's cooked their breakfast, and they'll be sitting in the cockpit to eat it in the sunshine. And then they'll be washing up and swabbing down the decks, and then they'll come sailing up the river to tell us all about it. Come on, Bridget. Miss Powell's toast'll be getting cold. I'll race you home to our breakfast."

"Five yards start," said Bridget, and she and Mother made a dead heat of it, off the hard, across the road by the inn, up the steep steps of the little garden of Alma Cottage and came to the door together. A boy with a leather belt outside his jacket was standing in the doorway talking to Miss Powell.

"There's a telegram for you, Mrs Walker," said Miss Powell.

Mother took the orange envelope and tore it open. Inside was a telegram dated from Berlin the day before. "MRS WALKER C/O MISS POWELL PIN MILL IPSWICH GETTING ALONG TED."

"Is it from Daddy?" said Bridget.

"Yes," said Mother. "And he sent it off yesterday. Bridgie! He must be crossing today. Oh dear, oh dear, I ought never to have let them go sailing. It's from my husband, Miss Powell. He was in Berlin yesterday. And there are all those children of mine afloat with Mr Brading. What bus shall we have to catch to Shotley to get over to Harwich in time to meet the boat?"

*

After breakfast, Mother took Bridget out on the hard again. The tide was well out, nearly low water, and they walked to the very end of it, where there was a narrow cement causeway, slimy with mud.

"I think I'd better hold your hand," said Bridget.

"All right," said Mother. "Then if one of us falls we'll both fall together, for company."

"You might be able to hold me up," said Bridget.

They stood on the end of the hard waiting for the tide to turn. At last the water began to creep in again over the mud.

"They may be starting any time now," said Mother, looking away down the river as far as she could see.

"Will John be steering?" asked Bridget.

"I should think perhaps Jim would let him. It's not blowing today like it was last night."

They waited a long time. The tide covered the end of the causeway and crept higher and higher, driving them back, foot by foot. One after another the loaded barges by the steamer, that had been waiting for the tide to help them, came beating up the river, the water foaming under their bows and

the sun lighting their brown sails and the scarlet
flags at their mastheads.

"There they are," cried Mother.

Far away down the river a little triangle of
red sail had come into sight.

"There they are," cried Bridget.

The triangle of red sail came slowly nearer. It
disappeared behind the moored steamer, showed
again, disappeared and showed once more.

"It's no good waving to them just yet," said
Mother. "They couldn't see you." Her voice dropped a note. "Even if it's them."

"It's sure to be them," said Bridget, who had
been trying to hurry them up.

Frank's boat slid alongside the hard, bringing
some gear ashore from one of the yachts. Mother
pointed to those red sails down the river.

"You know her better than I do," she said.
"Is that the *Goblin* coming up?"

Frank screwed up his eyes and looked.

"That's the *Emily*, ma'am," he said. "They
went out fishing the day before yesterday. Should
have been back last night. Held up by the fog, I
reckon."

For a moment Bridget thought that Mother
was going back to Alma Cottage. But she stopped
and turned again to the boatman.

"Will they be coming in here?" she asked,
"or going on to Ipswich?"

"That's their mooring," said Frank. "Just ahead
of *Coronilla*. The big blue boat. They'll be coming
in."

"We'll wait and talk to them," said Mother.
"They may have seen something of my sailors.

Of course, she isn't the *Goblin*. She's a yawl, and
the *Goblin's* a cutter. But she did look rather like
the *Goblin* because she hasn't got her mizen set.
Take care, Bridget. If you stand there, you'll have
the tide wetting your shoes."

"Shall I take them off?" said Bridget.

"You wouldn't like walking on the gravel, if
you did," said Mother, with her eyes on the distant
Emily. "You'd feel like the princess with peas in
her shoes, or the little mermaid who couldn't take
a step without being cut by sharp knives."

"I know that one," said Bridget.

Foot by foot they moved back as the tide crept
up over the end of the hard. They watched the
Emily come up the river. Three young men were
aboard her. One was steering and the others were
busy with her headsails. Down came the staysail
as the *Emily* came in among the moored yachts.
Down came the mainsail. Round she swung and
crept towards her buoy under jib alone. One of the
young men was on the foredeck, reaching with a
boathook for a mooring buoy.

"They did that very well," said Mother, as
the buoy came aboard.

A moment later the jib had been rolled up,
and the three young men were on the cabin roof
making a loose stow of the mainsail. Then all
three disappeared into the cabin.

"Oh, Bridget," said Mother. "Don't say they're
going to settle down to cook their dinner."

They came out again. The dinghy that had
been towing astern was hauled alongside. Somebody jumped into it. The others were passing down
bags and then a big straw basket.

"They're all coming," said Bridget, as the other two slipped down into the dinghy, which began to drift astern as they were getting their oars out.

"They're coming," cried Bridget again, as two of the men, each with an oar, began to pull for the hard.

But the one sitting in the stern with the bags suddenly pointed to the top of the *Emily's* mast, and the dinghy spun round and went back to her.

"They've forgotten to take down their flag," said Mother impatiently.

The dinghy waited alongside the *Emily* while one of the crew went aboard, hauled down the flag, and threw it in the cabin. At last they started off again. Bridget and Mother were waiting for them as they reached the hard.

"They've got lots of fish," said Bridget, looking at a shining silver mass in the straw basket.

"We had a jolly good day yesterday till the fog came," said one of the men, laughing at Bridget's eager face. "Would you like some?" and he held out a big codling. Bridget shrank back, and he laughed again.

"Do you know a boat called the *Goblin*?" asked Mother.

"Brading's boat?"

"I suppose you haven't seen her anywhere?" said Mother quietly, just as if it did not really matter very much. "Some of my young ones are in her with Mr Brading, and I was a little worried yesterday when it came on so thick after midday, and then all that wind and rain."

"They're all right," said the young man who had offered Bridget the fish, holding on to the

slimy, wooden piling at the edge of the hard to
keep the dinghy steady while bags and basket
were lifted out. "We came in yesterday soon after
the fog began and passed close to them. Spoke
to them, too. They're all right. Brading had his
anchor down, on the Shelf, just off the dock, out of
the channel. Couldn't have been in a better place.
One of them was playing a tin whistle."

"That's my Roger," laughed Mrs Walker. "If he
was playing his whistle there couldn't be anything
wrong."

"Brading knows what he's about," said one of
the others. "We ought to have done the same and
stayed there, but we tried to feel our way up, and
got on the mud and spent half the night on our
beam ends . . ."

"Don't tell tales," said another.

"All right, skipper. It was my fault as much
as yours."

"Well, I'm very much obliged to you," said
Mrs Walker.

"You never know what may happen in a fog,
and I was just a little bit worried about them.
Come along, Bridgie."

They walked together up the hard.

"Bridgie," said Mother gaily. "You've got a very
silly Mother. I ought to have known all the time
that everything was all right. But yesterday, with
that fog and then the wind and rain I just couldn't
help feeling that something awful was happening.
And there they were, anchored in a safe place, just
like I said, and enjoying every minute of it. And, of
course, they won't be back a minute before they
promised. Jim Brading said he'd be here at high

tide. They'll be coming up the river in time for tea, and after tea we'll all go across to Harwich together, just in case Daddy comes by the evening boat."

PIN MILL

CHAPTER XV

KEEPING AWAKE

ANOTHER hour of the night went by and still the *Goblin* was plunging gallantly through the dark. No more heavy splashes had come aboard. There had been no more rain. It was still blowing hard, but not so hard as to make the steering really difficult. More and more of the sky was clear of clouds and bright with stars. But Titty was not looking at them.

"Titty," said Susan.

"Titty," said Roger.

Titty, like Roger himself a little earlier, had fallen asleep in the cockpit. She woke in time to hear Susan saying to John that those two would be much better in their bunks.

"But we can't miss any of this," said Titty, with a bit of a shiver.

"You've missed some of it already," said Susan. "You were asleep just now ... And your hands are very cold. You won't miss any more by being asleep in the warm cabin than by being asleep on deck. So down you go."

"And you, too, Roger," said John. "It's quite all right for a sailor to take a watch below. You're off duty. You'll be wanted again later, and you won't be any use if you haven't been to sleep."

They may have thought they would have liked to stay up all night, but orders were orders, and anyhow they were very sleepy. Susan went down with them into the lighted cabin, and tucked them into their bunks as well as she could, wedging Roger in his place with a bundle of sail. She came on deck feeling easier in mind. No matter where they were, or what was going to happen to them, at least those two were going to get part of a proper night's rest.

"Are they all right?" John asked as she climbed back into the cockpit.

"Asleep already," she said, with half a yawn. She wedged herself into a corner of the cockpit on the starboard side, opposite John, and settled down to keep a good look out.

"Shut the doors," said John. "Easier to see without the light from below. You can keep the hatch open."

"Shall I go down and put the lamp out?"

"Better not," said John. "It'll show through the portholes, and even that's better than nothing in case of meeting steamers."

"The last one didn't see it," said Susan.

"Another one might," said John.

Ten minutes or so later he spoke to her again. "Susan," he said. "Are you all right?"

But he got no answer from the look-out.

Dimly in the darkness he could see where she was, a darker lump in the corner of the cockpit. But, unless in dreams, she was not keeping watch. Susan, tired out by worry, seasickness, and the shock of thinking John had gone overboard, had fallen asleep. Well, it was no good waking her to send her below like the others. She would never go. Poor old Susan. Best to leave her alone.

He settled himself to his steering and to keeping a look out at the same time.

With the doors to the cabin closed there was no light in the cockpit, except a feeble glimmer where the little candle-lamp, hidden from outside, threw a pale yellow glow over the compass card inside the window. South-east by east . . . South-east . . . South-east by south . . . South-south-east . . . The card never kept still for a moment. How could it, with the *Goblin* swaying on her way, and John easing her along as he had eased the little *Swallow* long ago, meeting her with the tiller when she tried to come round, stopping her when she tried to swing off, steering all the time as much by the feel of the wind as by the sight of the compass. He did his best. Roughly his course must be south-east, he thought. He could not be very sure.

It was not so hard to keep her steady as it had been, if you could call it steady, this regular swinging motion as she hurried along, wave after wave coming up on her quarter, lifting her, passing her, and racing ahead of her into the night. It was like keeping time to a tune, leaning on the tiller, letting it come back, leaning again. So . . . and back . . . So . . . and back . . .

The wind must be less than it had been. He was sure of that. Not that it wouldn't be more than hard enough if they had been going the other way and battling into it. Gosh! Those had been an awful few minutes. Poor old Susan! And then that reefing . . . Jolly lucky he had tied that life-line round himself when he went forrard. And everything had gone all right so far . . . The *Goblin* was still afloat . . . She wasn't leaking . . . Nothing had carried away, as it so easily might . . . He just would not think of what they would have to do next. Enough for now to keep her sailing safely along with her sleeping crew.

Her sleeping crew . . . Just for a second after leaning on the tiller he let it go and took a hurried peep over those closed doors and down into the lighted cabin. He could just see Roger's feet rolled in blanket, and a lump of red-tanned sail that Susan had used to stop him from sliding about in his bunk. Titty was out of sight in the fore-cabin. And here was poor old Susan asleep in her corner of the cockpit. All three of them were asleep. He was back at the tiller, leaning on it again. He took another look at the compass card under that dim yellow glow, wedged himself against the cockpit coaming with a foot against the opposite seat, looked up at the part of the sky that was full of stars, and a little ashamedly admitted to himself that he was happy.

Of course he ought not to be. There was all Jim Brading's chain and his best anchor on the bottom of Harwich harbour. There was Mother at Pin Mill and Jim Brading at Felixstowe not knowing what had become of them. But when they did know, Jim Brading would be pleased, except about that anchor and chain. The *Goblin* was all right, not bumping herself to pieces on a shoal as she very well might have been. No land sharks or pirates had had a chance of claiming salvage that might have cost Brading his ship. And Mother, when everything was explained to her, would be pleased that things were no worse. He had done his very best. And anyhow, here, at

night, far out in the North Sea, what could he do
other than what he was doing? If anybody could
have seen his face in the faint glimmer from the
compass window, he would have seen that there
was a grin on it. John was alone in the dark with
his ship, and everybody else was asleep. He, for
that night, was the Master of the *Goblin*, and
even the lurches of the cockpit beneath him as the
Goblin rushed through the dark filled him with a
serious kind of joy. He and the *Goblin* together.
On and on. On and on. Years and years hence,
when he was grown up, he would have a ship of
his own and sail her out into wider seas than this.
But he would always and always remember this
night when for the first time ship and crew were
in his charge, his alone.

So . . . and back . . . So . . . and back . . . Lean
and sway with this triumphant motion. Good little ship. Good little ship. He put a hand over the
edge of the coaming and patted the damp deck in
the darkness.

*

What was that?

Flash, flash, in the darkness far ahead. He saw
those flashes only when the *Goblin* was on the
top of a sea. There they were again. A flash, and
then, a moment later, another. Then darkness for
several seconds, and then again those two bright
flashes, close together.

It must be a lightship. Almost on the course,
too. If he kept on like this he would be passing it
fairly near. He wondered how far away it was. It
might turn out to be very useful. It might have

a name on its side, though without a chart that
would not tell him much. But supposing they were
near it when the dawn came, there would be no
harm in hailing, and perhaps the lighthouse men
would be able to tell him what course to steer to
get back to Harwich. That would help a lot. What
with the tides and steering to ease the *Goblin*
through the seas, John knew that his course from
Harwich would be more like a serpent's trail than
a straight line if he could see it on a chart. Gosh,
the lighthouse men might even be able to lend him
a chart if he came near enough. And they couldn't
very well hold the *Goblin* for salvage when they
themselves were in a vessel moored and fixed in
the middle of the sea. And in daylight it would be
safe to come near. They would signal to him if he
were standing into danger. He remembered the
signal for "You are standing into danger." . . . Two
shorts and a long. And then his mind went back
to last winter holidays and all the signalling with
Nancy and Peggy Blackett, and the expedition to
the North Pole, and he laughed, wedged there in
the cockpit, swaying to and fro, out in the North
Sea in the middle of the night, at the memory of
Nancy Blackett with the mumps and a face like a
pumpkin, earnestly signalling from her sickroom
window.

He looked again at the compass, when the
Goblin was pointing directly at the flashes. Just
a little east of south-east. That was near enough.
For the time being he would be able to do without
the compass and steer for those distant flashes.
Much easier not to have to keep peering at that
glowing card and at the same time to keep as good

a look out as could be kept by a busy steersman
in the dark.

*

So and back ... So and back ... He sat there
swaying with the tiller. Sea after sea rolled up
astern, lifted the *Goblin* with a noise of churning
foam, dropped her, and rolled on. Now and then in
the darkness he could see the crest of a wave like
a grey ghost as it passed close by. Once or twice
he lit the big electric torch and flashed it over the
side to get an idea of how fast the little *Goblin*
was racing through the water. But mostly he was
content to keep up that easy, rhythmical steering,
to know by the feel of the wind that there was no
danger of a jibe, and to look far ahead for that
winking light ... flash, flash, one after another,
arrows of light over the water, then black for a
few seconds, and then again those sudden sharp
piercings of the darkness.

He wondered what the lightship would be like,
remembering those he had seen in Harwich harbour and at Falmouth, big red hulls, with thick
masts amidships, and lanterns on the masts like
huge cages, and some of them with balls and
things at the masthead. He thought of the lighthouse men aboard her. Of course, they couldn't
see the *Goblin* bustling along towards them in the
dark. Some of them would be watching, surely, but
the rest would be lying in their bunks asleep, like
Titty and Roger asleep down below in the cabin of
the *Goblin* ... Asleep ... John suddenly felt his
own eyes closing. He opened them again, extra
wide, and stared in the darkness towards the

other side of the cockpit where, though he could see nothing but a lump perhaps a little blacker than everything else, he knew that Mate Susan, hunched down in her oilskins, was herself asleep like the rest of the crew.

LIGHTSHIP AT NIGHT

On and on. Was that one flash or two? His eyes must have closed again for a moment without his knowing it. This would not do. He straightened his back. With his fingers he opened his eyes as wide as he could, hoping that perhaps they would stay so. Again he found them blinking. He stared ahead into the darkness and tried to count the seconds between one pair of flashes and the next. He counted seven before the flashes came again. The next time he counted five, the time after that six. Then another seven. Then eight. Then six again. How hard it was to keep counting at the same pace. This was a very good way of keeping awake. For a long time he went on counting, beginning afresh each time those two flashes broke out of the darkness. And then, suddenly, he realised that he had counted up to twelve. He must have missed seeing one pair of flashes altogether.

He rubbed his eyes really hard, blinked them rapidly, looked at the compass, and stared ahead into the night. By now, even when the lightship was not sending out those stabbing flashes, he could see a faint glimmer from her lantern. He would keep those flashes on the starboard bow. It wouldn't do to pass too near if they were going to reach the lightship while it was still dark. Whatever happened, he simply must not go to sleep. If only he could sing it would be easier to keep awake. But he could not sing because of waking Susan.

Suddenly he started. A sail was clapping like thunder. The wind was blowing not from behind him but into his face. The tiller was kicking this way and that and the *Goblin* was plunging up and down like a mad thing. Two bright flashes shone out not on the starboard bow but somewhere away to port.

"John! John! What's happened?"

Susan had waked in terror.

"I fell asleep," he shouted into the wind. "It'll be all right in a minute. She's coming back."

Slowly he got the *Goblin* back on her course, with the flashes of the lightship once more on the starboard bow. The wind eased as he brought it aft. He looked at the compass. Pretty nearly south-east. That was all right.

"I say, Susan, I'm awfully sorry. I keep on dropping off."

"What are those flashes?" asked Susan.

"Lightship," said John. "I'm steering for it, and when daylight comes we'll ask them what we'd better do."

"How long have I been asleep?" said Susan.

"Good long time," said John. "Are you feeling all right now?"

"Ever so much better," said Susan, with half a yawn. She looked down through the hatch at the feet of the sleeping Roger in the cabin. "They haven't been up, have they?"

"No."

She opened one side of the door a little way so that she could see the clock.

"I say, it's after two o'clock. You must be awfully tired."

"Only sleepy," said John. "My eyes will keep shutting. Look here. It'll be all right if you talk to keep me awake."

Susan began talking.

"What do you think the lightship people will say?"

"I don't know ... Perhaps they'll lend us a chart ... Anyhow they'll tell us how to steer for Harwich ... We've been wiggling about a good deal ..."

He yawned desperately.

Susan went on.

"It isn't as rough as it was. I wonder if I'll be able to get them something hot for breakfast. They'll be pretty hungry when they wake up ..."

"Roger always is ..."

"I say, John, do you know that today is the day we ought to be back at Pin Mill? In time for tea. It'll be too awful if Daddy comes back and Mother doesn't know where we are ... John ... JOHN!"

He started violently. Already the flashes of the lightship had shifted back to the port bow.

"Sorry."

Again he brought the *Goblin* back to her course.

"It'll take ages to get back," said Susan. "We must have come a very long way."

"She's jolly fast," said John. "And she steers beautifully. Some day I'll have a boat like her. She steers nearly as easily as old *Swallow*. Do you remember how we used to watch for waggles in each other's wakes ... when we were ... when we were learning, I mean ... ow!"

A sharp pain caught him just above the knee. Susan had reached out and pinched him as hard as she could.

"Good," he said, when he knew what had happened. "Go on. Do it again. Do it every few minutes. What was I saying?"

"You'd stopped saying anything," said Susan. "You were asleep."

"Well, go on pinching," said John. "OW! You

needn't do it quite so hard while I'm awake."

"I can't see in the dark whether you're awake or not."

"Pinch whenever those lights get on the wrong side of the bowsprit. I want to keep them on the starboard bow."

"There's another steamer," said Susan.

Far away to the south they could see the two masthead lights. For some time John kept awake, watching anxiously to see the steamer's red and green navigation lights. But she was too far away and presently even the masthead lights disappeared.

John found Susan jerking at his arm.

"Look here, John. It's no good. You'd better let me steer for a bit. You can't go on for ever."

He hesitated.

"See if you can," he said at last, and made room for her in the steerman's seat. He was so stiff that he could hardly move. "That's right. Here's the tiller rope. It helps a lot when she's really pulling. Don't try to hold her too hard. Keep her going as we are. Can you see the compass? Keep it about south-east ... That's right ... south-east and a bit east ... With the lightship on the starboard bow ... We'll be up to her quite soon."

"I can manage all right," said Susan after a minute. "You go to sleep for a bit."

"No," said John. "I don't want to now ... I'll keep a look out ..."

"When we come to the lightship, what shall we do next?"

"We'll go straight on till daylight. We'll still be in sight of the lightship and then we can come back till we're near enough to shout . . . I'm not going anywhere near her in the dark."

"You'd much better go to sleep," said Susan. "I'll wake you the minute I want help."

"No . . . No . . ." said John. He lifted his arms and stretched them. Lovely it was, just for a few minutes, not to be steering. And Susan was doing quite well. He peeped in at the compass, and then settled down in Susan's old place, in the corner of the cockpit, looking forward at the flashes from the lightship . . . Just for a few minutes . . . not steering . . . And then he would take on again . . . His head fell forward against the cabin, cold and damp . . . He let it rest there . . . Just for one minute . . . It wouldn't matter even if his eyes did close . . .

CHAPTER XVI

DAWN AT SEA

SOMETHING hard was pressing against his forehead. Someone was talking . . . saying his name. John woke with a jerk.

"John . . . John."

That was Susan's voice. He sat up and stared about him.

"Gosh!" he said. "Have I been asleep?"

"I've been keeping her going about south-east and a bit east," said Susan. "But we passed the lightship a long time ago. I kept straight on like you said. It's still dark, but there's something else to steer by now. A sort of glimmer right ahead. And there are searchlights in the sky right away over there . . . in the south-west . . . I put off waking you as long as I could."

John heard the pride in her voice. Everything had changed since he had let her take the tiller while he had a few minutes' rest. A few minutes? Why half the night had gone. When he had changed places with Susan they had had to feel their way about in the cockpit. He had had to take her hand and put it on the tiller. She had been just a lump of blackness in the dark. And now, though it was still night, he could see exactly where she was. He looked astern for the flashes of the lightship. They were gone. But ahead of them, dead on the bowsprit end, the loom of a light showed in the sky, though he could not see the sparkle

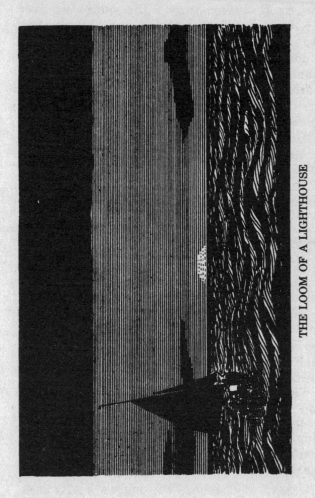

THE LOOM OF A LIGHTHOUSE

of the light itself. It must be still below the horizon. He looked away to the south-west, over the starboard quarter. Quick, one after another, two faint beams swung across the sky like the hands of a clock chasing each other round and round.

John stared at them, and then again watched for that sudden pale glow right ahead that gleamed and died and presently gleamed again.

"Gosh!" said John. "Those searchlights must be on land, and I bet that thing ahead's a light-house."

"Hadn't we better turn back at once?" said Susan. "It'll be daylight by the time we get back to that lightship."

John faced the wind and then looked in at the compass. South-east by east they were heading. With the wind as it was they would never be able to head north-west by west to get back over the same course.

"We'll keep on till daylight," he said. "We'd only get into a mess if we tried tacking before we can see the ropes and things. Look here, I'll take the tiller again. Are you all right in your inside?"

"Quite," said Susan. "Only a bit cold. Aren't you?"

"Rather."

"I'm going to try making tea," said Susan.

"What about cocoa?" said John.

"All right. If only the kettle'll stay put."

"I say," said John. "The night's nearly over. It's going to be daylight quite soon."

"I know."

Susan opened the doors at the top of the companion and, holding tight, went backwards down the steps into the warm glow of the lighted cabin. John steered for that glimmer in the sky that kept showing far ahead. South-east by east ... South-east ... South-east by east ... East-south-east ... Could they really have come right across? Were those searchlights somewhere in France ... or Belgium ... or Holland? He wished he could remember what the map looked like. Jolly cold it was, but who cared? Dawn was coming. Susan was all right again. The wind had gone down. The sea wasn't half as bad as it had been. And the *Goblin* was still afloat, swinging comfortably along just as if she had not found out that Jim Brading was not at her tiller. John's hands might be a bit cold, but there was a pleasant glow in his inside at the thought of how much worse things might have been. Things were very different now from what they had been in those dreadful moments when Susan and he had nearly quarrelled, when she had wanted to do one thing and he had known that they ought to do another, and Susan had cried, and Titty had had one of her heads, and Roger had been on the edge of being frightened, and Susan had been so dreadfully ill. He leaned forward and looked down into the cabin. Susan had got rid of her oilskin and was at the foot of the companion-steps, busy with the methylated spirit can, getting ready for the starting of the cooking stove. She was squirting the spirit into its little cup below the burner. She was putting the can in the sink. She was striking a match to light the stove. She was pulling to one of the doors to shield the blue flame from the wind. Now she was stooping at the foot of the steps, filling the kettle from the fresh-water tap. Good old Susan.

The stove in the galley burst into a roar. He saw Susan's hand putting the kettle carefully in its place on the top of it.

Voices sounded below.

"Yaw ... aw ... aw .... aw ... aw ... aw ..." Roger was giving one of his best and loudest morning yawns.

"Go to sleep!" That was Susan.

"Is it nearly morning?" That was Titty. And then, "She isn't bobbing about like she was. Are we back in harbour?"

"No."

"Shall I get up?"

"No. You lie still and keep warm. How's your head?"

"It wants to get up."

"How is it?"

"Not aching."

"It's still dark outside," said Roger.

"You lie down. There's no need for either of you to get up yet."

"What are you doing?"

"Boiling a kettle."

"Breakfast?"

"Cocoa."

"Good."

"You won't have any if you don't lie quiet till it's ready."

John, listening, smiled in the darkness outside. This was the old Susan indeed. If she was once again feeling like a ship's mate and keeping the

crew in order she couldn't have been pretending
when she said she wasn't ill any more.

He smiled in the darkness and at the darkness,
which was quickly growing less dark. It was jolly
cold all the same. He tried standing to steer with
the tiller in the crook of his arm and one hand in
his pocket getting warm while he used the other to
steady himself with a grip on the cockpit coaming.
After a few minutes he shifted to the other side of
the tiller to give the other hand a chance.

That glow in the sky, that he was sure must
come from a lighthouse on land, kept on coming every few seconds, but it was feebler than
it had been. The lighthouse couldn't be a ship
and moving away? No. Of course, the loom of it
was growing dimmer because over there in the
east the dawn was coming. He could no longer
see those revolving beams crossing the sky in the
south-west. Gosh! When the dawn did come they
might be in sight of land. And what land? Land
that they had never seen before. He stared all
round him, trying to see what there was where
sky and sea met each other.

Susan was arranging four of the red Woolworth
mugs in a row along one of the steps in the companion. John grinned again, remembering, now
that it was safely past, that awful moment when
the steamship had been heading for them in the
night and they had flashed the big torch through
the red Woolworth plate. Steam was coming from
the kettle. Little comforting clouds drifted away
from it, showing that the stove roaring away
beneath it was really doing its work. Susan was
sitting on the starboard bunk at the foot of the

steps, with a foot up against the opposite bunk to keep her steady. She had got out the bread-tin and was cutting thick slices, buttering each slice before she cut it. John knew suddenly that he was very hungry. Hullo, she was coming up to talk to him.

"John, let's have the ham ... Paper parcel in the open locker behind you."

He felt for it and could not find it. He saw something pale on the cockpit floor. He stooped and found a flabby lump.

"I say, it must have fallen out ages ago. I've been treading on it. I thought I felt something soft. And it's pretty well sopping wet."

There was a pause. Susan had gone back into the cabin to look into the cupboard behind that starboard bunk. There she was again.

"John."

"Yes."

"They'd better not have it if it's all wet. Do you think I ought to open one of Jim Brading's tongues?"

"Why not?"

"Do you think he'd want us to?"

"Jolly good idea," came Roger's voice from behind her.

With every minute now it was getting lighter. That faint glimmer under the bowsprit end was going to disappear altogether when darkness turned to dawn. And with the light they would have to bring the ship about and try to go the other way. All the time, though he had tried not to think of it, John had been dreading the moment when he would have to begin to find his way back. It was going to be very difficult. Wasn't there something better he could do? A new tremendous idea was forming in his mind. But what would Susan say to it? He looked back into the darkness and then forward again at that faint, promising glimmer.

*

A strong jet of steam was pouring across the companion from the spout of the kettle on the stove. John, looking down into the cabin, saw the lid of the bread-tin on the floor, with four thick slices of bread and butter on it and four large hunks of tinned tongue. Susan came to the companion again, lifted the kettle from the stove and began to pour boiling water into the mugs waiting in a row on the top step.

"Don't fill them too full," said John.

"Not going to. But she's ever so much steadier than she was."

She shovelled a heaped spoonful of powdered milk and cocoa out of a tin into each mug. She stirred them one by one and added a little more hot water.

"Can't we get up now?" came Roger's voice.

"All right. Come on, Titty. You'll both have to sit on Roger's bunk. Here you are, John."

John reached down for his mug, and put it carefully on the seat, close against the coaming so that it should not slide about. Lovely it was, just to feel the warmth of the mug with a cold hand. Susan handed up his slice of bread and butter with a hunk of tongue. Dawn was certainly coming. He could quite easily see the pale square of bread and butter when he put it down by the mug.

COOKING AND STEERING

In the lighted cabin he could see Titty and Roger sitting side by side on the port bunk, with their mugs of boiling cocoa cooling between their feet on the cabin floor. Susan, with her mug in her hands, was sitting on the bottom step of the companion. The *Goblin* was swinging easily along, but she had decided not to take the risk of putting things on the table. John grinned again, burnt his lips with his first sip of cocoa, cooled them with a bite of bread and butter and another of tongue, and attended to his steering. South-east by east ... Already the sky ahead of them was paling along the edge of the sea and it was hopeless to try to see the glimmer of the lighthouse. Never mind. South-east by east. He had only to keep her so and sooner or later he would see the lighthouse itself.

*

The sea was changing colour. It had been black as the night, so black that even the white crests of the waves had been invisible. Then they had shown like grey ghosts of themselves when a wave turned over and foamed by close to the *Goblin*'s side. It was still dark astern, but ahead, pale green sky showed on the horizon. The little world in which the *Goblin* had been moving all night was growing wider. He could see the waves alongside. He could see them ten yards away, twenty yards away. Even beyond that he could see their ghosts. The waves were the colour of the old pewter mug on the kitchen mantelpiece at Holly Howe. Further and further he could see. Waves everywhere, but waves somehow kindlier than they had been. The white crests were not roaring after each other. Wave after wave rolled by smooth-topped and harmless. Even where there were white crests, they were low and short, just little sudden churning bits of foam that turned to lacework on the back of a wave and slipped down into the trough behind it. Why, sailing out of Falmouth with Daddy when he had been quite a little boy, they had been among waves like these and Daddy had thought nothing of them at all.

Where was Daddy now? Lying in a train perhaps, jolting along, bang, bang, bangetty bang, getting nearer England every minute? But was he? You never knew with Daddy. What if he had managed to get across Asia and Europe quicker than he had expected? What if Roger had been right and Daddy had been sleeping in his cabin in that very steamer that had so nearly run down the *Goblin* in the night? He might be already at Harwich, where they were to meet him, and with every minute the *Goblin* was further and further away. The skin on the backs of John's hands went all tickly as he thought of it. How long would it take them to get back? Even if they could . . . He was more than ever certain that that new idea of his was right. But what would Susan say to it? He tried hard to see further than the light would let him over that pewter-coloured sea.

"Ready for some more cocoa?"

Susan's voice, now that she was back at housekeeping, giving people meals, sounded calm and cheerful. What would it be when he told her what he had in mind?

John passed down his mug.

"Hullo!" "Hullo!" shouted Titty and Roger from the cabin, both feeling much more like themselves with hot cocoa inside them and all that tongue and bread and butter.

"Hullo!" said John.

"We're coming on deck after our second mugs," said Roger.

"Finish your breakfasts first," said Susan.

*

Ten minutes later Mate and Able-seamen climbed up the companion-steps and out into the cockpit. Turning up the collars of their oilskins against the cool morning wind, for they were coming up warm out of the snug cabin, they looked about them. A long, narrow strip of cloud hung above the horizon. In the north-east the sky was brightening above it. The stars were fewer than they had been. They were going out one after another, vanishing even while they looked at them.

"Where's the land?" said Susan.

John pointed straight ahead.

"What land will it be?" asked Titty.

"France," said Roger. "Don't you remember? 'The further 'tis from England, the nearer 'tis to France.'"

"It may not be France at all," said Titty. "It may be just anywhere. It might even be uninhabited. You never know. There are uninhabited bits all over the place, even in England."

"It isn't uninhabited," said John. "There's a lighthouse. You can't see it now, but I could see the loom of it in the sky while it was still dark. Susan saw it too."

The brightness in the sky spread upwards. The darkness dropped towards the sea astern of them. A faint pink glow showed in the green. The cloud above the horizon ahead of them looked as if its edges had caught fire. They stared this way and that over a dull grey sea that seemed to stretch for ever. Fog, rain-squalls and then the night had shut them in with their ship. Now for the first time they felt how very large the sea was and how very small the *Goblin*.

"Aren't there any other boats?" said Titty.

"None in sight," said Roger.

"Isn't it light enough to turn back now?" said Susan. "You said we'd go back as soon as it was light, to talk to the people on the lightship."

"What lightship?" said Roger.

"One we passed in the night," said Susan. "Let's turn now. I'm sure I shan't be sick this time. It's not rough any more."

The moment had come. John looked at her.

"I don't believe we ought to turn back at all," he said. "We've come such a tremendous way. Wait a minute, Susan. Don't get in a stew. I'll turn back, if you like, but with the wind as it is we won't be able to head back straight for the lightship and we might easily miss it. We've only got to go on and we'll come to that lighthouse. Land can't be far away. I believe we'll see it when the sun comes up."

"But we've simply got to get back."

Roger and Titty stared at John. Neither of them said a word.

"I've been thinking," said John. "We've been sailing jolly fast all night and a lot of yesterday. Even if we could sail straight it'll take us just as long to get back. And we might get back to Harwich in the dark, which would be nearly as bad as the fog. No. Wait just a minute, Susan. The most important thing of all is to let them know where we are. Once they know the *Goblin*'s all right it won't be so bad. Today's the day we ought to be back and we can't be whatever we do. Mother'll be worrying like anything. And so will Jim. And Daddy may be there already. If we go on we're bound to come somewhere, and we'll be able to send a telegram."

"Perhaps they could send a wireless from the lightship," said Susan.

"But what if we miss it?" said John. "It'll be much safer to go on."

"If they knew we were all right it wouldn't matter so much," said Susan. "But are you sure we're near land?"

"Absolutely certain," said John. "You saw that light yourself. We've only got to keep on as we're going. It's perfectly clear. No fog. We'll go on and get into a harbour and send a telegram at once."

"And then Jim Brading could come to bring us home . . ." There was relief in Susan's voice and John knew that she was going to agree.

"I wonder if he'll have money to pay his fare to wherever it is," said Roger.

"I've got two pounds and seventeen shillings in the Savings Bank," said Titty.

"We'd better go on," said Susan.

*

The thing had been decided. From that moment
on not one of them looked astern, not even Susan.
Land, land, and the sooner the better. In spite of
everything a new excitement filled the *Goblin*.
Nobody had meant to go to sea, but here they
were, and an unknown land ahead of them.

"Properly," said Titty, "John ought to nail a
gold piece to the mast like Columbus did, and
the one who sees land first gets it."

"I haven't got one," said John.

"We'll keep a look out just the same," said Roger.

"I should jolly well think you will."

Far ahead on the horizon the flaming edge of
the long cloud had turned to gold. All the light
seemed to be coming from one point below it, in
the north-east. A spot of dazzling fire showed
under the cloud, and a long lane of blazing
sparks seemed to shoot out towards them over
the dancing sea.

The spot of fire widened and presently disappeared behind the cloud. The lane of light over
the water dulled. And then, above the cloud, the
sun rose round and red. A river of light poured
from it. The burgee that had been black at the
masthead all night shone out bright blue and red
and white. The red sails glowed warm. The sea,
no longer grey, was blue and green. The morning
sunlight bathed their eager faces, as the four of
them looked east and south for land. There was
not a sign of land, nor yet a ship. The new day
had begun and the *Goblin* was utterly alone.

Susan, Titty and Roger looked at John. Was
he mistaken after all?

"It's all right," he said at last. "We couldn't expect to see it yet. It'll be still below the horizon. But we know just where it is. Look here, Susan. You steer for a bit. Watch the compass. Keep her going south-east by east. There's much less wind. I'm going to let the reefs out again. And then I'll get the staysail up. She'll carry full sail easily now. The quicker we get there the better."

"What's that in the water?" said Roger suddenly.

"Where?"

"Port bow ... I mean starboard ... Sorry. I say, let's have the glasses."

"Floating log," said John. "Gosh, I'm glad we didn't charge into one of those in the night."

"There's another."

"And there's another on the other side."

John was tying the life-line round his middle. He was going to take no risks of giving Susan another fright while letting out those reefs. He stopped to look at a log as the *Goblin* passed it. Running into a thing like that would be as bad as running into a buoy. He wondered with a bit of a shiver how many of them they had passed in the night.

"Keep a good look out for them," he said.

"Aye, aye, sir," said Roger, leaning on the cabin top and looking ahead through the binoculars.

CHAPTER XVII

SHIPWRECKED SAILOR

"Where have they all come from?" said Titty, as another of those long timbers rocked past them. A squared end, orange with the wetness of the wood, lifted clear of the water and dropped into the smooth back of a wave.

"Deck cargo from a timber-ship," said John. "Norwegian probably, like the one we saw in the harbour. Jim says they roll like anything, and it was awfully rough in the night."

"First one side and then the other," said Titty, "and then a wave would come washing along and a whole lot of logs would be floating in the sea."

Susan was steering. John had made his rope fast with a bowline round his middle and was rummaging in the locker for the little brass handle of the reefing gear.

"There's a whole lot more," said Titty.

"There's something that isn't a log," cried Roger. "It's a box. Bother. I wish she'd keep still for a moment." He was trying to look through the binoculars and finding it very difficult, as the *Goblin* rose and fell, not to lose sight of the thing, whatever it was, that kept showing on the top of a wave ahead of them, disappearing in the trough and then showing once more.

"It's not a box," he said at last. "It's a sort of cage."

They came nearer and nearer to it, steering to

leave it twenty or thirty yards to port. "Don't go too near," said John. He did not mean the *Goblin* to bump even into a biscuit box, if he could help it, and this thing looked a good deal bigger than a biscuit box.

"It's a chicken coop," cried Titty. "How lovely. Don't you remember the poem about the pirates, after they'd scuppered the ship? . . . 'And hear the drowning folks lament the absent chicken coop.' It's the absent chicken coop that ought to have been there and wasn't." And then a graver thought struck her. "What's happened to the chickens? Eaten or drowned? I wonder which they'd mind most."

"They'd be eaten either way," said Roger. "If they were drowned some shark or other would be glad to gobble them up."

"But at least they'd be allowed to keep their feathers," said Titty.

"Hi!" spluttered Roger, trying to keep the binoculars steady. "There's something on it . . . There is . . . Do go a little nearer. Oh I say. It's a dead kitten . . ."

"Oh . . ."

"Drowned."

All four of them could see it now, as the chicken coop lifted and fell among the waves. It was no more than a scrap of wet fur plastered flat on the wooden slats. It drifted by perhaps a dozen yards away. They could see the head of the kitten, the fur on it sticking close to the skull, the slip of wet body, the hind legs stretched out as if they had no bones, the tail like a bit of wet string. They tried to look away from it, but their eyes came back to it in

spite of themselves. Even John, who had found his
handle and was in a hurry to go forward and get
the sail unreefed, stopped to watch it.

"How awful," said Titty.

"It must have been washed off with all those
logs," said John. "Perhaps the same big wave . . ."

"Asleep," said Titty, "and then in the water
and just clinging on till it was drowned."

John and Susan knew well enough how easily
they, too, might have found themselves struggling
in the water in the dark.

The chicken coop, with that soaking wisp of
fur on it, was already astern of them when Roger
suddenly shouted, "It's alive!"

"It can't be."

"I saw its pink mouth."

And then, as the chicken coop lurched away
astern, all four of them saw that pink mouth open
again, just a little, as if the kitten, too weak to
shout, were whispering a cry for help they could
not hear.

"We must save it," cried Titty.

John was already hauling in the mainsheet.

"*When there's a man overboard always jibe.*" He
could see the printed sentence as he had read it in
the book on how to sail. Gosh, he was glad the sail
was still reefed and easy to handle, and that the
wind had fallen light. "Now then, Susan, bring her
round. No . . . No . . . To port . . . Come on . . .
Round with her . . . I'll look after that backstay.
Don't lose sight of it, Roger . . . Look out for the
boom coming over . . . It's coming . . . Now . . ."

The boom swung over as the *Goblin* turned
sharp on her heel and headed back, close-hauled

into the wind. Frantically John made his backstay fast, let go one jib sheet, flung himself across the cockpit and hardened in the other.

"Where is it now? You haven't lost it . . ."

"Over there . . . It's a long way off . . . There . . . There . . ."

"We'll have to tack . . ."

"Can you manage it?" said Susan.

"We can't leave it to drown," cried Titty.

"We won't," said John.

It is none too easy to pick up small things at sea unless you have had a lot of practice. John had had none. Susan gave up the tiller to him, and he clenched his teeth together, and looked at that bobbing chicken coop and then up at the burgee at the masthead. No, they couldn't do better than this without going on the other tack.

"It's going further away," said Roger.

"Much further," said Titty. "Oh, John!"

"Ready about," said John, and the jib flapped and the boom swung across, and Titty and Susan threw themselves on the sheets. The *Goblin* was off again, this time coming nearer and nearer to the kitten and its raft.

"How are we going to get hold of it?" said Susan.

"Boathook?" said Roger.

"Have it ready," said John. "No. Don't. I'll go right alongside."

"You're going to pass in front of it," said Titty.

"No I'm not," said John.

"Hang on, Pussy!" shouted Titty, almost climbing up on the cabin roof.

"We'll knock it off if we bump the coop," said Susan.

"I know," said John. "Give me your shoulder to hang on to." He half stood on the seat in the swaying cockpit, steadying himself with a grip on Susan, who shouted to him not to go overboard. He was bringing the *Goblin* straight up into the wind, heading towards the chicken coop, just as if he were Jim Brading, bringing her up to her mooring buoy. He had to stand on the seat to be able to see the coop which was now close ahead.

"There it is . . . Now . . . Now . . ." gasped Titty.

The chicken coop touched the *Goblin*'s side, and there was a groan of terror from somebody. But it was only a touch. The next moment the coop was floating past the side of the cabin. John let go the tiller.

"Hang on to my feet," he cried. In another second it would be too late. He flung himself half out of the cockpit, reaching down across the side deck. The chicken coop lifted towards him. He grabbed the little cold wisp of wet fur. The kitten, with the last of its strength, hung on to the slats of the coop. One hand was not enough. John let go of the boat, to be able to use both. The next moment the chicken coop rolled slowly over and fell astern, and John hung there, more than half over the side, with the dripping kitten in his hands.

Titty and Susan hung on to his legs and hauled. Roger lugged at the rope that was tied round John's middle. John wriggled desperately, and, inch by inch, was pulled back into the cockpit.

He gave the kitten to Susan, and, a good deal

out of breath, took the tiller once more, glanced up at the burgee, looked round to see that they were in no danger of running into a log, and then kept his eyes on the compass.

Susan sat down with the wet little wisp of fur on her lap, shielded by her hands.

"He's nearly frozen," she said.

The kitten lay perfectly still, too weak to move.

"He can't have swallowed much water," said Titty, who was kneeling on the cockpit floor. "He hasn't got a stomach at all."

"Probably starving," said Roger.

"What do they do to people who are nearly drowned?" said Titty.

"Dry clothes and brandy," said Susan. "We've got no brandy."

"We can dry his fur," said Titty. "And what about Jim Brading's aunt's rum? . . . This *is* a medicinal purpose . . ."

"We'll take him down into the cabin and get him warm," said Susan. "You go down first, Titty, and I'll pass him to you."

"I'm going to get the rum," said Roger, and was half way down the steps in a moment.

Titty followed and waited at the bottom, while Susan carefully reached down and put the shipwrecked kitten in her hands. She was just going down herself when John stopped her.

"You can see it's no good trying to go back. Not until the wind changes. I'm heading her as near the wind as she'll go, and the best she'll do is south of west. On the other tack she'd be going much too far north, and to go back we want to head about north-west by west. It's no good going

RESCUE AT SEA

right up the North Sea. It's far better to go on as we were going and get somewhere."

"All right," said Susan. "I say, do you think it will be good for the kitten to give him rum?"

"See if it'll lick a drop off the end of your finger," said John. "And try it with the condensed milk. But look here, Susan, give me a hand to get back on the course. If you'll take the tiller, I can manage the rest ... And I *must* let those reefs out. We ought not to waste a minute. I was just going to do it when we sighted the kitten. If you'll take the tiller till I've done it, I'll be all right by myself. Those logs are easy enough to see ..."

Susan called down the companion to Titty. "Wrap him up, first in one bit of towel and then in another, to get the wet out of his fur. I'll be down in a minute ..."

*

In the cabin, Titty was sitting on the lee bunk with the kitten in her lap, tenderly mopping it with a towel. She tried to warm it by putting her hands round its empty little stomach. Roger had got the store-cupboard open and was hunting for that small flat bottle. Suddenly the *Goblin* heeled over on the other side, and Titty had to shift across, while Roger as nearly as possible dropped the bottle on the cabin floor in grabbing for something to steady himself.

"What's happened now?"

"It's all right," said Roger. "It's only that they've turned round again. We're going on."

"Do tell Susan to hurry up. I believe he's going to die after all."

"Susan," Roger shouted up through the companion. "Buck up. Titty says it's lost eight of its lives already."

"Coming," said Susan. "I say, John, I must. The kitten may really be dying."

"Go on down," said John. "But do be as quick as you can. I can't get the reefs out till you come back." He took the tiller once more, while Susan hurried down into the cabin.

The kitten lay between Titty's hands.

"He's still alive," she said. "Look. You can see a fluttering inside him. Stick to it, Pussy. You're quite safe."

Susan, with trembling fingers, was pulling the cork out of the flat bottle. "Rum. For medicinal purposes only." She read the label written by Jim's aunt. She pressed the mouth of the bottle against her finger and turned the bottle upside down and back again. A transparent golden drop stayed on her finger-tip. Tenderly, kneeling on the cabin floor, she pushed her finger into a corner of the kitten's mouth. She got another drop from the bottle and worked it into the kitten's mouth in the same way. The kitten gave a feeble splutter.

"Get a tin of milk," said Susan. "Spike two holes in the top of it. Go on. Use the spike of your knife." She scrambled up and got a spoon and a saucer out of the cupboard under the stove. She took a drop of water from the tap. Then, when Roger had spiked the milk-can with the marline spike on his scout knife, she poured some milk into the water and stirred it up.

"Now then, Pussy," she said, and dipped the kitten's mouth into the saucer.

The kitten spluttered again.

"He'll get it up his nose," said Titty. "You'll choke him."

But a thin pink tongue slipped out and in again like a tiny pink handkerchief. Susan took milk on her finger and smeared it on the kitten's mouth. Again that little tongue slipped in and out. The kitten opened its eyes and instantly closed them again. It opened its mouth and . . .

"Did you hear him?" said Titty.

"John," shouted Roger up the companion. "It's mewed."

"Salt water in his eyes," said Susan, and soaked her handkerchief in fresh water from the tap and gently wiped the kitten's face. Titty dipped her finger in the milk and the kitten licked her finger clean with a rough little tongue.

"He's going to recover," said Susan. She pushed the saucer under the kitten's chin. A lurch of the *Goblin* spilt some of the milk on Titty, who did not even think of wiping it off. The kitten's tongue shot out almost eagerly and began to lap.

"We mustn't let him have too much at once," said Susan. "Take another towel and go on drying him. I've got to go up to help John." Titty and Roger were left alone with the kitten.

*

"I'm going to sit on the floor," said Titty, when a little more milk had been spilt. "It'll be easier to keep steady."

"I will too," said Roger.

"He isn't half as cold as he was. Hullo. What's that? Susan's steering."

"John's gone forward," said Roger. "He was going to let out the reefs. I saw his feet go past the portholes. I wonder if I ought to go and help?"

"They'll shout if they want us," said Titty.

There was a good deal of thumping and banging overhead, the creak of a block, a squawk from the reefing gear which could very well have done with a dab of grease. Susan's voice rang out suddenly in fright . . . "Oh, do look out . . . You'll be tumbling again . . . John!" But she said no more, and the ship's doctors looking after the shipwrecked sailor down in the cabin knew that all was well. The block creaked again. They heard John's feet on the foredeck. The noise of the water on the other side of the *Goblin*'s thin planking began to change its note. For a long time now it had been quiet, except for the slop-slop of a wave coming up and splashing as it went by. The loud rushing noise they had heard through the planking when they had gone below to sleep and the *Goblin* was driving before the storm had died utterly away. Now it came again, not so loud, but unmistakably the hurrying, stirring noise of a boat moving fast through the water. They knew that John had unrolled the reefs and set the full mainsail once more.

Roger climbed up on a bunk to look out of a porthole.

"She's buzzing along like billy-oh," he said.

"Anything in sight?"

He scrambled past Titty and the kitten and had a look through a porthole in the fore-cabin.

"Only water," he said.

"Mix up some more milk," said Titty. "Sinbad's ready for another lot."

"Sinbad?" said Roger doubtfully, standing between the two cabins, with a foot against a bunk on either side, steadying himself with both hands.

"Shipwrecked sailor," said Titty. "Poor little Sinbad. Were you asleep on the chicken coop when it was washed overboard? Or did you find it just in time to save yourself from drowning?"

"It made a jolly good raft," said Roger.

"Mix up that milk," said Titty.

But just then there was a loud battering on the forehatch, and Roger, turning round, saw John's face on the level of the deck, looking in through a porthole. He was saying something, but with the porthole shut they could not hear it. Susan shouted down from the cockpit.

"You're to open the forehatch from below."

Roger scrambled forward and loosed the catch that kept the forehatch closed. The hatch was lifted from above, and there was John, sitting on the deck for safety's sake, with the life-line tied about his middle.

"Buck up," said John. "Pass up that bundle ... Staysail ... It's the top one ... There ... Just let me have an end of it. The end with all those brass hanks."

With a terrific struggle, Roger pushed the end of that bundle of stiff canvas up through the hatch, John pulling at it from above. Up it went foot by foot.

"It won't make much difference," said John, "with the wind so far aft, but every little helps, and when we were putting it away Jim said it

was the best pulling sail in the ship." The last of
the staysail went up on deck, and the hatch closed
down over Roger's head. It opened again an inch
or two. "Don't put the catch on," said John, and
down came the hatch once more.

Looking out from a porthole close beside the
mast, Roger got glimpses of a mass of red canvas, of John's legs, his head, and then his feet.
John was lying flat on the deck right in the bows,
hooking the hanks one by one on the forestay.

"Do hurry up with the milk," said Titty. "Sinbad's squeaked again."

Roger left the porthole and hurried aft, and
presently Sinbad's pink tongue was flicking in
and out of a fresh lot of milk and water, while
Roger watched and Titty stroked the drying fur
of the kitten's back.

"You can almost see him getting fatter," she
said.

"You don't think it'll burst?" said Roger.

The kitten finished that lot of milk and water
and then another.

The noise on deck had come to an end. John's
feet had passed the portholes. He was safely back
in the cockpit, busy with the staysail sheets.
Presently Susan came slowly backwards down
the companion-steps.

"John says he's all right by himself now," she
said. "I'm going to give the kitten some milk . . ."

Titty's face fell. "We've given him a good deal,"
she said. "Didn't you mean us to?"

And then Susan saw the kitten. Its fur was
dry. Its eyes were open. Its stomach was round. At
that moment it got up on its feet and, uncertainly,

because of the quick, swinging motion of the *Goblin*, it walked off Titty's lap to the cabin floor.

"He's all right," said Susan. "I didn't think we ought to give him too much at once. But anybody can see he's all right."

The kitten, its short, pointed tail jerking from side to side when it felt like flopping, was walking slowly along the floor.

"He's exploring," said Titty.

"Won't Bridgie be pleased with it?" said Roger, and with that the three doctors remembered where they were, and that with every minute they were further away from Pin Mill, and that Mother and Bridget would be watching for them coming up the river, and that Jim Brading would be looking for his boat, and that Daddy might get to Harwich before they could get back to meet him, and that . . . The more they thought about things the worse they seemed, until they seemed so bad that it was impossible to think of them at all.

"No," said Roger, putting a hand to head off the kitten. "Not down there. You'll get under the engine and covered with oil and grease."

The kitten turned, slipped, picked itself up again, and came unsteadily back along the cabin floor.

"Go on, Sinbad," said Titty. "Better have a look at everything in the ship, and make sure she's as good as your last. Probably not so big, but we'll make you very comfortable all the same."

She shifted her feet to let the kitten wobble past her.

It turned, came back, scrambled up on Titty's lap and began to lick its paws.

"He's going to live anyway," said Susan, watching it.

"I wonder how many of its lives it really has got left," said Roger.

"Perhaps the whole nine," said Titty. "Look. Look. He likes the *Goblin*. He's washing behind his ears, and they never do that unless they mean to stay in a place."

She bent her head close to the kitten and listened. Yes, there was no doubt about it. The kitten was licking its paws and rubbing its face, and from somewhere inside it came a steady, quiet rumble.

"He's purring."

Susan and Roger bent to listen.

John looked down into the cabin.

"Come on deck somebody," he said in a tense, eager voice.

"John," called Titty, "Sinbad's purred."

"Come on deck," said John. "Somebody come and have a look through the glasses. Fishing boats. A lot of them and very strange ones . . ."

"What about Sinbad?" said Titty.

"Bring him too," said Susan.

The three of them, bringing the new passenger with them, came up out of the cabin into the bright sunshine. *Goblin*, with all her sails set, was racing along over a blue, sparkling sea, and John was doing his best to steer with one hand while holding the binoculars steady with the other.

CHAPTER XVIII

LAND HO! WHAT LAND?

A THIN line of mist lay along the horizon, and out of that mist, away to the south of the *Goblin's* course, had come a fleet of fishing boats.

"Have a look, Susan," said John. "I can't keep the glasses steady and steer at the same time."

Susan took the glasses.

"What do you think they are?" said John.

"I've never seen any boats like them," said Susan. "I don't believe they're English. You have a look and let me steer."

She took the tiller. Titty, still thinking more of Sinbad than of anything else, wedged herself into a corner of the cockpit where the sunlight warmed the purring kitten on her knee. Roger sat beside her, holding on to the coaming and screwing up his eyes to see those distant boats. The *Goblin* was no longer alone on an enormous sea. Those boats were far away, but the mere sight of them, all sailing along together, made everything feel different.

"They're coming up this way," said Roger.

John, to see the better, stood on the top step of the companion and wedged himself in a corner of the open hatch, so as to have both hands free to manage the glasses.

"They aren't English," he said. "At least, if they are, I've never seen any like them."

"My turn for the glasses," said Roger.

"Shut up for a minute, Roger," said Susan. "What do you think they are, John?"

"They've got whacking great jibs," said John. "And little short gaffs to their mainsails . . . And the gaffs aren't straight, none of them . . . The sails aren't like English sails . . . And the boats aren't a bit like the fishing boats we used to see at Falmouth . . . Hullo . . . They aren't all the same. There's one with a sort of long snout pointing upwards. Most of them haven't got pointed bows at all . . . round like apples . . . I do believe they're Dutch . . . Gosh! How they roll . . . I say, Susan, we must be quite near land."

"Let's go and meet them," said Susan. "They'll tell us where we are."

"Look here," said John after a moment's doubt. "We can't. They'd grab the *Goblin* for salvage, just like Jim said. Remember how Jim's friend had to sell his boat to pay the Ramsgate sharks. It's bad enough to have lost his anchor and chain."

"They're coming up awfully fast," said Titty.

"They must have come out from somewhere near," said Susan. "And if we could ask them the way to the harbour . . ."

"It isn't as if there was only one of them," said John. "And they're bigger than the *Goblin* . . ."

"We'd be like the *Revenge* in the middle of the Spanish fleet," said Titty. "We wouldn't have a chance."

"And we haven't any guns," said Roger.

"But the harbour may be somewhere down there, where they've come from," said Susan. "And there isn't a sign of that lighthouse."

John looked ahead and then once more over the starboard bow at the fishing boats that were working up almost as if they meant to meet the little *Goblin*, a dozen or so of them, rolling heavily, plunging along, every now and then taking a sea, thump, on their bluff bows with a sudden explosion of white spray.

"We couldn't do a thing if they took us for salvage," he said.

"But we aren't wrecked," said Susan. "It'd be piracy."

"Oh I say," said Titty. "It really would be."

"They wouldn't care," said John. "And if we told them we were taking care of the boat for Jim, it would make it worse. They'd rescue us whether we wanted or not."

"If we only knew for certain about the lighthouse," said Susan.

"It must be there," said John. "I'm going up the mast to see."

"No ... No," said Susan. Even capture by piratical fishermen seemed better than that. She looked up the tall mast and the high red sail, swaying to and fro across the sky as the *Goblin* rushed along. She thought of John falling on the deck, breaking a leg, both legs, all his bones ... and then, perhaps, rolling off into the sea.

"It's no worse than a tree," said John. "Easier, with the mast-hoops to help."

"I'll hold the glasses," said Roger.

John had thrown off his oilskin and was climbing out of the cockpit.

"The life-line," said Susan.

"In the way while I'm climbing," said John.

"It's all right. There'll be lots to hang on to. It's only getting there." Already he was sitting on the cabin roof, working his way forward, gripping the handrail as he moved along. A moment later he had reached the foredeck, and had hold of the halyards with one hand and a shroud with the other.

Open-mouthed, in the cockpit, they saw him take a grip of the halyards with both hands high above his head and swing himself up off the deck, gripping the mast with his knees. He got a foot on the lowest of the mast-hoops. Up he went, hoop by hoop, as if he were climbing a ladder. The mast-hoops made good steps and hand-holds, and if only the mast had not been swinging about, climbing would have been easy.

"Susan," he shouted suddenly from half way up. "Don't watch me. Watch the compass and keep her steady if you can. I'm all right so long as you don't let her come round."

"Sorry," groaned Susan. She bent forward and kept her eyes on the compass card. Roger had long ago blown out the candle lamp, and the compass was lit now by the light pouring into the open companion. South-east by east ... And she had let the *Goblin* come round south of south-south-east. Back on the course, she steadied her. John was climbing again. She would not look at him. She must not look at him, but, though she kept her eyes on the compass card, she could not help knowing what that was, that thing she would not let herself see, higher and higher on the swaying mast.

"It's all right, Susan," said Titty at last. "He's

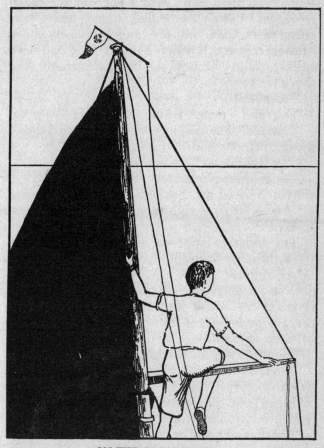

ON THE CROSS-TREES

got a leg on the cross-trees. Oh, well done, John!"

The next moment there was a triumphant yell from aloft. John, safe, with a leg over the cross-trees, had been able to look round. There was triumph in that yell, joy, and he hardly knew himself how much relief. For hours he had been sailing, telling himself the thing was there. And there it was.

"LAND HO!"

"Hurrah!" shouted Roger.

"Hurrah!" shouted Titty. "Sorry, Sinbad, I didn't mean to startle you."

"The lighthouse?" called Susan.

"Bang ahead," shouted John. "And there's a church . . . And another lighthouse. And another . . . And a steamer right ahead. Hi! Susan!"

"What?"

"I'm going to stay up here till you can see the lighthouse from the deck."

"All right."

Even if only one of them could see it, up there at the top of the mast, it made the land seem near for all of them. Land, dry land, was actually in sight.

"If only it was Harwich," said Susan.

"Never mind," said Titty. "It's somewhere, and we can't be very far off."

"I can see the steamer," said Roger, "but I can't see anything else."

"Another steamer broad on the starboard bow," shouted John from the cross-trees, and from the cockpit they saw a plume of smoke and a funnel and two masts beyond the fishing boats, and then the bridge and hull.

"We must be near a harbour," said Susan.

Meanwhile the fleet of fishing boats was working up as if to cross the *Goblin*'s course, and even
without the glasses, they could see the spirts of
spray as their round bluff bows crashed into the
waves.

"They've got leeboards," said Roger, sparing
a moment to look at them from sweeping the
horizon far ahead, trying to be the first to see
the lighthouse from the deck. "Like barges. But
they're not a bit like them in other ways."

"We're going to pass close to them," said Titty.
"Or will they get ahead of us? I say, Susan, you
don't think they're really pirates trying to cut us
off?"

"Of course not," said Susan, but she looked
anxiously enough at those big, bluff-ended boats,
wallowing to meet the little *Goblin*. It was going
to be awful if she had to steer through the middle
of the fleet. And, with the lighthouse in sight, she
no longer wanted to take the risk of asking questions.

"That steamer's coming this way too," said
Roger. "The other one's sticking just where it
was."

"That's all right," said Titty. "The pirates
wouldn't dare to touch us with two steamers in
sight. It's all right, Sinbad. There isn't any danger of anybody making you walk the plank. Did
someone make you walk the plank when you fell
into the sea? Perhaps you weren't washed overboard at all. Anyway, it would be very unfair if
it happened again."

"Land ho!" shouted Roger. "I say, I've lost it

again. No. There it is. Like a pencil sticking up
. . . And there's another thing sticking up a bit
to the left."

"John," called Susan. "Come down . . . We can
all see it . . . Come down . . . But do be careful."

John swung his leg off the cross-trees and
let himself down by the halyards. He waited a
moment at the foot of the mast. Yes. He could
see that slender pencil himself, sticking up out of a
thin line of mist along the edge of the sea. And that
distant steamer, almost exactly in a line between
the *Goblin* and lighthouse. He almost thought it
must be anchored. He worked his way aft along
the cabin roof and joined the others in the cockpit.

"All right, Susan, I'll take her," he said, as
he forced his arms into the sleeves of his oilskin.

"Those fishing boats are coming very near,"
said Susan, as she left the tiller. Titty and Roger
watched John's face.

"We won't alter course unless we have to," he
said, and paused. "Look here. We'd better show
we're English, just in case."

"Are we going to nail our colours to the mast?"
said Titty eagerly.

"I'll get the flagstaff," said Roger. "The ensign's
on it. I saw it on a shelf in the fore-cabin." He
pushed the glasses into Susan's hands and went
down into the cabin like a monkey. A moment
later the flagstaff, with the red ensign rolled about
it, came poking up through the companion with
Roger close behind it. Susan took it, unrolled it,
stuck the staff in its socket at the stern, made
the thin halyard fast to its cleat just inside
the transom, and let the scarlet ensign with

the union flag in the corner fly loose in the wind.

"It'd show a lot better if only the wind was blowing the other way," said Roger.

"Anybody can see it," said John. "That's all that matters."

"The enemy aren't flying flags at all," said Titty, "except those long streamers at the tops of their masts." Almost, and yet not quite, she had hoped that one at least of the approaching fleet would fly a skull and cross-bones.

On they sailed, their eyes now on the small steamer that seemed to stay just where it was, in a line with the thin pencil sticking up on the horizon, now on the fishing boats and on the much larger steamer coming up beyond them.

"Which are we going to meet first?" said Roger. "That steamer's coming an awful lick."

The fishing boats came nearer and nearer. John, glancing at them from time to time, held on his course as if they had not been there.

"We're going too fast for them," said Roger at last. "They couldn't catch us if they tried."

"Good. Good," said Titty. "Go it, *Goblin*."

The fishing boat that was leading the fleet was a hundred yards away, surging through the water towards them. A dozen others were scattered astern of her, big, varnished boats, their oaken topsides shining in the sun.

"They're shouting," said Roger.

"Telling us to stop," said Titty. "We jolly well won't. I wonder whether Sinbad knows their language."

"There's a boy with a red cap like Nancy's,"

said Roger. "They're all waving. What had we better do?"

"Wave back," said Susan. "It can't do any harm."

The whole crew of the *Goblin* waved as they swept past and left the fishing boats to cross their track astern of them, and on all the fishing boats arms were flung up, and a cheer came over the water from the fishermen to the little English boat that had come so far.

"They sound quite friendly," said Titty.

"Perhaps we could go and ask . . ." began Susan.

"They'd soon find out we were alone," said John, "and, anyhow, I can't now. I've got to look out for that steamer."

The huge black steamer, with red, rusty patches on her sides and a clatter of noise, was coming up from the south so fast that it was very near indeed when they had left the fishing boats astern. Black smoke poured from its funnel and they could hear the groan and throb of its engines.

"It's going to ram us," said Roger. "Hi! . . . Shall I get the foghorn?"

John clenched his teeth.

"They've seen us all right," he said. "There's the look-out above the rail, just above the anchor on this side. He was pointing at us. Steam gives way to sail. This isn't the river. We've just got to keep straight on." But it was not too easy to hold the *Goblin* to her course and to take no notice of that monster of a ship, those bows towering like a cliff, coming on and on, with the water spirting white on either side.

And then, ever so slightly, the huge steamer did indeed give way to sail, but not an inch more than she had to. That black cliff cut the water only a few yards astern of the *Goblin*. The bow wave caught the *Goblin* and threw her sideways. The black wall of the steamer's side, far above the *Goblin*'s masthead, cut off the wind. The *Goblin*'s sails fell slack. The boom crashed across and back again, and across once more. Far above them, officers on the bridge deck looked down at the crew of the little cutter thrown this way and that about the cockpit.

"Look out for Sinbad!" cried Titty, as she slipped from her seat, and the kitten, trying to save itself, landed on the floor in the general mix-up of everybody's legs.

Then, just as the wind caught them again round the steamer's stern, the wash hit them. Rolling across the regular seas, it came at them in steep-tossed hillocks. Crash ... crash ... Two seas, one after another, splashed aboard. Titty rescued Sinbad. John picked himself up and fought with the tiller. The boom swung back to the port side. The *Goblin* was sailing once more.

"Beasts! Beasts!" shouted Titty, shaking her fist after the steamer.

"They're nearly as bad as the ones that called us fishmongers," gasped Roger.

"Are you both sopping wet?" asked Susan.

"Hamburg," said John. "I couldn't read her name. That's where she's from. Hamburg's in Germany. Gosh. I wish I knew just where we were."

"We'll simply have to ask someone," said Susan, looking ahead at the steamer that was still in the same place between the *Goblin* and the lighthouse. Yellow sand dunes were showing now below the lighthouse. With every moment they were coming nearer to the land.

"There's water showing on the cabin floor," said Roger.

"Do some pumping," said John.

Roger pumped away busily, but after half a dozen strokes found he could pump no more. "It won't come," he said, lugging at the handle.

Susan had a try. It was no use.

"Choked," said John. "Never mind . . . I'll have a look at it in a minute."

He looked about him. There were no vessels in sight except the fishing boats, now far astern, the German steamer now far to the north, that steamer far ahead of them, and a few distant feathers of smoke that showed where other steamers must be below the horizon to the south. John, privately, was a good deal more than bothered. There was a new feel in the motion of the *Goblin*. The wind was certainly less, but the seas were steeper and shorter.

"How long do you think it'll be before we're in harbour?" asked Susan.

John would have liked to know the answer to that question himself. What was there between them and the land? It was dreadful having no chart, even if you didn't know much about how to use one. There might be shoals right out to sea, like the shoals off Harwich. All night, in open sea, John had been almost happy, but now he began to feel once more what he had felt in the fog, that awful horror of sailing in a place where you do not know what may be lurking out of sight for the wrecking of big ships and little.

"We must be getting into shallow water," he said at last. "The sea's changing colour too. Not nearly so blue as it was. Sandy. Keep a good look out for buoys or anything like that. It would be too awful if we went and smashed her up after all."

"We've got to get in now," said Susan. "Mother's expecting us at Pin Mill this afternoon. We've simply got to get a telegram off from somewhere."

John did not answer.

That growing line of sand dunes on the horizon terrified him. No signs of any harbour. The church spires looked as if they were far inland.

"That steamer's hardly moving," said Titty.

"Perhaps she's anchored," said Roger.

John made up his mind. "The water must be deep where she is," he said. "If only there isn't a shallow place first. I'm going to steer straight for her. When we're there we may be able to see where the harbour is."

"Anyway," said Susan, "there's no harm in asking how far we are from anywhere."

"From where?" said Roger.

"That's just it," said Titty.

"We can ask where she's from," said Susan. "That won't give anything away."

"So long as they don't spot there's anything the matter with us," said John. "It's not like asking a fishing boat. They won't try to come aboard."

"There are four of us," said Titty.

"We could bat their knuckles if they tried to come," said Roger. "They'd have to lower a little boat to come at all."

"I'm going to ask," said John, and held the little

Goblin straight on her course, while with grave, serious faces, her crew stared ahead of them at those rolling golden dunes in the hazy distance, and at that motionless steamer that might be friend or foe.

CHAPTER XIX

SIGNAL FOR A PILOT

"She's a long way off yet," said John at last. "You take over, Susan, while I go down and see if I can clear that pump."

"Can't we steer?" said Roger. "Jim let us."

"In a calm," said John.

"Well, it's not blowing hard now, and it's no good trying to look through these glasses. They're all full of water."

"We'll be awfully careful," said Titty. "And Susan can hold Sinbad when it's my turn."

"Don't let them jibe her, that's all," said John, and went down the companion-way, glad for a moment not to think about what to do next.

There was very little water showing on the floor, just a puddle, sloshing to and fro at the foot of the steps. He shed his oilskin, rolled his sleeve to his shoulder, and reached down under the engine into greasy, rusty water. Suddenly he, John, acting skipper of the *Goblin*, had a most dreadful shock. It was as if all his insides were trying to get up into his throat. He stood up, looking at his arm, all wet and stained. This would never do. Was Roger the only one to be free from it? It was all right for Titty and Susan to be seasick, but he was going to be a sailor anyway, and if he couldn't stand bending down below decks and a whiff of bilge-water and oil, well . . .! He held his breath, plunged his arm down once more, felt desperately about in the slush, and found the inlet pipe of the pump. His hand, slimy with grease, came up with a sodden lump of cotton waste that had been sucked against the holes of the inlet and closed them as well as if they had been sealed on purpose.

He straightened himself and held the rag up with one hand while he steadied himself with the other. Gosh, he was glad the pump had not choked when they were tossing about in the night.

"He's greener than you were, Susan," said Roger cheerfully. "I say, John, she isn't a bit difficult to steer. I'm going to steer again when Titty's had her turn."

"Chuck it overboard," said John, holding out the black greasy lump he had brought up. "And then have a try at the pump."

Roger took the thing in the tips of his fingers and dropped it over the side. He pulled at the pump. "It's working all right now," he said.

"I say, John," said Susan. "You're not going to be sea-sick too?"

"No," said John, wiping his arm, and climbing up into the cockpit dragging his oilskin after him, to put it on in the open air. He threw up his head to get all the wind he could. "It's only grovelling about below. Smell of engine mostly."

"Twelve, thirteen, fourteen, fifteen, sixteen," panted Roger, counting the strokes.

"I'll have a go," said John. "Seventeen, eighteen, nineteen, twenty . . ." Already he felt better again. He went on counting till he came to a hundred, when Susan took a turn and he stood by in case anything went wrong with the steering of the able-seamen.

At the hundred and seventy-third stroke there was a squelching, sucking sound, and the pump handle suddenly went up and down with nothing to stop it.

"Good," said John.

"She isn't leaking?" said Susan.

"Can't be," said John. "Look here, Susan. Will you steer while I go forrard? There's an awful mess of ropes on the foredeck, and the burgee's all cockeye, and the signal halyards are flying loose from the cross-trees. We simply must have her looking all right when we get near the steamer, so that they won't spot that anything's wrong."

"Put on the life-line," said Susan. "And don't go and get overboard."

"I won't," said John. He knotted the life-line round his middle and scrambled forward along the cabin top. He tightened the flag halyards so that the little flagstaff with the burgee stood up proud and straight above the masthead. But he could not reach those signal halyards that were waving far out of reach.

"Bring her round to the wind, Susan," he shouted. "Go on. Luff."

"I *am* luffing," shouted Susan.

Yes. The *Goblin* was coming round. That was the jib clapping. Flick. The halyards in their wild dance touched his face. If only they would do that again. His left hand would be the one to grab with. Up and down the little ship lifted and dropped. Up and down. He caught a glimpse of frightened

faces in the cockpit. And then, suddenly, the flying halyards were in his hand. He sat down hard
and unexpectedly on the cabin roof.

"Got them," he shouted. "Bear away again.
Get the sails full." Would they never hear him?

But they had heard him all right. The jib
clapped but once more, and then settled to quiet.
He made the halyards fast to a shroud.

Then, still sitting on the cabin roof, he had a
good look round to see what else wanted doing.
The coils of the jib halyards had come adrift, and
an end was trailing in the water. Starboard side,
too. What must those fishermen have thought?
And the mainsail somehow looked sloppy. The
main halyard soaked by the rain must have
stretched a good deal, and now the morning
sun had dried it. It was as slack as it could
be. No wonder the boom was drooping a bit.
No wonder the luff of the sail looked loose and
baggy. He tidied up the jib halyards and wedged
them in behind the mast. Then he tried to bowse
down the main. No good, with the sail full of wind.
They'd have to come round again to spill the wind
out of it, or he would never be able to get it up. He
looked at the steamer. Still a long way off.

"Susan," he called. "You'll have to bring her to
the wind again . . . just for a moment . . . Luff . . ."

Susan knew by this time exactly what was
wanted. She swung the *Goblin* round towards the
wind. The mainsail ceased to pull and John gained
six or seven inches by swigging down the halyard.
"All right now," he called, and Susan headed for
the steamer. John gave a swig at the staysail
halyard, too, and then went back to the cockpit.

"Don't know what they'll have thought we were doing," he said. "But perhaps they weren't looking."

"Even with a telescope they couldn't have seen much," said Titty.

"Hope not," said John, "but they'll have seen her yawing about."

"The sails look just right now," said Susan. "They look just like they did when we sailed down the river."

"Anyway, I can't get them any better," said John. "But we'll have to sail close up to the steamer, and everything ought to be as right as it can be."

"She looks simply fine," said Titty.

"Let's get the cockpit tidied too," said John.

"And I think I'll wash up ..." said Susan. "There isn't much. Only the mugs and a plate."

"We'd better not use fresh water for it," said Titty.

"We jolly well won't," said John. "Suppose they tell us there isn't a harbour."

"There must be," said Susan, but she could see no sign of one in that coastline of golden sand dunes, and was content to do her best with salt water, which John scooped in a saucepan from the top of a wave that rose alongside just when it was wanted.

More steamers were in sight now, away to the south and where the golden coastline seemed to come to an end. The only steamer in sight ahead of them was the one that seemed hardly to be moving.

"Perhaps the harbour's over there where those

other steamers are," said Titty. "We may be going the wrong way. This one may only be fishing."

"Let's have those glasses," said John suddenly.

"They're no good since they got all splashed," said Roger.

John wiped them as well he could with a damp handkerchief, let go of the tiller for a moment, and stared at the steamer ahead of them.

"We're all right," he shouted. "Have a look, Susan. Isn't that a pretty big flag she's got at her masthead?"

Susan looked through the misty glasses and put them down, to be grabbed by Roger. "I can see better without. It's two flags, one above another. No. It's one, a huge one."

"She's a pilot vessel," shouted John. "Remember the pilots at Falmouth. We're all right now . . ."

"They'll know where we are anyway," said Titty.

"It isn't that," said John. "We can take a pilot to wherever we want to go. It isn't like asking for help. Jim said so himself. It's quite all right to signal for a pilot. Even liners do it. Where's that roll of flags?"

"Behind my bunk," said Titty. She pushed Sinbad into Susan's hands and dived down the companion.

She was up again a moment later with the canvas roll and opened it on the cockpit floor.

"S for a pilot," she said. "Here it is." She held up a small roll of blue and white.

John hurried forward to the mast, and, sitting on the cabin top, unfastened the signal halyards. When he had caught them and made them fast for tidiness' sake, the very last thing he had thought was that he would be using them so soon. He bent on the square pilot flag, and, doing his best to send it up hand over hand in professional style, had it fluttering a moment later from the cross-trees.

SIGNAL FOR A PILOT

"We're in for it now," he said, looking at the steamer, now quite near, and then up at that fluttering blue square with its white border.

"Will you let the pilot come aboard?" asked Roger.

"Yes," said John.

And then doubts began again.

"What land do you think it will be?" asked Titty.

"There are lots it might be," said John.

"It can't be England," said Roger.

"Not unless that compass is altogether wrong," said John.

"It'll have a harbour anyhow," said Susan. "Or there wouldn't be a pilot boat about."

"What language will you talk to him?" said Roger.

John's mouth fell.

"I know a little French," he said. "But jolly little. I'm always bottom for it at school."

"What's harbour?" said Titty. "S'il vous plaît, montrez nous le rue à une . . ."

"Porte," said Roger hopefully.

"But it isn't montrez," said John. "We want him to take us there."

"Prenez . . .," said Titty. "Prenez nous à une porte . . ."

"But perhaps he won't know French," said John. "And we ought to tell him what port we want to go to. And we don't know. It's going to be jolly difficult. If we let out we don't know, he may just turn beastly and take charge, and Jim'll have to pay salvage, and you know he couldn't buy oil because he had only just enough money for petrol."

"But can a pilot grab us for salvage?" said Roger.

"Anyone could," said John, "if they knew what had happened. It's all of us being so beastly young."

"Let's not have him on board," said Titty. "Can't we manage without? He may not have seen the signal yet. Let's take it down."

"We *must* have him," said Susan. "We can't help it, with Mother not knowing what's become of us. And the weather may go bad again. And every minute matters. We've simply got to get somewhere where we can telegraph."

All minds turned to Pin Mill, and the quiet anchorage, and the barges on the hard, and the Butt and Oyster, and Miss Powell's cottage, and Mother probably making sketches of boats, watching to see the *Goblin* come sailing up the river and Bridget splashing about in her sea-boots in the little stream by the boat-builder's sheds. They thought of Jim coming to Pin Mill with the news that he had lost them, *Goblin* and all.

"And I wouldn't be surprised if Daddy was in that steamer that called us fishmongers last night," said Roger.

"It's too late now, anyway," said John. "They've seen it. They've lowered a boat."

A boat, lowered on the other side of the steamer, dropped astern of her, and came rowing to meet them.

"Two men in her," said Roger. "Oh, bother these glasses."

Now and then the boat almost disappeared, and then showed again on the top of a sea, spray spirting from under it and two pairs of oars lifting it along.

"I say," said Roger. "The pilot *is* French. Look at the stern of the steamer. Her ensign is red, white and blue."

Titty looked through the glasses. There was doubt in her voice as she asked, "Don't the French red, white and blue go up and down? These go crosswise."

"She's Dutch," said John. "And those fishing

boats were Dutch too. I thought they were."

"Gosh!" said Roger. "Holland!"

"Windmills," said Titty, "and dykes to keep out the sea . . . And wooden shoes . . ."

"So long as they've got telegraph offices," said Susan.

"Look here," said John. "We've not got to let him know what's happened. There's only one thing to do. You'd better all go below."

"Below?" said Roger. "Oh, I say!"

"Can't be helped," said John. "With all four of us in the cockpit anyone would begin to ask questions. I've got to stay, because somebody has to be steering. But you'd better go below. And shut the doors. And close the hatch. You'll be able to see out through the portholes."

"Pretend not to be there?" said Titty.

"No. No. Make a noise. Make noises as native as ever you can. So that he'll think there's a captain and crew in the cabin and that I'm a sort of Roger . . ."

"Shall I play my whistle?" asked the real Roger.

"Good idea," said John. "Lots of natives play it quite as badly. You can't tell how old a person is by listening to a penny whistle. And stamp with your feet. Kick up all the grown-up row you can."

"Come on," said Susan. "John's right . . . Once we're in harbour they can't grab us . . . If only the pilot doesn't guess something's wrong and want to come down into the cabin."

"Come on Sinbad," said Titty.

"You'll have to mew like an old cat," said Roger.

A moment later John was alone in the cockpit, watching the rowing boat bouncing nearer and nearer over the waves. Susan closed the hatch over her head and pulled the doors to.

One door opened again. John saw her serious face.

"John. If you do have to explain, it can't be helped. Getting in matters more than anything else. Even if we have to save up for years and years to pay for the salvage."

"It'll be all right if only he doesn't guess," said John. "But I wish I knew enough Dutch even to say Good morning."

CHAPTER XX

GROWN-UP NOISES BELOW

JOHN tried his best to feel that he was not in charge of the ship but was only a ship's boy with nothing to worry about except his steering. Whatever happened he must not look bothered when the pilot came aboard. He tried to whistle, but remembered in time that sailors did not whistle unless for a wind, and, for the time being, he had all the wind he wanted. He tried to sing, but something went wrong with the words of the only tunes that came into his head. "What shall we do with a drunken sailor?" That started all right, but the second line ought to be the same as the first, and instead it came rather differently. "What shall we do with a drunken pilot?" John bit his tongue and went off into "Spanish Ladies," but found himself singing Holland instead of Scilly ... "From Ushant to Holland is thirty-five leagues." And, of course, it isn't. Just about right, though, counting from Harwich, though it had seemed much further ... "From Harwich to Holland is thirty-five leagues." But whereabouts in Holland? If he only knew ... What was he to say when the pilot asked him where he wanted to go? To a harbour. To a port. But what port? And in another minute he would have to be ready with the answer ...

He was steering to meet the little broad-beamed rowing boat that had left the pilot steamer. One

of the men in the boat was pulling in his oars.
He stowed them and moved to the stern-sheets,
while the other went on rowing. That man in the
stern was signalling to the *Goblin*. Telling her to
heave-to. It couldn't be anything else. But how?
Jim had never shown him anything about that.
Better not to try than to make a mess of it and
betray how little he really knew. But he would
have to stop the *Goblin* somehow. She was going
much too fast through the water. The only thing
he could think of was to bring her right up into
the wind as Jim had done when he was bringing
her up to her mooring buoy. He swung her round,
bit hard on his own teeth, looked out of the corner
of his eye at the boat tossing close by, pretended
not to see the signals, and kept the jib flapping and
the mainsail all of a shake. They were shouting at
him from the rowing boat. The man at the oars
was pulling like mad. John let go of the tiller,
grabbed one of the rope fenders and dangled it
over the side.

Bump.

What would Jim have said to that? Another bump. A round bundle of oilskin landed in
the cockpit with a thud. Big hairy hands, with
mottlings of blue under the hair, grasped the
coaming. There was a shout in a foreign language. The rowing boat drifted astern. A broad,
blue-clothed, red-faced man scrambled into the
cockpit.

The moment had come. What harbour was John
to name? Awful if it happened to be a hundred miles away on some other part of the coast.
The pilot would know at once that there was

something wrong. John thought of one Dutch harbour after another. Amsterdam, Rotterdam, the Hook ...

"Good day, mynheer," said the pilot, reaching for the tiller, "You want me to take you into Flushing? ..."

John felt his ears grow suddenly hot with relief. The question had been answered for him. And in English too. The pilot had seen the little scarlet ensign fluttering from the jackstaff in the stern.

"Yes, please," he said, moving forward in the cockpit to leave more room for the pilot, who had already taken the tiller, glanced at the compass, swung the little vessel round, quieting her sails, and now headed her not on her old course towards the distant sand dunes, but well to southward of it where John could see no land but only a thin line of haze.

John picked up the oilskin bundle and put it on the lee seat in the cockpit.

"Thank you, mynheer," said the pilot. "Where from?"

"Harwich."

"Your capten pick his weather bad to make crossing in so little boat."

John said nothing. He was listening for a good grown-up noise from the cabin, to keep the pilot thinking there was indeed a captain aboard.

"Bad blow we had yesternight. Where was you?"

"Outside Harwich," said John. That, at least, he knew for certain.

"No hurt? Many fishing boat lost sails."

"We were all right," said John. "Reefed ..." He made a motion to show sails coming down.

Why wouldn't those donkeys in the cabin make themselves heard?

"Little boat," said the pilot. "But ver' good." He patted the oaken tiller.

"Yes. Jolly good," said John.

And then, at last, the noise of a penny whistle came from the cabin, clear, though not very loud, through the open porthole by the compass. There was a noise of thumping. Of course, they had had to hunt for that whistle among all the things that had got swept on the floor in the worst of the storm and been bundled together anyhow in tidying up. They had not liked to sing or talk, for fear their voices might not be native enough. But now, a little jerkily, and not too certain of his fingering, Roger was playing the tune he thought he was best at . . . "We won't go home till morning." This is a tune that is not too bothersome about the high notes, and a lot of it is easy to remember and to play, just running up the scale and down again. The others were helpfully banging with their feet on the cabin floor.

"Merry barty," said the pilot.

"Very jolly," said John, and just then Roger, thinking it well to change his tune, began his next best, which was "Home, Sweet Home!" This was not so successful, for in the short choppy sea the long-drawn notes of "Home, Sweet Home!" did not sound quite as they should, when unexpected lurches of the boat made the musician take his fingers from the holes of the whistle and grab for something solid. There would be a short silence and then a few notes played very fast while Roger was trying to catch up. Then, when he felt he had drawn level, there would be slow time again to recover the pathos he had lost by the necessary burst of speed.

The pilot smiled. "Someone play trick, hey?" he said. "Music not so good."

John did not know how to answer. He was still trying to think of something to say, when the pilot flung up a large hand and pointed forward.

"Deurloo buoy," he said.

It was a big buoy, with red and black stripes on it going up and down, and a staff with a big triangle sticking up above it, and a square on the top of everything.

John nodded, as if he had been expecting to see it.

Then he saw other buoys, black can buoys and red buoys with pointed tops. The haze seemed to be clearing ahead of them. Land, a long low line of it, was showing to starboard. Those sand dunes which they had left far away to port were closing in on them. There were houses. He knew they must be coming up the channel in the mouth of a huge river. Where was Flushing? John tried to remember the names of the rivers of Holland, but could not think of any except the Maas.

There were more steamers now, close along the land in the south, and others far ahead. John leaned on the closed hatch above the companion, blinking in the sunshine, wondering what he had better do when the pilot asked for the captain. He might ask for him at any minute.

There had been a pause in the penny-whistling. Roger had been looking out of a salt-crusted porthole. Now he was working away again at one of his

latest show pieces, a great part of which he knew
almost for certain, though in other parts he still
had to find his way by experiment. "Way down
upon the Swanee river." He could perform one of
the twiddley bits in that at astonishing speed, and
anybody could have guessed that he was making
of it a song of triumph, a fanfarronade of victory.
Holland in sight! Houses! Windmills! "Way down
upon the Swanee river . . . Way . . ." A note well
held. Diddle, diddle dee dee diddle at racing pace.
"Far, far away . . ." Notes held so long that at least
one was cracked in the middle. John knew what
the tune was meant to be, but the pilot listened
with a puzzled face.

They came close by a large cage buoy with a
light on the top of it like the Beach End buoy
off Harwich. The shore on the port side was now
quite near . . . Hotels . . . A pier hung with flags
fluttering in the sun . . . A man on a bicycle who
seemed to be riding along the top of a wall . . . A
short grey tower rising out of the water . . . A fort
. . . Guns . . .

"Where will you go, mynheer?" said the pilot
. . . "Middelburg Canal?"

"Is there a consul at Flushing, a British consul?"
stammered John.

"Very fine man," said the pilot. "Now you go
call your capten."

John shook his head. He did not know what to
do. They would have to pay the pilot. And after
paying him, would there be enough money to send
the telegram? He felt the half-crown in his trouser
pocket. How much had Susan got? And how much
would a telegram cost from Holland to Pin Mill?

And what, oh what would happen when the pilot found out that there was no captain and that the four of them were alone on board? They were not in harbour yet. John shook his head, not by way of answer, but just because he had too many questions to think of at once.

The pilot laughed. "Your capten give orders not to disturb. Very fierce man, hey? I knew such one when I was boy in sailing ship." He waggled an end of the mainsheet and blew between his half-closed lips. "Very sore." He laughed again. "Ver' well. You say nodings. I call your capten mine self. When we want engine. Till den, merry barty and we leave him be."

"We've run out of petrol," said John. "No petrol."

"Ach," said the pilot. "Good wind. We sail into Outer Harbour. Old style. Hey?"

It seemed now to be understood that the captain was below, making merry in the cabin, and that the pilot, in order not to get John into trouble, would put off calling him on deck until the last possible moment. In some ways this seemed almost worse than if the truth had come out at once. John worked his way forward along the side deck. He wanted to be as far away from the pilot as he could get, so that there would be less chance of having questions to answer.

Where was the pilot taking them? They passed the mouth of a harbour. John saw the crowded masts of fishing boats. No. They were not going in there. The penny-whistling had stopped. John looked down between his feet and saw a nose flattened on the glass of a porthole. Titty. He looked down at the porthole on the other side of

the mast and saw another flattened nose. That
was why the penny-whistling had suddenly come
to an end. Well, there was no need for it now.

The little *Goblin* was swooping along under
the steep grey wall of a stone pier. A Dutch boy
in wide blue trousers shouted from the top of the
jetty and waved. The pilot solemnly lifted a huge
hand and dropped it again. They passed a beacon
on the end of the breakwater. The pilot was hauling in the mainsheet. Jibing. John wanted to go
and help, but it was over too quickly. He wriggled
himself out of the way on the cabin roof as the pilot
brought the headsails over. A huge open space of
smooth water opened before them. The *Goblin*
was on an even keel. Away to the left behind
the breakwater were the gates of a lock and a
couple of steam ferryboats. The high breakwater
shut off the wind. There was an almost startling
peace. But only for a moment. There was the sudden roar of a chain as a crane lowered a crate into
the hold of a liner, a huge, two-funnelled liner,
that was lying alongside a pontoon. It was the
last crate of the cargo. The pilot pulled out his
watch and looked at it, and pointed towards the
liner.

"Sailing for Harwich ... Where you come
from," he called out proudly to John. "Nederland
steamer."

And John looked up at the steep black sides
of the great steamship, at her funnels with their
bands of the Dutch red, white and blue, at the
high bridge, where an officer paused in his walk
and looked down. Below the bridge was the rail
of the boat deck, and below that yet another

rail, with passengers leaning on it, and stewards
bustling by. Yes. The pilot was right. The liner
was on the point of leaving. A crowd of people
on the pontoon were waving handkerchiefs and
cheering their friends. That big crane was moving
off. A bell struck. Someone ashore was blowing a
tin trumpet. A whistle sounded. Huge wire warps
that had been taut, drooped slack from the liner's
bows. She was casting off. A wild idea came into
John's head. If only they could have put one of
them aboard her, Titty, or Roger, to go home and
explain what had happened. But with only a few
shillings between the lot of them, they could do
nothing of the sort. And anyhow it was too late.
And there was the pilot to pay, and that telegram.

They were slipping up the harbour past the
great liner, when John noticed a ship's officer
and a passenger come to the rail of one of the
upper decks, and lean over it, talking together.
The passenger was in light grey clothes, not looking at all as if he had anything to do with the sea.
But his face was sunburnt to a dark brown, and
he flicked off his soft tweed hat and shot his fingers upwards through his hair with a trick that
seemed to John somehow familiar. The passenger
far away up there high above the little *Goblin* was
looking down at her, staring. Suddenly he seemed
to stiffen. A voice accustomed to be heard in a gale
of wind rang out across the water:

"Ahoy there! JOHN!"

"Daddy!" John gasped. "Ahoy! Ahoy!"

Neither John on the foredeck of the *Goblin*, nor
Daddy aboard the liner, could have heard another
word. There was a spirt of steam from beside one of

the funnels, and the big steamship's siren loosed a terrific throbbing shriek that seemed to go on for ever.

John, hardly knowing what he was doing, raced back to the cockpit. The liner was beginning to move. Daddy had disappeared. Was that him on the deck below, dodging through stewards and luggage and passengers? He was gone again.

"Fine voice," said the pilot genially. "Sailor, eh? You know him?"

"Yes," said John. There was nothing to be done. Oh, if only the *Goblin* had got in ten minutes earlier.

"Very fast ship," said the pilot. "Dey will have quick passage to England. Fine weather. What de matter?" And then the pilot chuckled to himself, and beckoned John to come nearer. The pilot bent towards John and half hid his mouth with a huge hand.

"I understand," he said in a great windy whisper. "Your capten very glad. Great storm. Very little boat. And all right ... Prosit!" And then he made as if he were tipping a bottle down his throat ... "But not right to leave boy to bring ship in alone wid de pilot. We will show him, hey? What he say, mynheer, when he find we tie up ship widout him? I will den have one small word wid him. But now, mynheer, we say nodings. We bring de ship in. Anchor, no need. We tie to buoy. You have rope ready forrard. You will bring down sails fore de mast when I make so ..." He made a sweeping downward motion with his free hand.

"Aye, aye, sir," said John desperately, trying

to remember what Jim had told him about rolling up the jib, and at the same time watching the towering stern of the Flushing-Harwich liner already clear of the pontoon. The *Goblin*, with the flood tide taking her up, was already far beyond the steamer berths.

"And now, you, boy, go forrard and watch ... I will not shout ... No. No. I will say nodings. And you will say nodings. And your capten, he will ..." The pilot closed both eyes. "Ah, no," he said. "He wake ... but come not on deck. He play de national hymn, is it not so, mynheer? God save de King!"

And indeed the penny whistle was at work once more, this time with great confidence, the performer no longer needing to hang on to anything even with an elbow, and the tune being one that he could play without need for experiment.

"Go forrard, boy. We will surbrise him."

John, puzzled a little at being called sometimes "Boy" and sometimes "Mynheer," though he rightly guessed that the pilot meant "Mynheer" more or less as a joke, went forward thinking miserably of Daddy on his way to England. Mother and Bridget would be meeting him at Harwich alone with all their plans gone wrong. And in a very few minutes now they would have to let the pilot know the truth.

The short length of rope he had used when he had tried to anchor was still on the foredeck, coiled round the windlass. He uncoiled it, made one end fast and cast loose the other end which had been tied to the anchor. The *Goblin* was gliding up the harbour. They were passing some moored lighters.

AHOY! AHOY!

John could see no mooring buoy. And then he
saw it, some way ahead, a big black buoy with an
iron ring on the top of it. He glanced back at the
pilot. The pilot nodded. Then the big hand made
a sharp gesture, downward. John struggled with
the staysail halyard. He had belayed it firmly,
for fear it should come adrift, and now, when he
wanted to free it in a hurry his fingers had to fight
with a tight half hitch of stiff rope. It was free at
last and down came the sail. Yes. The pilot was
signalling to furl the jib. He had let the sheets
fly, and the jib was flapping idly like a flag. John
stooped, risking a blow from dancing blocks, and
took hold of the furling rope. What had Jim done?
Simply pulled? John pulled as hard as he could,
and the sail rolled up, and the blocks danced
no more. Quick. Quick. Already the *Goblin* was
rounding up towards that buoy. John glanced aft
again. The pilot, standing in the cockpit, made a
ring with finger and thumb and poked the end of
the mainsheet through it. John understood. The
buoy was nearer and nearer. He could not reach it
from the deck. He slipped down by the stemhead,
under the bowsprit, got his feet on the bobstay,
and hanging on to the bowsprit with one hand,
waited with the end of the rope ready in the other.
Nearer and nearer. The *Goblin* was losing way.
Would she reach the buoy? Another foot would
do it. Another inch. John reached out, put the
end of the rope through the ring on the buoy,
grabbed it again, hauled some slack through the
ring, and a moment later had clambered back on
deck and was making fast.

"So," said the pilot. And then he winked at

John. "NOW, CAPTEN!" he shouted at the top of his voice, and thumped with a large flat hand on the sliding hatch of the cabin.

The seventeenth verse of "God Save the King!" came to a sudden stop.

CHAPTER XXI

SURPRISES ALL ROUND

FROM the moment that Susan closed the cabin doors and pulled across the sliding hatch, those below decks could hear nothing of what was going on in the cockpit. Through the portholes they caught a glimpse of the rowing boat leaping in the waves. They felt the bump as she came alongside. They heard the heavy thud of the pilot's bundle on the cockpit floor. But they did not hear the pilot's cheery "Want me to take you into Flushing?" They did not know how John had managed to talk to him. They tried to see what he had done with his boat, but the *Goblin* had turned away and left it astern and they could see nothing of it. They knew only that the pilot was aboard. Otherwise John would have opened the hatch and told them they could come out.

"It must be all right," said Susan, after a few breathless minutes. "We're sailing on again."

"Where to?" said Roger.

"John must know," said Susan. "He's managed the pilot somehow."

"I wish we knew," said Roger.

"What about the native noises?" said Titty.

"Sorry," said Roger, and, wedging himself in a corner of the lee bunk, let himself go on the penny whistle.

"Will they hear it?" said Susan doubtfully. "We can't hear them."

WHAT THEY SAW THROUGH THE PORTHOLES (I)
THE PILOT STEAMER

"It's pretty deafening," said Titty. "I expect they can. Sinbad's stopped purring. He doesn't like it at all."

"Cats aren't musical," said Roger, stopping to take breath.

"Sinbad may be," said Titty. "That's twice you've got the wrong note. Never mind. It's the noise that matters. They'll hear it. The compass porthole's open."

"But we don't hear them," said Susan.

"They're not trying to make us," said Titty. "But we'd better help. Let's bang with our hoofs. It's all right, Sinbad. Don't be frightened. Look here, Susan. Will you do the stamping? It jerks him too much if I do."

"We'd all better stamp," said Susan. "Put him on the floor for a bit."

For a long time they worked hard, stamping three pairs of feet and occasionally banging on an empty biscuit tin, while Roger whistled on and on, for once with the full approval of his audience.

The land, seen through the portholes, was coming nearer, no longer a wavy yellow line along the edge of the sea, but real land, houses, spires, a beach, and windmills. The motion of the *Goblin* was getting easier. Roger and Titty knelt on the bunks to look out, but it was hard to thump the floor while kneeling on a bunk, and harder still to play the penny whistle.

"It's Holland all right," said Roger, on seeing the windmills.

"Keep on playing," said Susan. She, too, looked out at the approaching land. But a new and dreadful thought had struck her. She dug into the knapsack stowed under the pillow on her bunk and pulled out her purse.

"We'll have to pay the pilot," she said. "Pilots don't take people in for nothing. We'll have to pay him even if he doesn't grab us for salvage. And we may not have enough. And even if we have there may not be any left for the telegram."

"What do pilots cost?" said Roger.

"I don't know," said Susan. "And a telegram from Holland to England may cost pounds. Titty, how much money have you got?"

"I've got two shillings and sevenpence," said Roger, stopping in the middle of a bar.

"Oh good," said Titty.

"But it's at home," said Roger, and his sisters turned impatiently away.

Titty and Susan emptied their purses. Susan had very nearly five shillings. Titty had a shilling, a sixpence, four pennies, one halfpenny, and a half-crown postal order that had been sent her by her godmother to buy a new drawing-book. "If only I'd changed it before we started," she said.

"John may have some," said Susan.

"I don't believe he has," said Roger. "Anyhow not much. He had to get next month's pocket-money in advance when he was buying his new knife."

"Keep on playing," said Susan. "We'll have to ask the pilot to wait. The telegram's got to go first. We'll have to ask Mother to send us some money for the pilot. We'll have to ask him to wait."

"He can't take us out to sea again if we're once in harbour," said Titty.

"But how on earth are we going to explain?" said Susan, and counted the money again.

"People bathing!" cried Titty.

"Look at the flags on that pier," said Roger.

"Don't stop playing," said Susan. "We'd play if we could, but we can't."

"Oh, all right," said Roger, played through "Swanee River" at breakneck speed, and cut the chorus in half to bring the others across the cabin to look at a huge buoy.

"We're close in," said Titty.

"We're not at sea any more," said Susan. "If only we knew what to say to him."

Grey stone walls and battlements showed up on the port side, forts with guns above their ramparts, houses with steeply rising roofs, women with enormous white sunbonnets, men with wide blue breeches, children – Dutch children – riding bicycles. Then, right past their noses, John's feet went by. He was on his way to the foredeck.

"We must be just arriving," said Susan.

"Oughtn't we to go and help?" said Roger.

"Not until he calls us," said Titty. "I say, Susan, we'd better have the money all ready to show the pilot when we come on deck."

"He'll only think it's all for him," said Susan. "And we must send that telegram."

"We're in the harbour," cried Roger. "Gosh! What a ship!"

The *Goblin* had rounded the end of the breakwater and was moving past the steep black sides of a big liner.

"Two funnels," said Roger.

The tremendous blare of a siren high above

them set their ears throbbing even in the closed cabin.

"She must be just starting," said Titty.

"Will we get out of the way in time?" said Roger.

And then, suddenly, they heard John's voice, shouting in desperate excitement.

Was he shouting for them? No. He couldn't be. That siren blared out again. John's feet pattered across the cabin roof. He must be talking to the pilot. Then they saw his feet again, going forrard past the portholes. What was happening now? Looking out forrard through the portholes at each side of the mast they saw the red staysail come down, and John bundling it to one side. They saw the jib roll up. They saw John, to Susan's horror, let himself down over the bows and disappear. They saw him come scrambling back with the end of a rope and make it fast. The *Goblin* was no longer moving. They saw that the huge, two-funnelled liner had left the quays and was steaming slowly out, dwarfing the tugs and ferryboats, and making even this big harbour look small.

And then came that thundering bang on the sliding hatch above the companion. A big voice roared:

"NOW, CAPTEN!"

The hatch slid back. The doors were pulled wide, and they saw the Dutch pilot looking in at them, and John's worried face behind him.

"How do you do?" said Susan, too bothered even to think of trying French.

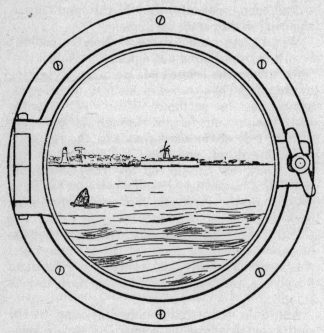

WHAT THEY SAW THROUGH THE PORTHOLES (II)
FLUSHING

"How do you do?" said Titty.

"Can we come out now?" said Roger, looking at John.

They came out: first Susan, then Titty with Sinbad, and then Roger, who had stopped for one moment to hide the penny whistle away in the shelf over his bunk.

"Susan," said John, "Daddy's on that steamer. He saw us, and shouted, but it was too late."

"Daddy! Oh no. It can't be."

They stared miserably at the big steamship, now slowly turning beyond the breakwater, to head for the North Sea and home. This was the worst thing that had happened yet. So near, but he might as well have been a hundred miles away. The liner loosed a last long hoot on her siren. It was like a jeer. She was gone, and Daddy with her, and they saw her masts go by, moving faster and faster, beyond the distant piers.

The pilot was looking past them down into the little cabin.

"So many children," he said. "But where is de capten?"

John looked at Susan, but said nothing. He could not think of anything to say. It was Susan who made the decision. "We'd better tell him everything," she said, and then, turning to the pilot, she began. "There isn't one. At least John is really. You see we didn't mean to come. And now we have to send a telegram, and will you please tell us how to send it and how much it will cost, because I'm not sure if we've got enough money. Of course we will have when we've telegraphed. Mother'll send us some from home."

John watched Susan gratefully. She was quite right, and she was doing it much better than he could have done. But he would have to ask how much they ought to pay the pilot.

The pilot's mouth had dropped open. He was staring at Susan. Then, leaning down into the companion, he looked right forrard, through both cabins.

"No capten," he said. "No capten! Four children . . . and dat small cat . . ." He was looking at the kitten that was blinking back at him out of Titty's arms.

"We rescued Sinbad on the way," said Titty.

"Four children alone . . . and you cross de Nord Sea . . . four children . . . and it blow yesternight . . . I would not cross de Nord Sea mine self in so small a boat . . . And I dink de capten too merry in de cabin . . . And de capten was all de time *you*, mynheer," and he suddenly startled John by taking him by the arm, and holding him, as if to have a better look at him. "And you fool de old pilot. He dink de capten down below . . . wid de bottle perhaps . . . and you de boy . . . Dere is not one boy in all Holland dat take a boat across de Nord Sea."

They were all watching the pilot's face. He seemed to be quite pleased at being taken in by John, and he had not said anything about salvage, but Susan, with her money and Titty's clasped in her hand, knew how very little it was. What would the pilot say when he knew too? Not one of them noticed the "Brrrrrr" of a motor-boat that was humming up the harbour towards them. Too much depended on what the pilot would say.

With Daddy already on his way to Harwich, it was more than ever important to get a telegram to Mother sent off at once.

"Ahoy!"

They started almost as if something had run into the *Goblin*.

"Ahoy!"

The little motor-boat was circling round to come up alongside, and sitting in it, holding on his grey felt hat, was . . .

"DADDY!" they all four shouted at once.

In another moment he was aboard. The Dutchman in the motor-boat handed John a painter, and John was making it fast while the motor-boat dropped astern.

"Hullo!" said Daddy. "What's all this? Whose boat? I never thought of anyone bringing you across to meet me."

"We didn't mean to go to sea," said Susan.

"It was in the fog," said John.

"We couldn't help it really," said Susan, and, looking at Daddy, with his weather-beaten, brown face, and the wrinkles round his eyes, some from laughter, some from looking into wind and sun at sea, she knew that whatever had happened everything was all right now. The relief was too much for her. She felt her lip moving in spite of herself, a hotness in her eyes, and, worst of all, a wetness on her cheek. She choked a sob, and bolted down into the cabin.

"Hold up, old girl," said Daddy, but Susan was out of sight, pressing her face into a pillow.

"It isn't her fault," said John. "She was dreadfully ill part of the time."

"Across de Nord Sea dey come," said the pilot.
"By demselves across de Nord Sea. I would never
have believe it. But I see it mine self. Dey fly de
pilot flag for me, and I come, and, de capten here,
he was steering de ship alone."

Daddy's eyes ran quickly here and there over
the rigging and then back to John and Titty and
Roger. He did not show that he was surprised in
any way. All he said was, "You must tell me about
it some time. Lucky I saw you coming in just in
time to make a pierhead jump the other way. A
minute later I couldn't have done it. What do you
propose to do now?"

"Have you got plenty of money?" said Roger.
"We haven't much, and Susan wants to telegraph
to Mother, and we haven't paid the pilot."

Daddy turned to the pilot. "Of course," he said.
"Well, pilot, what's your fee for bringing in the
liner?"

Susan, ashamed of her flight, had wiped her
eyes, and came up the companion-ladder. She
offered Daddy the handful of small change.

But the pilot thumped his knee with an enormous hand.

"Nodings," he shouted. "Nodings. You haf dam
fine children, mynheer . . . I give my congratu-
lations to your wife . . . No . . . No . . . I tell you
I will not take a guilder . . . No . . . I will take
nodings at all . . ."

"Have a drink, anyway," said Daddy, and hesitated, looking at Susan. Was there a drink on
board?

"There's the medicinal rum," said Titty. "Sinbad
only had the tiniest drop."

"I'll get it," said Susan. Once more she dropped
down into the cabin and came up again at once
with two mugs and that flat bottle labelled "For
medicinal purposes only." Daddy looked at it, read
the label twice, pulled out the cork, sniffed at the
mouth of the bottle, and poured out the doses.

The pilot and Daddy looked at each other,
touched mugs and drank. Then the pilot turned
to John.

"Your good health, Herr Capten. I am proud to
have pilot your vessel into Flushing. I will remember it all my life. Your health, Herr Capten."

John turned a very deep red under his sunburn,
spluttered, caught his father's gravely smiling
eyes and said, "Thank you very much."

The next minute Daddy was talking to the
pilot about tides. Then he turned to John. "What
charts have you aboard?"

"Only English ones," said John. "Harwich to
Southampton."

Daddy's eyes flickered, but he only said, to the
pilot, "I suppose I can buy a North Sea chart in
the harbour." Then he turned to the others and
asked, "When did you last have something to eat?"

"We had hot cocoa and tongue," said Roger,
"a long time ago."

"And we must get a telegram off to your
Mother at once," said Daddy. "I think we'd better
go ashore."

The pilot spoke in Dutch to the man in the
motor-boat. Then he turned and looked first at
Daddy, but spoke with grave respect to John.

"Capten," he said, "you will better take your
boat drough de lock into de inner harbour. Den

you will be able to lie alongside. Now if you cast off from de buoy, dis man will tow you. Better lower de mainsail, what you dink?"

"Can I give you a hand, Skipper?" said Daddy, and a minute or two later the mainsail was lowered, Daddy and John were putting tyers round it, and the *Goblin*, steered by the pilot, was being towed down the harbour.

"I can't believe it's Daddy really," said Titty.

"Of course it is," said Roger.

"I know," said Titty, "but I can't believe it all the same."

CHAPTER XXII

IN A FOREIGN PORT

THE pilot steered, shouting a word now and then to the man in the little motor-boat who was towing the *Goblin* round to the lock. Susan, Titty, and Roger watched their father quietly helping John to stow the mainsail. It had been a long time since they had seen him, but Daddy had not changed a bit. He looked the same and he was the same, taking everything as it came, just as if it had been carefully planned that they were to cross the North Sea and meet him in a Dutch harbour. No one could have guessed from looking at him that it had been any sort of surprise to him to look down from the upper deck of a Dutch liner at a little yacht coming in, and to see his son standing on her foredeck. He was behaving as if he had expected nothing else, and Titty, watching him, found herself smiling in the funny quiet way Mother sometimes smiled when she talked of the things Daddy had done long ago. Daddy was certainly very unlike anybody else. Captain Flint could be counted on in the same sort of way, but even Captain Flint, if he had met them all in some place where he had least expected them, would have called them all by name, Captain John, Mate Susan, Able-seaman Titty, and would have asked at once about the parrot and Gibber, and whether the ship's boy was hungry, and then he would have been in a hurry to know all about it,

how it had all happened, and so on. But Daddy, in
the presence of the pilot, was asking no questions
at all. He had come aboard just as if he had left
them only for a few minutes instead of being away
in the China Seas for ages and ages. Titty could
hardly believe he had ever been gone, as she saw
him hauling aft a bunt of sail and waiting, saying
nothing, while John, equally silent, put a tyer
round the part that was already rolled up. Silent
they both were, John and Daddy, but she knew
by the way they looked at each other across the
sail they were stowing how glad they were to be
together.

Susan was happier than she believed she could
have been before getting back to Pin Mill, but she
was in a fever to get that telegram off to Mother,
and could think of nothing else. She would have
been happier still if Daddy had asked a hundred
questions, had learnt all the truth at once, and,
like her, was in a frantic hurry to get to the
telegraph office.

The huge gates of the lock were open and
the *Goblin*, turning in from the outer harbour,
slipped slowly along under steep grey walls with a
high-water mark of green slime. Faces were looking down on them from above, smiling Dutch faces
under flat, uniform caps. Daddy on the foredeck
had coiled the rope John had used to tie up to
the buoy. He threw it up and one of the locksmen
caught it.

"What about fenders, skipper?" said Daddy.
"I've brought one forrard, but you'll want another
amidships."

John, after a smiling glance at Daddy, called

IN THE LOCK AT FLUSHING

out, "Susan, Mister Mate, let's have another of those fenders."

The pilot, rummaging in the rope locker aft, threw the best warp he could find up to another of the locksmen. The *Goblin* came gently to rest against the wall of the lock. The fenders held her off and saved her paint. Her little tug lay just ahead of her. The lock gates were already closing astern.

"Look at the jelly fish," cried Roger, "and the crabs."

Titty, Susan, and even John, who had a lot on which to think, looked down between the *Goblin* and the wall to see a crowd of small jelly fish, waving rings of filmy threads, hollowing themselves and filling themselves out again, moving slowly along in short jerks, while crabs of all sizes were climbing up under water, sideways, with busy, flickering legs, coming nearly to the surface and then dropping back out of sight.

The water began to rise and swirl in the lock, and the *Goblin* rose with it, swinging about so that John and Daddy and the pilot were kept busy fending her off from the wall.

Meanwhile the pilot was talking in Dutch to the locksmen, who were shortening the ropes as the *Goblin* rose. The locksmen called to other people somewhere up there on the top of the lock, and presently a crowd of heads were looking down at the little boat that had come across the North Sea with so strange a crew. And then a man in blue uniform pushed through the others and saluted, and asked for the captain and the ship's papers. Daddy looked at John.

"I know where he keeps them," said John, and hurried aft and down into the cabin, to come up again with a long envelope marked "SHIP'S PAPERS," which he passed up to the harbourmaster.

The harbourmaster pulled out the papers and looked at them, and then looked in a puzzled way at John and then at Daddy.

"Which of you is Mr Brading?" he said.

"He'll take you for a pirate," said Daddy quietly, but there was no need for John to say anything or even to begin to explain that Jim Brading wasn't there. The pilot was doing all the talking, and the harbourmaster was listening to him, every now and then looking all over the ship, at John and then again at Daddy. Was there going to be some awful trouble? The harbourmaster was asking questions. Daddy was filling a pipe as if nothing else mattered. Suddenly the harbourmaster reached down and handed the papers and their envelope back to John.

"Tonnage?" he asked.

"4.86," said John, who by this time knew by heart the figures carved on the main beam down in the cabin.

"Name?"

"*Goblin.*"

"From?"

"Harwich."

"That will be all right, Captain," said the harbourmaster, saluting again. "Welcome to Flushing!" He handed down a slip of pale buff paper. "The pilot says you leave again today or tomorrow . . ."

John looked at Daddy.

"What sort of weather forecast have you got?" asked Daddy, looking up at the harbourmaster with a smile.

"Wind veering north and east . . . Smooth sea."

"Better take our chance, eh, Captain?" said Daddy.

"Let's start today," said John.

"At once," said Susan, and then, "We must send the telegram off first."

"No dues to pay," said the harbourmaster. "The lock will open for you when you want to leave. Day or night. You will find a good berth by the pilot-boat . . ."

"I will show de Capten," said the pilot.

The water stopped rising. The gates at the other end of the lock opened. There was a sudden buzz from the motor-boat, fussing to be off.

"All clear."

The warps came tumbling down. John coiled one, and, in the cockpit, Roger did his best to coil the other. The motor-boat went slowly ahead. The tow-rope tautened. They were moving again, out of the lock into the inner harbour. Children were fishing from some stone steps. There was a battleship, long and grey, flying the Dutch flag. A long, black barge with a tug ahead of her, and a high deckhouse in her stern with tubs of scarlet geraniums by way of a garden, was moving slowly towards the lock. The motorboat led them away to port, where a street ran along the side of the harbour, with trees and green grass between the roadway and a row of wooden piles with white tops standing well out in the water. A gangway

ran all along the piles, and a long row of all kinds
of small vessels were tied up there, yachts and
plump Dutch traders, spick-and-span with clean
paint and shining windows in the deckhouses on
their poops. Last in that long row was a black
steamer, exactly like the pilot steamer they had
signalled to in the morning, except that she had a
different number on her bows. There was a space
ahead of her, not big enough for a Dutch trader,
but quite big enough for the *Goblin*, and presently the motor-boat had turned in a half-circle and
brought her round, and the *Goblin* slid up against
the piles, which, almost as if they were expecting
her, had big black motor tyres slung in front of
them as fenders. Daddy and John made fast to
the piles. Daddy gave some money to the man in
the motor-boat who had come up alongside. The
motor-boat shot off again back to the lock.

The pilot shook hands with all of them, beginning with Susan, then Titty, then Roger, then
John, then Daddy, and then John again.

"No need to buy charts, Capten," he said. "I
will bring you chart for de Nord See. No need
to pay nodings."

"Oh, I say," said John.

"Plenty in my house," said the pilot. "My sister's
son a capten too, and we will give you one to take
you home. So long, Capten. I will see you later."
He took his oilskin bundle, stepped across to the
gangplank that ran along the piles, and saluted.
Daddy stepped across with him, and asked him a
question.

"Half ebb and you will be all right," they heard
the pilot say. And with that he was gone, across

TIED UP IN HARBOUR

one of the smaller gangplanks that led from the piling to the green grass and the street. In a minute or two he was out of sight.

Roger bounced ashore and stamped firmly on the gangway, opened his eyes wide at finding he was not so safe on his feet as he had thought, and came aboard again in a hurry.

"I've been in Holland," he said uncertainly.

"Daddy, what about that telegram?" said Susan.

"We must make up our minds what we're going to say," said Daddy. "Will you lead the way below."

*

"Jim Brading? Haven't heard of him."

They were finding it difficult to explain to Daddy just how little Mother knew, and how it had happened that they had come sailing into Flushing just as he was leaving on the liner for Harwich.

Daddy was sitting on the port bunk with John and Susan. Susan had him firmly by one arm, but John kept getting up every now and then, unable to stay sitting down when there was so much to say and such a hurry to get it all said. Roger and Titty and Sinbad were on the starboard bunk. At least Titty and Sinbad were, but Roger kept hopping up to look out of the portholes at the shipping in the harbour, and at small Dutch boys paddling about in canoes. He was seldom in one place for very long, though he was listening to what was being said and sometimes putting in a word himself.

They explained Jim Brading.

"And then what happened? He went ashore and you drifted off in the fog. H'm. And when the

fog lifted . . . he'll have found his boat gone and
his crew with it . . . He may have gone to see if
anybody had seen anything of you at Pin Mill . . ."

"And Mother . . ." Susan's voice shook.

"She'll be in an awful stew," said Roger.

"Jim too," said John.

"He will, poor chap," said Daddy. "The only
hope is that he's in too much of a stew to tell her.
He'd go to the harbourmaster first for news of his
boat . . ." And then another idea seemed to strike
Daddy. "Funny he didn't make a shot at coming
off to you in the fog," he said. "Is he a seaman?"

"Jolly good," said John. "He brought the *Goblin*
from Dover all by himself."

"H'm. Something may have happened to keep
him ashore."

They looked at each other.

"I don't know what could have," said John.
"He only went to the dock for petrol."

"He'd been gone a long time before the fog
came," said Titty.

"Got to bear it in mind," said Daddy, pulling out
his pocket-book and making notes for a telegram.

"We've got to let your Mother know you're
all right," he said, crossing out some words and
writing others instead of them. "And Jim too, in
case he's gone to Pin Mill. But we won't worry her
with the North Sea, just in case he hasn't. And
anyhow we don't want your Jim coming over on
the night boat when we're on our way back. And
with the forecast the harbourmaster gave me, we
ought to be off this afternoon . . . Can you stick
another night passage?"

"Of course we can," said John.

"Did you get much sleep last night?"

"We got some," said Susan. "John didn't get much."

"Nor did you," said John, "but we're all right."

"Titty and I got lots," said Roger.

"There's another thing," said Daddy. "Your telegram mustn't come from Holland or your Mother'll be throwing fits."

"But we must send one," said Susan.

"We will," said Daddy. "But we'll have it sent from nearer home. What about this?" . . . He read out what he had written in clear capital letters that John and Susan read for themselves . . . "CAPTAIN CURTLEDGE SHOTLEY ENGLAND PLEASE SEND FOLLOWING TELEGRAM UNSIGNED QUOTE WALKER ALMA COTTAGE PIN MILL. . . . That's the right address? . . . She's at Miss Powell's, isn't she? . . . GOBLIN AND CREW ALL WELL RETURNING TOMORROW UNQUOTE ANSWER NO QUESTIONS TED WALKER. Curtledge is an old friend. He'll do it all right. Your Mother'll be pretty mad with you, but I can't help that. Better have her mad than worried. Any suggestions? Eh, Titty?"

"Put in about Sinbad. So she'll really feel nothing can have gone wrong."

"Good idea." Daddy smiled, and altered the telegram. "Now, the telegram she'll get'll read like this: WALKER ALMA COTTAGE PIN MILL GOBLIN AND CREW INCREASED BY KITTEN ALL WELL RETURNING TOMORROW NIGHT . . . That gives us a bit more time. We don't want to have her expecting us first thing in the morning."

"Aren't you going to send her a telegram yourself?" said Titty.

"Lucky I haven't already," said Daddy. "I sent one yesterday from Berlin. I meant to send a wireless from the boat." He wrote another telegram: "WALKER C/O MISS POWELL PIN MILL IPSWICH ENGLAND SO FAR SO GOOD TED . . . She'll see I've got as far as Flushing, and if she makes enquiries she'll know I've missed today's boat. We're all in a scrape together, but that's the best I can think of to get us out of it."

"Let's send the telegrams off at once," said Susan.

"All in a scrape together." It was the most extraordinary thing, but, though he had never said so, they all knew that for some reason or other, Daddy was rather pleased with them than otherwise. There was something in the way he looked at John.

"Come on," said Daddy, glancing up at the *Goblin*'s clock. "You can tell me the rest of the yarn later on."

"What about Sinbad?" said Titty. "I'd better stay with him."

"Don't you want to see Holland?" said Daddy.

She did, but she couldn't leave Sinbad to wander off ashore and get lost, or to fall overboard and be drowned in harbour after so very nearly being drowned at sea.

"I don't mind staying," she said.

Daddy pulled open a drawer under Titty's bunk in the forecabin. "Here you are," he said. "We'll empty all this on the bunk till we come back. Make a bed for it with a towel . . . And we'll leave the drawer not quite shut. If it's going to sea again at once it'll do it no harm to have a little sleep."

"He's nearly asleep already," said Titty.

"It'll do," said her father. "Now then, has your Jim Brading a milk-can aboard? Bring it with us. If that kitten's got any sense, it'll like honest cow's milk better than condensed."

CHAPTER XXIII

DUTCH AFTERNOON

ALL four of them nearly fell into the water in crossing the gangplank from the piling to the shore. The black tarred plank seemed to ripple like a strip of tape, now coming up to meet their feet before their feet expected to meet it, and now doing just the opposite. John staggered, fixed his eyes on the shore, and walked along the plank as if he were on a particularly uncertain kind of tight-rope. Susan swayed hurriedly after him. Titty stopped dead for a moment, and went on moving each foot about six inches at a time. "It would be all right if only I had four feet," said Roger, and, remembering the ways of Gibber (who was now spending his time spinning nautical yarns to the other monkeys in the Zoo), took hold of the edges of the plank with his hands, and so came ashore four-footed in perfect safety.

"Come along," said Daddy. "You'll soon get your shore legs again."

"Hurry up," said Susan. "Every minute matters till we get those telegrams sent."

On the other side of the road, just opposite the place where the *Goblin* was moored, there was a small shop, with a lot of wooden sabots hanging in the doorway. Roger, now standing on his hindlegs, pointed them out, but did not stop. Daddy was already striding along the road.

"Do you know the way to the Post Office?" asked Titty.

"Unless they've moved it since breakfast-time," said Commander Walker. "I had a walk round after my train got in. To stretch my legs after sitting still for twelve days . . ."

"Twelve days?" said Titty.

"And nights?" said Roger.

"As a matter of fact I slept a good part of the days as well as the nights," said their father. "So I'll be quite glad of a night watch at sea for a change . . . Now, tell me, John, what made you come to Flushing?"

"I didn't really try for anywhere," said John.

"Did you set a course at all?"

"About south-east," said John. "We tried to stick to that but we couldn't help wobbling a good deal."

"Why did you choose that?"

"It looked about right for getting clear of the shoals in the fog," said John. "You see we had a chart of Harwich, and when we were near that Cork lightship the chart showed shallow places almost everywhere except that way."

"You were a bit lucky," said his father, "but it wasn't a bad idea."

"I couldn't think of anything else to do," said John. "You see, she isn't our boat, and we couldn't see anything in the fog, and I didn't want to go aground."

"Quite right, though perhaps your mother wouldn't say so. Come on. Round this corner. But what made you keep on the same course once you were clear outside?"

"We meant to turn round and get back when the fog stopped, and I thought if we kept on one course we'd be able to get back to where we started from by going the opposite way."

"And the wind wouldn't let you?"

"It wasn't only that," said Susan. "It was my fault. I was sea-sick, and when we turned round it was too awful . . ."

"Head sea," said Daddy. "Beastly. And then it would be getting dark . . ."

"It was blowing much worse," said John. "And I thought we ought to reef."

"Good . . . Manage all right?"

"I had a life-line," said John.

"He nearly went overboard," said Susan, paling even now as she remembered it.

"But didn't," said Daddy. "Go on."

"We kept on like that all night. Susan steered a lot of the time. And then in the morning, before the dark went, we saw a light in the sky, and it was right ahead. And then when the day came we sighted the lighthouse."

"John went up the mast."

"And then?"

"We saw the pilot steamer, and we signalled for a pilot. We were nearly sure it was the right thing to do."

"It was. This way . . ."

"Wasn't it lucky we kept going straight?" said Titty. "We'd never have seen Sinbad if we hadn't . . ."

"A lot of things were lucky," said Daddy, and suddenly, while they were walking along, brought his hand down on John's shoulder and gave it a bit of a squeeze. "You'll be a seaman yet, my son."

And John, for one dreadful moment, felt that something was going wrong with his eyes. A sort of wetness, and hotness . . . Partly salt . . . Pleased though he was, he found himself biting his lower lip pretty hard, and looking the other way.

They were walking now through the streets with little trees along the pavements. Here and there were cafés, with tables and chairs out in the open air. Girls with enormous fluttering white muslin sunbonnets and skirts like black balloons went by on bicycles. Men with flat caps, short jackets, and wide baggy trousers that came in at the ankles, strolled along, each one of them with a cigar in his mouth. A small boy, no bigger than Roger, was leaning against a lamp-post, and took a huge cigar out of his mouth, because he wanted to open his mouth to stare better as the crew of the *Goblin* went by.

"He's smoking," said Roger.

"They start them in their cradles," said Daddy.

A hand cart piled high with vegetables was rattling down the street at a good pace, pushed by an old man, who was puffing away at his cigar as he hurried along. He had almost passed them when they saw a large dog, harnessed, trotting along under the cart, between the two wheels, straining at the traces and doing its full share of the work.

"Look at that dog!" exclaimed Roger.

"Hard-working country," said Daddy. "Even the dogs earn their living."

"Don't let's wait," said Susan, as Titty turned to watch the dog.

"You'll see plenty more," said Daddy, "and we'll have those telegrams on their way in a minute."

They turned one more corner, and Daddy led the way into a big building. Inside it there was a large hall, and all round the hall were grilles with labels over them, some for telegrams, some for stamps, some for money orders. By each grille a queue of people were waiting.

"Taking turns to see what's in the cages," said Roger.

"That's the animal we want," said Daddy, and took his place at the end of one of the queues.

"What about Dutch money?" said Titty.

"I think I've got more than enough. I kept some to use aboard the boat, and I shan't want it if I'm going to be a passenger in the *Goblin*."

"Hurry up. Hurry up. Hurry up." Susan's lips were moving, but no sound came out of them. She was secretly saying to herself what she would have liked to say to the old woman whose turn came before Daddy's.

The old woman was satisfied at last, and Daddy pushed his two telegrams through under the grille. The animal inside the cage gave no sign of excitement. He took them as calmly as if they did not matter at all, counted the words with a pencil, and then told Daddy that he must copy the telegrams out on proper telegraph forms.

"Oh!" said Susan in despair as she saw the telegrams pushed back.

Daddy said nothing at all. He went to a table, took two forms, copied out the telegrams, and took them back to the cage, where, luckily, no one else was waiting a turn at the moment. The animal inside counted the words all over again. Daddy handed through what seemed a lot of money and turned away.

"Now," he said. "We've done all that can be done to put things right, and we've got another two hours before starting back. It's no good worrying when worrying won't help. Cheer up, Susan. Let's enjoy ourselves. What about a bit of stowage?"

"Stowage?" said Titty. "Where?"

But Roger grinned up at his father. "I've got room," he said.

"Thought you might have. And we may not be able to do much cooking under way."

They went out, and down the steps of the Post Office. Something seemed to have happened to the day. The sun was brighter. Everybody in Flushing seemed to be smiling or laughing. Even the colours of the shops shone out more clearly. The crew of the *Goblin* stood, looking up and down the street, as if they had just come out of school to begin an unexpected holiday. Already those telegrams would be flashing along the wires to let Mother know that nothing had gone seriously wrong.

They sauntered along the pavement till they came to an open square, with a forest of masts sticking up out of a harbour at one side of it. They looked down over a low wall on a crowd of Dutch fishing boats, like those they had seen in the early morning, packed side by side, close together, with red nets hauled up above the decks to dry in the sunshine. Dutch fishermen, two and three together, were leaning on the wall above their boats, talking and smoking their cigars. Dutch women with those big spreading muslin sunbonnets, and gold ornaments at each side of their foreheads, were doing their marketing, chaffering over the fish, and filling their baskets from the wooden booths in the square.

At the far end of the square was another of those cafés with an awning out over the pavement, and tables with white cloths under the awning. Here they stopped, and in a moment a Dutch waiter (who looked quite like an English one) had put two of the small tables side by side, making a big one, and they had sat down, and Daddy had pointed to things on the menu, and the Dutch waiter was hurrying off into the café.

"Can't go far wrong with soup and steak," said Daddy. "You never know what you get when you try something with a fancy name."

Roger had known he was hungry before, but the others knew they were as hungry as Roger the moment they were sitting at that café table. They began at once, nibbling the crackly brown rolls that looked like English rolls but tasted different. Their mouths were watering for food. After all, it was a long time since they had had hot cocoa and tinned tongue and seen the sun come up out of the sea. It seemed almost as long, though it was only a few minutes, before the waiter came out again with a huge tray and plumped a deep plate of steaming soup before each one of them.

"Set to," said Daddy, and five tongues were burnt at the same moment. The soup was nearly boiling.

They nibbled more bread and waited. And

then, altogether unexpectedly, John felt his eyes closing. He opened them and looked all round him. They closed again. His head felt somehow much heavier than usual. He propped it with a hand . . . with both hands. Nothing would keep it up. Down it went, down . . . down. Daddy reached out just in time to move John's plate before he dipped his hair in it. John had fallen asleep with his head on the table.

"Skipper's been a long time on the bridge," said his father quietly.

"That's what happened to Jim Brading when he came to supper," said Roger.

"He'd sailed all the way from Dover," said Titty.

"And you've sailed a lot further than that," said Daddy, and smiled as he caught the eye of a Dutchman who was sitting at one of the other tables and had seen John's nodding head go down.

Susan, who was herself very sleepy, had been on the point of waking John, but if Daddy didn't mind John going to sleep in public, she knew it didn't really matter. The waiter came with four glasses of lemonade and one of lager beer. No one could have told from looking at him that people did not go to sleep with their head on his tables every day of the year.

"It's not too hot now if you blow it a bit," said Roger presently.

John started, opened his eyes and sat up very straight. He began to say "Sorry," but found himself biting on a yawn.

"All right, old chap," said Daddy. "You'll feel better when you've had some soup."

The hot soup, with scraps of carrot and potato

and onion floating about in it, cleared sleep away
like magic. Everybody was ready to talk about the
voyage, and things that had seemed awful at the
time seemed almost jolly now, as they sat with
Daddy under the awning on the pavement, while
the sunshine poured down on the busy square and
little puffs of wind tried to lift the corners of the
table-cloths. Bit by bit, Daddy, without asking a
lot of questions, pieced the whole tale together.
"Fishmongers, they called you, did they? . . . That
lightship must have been the North Hinder . . .
You must have passed fairly near Thornton Ridge
buoy . . . Lucky you didn't turn south after those
searchlights . . . Much further away than you
thought. They were the big light at Ostend . . .
And a nasty lot of banks between you and them
. . . Sinbad? . . . I don't suppose your mother'll
mind . . ." And then he looked at his watch. "It's
that Jim Brading of yours I'm worried about . . .
If he's gone and told your mother he's lost you . . .
Well, hurry up, Roger. The sooner we put to sea
the better . . ."

Steak had followed soup, and pancakes had
followed steak, and as Roger scooped up the last
drops of pink liquid left from a strawberry ice he
felt he could quite well last till teatime.

Daddy paid the bill. Titty picked up the milk-
can that she had put under her chair, and they
were off on their way back to the inner harbour
and the *Goblin*.

"We must keep a look out for a milk-shop,"
said Titty.

"What about our own suppers?" said Daddy.

"We've eaten all the bread," said Susan. "But

there's lots of tins of pemmican, and steak and kidney pudding, and fruit and things. All belonging to Jim. He's got plenty of tea and sugar, and we've still got half a tin of cocoa."

"We must make sure about water," said Daddy. "And we must fill up that petrol tank. No waiting about in calms for us on this trip. What sort of an engine is it?"

"Handy Billy," said Roger. "And it always starts first buzz. At least it did . . ."

"Good . . . Come along in here, Susan, and buy some bread for us."

They came out from a little bakery with a loaf of bread long enough to make not only Roger but everybody laugh.

"Now for the milk," said Daddy. "Bound to find a milk-shop somewhere near."

They found something better than a milk-shop. Round the corner of the street came a milk-cart, with an enormous dog between the shafts and a man in wooden shoes walking beside it. Daddy handed out some money, and Titty and Roger raced across the road. They had forgotten that they did not know Dutch, but the man seemed to understand. He stopped his cart, and the dog looked gravely round at them, while the man began drawing milk into a jug from a tap at the side of his cart. There was a hole there, as Roger pointed out, and the tap of a milk-churn poked through it. "When one churn's empty, he simply puts another in the same place," said Roger. Jug by jug the man measured out the milk into the can. When it came to paying, Titty simply held out her hand with all the Dutch money in it, and the man poked it about with a finger and picked out the bits of money he thought right.

THE MILK-CART

They came back to Kanaal Street, which runs alongside the inner harbour, and there was the *Goblin* where they had left her, tied up to the piling, just ahead of the pilot steamer like the one they had met at sea. But something seemed to be happening. There was a crowd of children on the grass between the street and the water, and ... no ... yes ... there was someone actually aboard.

"Hi," said Roger. "Pirates."

"Steady," said Daddy, and the next moment they saw it was their friend the pilot, who was sitting on the cabin roof with a rolled up chart across his knees, smoking a cigar and talking to a row of Dutch boys and girls who were looking down at him. He may have been telling them about the voyage of the *Goblin*, for all the Dutch children turned round as the crew of the *Goblin* crossed the road and came to the gangplank, and they heard the words "Nord See" said several times with great respect.

"Well, Capten," said the pilot to John. "These boys and girls dey not believe you bring your ship across de Nord See. Hey? But I tell dem. And here I have a chart for your fader. De wind go round and you will have fine passage home."

And then he unrolled the chart on the cabin roof, and pointed out the lightships marked on it, and told Daddy that he had put right the descriptions of the lights. "Some dey change last year. It is an old chart, but you will find it marked right now."

Daddy spoke of petrol and water, and the pilot turned to the crowd of children at the waterside. In a moment two of the boys were racing each other along the street, and two more had run across and into the little shop where the wooden shoes were hanging in the doorway.

A man came to the door of the shop and shouted something in Dutch to the pilot. The pilot shouted back.

"All right," he said to Daddy. "Dis man give you all de water you want." He shouted again, and the man went back into his shop, and presently a boy came staggering across the road with a can of water that slopped over in the dust about his feet. He carried it along the gangplank, and passed it on board, and Susan and John between them poured it down into the water tank under

the cockpit floor. The Dutch children fought for
the can when they passed it back, and two small
girls brought the next load. Then another boy
had a turn, and so on, till the water showed in
the bung-hole of the tank, and the *Goblin* had no
room for any more.

There was very nearly an accident with the
petrol. Daddy had said "Petrol" to the pilot, and
the pilot had shouted "Petrol" to the children
ashore, and the boys came back with a young
Dutchman carrying two big green tins. Daddy
unscrewed the cap of one of them, opened the
empty petrol tank, and began to pour the stuff in
through a funnel, when he noticed that instead of
being clear, like water, the petrol was bright blue.
He stopped pouring instantly and sniffed.

"But this is paraffin," he said. "Where's the
paraffin tin, John? We'll want some of this for
our navigation lights."

The pilot roared with laughter. "Ah," he said.
"It is benzine you want . . . not petrol . . .," and
the young Dutchman who had brought the tins
laughed too, and went off and presently came
back with two more.

This time Daddy sniffed before pouring. "That's
the stuff," he said.

"Some engines take petrol," said the pilot, "and
some take benzine, and what you call petrol we
in Holland call benzine . . . dat is de difference."

"Well, I'm glad you colour it blue," said Daddy.
"We'd have been in a mess if we'd filled the tank
with the wrong stuff."

At last everything was ready and the benzine
paid for. Daddy looked across the road where the

shopman was smiling in his doorway. "What about paying for the water?" he said.

"He give you dat," said the pilot. "Eh?" He shouted across the road, and the man smiled still wider, and threw out his hands in a manner that said clearly without any words at all that he was not going to charge them anything.

"Half a minute," said Daddy. "Didn't somebody say he'd like wooden shoes? You'd better take something back from Holland now you're here. Let's see if he's got anything that would do for Bridget."

All four of them went ashore by the plank. "It's a good plank to walk," said Roger, "and no sharks." Daddy went too, counting up how much Dutch money he had left. There was just enough for five pairs of wooden shoes (one pair two sizes smaller than Roger's, which Susan thought would be about right for Bridget), one toothbrush, a box of cigars and a small Dutch doll dressed exactly like one of the little Dutch girls who stood and giggled in the doorway of the shop, watching Roger try on his wooden shoes.

They went back, laden, to the *Goblin*, and Roger put childish things, like wooden shoes, behind him. He had to explain to Daddy just what Jim Brading did before starting the engine.

"There's plenty of oil in it already," he said. "He'd only just filled up with oil when the petrol ran out. But he said never to start it without having a look at the stern tube and screwing in more grease."

"Well, have a look at it," said Daddy. Roger lifted a door in the floor of the cockpit, and reached down to give a turn or two to the greaser. "Better you than me," said Daddy. "These clothes aren't meant for engine-rooms. Now then. All clear there." He slipped down into the cabin. "Petrol on. Here goes . . . Well, that's an engine worth having aboard." The little Handy Billy under the companion-steps went off at the first swing, chug, chugging away as if it had been only waiting for its chance.

Daddy came up again.

"Cast off forrard, John . . . Stern rope . . . Thank you."

One of the small Dutch boys handed the stern warp aboard.

"Well, goodbye, pilot, and thank you very much."

"I come wid you to de lock," said the pilot. "See you drough. Perhaps I take de tiller. Yes?"

The *Goblin*, her engine chug, chugging quietly, slid away from the piling. The pilot headed out into the harbour and then turned towards the locks. "You must give de signal," he said. "Sound de horn."

Roger rushed down into the cabin, nearly tumbling over Titty, who was giving Sinbad a good feed of milk while they were still in the smooth water of the inner harbour. He rushed back with the foghorn, hauled out the plunger and drove it in. There was a mighty roar. Almost at once they saw the lock gates opening.

"Shove her out of gear," said Daddy. "Go on, Roger. You're the engineer."

The *Goblin* slid slowly in, and John and Susan were ready with the fenders, and Daddy threw the warps up to the locksmen as the little ship once more came to rest under that steep grey wall.

"You not stop long in Holland, Capten," said one of the locksmen, looking down.

"We'd like to but we can't," said John, when he saw that the locksman was speaking to him and not to Daddy.

Just then there was a clatter of wooden shoes on stone, and all the Dutch children who had been helping in the inner harbour, and had raced round by land, arrived, panting and smiling to watch the *Goblin* put to sea.

Daddy and the pilot had gone down into the cabin while they were waiting for one pair of gates to close and the other to open. Daddy was fixing the North Sea chart on the table with two lengths of string. He had rummaged in the shelves and found Jim Brading's parallel rulers and protractors. He had pulled Jim's Nautical Almanac from its place and was looking up the tides. There would be no trusting to luck about the *Goblin's* navigation on her voyage home.

"Hi," called Roger. "The gates are opening to let us out."

In another moment the pilot was climbing up a ladder in the side of the lock, after shaking hands once more with all the crew.

"Goodbye, Capten," he said. "You will take me for pilot, I hope, when you come dese ways again."

"Goodbye, goodbye ... And thank you very much indeed."

They could hardly believe that they had been so nervous when he had come aboard, with John waiting alone for him in the cockpit and the others shut down below to make native noises for their very lives.

"Goodbye . . . Goodbye, English," shouted little Dutch boys, running along the edge of the quay.

Daddy called out, "Ahead!" and Roger shifted the gear lever; "Full!" and he opened the throttle. The chug, chugging of the engine quickened to a livelier, louder tune, and the *Goblin* passed through the gates and was at sea.

Titty held up Sinbad, who, after all, had seen less of Holland than any of them, and the Dutch children waved their caps and called, "Goodbye, English," till the *Goblin* was almost out of hearing.

"We'll come across again some other time," said Daddy, as if he knew they were all thinking that though they had been in foreign parts they had not stayed there very long.

"Nothing matters now except getting back quick," said Susan.

"Another time we'll bring Mother and Bridget with us," said Titty.

They were rounding the outer pierhead.

"If you'll take her, Skipper," said Daddy, "I'll make sail, though we shan't get much wind till we're clear of the land. We'll keep the engine going."

Chug, chug, chug, hummed the little engine, and in the afternoon sunshine the *Goblin*, with the ebb-tide to help her, soon left Flushing astern. Up went mainsail, jib and staysail, and with Daddy to swing on the halyards they somehow looked a good deal better than when John had had to hoist them as best he could alone. The wind had veered as the harbourmaster had said it would. It blew soft over

the roofs of the old Dutch town. The windmills
were turning slowly. The flags were fluttering on
the promenade pier. The *Goblin*, running easily
in the channel under the land, heeled a little as
she began to feel her sails.

"She's going beautifully," said Roger.

"She's going home," said Titty.

"Better leave that buoy to port, Skipper," said
Daddy, and, after glancing round at the set of the
sails, dived down into the cabin to have another
look at the chart.

CHAPTER XXIV

HAPPIER VOYAGE

THE *Goblin* was a happier ship now that she was homeward bound. Instead of knowing that she was going further and further into unknown seas where she had no right to be, everybody aboard her wanted her to go just as fast as she could. It was awful to think of Mother and Bridget and Jim waiting at Pin Mill not knowing where she was. But the sending off of those telegrams had made everybody feel better, and it was as if the *Goblin* herself were doing her best to help, hurrying, hurrying home to rejoin her lawful master. Not a moment was wasted. The chug, chugging of the engine, horrible noise though all of them (except perhaps Roger) thought it in the ordinary way, was now a cheerful song of haste, as the *Goblin* foamed along under the lee of the land before heading out through the channel into the North Sea.

The wind blew harder as they left the land behind them, and the tall tower of West Kapelle light, built on the top of a church, turned once more to a pencil rising out of the sea, grew smaller, vanished as the night came up, and at last flashed out far astern, a dim loom in the sky, to remind them of the Holland they had left.

For a long time they kept the engine running, really because of that encouraging bustling noise.

"Roger," said Daddy at last, when he had lit

the navigation lamps, and put them in their places, red and green, in the port and starboard shrouds, "Roger, you're the engineer. Nip down and turn the petrol off. We'll be going as fast without it."

Roger nipped down, turned off the petrol cock and waited. The noise of the engine changed as Daddy shut down the throttle and pushed the gears into neutral. "Chug . . . chug . . . chug . . ." The noise of the engine faded into silence, and they heard instead the steady swish of the water past the *Goblin*'s sides.

"Going fine," said Daddy. "And now, to bed with the lot of you. Roger and Titty first."

"Two more mugs to wipe," said Susan sleepily.

Susan was happier than she had been since Jim had anchored the *Goblin* in the sunshine off Felixstowe Dock. She had been afraid that she would be sea-sick again on the homeward voyage, but she had not been long enough ashore to lose her sea-legs, and she had not been sick at all. She had felt a bit peculiar just at first, but by the time they left the land she was better again, and knew that she was cured for this time at any rate. Why, she had been able to sit at the top of the companion, above the throbbing engine, to boil a kettle and make tea, and to hold a big saucepan steady on the stove while a tinned steak and kidney pudding had been hotting up inside it. She had even been able to eat her share of the pudding.

Titty, with Sinbad to look after, had not had time to think of sea-sickness or headaches, and now, when Daddy said it was time for bed, she took the kitten into her bunk, and in two minutes they were asleep together.

Roger had had a busy time. Twice he had burrowed down under the cockpit floor to give an extra turn to the greaser on the stern tube. Once he had poured a little more oil into the crank case. Besides that, while John was steering, he had helped Daddy to pour paraffin into the navigation lamps, a smelly job from which his sisters shrank.

"I'm not a bit sleepy," he said, but orders were orders, and he rolled into his bunk, was comfortably wedged in with the trysail by Susan, and fell asleep while he was still amusing himself by wriggling his toes under the blankets.

Susan was next to bed, and she, too, fell almost instantly asleep. She had slept longer than John the night before, but she was very tired. Seasickness was not the only misery from which she had escaped. Daddy was here, in the *Goblin*, and she no longer had that dreadful feeling that it was somehow her fault that they were at sea. They were going home as fast as they could, and Susan fell asleep almost as happily as if they had never left Harwich harbour.

John lingered in the cockpit.

"You too, old chap," said his father, and then, "But first take the tiller while I make sure about those tides. West by north . . ."

"West by north it is," said John, and steered while Daddy slipped down below to say good night to the rest of the crew, or rather not to say it, since he found all three were already asleep, and to rule a few lines on the chart, fixed on the table under the cabin lamp. John glanced down the companion to see Daddy using the parallel rulers and making notes on a scrap of paper. It was easy steering when you knew you had nothing to worry about and were going below in a minute or two.

"I could go on all night," said John as his father came up, glanced at the compass, and went forward over the cabin top to see that the navigation lights were burning properly.

"Dare say you could," said Commander Walker, "but I think you've done your whack and earned your watch below. I've been sleeping for the best part of a fortnight."

"Good night, Daddy," said John, taking a last look round into the night.

"Good night, old skipper," said his father.

Two minutes later John was in his bunk. He dozed off at once, but woke a moment or two later, feeling for the tiller, afraid he had let the *Goblin* off her course. He was on the point of shouting out when he remembered that he had a trusty seaman at the helm. He lay there, looking up out of the lighted cabin at that square of darkness outside the companion. To the right of it he could see the glimmer of the little candle-lamp that lit the compass. But in the opening there was nothing but the dark. Then, suddenly, there was the red glow of a lit match shielded by his father's hands. He saw his father's face as he lit one of the Dutch cigars. The match went out, but there was the cigar-end red hot in the darkness. Now and then, as Daddy took a puff at the cigar, that red-hot end glowed brightly enough to let John see Daddy's face behind it. Then it faded slowly.

Then it slipped sideways and disappeared. Then, glowing bright once more, it showed again.

John lay there, tired but content. Gosh, how awful it would have been if Daddy had not been able to jump ashore as the liner was leaving Flushing for Harwich. He would have been at Pin Mill by now, and Mother would have known that they were alone at the other side of the North Sea. Now, with Daddy aboard, the only thing that mattered was getting home quick. John listened to the water swirling by at the other side of the planking. He put his hand on the planking as if to feel that hurrying water. The *Goblin* was doing her best. And Daddy had known without any explainings that they had done theirs. Almost it had seemed that he was pleased with them. "You'll be a seaman yet, my son." John said those words over again to himself, as if they were a spell. And then he heard another noise beside the swirl and rush of the water so close at hand as he lay in his bunk. Daddy was singing to himself up there in the cockpit, out in the dark with the glow of the compass lamp, the glow of his cigar, the wind and the starry night. He was singing very low, more like humming than singing, the old sea songs they had all learnt in the nursery.

"Away to Rio . . . Away to Rio . . .
Oh, fare you well, my bonny young maid,
For we're bound to Rio Grande . . ."

And then a little louder, beginning to forget his sleeping crew . . .

"There's a Black Ball barque a-coming down
the river,
 Blow, bullies blow.
There's a Black Ball barque a-coming down
the river,
 Blow, my bully boys, blow."

And after the end of that song Daddy seemed
to have forgotten that he was not alone in the
ship, for he was singing very heartily, steering
with one hand, with the red glow of the cigar in
his other hand weaving circles in the dark . . .

"In the Black Ball line I served my time,
 To me hoodah. To me hoodah.
In the Black Ball line I served my time,
 Rah, hurrah, for the Black Ball line.
 Blow, my bullies, blow,
 For California O.
 There's plenty of gold
 So I've been told
On the banks of the Sacramento."

There was stirring in the fore-cabin.
"Sh! Sinbad," John heard Titty whisper. "It's
all right. It's only Daddy."
"John," whispered Susan. "He can't think it
was our fault, or he wouldn't be singing like
that."
"He's been away from home a long time," whispered Titty. "He's singing because he's nearly
back."
Roger never woke, and presently the others
dropped off again to sleep.

Roger's turn to wake came later in the night, when something cold and hard tapped him lightly on the head. He had too much hair for the parallel rulers, that had slipped off the table, to do him any harm. But he woke with a start to find Daddy peering at the chart with a pocket torch. The cabin lamp, turned low, did not give enough light to let Daddy read the notes the Dutch pilot had scribbled in red ink beside the little pictures of the lightships.

"Sorry, old chap," said Daddy.

"Who's steering?" said Roger.

"Steering herself at the moment."

"Are we nearly home?"

"About half way. But the wind's dropping a little. You go to sleep . . ."

"Call me if you want to start the engine," said Roger sleepily.

"I will," said his father, reached over Roger to put the rulers in the rack, and was gone.

*

A splash of sunlight was playing round the cabin. It came in through the open companion, danced over the clock and the barometer, and through into the fore-cabin, and danced out and back again as the *Goblin* rose and fell.

"Show a leg, the watch below!"

Gosh! Daylight already . . . broad daylight and the sun shining. The watch below were out of their bunks, rubbing their eyes and, in the case of Sinbad, calling loudly for breakfast. They hurried into their clothes and up on deck to find a blue, sunlit sea, and right ahead of them a lightship.

Away to the south a feather of smoke showed where a steamer must be.

"Where are we?" asked John.

"Coming in to the Sunk lightship," said Daddy. "Here, you can take over. Keep her going for the lightship. I want to stretch my arms. And what about breakfast, Susan? Think the kettle'll stay put? Hullo, Pussy . . . Hungry?"

"Very . . . Aren't you, Sinbad?" said Titty.

"We'll have breakfast in peace, and then turn the engine on," said Daddy. "Wind's been dropping for some time, and if Roger'll get her greased up . . ."

"How long before we see land?" asked Susan.

"Not long now . . . but we'll see it sooner with the engine earning its keep." Daddy left the cockpit and sat on the top of the cabin, and stretched his arms and yawned. "That's right, John . . . Head up a little bit to allow for the tide."

Titty went below to feed the hungry Sinbad. Roger lifted the board in the cockpit and burrowed down to get the screw cap from the stern tube, fill it with grease as he had seen Jim fill it, and screw it down again. Susan lighted the stove, put the kettle on, and sat at the top of the companion-steps to see that the kettle did not slip off. John, in the light north-easterly wind, was finding the steering very different from the struggle it had been in the rough water and hard squalls of the outward passage.

They were eating their breakfast in the cockpit as they passed close under the stern of the Sunk lightship. It was a proper breakfast of cocoa, Dutch bread and English butter, potted meat and Pin

Mill eggs. If they had been by themselves, Susan would have taken the easy way and boiled those eggs, but she remembered something from the last time Daddy was home, and she took the big frying-pan that had served as a bell in the fog, and melted the last of the butter in it, and broke six eggs into the butter and stirred them with a fork, only once letting a little slop over to hiss and splutter on the stove. Daddy, sitting on the cabin roof, did not see what she was doing, but when breakfast was ready, and she handed the mugs of cocoa out into the cockpit, and then five deep saucers full of scrambled egg, he laughed.

"I'd been counting on scrambled eggs tomorrow," he said. "I didn't expect them today. Good ones, too. Thank you, Susan."

As they passed the lightship they exchanged "Good mornings" with the men on board who came and looked down over the stern to see the little ship go by.

"Fare to be good weather now," called one of the men. "Had a good crossing?"

"Nothing to complain of," shouted Daddy.

"Pretty bad, night before last," shouted the man.

"It jolly well was," said John quietly.

"Did you see them on the way out?" asked his father. "You must have passed them pretty close."

"We only heard them," said John. "We didn't see any of the lightships till that one in the middle of the night."

"We couldn't see anything in the fog," said Susan.

"Only buoys," said Roger. "Just in time not to bump them."

MEETING THE SAILING SHIP

"We heard the lightships making their noises," said Titty.

On they went, and Daddy altered course just a little, after having another look at the chart and the clock and the Nautical Almanac.

"About half flood," he said. "We'll have the tide with us to carry us in."

By the time they had finished breakfast the Sunk was far astern.

"Come on, Susan," said Daddy. "We'll do the washing up in the cockpit, but we'll have that engine going first."

Yes. Daddy was in a hurry too. And a minute later the engine began its quick chug, chug, chug, the wash suddenly lengthened, and a foaming narrow wave spread from the bows of the *Goblin*.

"We shan't be long now," said Daddy. "A bob for whoever first sights the Cork."

Roger, who had been on the very point of speaking, held out one hand and pointed ahead with the other.

"Jove," said Daddy, after taking a look through the glasses, "you're right. Good eyes. Well, another bob for whoever first sights land."

Very soon after the Cork lightship was clear for all to see there was such a general shout of "Land ho!" that the only thing to do was to hand out shillings all round, if only there had been enough shillings. But as there were no more, they agreed to trust Daddy until he could change some money at Pin Mill. The tall wireless masts at Bawdsey were showing, and a chimney behind Harwich, and then the cliff just north of Felixstowe.

"Better get up the quarantine flag," said Daddy.

"We'll have to be cleared by the Customs, coming in from foreign."

"I'll get it," said Titty.

"Know which it is?"

"Of course," said Titty. "It's the yellow one. We had to hoist it when Nancy was having mumps."

She dived below for the roll of signal flags, and came back with the little square of yellow bunting. John went forward, and presently it was fluttering from the cross-trees.

"Ship on the starboard bow," yelled Roger.

"It's a sailing ship," cried Titty.

"With a tug," said Roger.

Coming out beyond the Cork was one of the last of the old sailing ships, a four-masted barque, being towed out clear of the shoals before setting sail for the Baltic.

"In ballast," said Daddy. "See how high she is out of the water. She'll have left her grain at Ipswich. She'll have come round the Horn from Australia, and now she's going home."

"So are we," said Titty. "Oh, Daddy, do you think there's a chance that we're going to get home before Mother knows we've been to sea?"

"Not much," said Daddy. "Two days and two nights away ... That young man of yours'll be bound to have told her he's mislaid you."

With grave, disturbed faces they watched the barque, with the sailors out on the yards of her, ready to loose her white sails. They read her name through the glasses ... "*Pommern.*" They listened to Daddy telling them of the island harbour of Mariehamn in the Baltic to which the barque belonged. They read the name "CORK" in huge white letters on the red hull of the lightship whose bleats had frightened them into heading out to sea. They saw the buoys they had so nearly run into. They watched the houses of Felixstowe growing clearer, the long pier, Landguard Point running out into the sea, Harwich church ... One by one they passed the buoys that mark the outer shoals. Daddy had brought the boom over by the Cork, and they were running along the land towards a big conical buoy that seemed far out to sea.

"Got to go outside that one," said Daddy. "That's Beach End buoy ..."

"Beach End buoy."

They looked at each other, remembering the awful moment when they had last seen it.

"It came charging at us in the fog," said Roger.

"That was how we knew we were at sea," said John.

Little else was said as they hurried towards it. Sinbad alone was not thinking of Jim Brading who had lost his ship, and of Mother who ... if Jim Brading had told her, not one of them could bear to think of what she must be feeling.

"Cheer up," said Daddy at last. "She'll have got our telegrams yesterday."

Sinbad mewed loudly for more milk.

CHAPTER XXV

LOST! TWO DAYS AND A BOAT

JIM BRADING was coming to himself. There had
been a sudden burst of light into his room as the
curtains were drawn ... He remembered that
... and someone with an arm round his shoulders while someone else was pushing pillows in
behind his back ... a tray with a white cloth on a
bed-table across his knees ... a spoon pushed into
his fingers ... A bowl of bread-and-milk ... It was
nearly empty ... Had someone been feeding him?
He scooped up the last spoonful ... There was still
a drop of milk in the bottom of the bowl. He chased
it round with the spoon, but could not catch it, and
gave it up, feeling very tired. The spoon slipped
from his fingers. For some minutes, hardly seeing
it, he looked at a glass with a bright orange liquid in it. Raw eggs beaten up? Orange juice? He
reached for it and brought it to his lips. He tried to
sniff at it. Gosh, what a headache! Whatever that
orange stuff was, he wanted it. With a shaking
hand he tipped it into his mouth, and drank it off,
spilling a little down his chin and on ... What on
earth was he wearing? A white nightgown? Jim
looked at his sleeves with great disgust. He had
never worn a thing like that. Had he turned into
somebody else without knowing it?

The door opened and a nurse bustled in.

"That's better," she said. "Now, I'll take that

tray, and you'll lie quiet till the doctor comes to say good morning to you."

Jim stared at her. Doctor? What doctor? And what was this neat white room?

"Where am I?"

"In hospital," said the nurse. "And you've come off very lucky, too. Good hard skull, you've got, the doctor says. Now you're not to start talking till he's seen you."

And she was gone.

Jim felt his head, a mass of thick bandaging. What had happened to him? Suddenly he remembered that he had come ashore to get petrol for the *Goblin*. But when . . . WHEN? There had been no petrol in the dock. He had taken a bus to the nearest petrol station. Just time to nip across the road and get his can filled and catch another bus back. He remembered an old lady getting up in the bus and blocking the gangway when he had been in such a hurry to get out. After that . . . But was that yesterday or this morning? A dim memory of someone in the darkness, talking, told him it must have been yesterday. Had he been in this place all night?

And those children aboard the *Goblin* by themselves . . . Oh, how his head ached. By themselves in the *Goblin* . . . All night . . . And he had promised Mrs Walker to look after them.

He threw off the blankets. Again that nurse came into the room.

"No, no, no," she said, putting the bedclothes back and tucking them in at the sides. "You must lie quiet a little longer."

"But I can't," he spluttered. "I can't. I've got

to go at once. To the harbour . . . I've left them all alone . . ."

"The doctor'll be coming presently," said the nurse kindly. "He gave you an injection last night. You mustn't stir till he comes. He won't be pleased if he finds you feverish . . ."

"But . . ."

The nurse smiled at him and closed the door behind her. He was alone.

He threw the bedclothes off once more. Why, every minute mattered. He must go now, at once. They had no right to stop him. He got out of bed, slowly, but as fast as he could. Why couldn't the room keep still, instead of spinning round him?

"Steady," he muttered to himself, and got somehow to the window and looked out. Bright sunshine flooded a street of red-brick houses. He knew that street. He tried to remember the name of the hospital. "But I never came here," he muttered. "Where are my clothes?"

He tottered back and caught hold of the rail at the foot of the bed. There was a card hanging from it, a printed form. He read: "Patient's name . . ." Someone had written in ink, "Unknown Seaman.? Dane?? . . ." Then he saw the word "Pulse," and after it a row of figures . . . "Temperature," and another lot of figures. "Notes." Under that someone had written, "Injection A.2," and "Sleeping Draught, 9 p.m." Then he saw that someone had drawn a line in pencil from the space for "Patient's Name" down to the bottom of the card, where, in round, clear handwriting, he read the words, "Talks English."

"Well, I do like that," said Jim Brading.

There was no furniture in the room except
the white hospital bed, and a washing basin,
and the white bedside table with a glass and a
carafe of water, and one white chair. Had they
stolen his clothes? And then, in the white wall,
he saw a white-painted door, with a lock and a
key in the lock. He opened the door and found
a built-in cupboard, with hooks in it, and there –
oh, thank goodness for that! – his sea-boots, his
jersey, and his flannel trousers.

He tottered across to the door of the room. It
had no lock on it, and he knew that the nurse and
perhaps the doctor might come in at any moment.
He tried to put on his trousers, and found he had
to sit on the chair to do it. Usually putting on
trousers was a matter of a swift left and right,
first one leg and then the other, haul up and
buckle tight. Today he somehow could not make
a good shot with one foot while trying to balance
on the other, and if he hung on to the end of the
bed he was a hand short for holding the trousers.
Sitting on the chair he managed it, but it was a
slow business and he was in a desperate hurry.

That horrible white nightgown came off easily
enough, but it was a painful, slow job to work
his huge bandaged head through the neck of his
jersey. A steam hammer seemed to be pounding
inside that head of his. Then his sea-boots. When
he stamped his heel down it was as if someone
had hit him on the point of the chin.

He swayed across the room to the door, and
opened it a chink, with one hand on the doorpost
and the other on the handle. They had no right
to keep him here. He had never asked to come.

And the *Goblin* anchored out in the harbour all night, with those children all by themselves. He listened. Someone was coming. The steps passed his door. He waited a moment, and tottered out, just as the nurse turned a corner somewhere away to the right. To the right. He turned left, and, with a hand against the wall, hurried weakly along the corridor. At the end of the long corridor there was a landing and steps down into the hall. People were talking down there. A flood of sunshine poured in from the open door. He heard a nurse say, "If you will just wait in here, I'll go and fetch the matron." Dimly he saw someone go into a doorway, and then a flurry of white as the nurse came towards the foot of the stairs. For a moment he thought she was coming up, but no, the matron must have been somewhere on the ground floor. Now was his chance. He must get down those stairs and out before the nurse and the matron came back. If only he were not so wobbly at the knees.

Down he went, almost losing his balance half-way, but saving himself with a hand on the banister and another on the wall. Through a doorway on the right he saw someone, a patient or a visitor, sitting on the edge of a chair staring at him as if he were a sort of monster, as indeed he must have looked, in jersey, flannels and sea-boots, with a huge white-bandaged head.

Footsteps sounded behind him on a concrete floor. The matron and the nurse were coming. He had not a moment to lose. He crossed the hall and went out through the open door. The sunlight was like a blow in the face for him.

He blinked, stumbled, but found himself in the street. He hurried along it. His feet were beginning to behave as if they were his own. He turned a corner and was out of sight from the hospital.

This street came down to the main road to Felixstowe Dock. He came to the corner just as a motor-bus was pulling up to set down a passenger. He clambered in.

"Hold tight now," said the conductor, and the bus was off again on its way to Felixstowe Dock.

Jim felt in his pockets. Yes, his money was still there, and he took out a penny for the fare.

"Glad to see you're no worse," said the conductor, smiling at him. "And Bill'll be glad too. That he will. They tell him that might be a long whiles before you'd be about again . . ."

"Bill?" said Jim, who did not know what the conductor was talking about.

"He drive that bus you try to capsize," said the conductor. "Police at him about it, and you'll have to tell them you run into him. Lucky you didn't smash that bus. It wasn't Bill's fault. But he's been in a taking about it. He think he'd killed you first go off. But he hadn't a chance, Bill hadn't, not with you running into him like that . . ."

And then, while Jim was thinking all the time of the *Goblin*, and those four children alone aboard her in the harbour, the conductor went on to tell the other passengers all about it. "He get out of my bus in a hurry, with his petrol-can, and run right across, that he do, bang wallop into old Bill's coming t'other way. Might have been killed, that he might. Made a proper dint in old

Bill's mudguard. And old Bill, he turn white as a
sheet and empty his breakfast out in the road like
it were him what were hit. And this young man
laid out flat, till they take him round to hospital
on a door from the garage. Look like croaking
any minute if they wait for the ambulance. All's
well as ends well, as they say. Good job he's come
through sound in mind and limb . . . Here you are
. . . Felixstowe Dock . . . Yes . . . That's the way
to the ferry . . . No, ma'am. It'll be ten minutes
before we leave . . . Thank you . . ." He helped Jim
out. "Good day to you. You're safe here. Terminus.
You ain't got old Bill's bus to run into this time."

Jim, as fast as he was able, crossed the wide
square in front of the Pier Hotel. Had the *Goblin*
shifted? When he had come ashore with the petrol-
can, surely he had been able to see her through
those railings. He hurried round the dock offices
and out on the little pier, hardly looking at the
steam ferry that was taking aboard passengers
for Harwich at the float below him in the dock.
He dodged round a railway truck and a heap of
coal, and looked across the harbour, and looked,
and looked again.

She had gone.

Jim Brading steadied himself with a hand on a
bollard on the edge of the pier. She must be there
somewhere. He looked across to Harwich town,
trying to see her among the fishing boats anchored
beyond the Guard buoy. He looked up towards the
mouth of the Orwell. Nothing by Shotley Spit but
anchored barges. He looked at the mouth of the
Stour. There was the Trinity House steamer on
her moorings, an anchored dredger, a big white

steam yacht, but never a sign of his own little ship.

The *Goblin* was gone as if she had never been there.

Jim staggered back to the dock. The ferry was just casting off to go across to Harwich town.

"Half a minute," he called, and, with most uncertain feet, got down the steps to the float and aboard. The harbour-master at Harwich would know where she was. But, already, dreadful thoughts were beating in his aching head. Run down? A barge might have put her under in the night. Would John have lit the riding light? Was there any oil in it? He flopped on a seat, looking in all directions as the little ferry boat steamed across the harbour. The mate of the ferry boat came for his ticket. He had not got one, but the man knew him and told him to buy a ticket at the other end.

"Been in the wars?" he said.

"Where's the *Goblin*?" said Jim.

"Haven't seen her," said the mate.

"But I left her anchored on the Shelf yesterday morning."

"I was off duty yesterday," said the man. "She's not been in the harbour today . . . Hey, Bob, seen anything of the *Goblin*? Little cutter anchored on the Shelf yesterday morning."

"Never see her," said the skipper.

Jim's head felt as if it were going to crack across the top. How could they not have seen her? It was no use arguing. He said no more. The harbourmaster would know. As the little steam ferry throbbed her way across the harbour, he

stared up the Orwell and up the Stour, looking
for that white hull with the slightly raking mast,
looking for that well-known triangle of dark red
sail. But surely that boy John would never have
had the cheek to hoist sail on her alone. Surely
he would have known that he had nothing to do
but wait till her owner came back. Ten minutes
he had said, and that was yesterday morning . . .
A long time for them to wait . . . But still . . . Oh,
if only his head would let him THINK.

The little ferry steamed into the camber at
Harwich, and Jim pulled himself up, went ashore
and up the wooden steps to the top of the pier and
so to the harbourmaster's office.

The harbourmaster was at his desk, and looked
up as Jim came in. He laughed.

"That's a fine lot of bandaging you've got
on. Somebody cracked your head with a marline
spike?"

But Jim could make no jokes about cracked
heads.

"Where's the *Goblin*?" he asked.

"The *Goblin*?"

"My boat. Bermuda cutter. Seven tons, Thames.
4.86 registered. No. 16856."

"Came in from Dover on Tuesday," said the
harbourmaster.

"No. No. Since then," said Jim. "I brought
her down from Pin Mill to Shotley, and anchored
her on the Shelf yesterday morning while I went
ashore . . ."

"Leave anybody in her?"

"Four children," groaned Jim.

"I remember her now," said the harbourmaster.

"But that wasn't yesterday. There was no cutter on the Shelf yesterday. That was the day before. You were anchored off Shotley pier for the night. I saw you bathing off her next morning. And pretty early you took her down harbour and anchored off Felixstowe Dock when it come calm. Just before the fog that was. But not yesterday. That was the day before . . ."

"The day before yesterday . . ." repeated Jim. "Fog? But there's been no fog."

"No fog," laughed the harbourmaster. "We had a proper thick'un come in with the tide day before yesterday, before that blow. That blow pretty fierce in the night. Why, where have you been not to know it?"

Fog. And a night of wind. He must have been two whole days in hospital instead of one.

"Got knocked down," said Jim. "I've been in hospital. But the *Goblin*? What about the *Goblin*? Where did she go after the fog?"

"She'd cleared out before the fog lifted," said the harbourmaster. "I was across twice that night, and there was no yachts about at all. They'll have felt their way up the river when it began to come thick. Or gone into Felixstowe Dock out of harm's way. You didn't look there, did you?"

No. He hadn't. His eyes had been all for the harbour. He remembered that there had been some small craft anchored at the top of the dock. There often were, but he had never thought of looking that way.

He never knew how he got out of the harbourmaster's office. He remembered only the loud ringing of a telephone bell somewhere close by.

He got back to the camber in time to buy his ticket and get aboard the ferry.

"Found her?" asked the mate.

"No," said Jim, and then, "That fog . . . When was it?"

"Day before yesterday," said the mate, and Jim groaned. Had he really been two days and two nights in that white room? What could have happened? They couldn't have got ashore without a dinghy. Had they hailed another boat to tow them back to Pin Mill? Or to take them into the dock? Why, it was yesterday he had promised they should be back. And what if they were not in the dock, or at Pin Mill? In a fog anything might have happened.

As the ferry came through the pierheads at Felixstowe, Jim looked at the little bunch of boats on moorings up at the far end of the dock. The *Goblin* was not there, but he saw his own little black dinghy, the *Imp*, tied to a chain. Somebody must have shifted her for him. He went ashore, stumbled up the steps, and met the man in charge of the dock.

"Do you know where my boat is, the *Goblin*, seven-ton cutter? She was anchored on the Shelf yesterday . . . No, no . . . the day before yesterday . . ."

"Before the fog . . . I see her," said the man. "White-painted boat with bowsprit following her sheer. Yes, I see her just before that come on thick. She was gone next morning. Reckon your crew take her up the river."

"But there were only children aboard," groaned Jim.

What was he to do? Telephone to Mrs Walker? No good, if the *Goblin* was at Pin Mill. Worse, far worse, if she wasn't. No, he could not telephone. He would have to go and tell Mrs Walker . . . now . . . at once. But Pin Mill was on the Shotley side of the river. And his dinghy was here . . . He would want the dinghy anyway . . . The *Goblin* MUST be at Pin Mill. He hurried along to the head of the dock to get hold of the *Imp*. Yes, that was the only thing to do. He could never row all that way. Take too long. He would row across to Shotley, leave the *Imp* there and take the bus up that side of the river, to explain to Mrs Walker how it had happened that he had left them aboard by themselves.

He cast off the *Imp*'s painter, put the oars in the rowlocks and rowed out of the dock, his head thumping at every stroke he took.

It was going to be a long pull, even to Shotley. Good thing the tide was with him. The sun blazed off the water into his eyes. He looked over his shoulder, headed for Shotley, took marks on land over the stern and settled down to row. What, oh what, was he going to say to Mrs Walker?

"Ahoy there!"

The hail came from behind him. He stopped rowing and looked round. A fast launch was rushing towards him, water spirting from her bows. The Customs launch. He knew her and he knew the Customs officers aboard her.

"Ahoy there! Looking for your ship? The harbourmaster just passed us the word. There's a small cutter reported coming in from the Cork . . ."

"From the Cork?"

"Aye ... There she is, coming past Landguard ..."

The man pointed out to sea. And there, beyond Landguard Point, heading towards the Beach End buoy, Jim saw a triangle of red sail, a white boat ... and knew her in a moment for what she was.

"Thank you," he shouted, spun the *Imp* round, and headed out against the tide to meet her.

The Customs officer gave a short wave of the hand, and the launch shot suddenly ahead in a flurry of foam.

Coming in from the Cork? From the open sea? But who on earth could have borrowed her? Who would have dared to take her out? And what had become of the crew? It was no good ... That head of his simply would not work. But there was the *Goblin* dancing in between the outer buoys, and her desperate owner rowed to meet her.

CHAPTER XXVI

"NOTHING TO DECLARE . . ."

"Beach end."

They read the name on the buoy as they swept past it. How differently they had felt about it when they read it last. Then it had meant that everything was all wrong. Now it meant that things were on their way towards being put right. Nothing could be very wrong with Daddy there, aboard, hauling in the mainsheet.

"Ready?" he asked. "All right. I'll look after that backstay. Now then, John, bring her round."

John put his tiller up. The boom swung over, and the *Goblin* headed in for the harbour. There was a moment's business with headsail sheets.

"Motor-boat on the starboard bow," shouted Roger. "Coming at a good lick too."

"Where you from?"

Daddy was on the point of answering, but, instead, looked at John. "Sing out, Skipper," he said quietly. "I'm only a passenger . . ."

"Flushing," shouted John.

"What's that?" shouted the man.

"Flushing," shouted John . . . "Holland . . ."

"We'll come aboard . . . Will you bring up at Shotley?"

John looked at his father. "Tell them you'll bring up inside Shotley Spit, as we're bound up river to Pin Mill."

"We'll anchor inside Shotley Spit," shouted John.

"Right oh. We'll be along to clear you at once . . ." The launch swung round and was off, but, as her engine roared again, they heard another shout from the man. What with the engine from the launch and their own Handy Billy still chugging away below, they heard only three words of what he said, but those three words were enough – "asking for you!"

In horror they looked at each other. Who had been asking for them? Jim? Mother? They saw Mother going first to one place and then to another, asking if anyone had seen a little cutter with four children aboard. The very worst must have happened.

ENTRANCE TO HARWICH

Roger sang out again. "Boat ahead . . ." and then, "I say, is this really Harwich? There's a native in that boat . . . wearing a turban."

They were well inside the point now, steering to pass close by the moored seaplanes and the huge gantry on the Felixstowe side of the harbour. With their eyes on the Customs launch they had not at first seen that small dark speck on the water. Now it was already quite near, a little dinghy with a man in it, rowing hard against the tide, his oars flashing and, yes, Roger was right, he really did seem to have a huge white turban on his head.

"It's the *Imp*," cried John. "It's Jim Brading."

"It's Jim," cried Titty, at the same moment.

"What's he wearing a turban for?" said Roger.

"Ahoy! Ahoy!" they all shouted together.

The white turban stopped bobbing backwards and forwards with each stroke of the oars. Jim looked over his shoulder and then, with a dip of one oar, spun his dinghy round.

"That the fellow who lost you?" said Daddy. "Looks to me as if he's been in trouble. Somebody's cracked his skull for him."

"He may have been bathing," said Susan.

"Drying his hair," said Titty.

"I suppose we'd better pick him up. Stop the engine, Roger. We'll heave to for him, eh, Skipper?"

John nodded. Now he would see how it was done and would know another time. Roger was already below. The engine stopped. The *Goblin* under sail alone was close to Jim in his dinghy. Daddy hauled in the starboard staysail sheet, bringing the sail across. Then he hauled in the mainsheet just a little. "Let her come up in the wind now," he said, and John put the helm down and the *Goblin* swung round to meet the wind, but did not swing too far, because the wind caught the staysail aback, so that the staysail pushed one way and then the mainsail pushed the other. The *Goblin* came almost to standstill, and lay there, drifting with the tide. So that was how it was done. Another time, when he had to pick up a pilot, John would know how to do it for himself.

Jim Brading paddled the *Imp* alongside. He looked ill and pleased and puzzled all at the same time. Who was this thin, sunburnt man who took the painter from him and with two turns of his wrists had it on a bollard in a clove hitch? He looked at the others, all four of them there. He looked up and down the *Goblin*, and then again at Daddy. They could almost see that he was just going to say, "What do you mean by grabbing my ship?" They all began telling him at once.

"We didn't mean to go to sea . . . This is Daddy . . . I've lost your anchor . . . and all the chain . . . We drifted away in the fog . . . Couldn't get back . . . You know what you said about shoals, getting outside them . . . But what have you done to your head? . . . Quick, Daddy, he's ill . . ."

Commander Walker was just in time to catch Jim by the arm as he clambered aboard. A moment later and he would have slipped back into the water or capsized the *Imp*. But he was pulled safely into the cockpit, where he sat for a minute, dazed and oddly green about the eyes.

"All right, old chap. Don't talk. Plenty of time for that. Cast off that staysail sheet, Susan. Let her pay off again, John."

The *Goblin* was once more sailing up the harbour, with the little black dinghy towing astern, as it had been when they started from Pin Mill. But Jim Brading, sitting there silent in the cockpit, looking dreadfully ill, was very different from the quick, efficient skipper they had known.

"He's had a bit of a shock of some kind," said Daddy. "Leave him alone. Don't ask questions." And then he himself asked the question that was on all their lips. "Does my wife know?"

Jim looked at him as if he hardly understood. Then his lips moved. "I couldn't tell her," he said slowly. "They put me in hospital. I only got away this morning . . ."

"Thank God for that," said Daddy.

It was as if a heavy weight was lifted from their hearts. Mother might have been worried, but at least she had not known the very worst. Then they thought of Jim. In hospital? What could have happened to him? Something pretty bad.

"I think he ought to be lying down," said Susan.

"Good idea," said Daddy. "Take it easy."

Jim let himself be helped down the companion-steps and lay down on John's bunk. Susan put a couple of cushions under his head.

"I'll be all right in a minute," he said.

"What about fishing for his anchor and chain?" said John. "I know where it was. We've just passed the place. Over there. Just opposite the dock."

"We'd better report to your Mother first," said Daddy. "Anchors can wait. Even Jim's."

So the *Goblin* sailed on, up the wide harbour, past the Guard buoy, past the other big buoy that marks the end of Shotley Spit, and was presently slipping in towards the Shotley shore of the Orwell where half a dozen barges were lying to their anchors.

"We'll put our hook down just ahead of them," said Daddy. "Where's the warp? That bit of hal-yard's no good."

"We couldn't find anything else," said Susan.

Daddy put his head in at the companion. "Got a warp for your kedge?" he asked.

"In the stern locker," said Jim.

Daddy had found the latch in a moment, and opened a locker they had never noticed, under the short after deck.

"That's why we couldn't find it," said Susan, as Daddy hauled out a huge coil of thick grass rope strong enough to hold a boat much bigger than the *Goblin*.

Daddy went forward, taking the coil with him. He stocked the kedge anchor and made the warp fast to it, while John steered and watched as well as he could at the same time. Then the staysail came rattling down, the jib was rolled up, and Daddy looked over his shoulder. "All clear here," he said, and seemed to be waiting for an order.

It seemed all wrong to John, to be skipper now, when Jim was back aboard. But Jim was in the cabin with two nurses, one of whom, Susan, had slipped down, thinking he might like a drink of water, and the other of whom, Titty, was puzzling him very much by showing him a kitten. Several times that morning Jim had thought he had gone mad, and this kitten, aboard the *Goblin*, seemed to him almost to settle the question. John, for a moment, looked down into the cabin at the white turbaned head resting on the *Goblin's* red cushions, at Susan with her glass of water, at Titty carefully lowering Sinbad till his claws caught hold of Jim's jersey, at Jim staring at the kitten and putting out a doubtful hand to feel its fur. No, it was clear that the order for anchoring was to come from him and from him alone. He looked at the last of the barges, judged his distance from the shore, and brought the *Goblin* round into the wind.

"Let go!" he called.

Down went the anchor with a splash.

*

They had just had time to lower the mainsail when they saw the Customs launch racing towards them.

"Half a minute while I get the fenders," shouted John.

"We won't bump you," said one of the men on the launch, pointing to the enormous rope fenders that hung along the side of the launch and made the *Goblin's* fenders look like toys.

The launch slid up to them, her engine purring, and a Customs officer stepped aboard.

"We're only lying to a kedge and light warp," said Commander Walker quietly. "I think they slipped their cable . . ."

"Slipped their cable . . ." Gosh, as Daddy said it, it sounded almost a normal thing to do, not at all like those frantic moments when the chain had gone smoking through the lead and John had been flung on his back when he had tried to stop it by putting a foot on it.

"That's all right," said the Customs officer. "We'll not make fast to you. Come on, George."

A younger officer stepped aboard, carrying a leather case.

"Come on out, Susan," said Daddy. "We'll be wanting the cabin table . . . No. No. Sick men don't stir," he added, seeing that Jim Brading was making as though to get up.

Susan came out into the cockpit. Titty was just going to do the same, but thought better of it and slipped into the forecabin with Sinbad. Roger,

TURBANED NATIVE

who was on the foredeck, dropped hurriedly down
the forehatch. He was not going to miss anything,
and Titty was in time to catch one of his waving
legs and steer it to a foothold as he lowered himself
into the fo'c'sle.

"Now," said Daddy, and the two Customs officers went down into the cabin. Daddy followed.
"Come on, John," he said.

"Pretty nasty crack you had from what they
tell me," said the elder of the Customs officers
to Jim. "We heard about that on the Felixstowe
bus, but they didn't know who it was. Who took
your ship to Holland for you?"

Jim was looking very dazed.

"All right, old chap," said Daddy. "We'll do
the talking."

"We didn't mean to," said John.

"Piracy," said the Customs officer. "That's what
it was . . . Well, who'd have thought it . . . piracy
in Harwich harbour . . . If the owner likes to prosecute . . ."

The two Customs officers were sitting on the
port bunk behind the table. Daddy was sitting
beside them. John was at the foot of the stairs.
Susan was looking down from the cockpit. Roger
and Titty were in the doorway to the forecabin,
listening and watching.

"Yes," said the second Customs officer. "Rank
piracy. If the owner likes to prosecute . . ."

"I say," interrupted Titty. "It really was piracy
. . . We never thought of it, but of course it was
. . . We'll all be hanged at Execution Dock . . . in
chains . . . jangling in the wind. Oh, I say, Jim,
do prosecute. Nancy'd be simply delighted . . ."

The Customs officers laughed. "Let's get to business," said the elder of the two. "Anything to declare? ... pirates or no pirates ..."

"Nothing to declare," said Daddy ... "Oh, yes ... Five pair of wooden shoes ... One Dutch doll ... Box of Dutch cigars ... I've smoked some ... Help yourselves ... And a kitten ... Nationality unknown ... Bring out the souvenirs, Titty."

He put the box of cigars on the cabin table, and Titty and Roger brought Bridget's doll and all the shoes and put them on the table beside it. Titty held up Sinbad.

"He's a distressed sailor," she said, "shipwrecked and rescued at sea."

"Better put the shoes on, then we shan't have to charge you," said the second Customs officer, lighting one of the cigars and holding a match for his chief to do the same.

"What about the Dutch lady?" said the elder man.

"She's for Bridget," said John ... "Our sister. She stayed at home."

The Customs officer tilted the little doll on her back, to see if her eyes closed, which they did not. He opened the leather case which was full of printed forms.

"Let's see the ship's papers," he said.

"They're in the drawer under Susan's bunk."

Roger already had the drawer open and passed the big envelope into the cabin. The Customs officer pulled out the papers, unfolded them, and looked at them. Then he looked across at Jim Brading.

"Owner?" he said.

"I am," said Jim.

"Who's the skipper? That's what matters. You didn't pick up the owner till you came back." He looked at Daddy, but Daddy shook his head.

"Not me ... I'm only working my passage. Count me a deckhand if you like ... Here's the skipper."

Both Customs officers looked at John.

Commander Walker took his passport out of his pocket and handed it over.

"We heard you were coming, sir," said the elder man as soon as he had read the name in it.

"Here I am," said Commander Walker. "Took a passage with my son from Flushing. He's the skipper."

"Daddy brought her back," said John.

"Under orders," said Daddy.

"But who took her across to Holland?"

"We did," said John. "But we didn't mean to go to sea at all. We'd promised ..."

"You four children took her across to Holland? Where were you the night before last?"

"At sea," said John.

"Bless my soul," said the younger man.

"Shake," said the elder, and John found his hand being given a pretty hard squeeze.

Daddy was not exactly smiling. But all four of his children knew that he was somehow rather pleased.

The elder Customs officer took some of the printed forms out of his leather case, put two of them together with a sheet of carbon paper between them, and began filling them in.

"You'd better come here," said Daddy, and made

room for John between himself and the Customs
officer, who was going through the form, filling in
the spaces with a hard copying pencil.

CERTIFICATE OF PRATIQUE

I hereby certify that I have examined Mr ...
"Name?" "John Walker." JOHN WALKER, Master
of a Vessel called the GOBLIN, lately arrived
from FLUSHING, and that it appears by the verbal
answers of the said Master to the questions put to
him that there has not been on board during the
voyage any infectious disease demanding deten-
tion of the Vessel and that she is free to proceed
... "Have you any infectious diseases on board?"
"No," said John. "Susan was jolly sea-sick," said
Roger, "and she may have caught it from Titty."
... "We don't count sea-sickness," said the Customs officer. "And the night before last might have
turned up anybody ..." He filled in the last spaces
... Given under my hand at Harwich ... this ...
"What's the date, George?" ... (Signed). He wrote
his name ...
    Preventive Officer of Customs and Excise.

"There you are, Skipper," he said, handing the
form over to John, and putting the copy away.
"You're all clear now and can go where you want.
I don't know what your owner'll be saying to you
for taking his ship across to the other side, but
we'll leave that to him ... Good day to you,
Commander. Shall I let them know at Shotley
you're here?"

"I'll telephone from Pin Mill," said Daddy. "But,

look here, young man (he turned to the turbaned figure of the owner on the starboard bunk), didn't you say you'd bolted from that hospital of yours? There'll be consternation and monkeyhouse when they find you've gone. Better let them have word at once, or they'll be raising Cain, and I don't blame them."

"Could you tell them I'm aboard my boat and I'll explain later?" said Jim. "But I'm not going back there . . ."

"We'll give them a ring right away," said the Customs officer. "And tell them you're as fit as a fiddle."

The Customs officers shook hands and went up the companion. Everybody but Jim went up too. The Customs launch slid alongside. The two men jumped aboard her, waved their cigars, and a moment later were foaming back to Harwich.

"That's that," said Daddy. "And now to make our peace with your Mother."

Jim's bandaged head appeared in the companion-way.

"I don't know what I'm to say to Mrs Walker," he said wretchedly. "I promised to look after them."

"You leave it to us," said Daddy. "Nobody's drowned."

CHAPTER XXVII

COIL DOWN

THE Customs had gone. The ship was cleared. John hauled down the yellow quarantine flag and gave it to Titty, who stowed it away in its proper pocket in the roll of signals.

"Look here," said Daddy. "Tide's turning. We'll have it against us going up the river, and there isn't enough wind to push us over it. We shan't want the sails again. We'd better make a harbour stow while we're about it." He felt the canvas of the mainsail. "Dry as a bone. We'll put the cover on. No, Jim. We'll manage. You lie quiet and leave us to it."

Everybody set to work. Susan and Titty went down below to ram the crew's belongings into the knapsacks ready for going ashore. Daddy unrolled and re-rolled the jib, and went out on the bowsprit and put a tyer round it. John stowed the staysail away in the fo'c'sle. Together they flaked the mainsail along the boom, and rolled it neatly up with no wrinkles on the outside, and laced the long green sail cover over it to keep it dry till it should be wanted again.

"The barges are swinging already," said Susan, bringing up a packed knapsack. "Sorry, Roger." She had almost trodden on him as he lay on the cockpit floor reaching down to give a turn to the grease cap on the stern tube.

The barges were no longer pointing down the

river. They were pointing all ways, slowly swinging round, the *Goblin* with them, till every vessel
in the anchorage had its head upstream. The tide
had turned. There was hardly wind enough to stir
the reflections of the barges in the smooth water.

"Well, Skipper," said Daddy. "What about it?"

"We're ready," said John.

Roger scrambled to his feet after forcing the
screw cap round with a spanner.

"You've got a lot of grease on your face," said
Susan.

Roger wiped it with a handful of cotton waste.

"You've made it worse," said Susan.

"What about dinner?" said Roger.

Susan laughed in spite of her worries.

"That's right, Roger," said Daddy. "Put the cook
in her place. Engineers can't help being greasy.
Never knew a clean one yet."

He slipped down and started the engine.

"Can you use the stove with the engine at
work?" he shouted from the foot of the companion
with the noise of the engine chug, chugging in his
ears.

"I used it last night," Susan called back.

"Of course you did," said Daddy. "What about
inviting Mother and Bridget to a meal aboard? If
the owner doesn't mind."

"Do you think they'll come?" said Jim dully,
"after what I've gone and done."

"Cheer up," said Daddy. "Of course they will.
The only thing you did wrong was to go ashore.
Captain shouldn't leave the ship . . . Not without
a mate in charge with his master's ticket in
his pocket . . . You should have sent John in

the dinghy for the petrol ... But," he added, looking at Jim's bandaged head, "I'm jolly glad you didn't. Ticking over all right, isn't she? Fine engines, these Handy Billies. We'll be home in no time now, as soon as I get the anchor off the ground."

He went on deck, up through the forehatch, and John hurried forward to help coil down the warp as Daddy hauled it in.

"Anchor's atrip," said Daddy presently. "Better go to the helm and tell your engineer to put her half ahead."

Roger pushed the gear lever forward. The noise of the engine changed. There was a clank under the bobstay, and they saw the anchor come aboard. The *Goblin* was moving.

Presently Daddy came aft. "What about washing the mud off the foredeck?" he said. "Ready for visitors. Don't worry about the cooking for a few minutes, Susan. Straight up the river, John. Leave that black buoy on the point to port. I'm going down to have a talk with Jim."

"But I say ..." said John at the tiller.

"Carry on, Skipper," said Daddy. "If you can take this ship to Holland under sail, you can take her up the river under power."

*

Chug, chug, chug. The little engine settled to its work. The *Goblin* moved slowly up the river over the ebb. John stood at the tiller, hardly able to believe that only three days had gone by since he had sailed in the *Goblin* for the first time, past these very shores, listening eagerly for orders. And now, he had been to Holland and back, and Daddy and Jim were down below, Jim lying on his bunk, Daddy sitting opposite to him, smoking a Dutch cigar, and neither of them seeming to take the least interest in what was happening on deck, but trusting the ship to him as if he had been sailing her all his life.

Susan, remembering how awful it had been to see John clinging to the heaving deck, could hardly believe that it was the same deck as that on which she herself was standing up, dipping a bucket over the side on the end of a lanyard and sluicing Orwell mud off the anchor. Titty was going round the side decks with a mop, spinning the mop sometimes, to see the sunlight make rainbows in the flying drops of water. Roger was fiddling with the throttle-lever, finding the point at which the engine seemed to be happiest. Gosh, when he got back to school, he was going to have something to talk about to that engineering friend of his.

Presently Susan went down through the fore-hatch. A few minutes later, her plans made for dinner, she came up the companion-way and began to start the stove.

"We're going to have tea going anyhow," she said. "And grog for anybody who wants it, and there's a huge glass of brawn we never found, and Jim says it's just the thing he feels like eating. And I thought of hotting up some peas."

"And we've still got about a mile of that Dutch loaf," said Roger, "and eleven oranges. More than enough to go round."

Titty, her swabbing done, stowed the mop and sat herself on the cabin top, watching the smooth water go by, watching the *Goblin*'s wash go rippling through the reflections by the shores. A cormorant, spreading its wings like a German eagle, was perched on the buoy at the bend.

"John," cried Titty. "There's a steamer coming down."

"I've seen it," said John.

It was a little cargo steamer, and they met it just after rounding the buoy. For a moment John thought of calling Daddy. The steamer hooted twice. He remembered ... "Two hoots ... Turning to port." He turned a little to port himself, to show the steamer he had understood. Looking down into the cabin, he saw his father half get up, glance through a porthole and settle again to his talk and his cigar.

Two yachts were motoring down in the calm, their sails flapping. One of them he did not know. The other was the blue *Coronilla*, with the natives aboard it who had seen them start.

He heard a hail.

"Ahoy! *Goblin*! Have a good time?"

"Yes, thank you," shouted John, and he and Titty and Roger waved back to them.

"They don't know where we've been," said Roger. "Shall I tell them?"

"No," said John, and the *Coronilla* went on down the river, little thinking that the *Goblin* was coming home from foreign parts.

Again they saw porpoises plunging down with the tide.

"We never saw any at sea," said Roger.

"They were probably keeping down below out of the storm," said Titty.

Far up the creek on the northern side of the river, they saw the gleaming bodies of bathers. On and on they went, fast through the water, but slowly past the land, because of the outgoing tide. It was so soon after high water that the mudflats were still covered, and the shining river stretched from the woods on one side to the woods on the other. The same big steamer from the River Plate was still moored between the buoys, unloading into barges. The *Goblin* passed close by her, so that they heard the rattle of the derricks and the shouts of the stevedores at their work.

Daddy came up from below, driving Susan before him, to have a private word.

"Your owner," he said, "seems to have made up his mind that fourteen tugs won't get him back to that hospital. We'll have to have a word with the doctor there when we get in, but it looks to me as if he's not much the worse. Tough skull he must have got. Hurt the motor-bus a bit, I should think. Anyhow, he's made up his mind to stay aboard, and I don't see why not, if some of you people come and cook his meals for him."

"Of course we will," said Susan.

"Susan's got her first-aid box at Miss Powell's," said Titty. "We'll make the *Goblin* into a hospital ship."

"He won't mind that," said Daddy, "but he gets all of a stew when he thinks of that place at Felixstowe and starts worrying about two days he says he's lost. He'll be better lying quiet in the cabin."

"The water's boiling," said Susan. "I'll put the peas in now, and we'll be able to give them dinner as soon as we get tied up."

Daddy looked ahead. Already they were passing the boats anchored below the hard. They could see the boat-builder's sheds, and the old Butt and Oyster Inn at the water's edge, and the crowd of moored yachts.

"Do you know where to look for the *Goblin*'s buoy?" asked Daddy.

But Jim Brading's big white-bandaged head was coming slowly up out of the companion.

"I'm going to take her in," he said. "I know just what she'll do."

"There's Mother and Bridget on the shore," shouted Roger. "Can't I hoot the foghorn to make them look this way."

"They've seen us," said Titty.

Daddy ducked suddenly down below the cabin top.

"Look here," he said. "We don't want to give her too many shocks at once. Can you manage without me?"

"I can take her in all right, sir," said Jim, "if John'll get the buoy aboard."

"Aye, aye, sir," said John.

"Better not show that bandaged head of yours more than you can help," said Daddy. "Not right away. You'll have to leave John to moor her."

"I'll take her up to the buoy and then come below," said Jim. "But I wish I knew what to say to Mrs Walker."

"Cheer up, man," said Daddy. "She isn't a

dragon. And a chap like you who doesn't mind ramming motor omnibuses . . ."

Jim grinned doubtfully.

"I'll be standing by in case of trouble," said Daddy, and disappeared into the cabin.

"You go forrard, John," said Jim Brading. "Get hold of the buoy with the boathook. Haul away on the buoy rope, and make fast as soon as you've enough of the chain aboard."

"Aye, aye, sir," said John, very glad to be skipper no more, as the *Goblin* threaded her way in among the moored boats.

He went forward, freed the boathook from its tyers, and stood, waiting.

They were in the middle of that crowd of yachts. They passed between a ketch and a yawl, close by a tall Bermudian cutter, close by a big motor cruiser all glass deckhouses, high above the water. The chug, chug of the motor softened. Jim had shut down the throttle. There seemed to be a boat on every mooring in the anchorage. John looked in all directions for the black buoy with the name GOBLIN painted on it in green. Hullo! That must be it. Two more boats to pass. He glanced back. Yes, Jim had seen it. The noise of the engine changed again and it seemed to be running much quicker. Jim had told Roger to throw it out of gear.

"Mother's got a dinghy," cried Titty. "They're just getting into it."

John glanced towards the shore, but only for a moment. Jim never turned his head. Roger was standing by with his hand on the gear lever, waiting for orders. Susan and Titty had eyes only for Mother and Bridget, pushing off in the borrowed dinghy. Titty held Sinbad up to see them.

The *Goblin* passed the first yacht, and the second, that lay between her and her buoy. She was moving more and more slowly.

"Ahead," said Jim quietly.

Roger pushed the lever forward.

"Enough."

He pulled it back again.

John was holding on to the forestay, watching the buoy. Nearer and nearer it came. It was close under the bows. The *Goblin* was hardly moving. Was she going to reach it? Just as she stopped, John reached down with the boathook, caught the buoy, lifted it aboard, put down the boathook, and began hauling in hand over hand. Headache or no, Jim Brading had made a beautiful job of picking up his moorings.

The rope was in the fairlead at the stem. In it came. There was a sudden rattle. Chain, muddy wet chain, was following it aboard, a yard of it, two yards. John took a turn with the chain round the winch, another, and made fast.

"All fast," he called, and looked round in time to see a large, white turban disappear. The engine coughed and stopped. The *Goblin* was at home again. John, Susan, Titty, and Roger were alone on deck.

*

John looked towards the shore. Mother and Bridget in the dinghy were already half-way out to them. He looked aft at Susan, Titty and Roger, waiting in the cockpit. The forehatch was pushed up close beside him.

"Don't try to tell her everything at once," said Daddy from below.

*

Mother was rowing hard, as if she was in a hurry. Bridget, sitting in the stern of the dinghy, was waving, but only Roger waved back. The others were thinking of all that had to be explained. It was a good thing that Mother had not known that they had been at sea alone, and that Jim had been knocked down and in hospital. But she would have to be told now. And except for yesterday's telegram, she had heard nothing from them since they had talked with her on the telephone that first evening. And they had all promised not to go to sea, and to be back in time for tea the day before.

Mrs Walker steadied the dinghy a few yards from the *Goblin*, and turned to see the four of them looking gravely down from the cockpit. She spoke very quietly, but they knew at once that she was dreadfully upset.

"John, Susan, didn't you promise me that you would be back yesterday? I should never have let you go if I hadn't been sure I could trust you. I know you couldn't come up the river in the fog, but it was a wild night and you must have known we'd be worried about you. You could have telephoned in the morning. And you had no excuse for not coming home yesterday afternoon. It was rather too bad, don't you think, just to send a telegram. You could have telephoned first thing, and then you could have come back by bus from Shotley if Mr Brading didn't want to bring his boat . . ."

"But we couldn't," said John. "We really couldn't . . ."

"We weren't at Shotley at all," said Roger. "Not yesterday."

"Do you know I had a telegram from Daddy the day after you left, a telegram from Berlin? He might have been here yesterday morning. And then yesterday there was a telegram from Flushing. He must be on his way now. He may even have arrived already . . . Oh, what have you done to your head?"

Jim's monstrous bandaged head had come slowly up out of the companion.

"It wasn't their fault, Mrs Walker," he said. "It was all mine."

"What are all those wooden shoes?" asked Bridget, looking up at the shoes, which Roger had arranged in a neat row, five pairs of them, beside the handrail on the cabin roof.

"Of course," went on Mrs Walker, "if you had an accident and hurt your head, you were quite right not to sail. But they ought to have come home from Shotley . . . And you could have telephoned instead of just sending a telegram to say they were going to stop an extra day . . ."

Mother turned again to John. "Daddy may have crossed by the night boat. He may be waiting, wondering why there's nobody to meet him . . ."

"He knows all about it," said Titty. "And he doesn't mind, and he says he doesn't think you'll object to Sinbad . . . Oh! where *is* Sinbad? He's gone . . ."

The kitten had been climbing about on the knapsacks piled on one of the seats in the cockpit. It had climbed over the coaming and wandered along behind the cabin top.

"Oh, look!" cried Bridget. "They really have got a kitten."

Mother looked away from those wretched children of hers who had caused her such dreadful worry in the fog and the storm, and then, instead of coming home in time, had calmly broken all their promises and sent her a telegram to say cheerfully that they were going to stop away another twenty-four hours. Like Bridget, she saw the fluffy Sinbad come unsteadily round from behind the cabin and out on the foredeck. And then she saw something else. Someone must have seen Sinbad go past the cabin portholes. A hand, a lean, brown hand, came up out of the forehatch and felt this way and that for the kitten.

Mother's mouth dropped open, just as Titty's always did when she was thoroughly surprised.

"Ted!" she cried.

A head followed the hand.

"Hullo, Mary," said Daddy. "Don't be too hard on them. Nobody's drowned. And nobody's really to blame."

"I'm coming aboard," said Mother. "Though I didn't mean to. You take that painter, John. You awful children. Did you meet him in Harwich?"

"No," said Roger, unable to resist his chance, while the others never took their eyes off Mother's face. "No . . . We met him in Holland."

"Rubbish," said Mother, lifting Bridget up to Daddy, who had climbed out of the forehatch and

come aft to take her. Daddy planted her beside the
wooden shoes on the cabin roof and put the Dutch
doll in her hands. The next moment he had swung
Mother aboard and kissed her.

"I don't think I ought to kiss any of you
others," she said, but with the beginning of a
laugh in her voice.

"You can kiss the whole lot of them here and
now," said Daddy. "You can take it from me they
deserve it."

"Oh, well," said Mother, "I suppose I've got to
forgive them now you've come back." She did as
Daddy said, and shook hands with Jim Brading
and said she hoped he hadn't hurt himself badly.
"Was it the boom?" she asked. "It can give you a
nasty bump."

"No," said Jim Brading. "It wasn't that."

"If only they'd kept their promises," said Mother, turning to Daddy again. "We'd planned all to
meet you in Harwich, instead of these four bad
lots by themselves."

"Didn't you hear?" said Roger again. "We didn't
meet him in Harwich. We met him in Holland."

"Oh, yes," said Mother, quite clearly not believ-
ing a word of it, thinking it was just one of Roger's
jokes. "What a lovely doll, Bridget."

"Now look here, Mary," said Daddy. "We've
a grand spread nearly ready in the cabin, and
the owner and the skipper and the crew and the
passengers want you and Bridget to honour them
by lunching aboard. Isn't that so, Jim?"

Jim's turbaned head nodded slowly. He could
not trust himself to say a word.

John, Susan, and Titty were in time to see

their father give both Jim and them something very like an encouraging wink.

"We'll be very pleased," said Mother. "But we'll have to go ashore and tell Miss Powell first."

Roger thought Holland was falling very flat indeed.

"Don't you understand we met him in Holland?" he said.

"Oh, yes," laughed Mother. "And I suppose you bought all those wooden shoes yourselves and tried them on in a Dutch shop."

"They did indeed," said Daddy, and Mother, looking at his face, saw that he meant it.

"Jim!" exclaimed Mother. "You don't mean to say you took them right across the North Sea in that awful weather, when you'd promised me not to take them out of harbour?"

"I ... I," Jim stammered, and put a hand to his head. This was too much for him.

"Jim wasn't there," said Daddy. "And that reminds me, I've got some telephoning to do on his behalf ... Now then, Mary, don't say another word till you know what really happened. I'm going to row you ashore, and I'll tell you all about it."

He jumped down into the dinghy, and Mother, dazed and puzzled, joined him there.

"Back in a quarter of an hour," he said cheerfully. "You others'll have the grub ready by then."

A moment later he was pulling away from the ship.

Bridget had scrambled off the cabin roof and, with the Dutch doll clasped to herself with one hand, was holding the rail with the other, and making her way to the foredeck. The others, in the cockpit, watched the dinghy, with Daddy rowing and Mother sitting in the stern, going away towards the shore. Now and then they saw Daddy rest on his oars, while he leaned forward to talk to Mother. More than once they saw her turn to look back at the *Goblin*.

"Do you think she'll ever forgive me?" said Jim.

"Daddy's explaining everything," said John.

"It's going to be quite all right," said Titty.

"Daddy'll tell her we didn't mean to go to sea," said Susan.

"He said they'd be hungry when they got back," Roger reminded her.

"What's the name of the kitten?" asked Bridget from the foredeck.

THE
ARTHUR RANSOME
SOCIETY

The Arthur Ransome Society was formed in June 1990 with the aim of celebrating his life and his books, and to encourage both children and adults to take part in adventurous pursuits – especially climbing, sailing and fishing. It also seeks to sponsor research, to spread his ideas in the wider community and to bring together all those who share the values and the spirit that he fostered in all his storytelling.

The Society is based at the Abbot Hall Museum of Lakeland Life and Industry in Kendal, where there is a special room set aside for Ransome: his desk, his favourite books and some of his personal possessions. There are also close links with the Windermere Steamboat Museum at Bowness, where the original *Amazon* has been restored and kept, together with the *Esperance*, thought to be the vessel on which Ransome based Captain Flint's houseboat. The Society keeps in touch with its members through a journal called *Mixed Moss*.

Regional branches of the Society have been formed by members in various parts of the country – Scotland, the Lake District, East Anglia, the Midlands, the South Coast among them – and contacts are maintained with overseas groups such as the Arthur Ransome Club of Japan. Membership fees are modest, and fall into three groups – for those under 18, for single adults, and for whole families. If you are interested in knowing more about the Society, or would like to join it, please write for a membership leaflet to The Secretary, The Arthur Ransome Society, The Abbot Hall Gallery, Kendal, Cumbria LA9 5AL.

SWALLOWS AND AMAZONS FOR EVER!

Other great reads from **Red Fox**

Further Red Fox titles that you might enjoy reading are listed on the following pages. They are available in bookshops or they can be ordered directly from us.

If you would like to order books, please send this form and the money due to:

ARROW BOOKS, BOOKSERVICE BY POST, PO BOX 29, DOUGLAS, ISLE OF MAN, BRITISH ISLES. Please enclose a cheque or postal order made out to Arrow Books Ltd for the amount due, plus 75p per book for postage and packing to a maximum of £7.50, both for orders within the UK. For customers outside the UK, please allow £1.00 per book.

NAME_____

ADDRESS_____

_____

Please print clearly.

Whilst every effort is made to keep prices low, it is sometimes necessary to increase cover prices at short notice. If you are ordering books by post, to save delay it is advisable to phone to confirm the correct price. The number to ring is THE SALES DEPARTMENT 071 (if outside London) 973 9700.

Other great reads from **Red Fox**

Enter the gripping world of the REDWALL saga

REDWALL Brian Jacques

It is the start of the summer of the Late Rose. Redwall Abbey, the peaceful home of a community of mice, slumbers in the warmth of a summer afternoon.

But not for long. Cluny is coming! The evil one-eyed rat warlord is advancing with his battle-scarred mob. And Cluny wants Redwall . . .

ISBN 0 09 951200 9 £3.99

MOSSFLOWER Brian Jacques

One late autumn evening, Bella of Brockhall snuggled deep in her armchair and told a story . . .

This is the dramatic tale behind the bestselling *Redwall*. It is the gripping account of how Redwall Abbey was founded through the bravery of the legendary mouse Martin and his epic quest for Salmandastron.

ISBN 0 09 955400 3 £3.99

MATTIMEO Brian Jacques

Slagar the fox is intent on revenge . . .

On bringing death and destruction to the inhabitants of Redwall Abbey, in particular to the fearless warrior mouse Matthias. His cunning and cowardly plan is to steal the Redwall children—and Mattimeo, Matthias' son, is to be the biggest prize of all.

ISBN 0 09 967540 4 £3.99

MARIEL OF REDWALL Brian Jacques

Brian Jacques starts his second trilogy about Redwall Abbey with the adventures of the mousemaid Mariel, lost and betrayed by Slagar the Fox, but fighting back with all her spirit.

ISBN 0 09 992960 0 £4.50

Other great reads from **Red Fox**

Dive into action with Willard Price!

Willard Price is one of the most popular children's authors, with his own style of fast-paced excitement and adventure. His fourteen stories about the two boys Hal and Roger Hunt in their zoo quests for wild animals all contain an enormous amount of fascinating detail, and take the reader all over the world, from one exciting location to the next!

Amazon Adventure
ISBN 0 09 918221 1   £3.50

Underwater Adventure
ISBN 0 09 918231 9   £3.50

Volcano Adventure
ISBN 0 09 918241 6   £3.50

South Sea Adventure
ISBN 0 09 918251 3   £3.50

Arctic Adventure
ISBN 0 09 918321 8   £3.50

Elephant Adventure
ISBN 0 09 918331 5   £3.50

Safari Adventure
ISBN 0 09 918341 2   £3.50

Gorilla Adventure
ISBN 0 09 918351 X   £3.50

Lion Adventure
ISBN 0 09 918361 7   £3.50

African Adventure
ISBN 0 09 918371 4   £3.50

Diving Adventure
ISBN 0 09 918461 3   £3.50

Whale Adventure
ISBN 0 09 918471 0   £3.50

Cannibal Adventure
ISBN 0 09 918481 8   £3.50

Tiger Adventure
ISBN 0 09 918491 5   £3.50

Other great reads from Red Fox

Chocks Away with Biggles!

Squadron-Leader James Bigglesworth – better known to his fans as Biggles – has been thrilling millions of readers all over the world with all his amazing adventures for many years. Now Red Fox are proud to have reissued a collection of some of Captain W. E. Johns' most exciting and fast-paced stories about the flying Ace, in brand-new editions, guaranteed to entertain young and old readers alike.

BIGGLES LEARNS TO FLY
ISBN 0 09 999740 1   £3.50

BIGGLES FLIES EAST
ISBN 0 09 993780 8   £3.50

BIGGLES AND THE RESCUE FLIGHT
ISBN 0 09 993860 X   £3.50

BIGGLES OF THE FIGHTER SQUADRON
ISBN 0 09 993870 7   £3.50

BIGGLES & CO.
ISBN 0 09 993800 6   £3.50

BIGGLES IN SPAIN
ISBN 0 09 913441 1   £3.50

BIGGLES DEFIES THE SWASTIKA
ISBN 0 09 993790 5   £3.50

BIGGLES IN THE ORIENT
ISBN 0 09 913461 6   £3.50

BIGGLES DEFENDS THE DESERT
ISBN 0 09 993840 5   £3.50

BIGGLES FAILS TO RETURN
ISBN 0 09 993850 2   £3.50

Other great reads *from* **Red Fox**

Share the magic of The Magician's House by William Corlett

There is magic in the air from the first moment the three Constant children, William, Mary and Alice arrive at their uncle's house in the Golden Valley. But it's when they meet the Magician, William Tyler, and hear of the Great Task he has for them that the adventures really begin.

THE STEPS UP THE CHIMNEY

Evil threatens Golden House in its hour of need – and the Magician's animals come to the children's aid – but travelling with a fox brings its own dangers.

ISBN 0 09 985370 1   £2.99

THE DOOR IN THE TREE

William, Mary and Alice find a cruel and vicious sport threatening the peace of Golden Valley on their return to this magical place.

ISBN 0 09 997390 1   £2.99

THE TUNNEL BEHIND THE WATERFALL

Evil creatures mass against the children as they attempt to master time travel.

ISBN 0 09 997910 1   £2.99

THE BRIDGE IN THE CLOUDS

With the Magician seriously ill, it's up to the three children to complete the Great Task alone.

ISBN 0 09 918301 9   £2.99

Other great reads *from* **Red Fox**

Have a bundle of fun with the wonderful Pat Hutchins

Pat Hutchins' stories are full of wild adventure and packed with outrageous humour for younger readers to enjoy.

FOLLOW THAT BUS

A school party visit to a farm ends in chaotic comedy when two robbers steal the school bus.

ISBN 0 09 993220 2   £2.99

THE HOUSE THAT SAILED AWAY

An hilarious story of a family afloat, in their house, in the Pacific Ocean. No matter what adventures arrive, Gran always has a way to deal with them.

ISBN 0 09 993200 8   £2.99

RATS!

Sam's ploys to persuade his parents to let him have a pet rat eventually meet with success, and with Nibbles in the house, life is never the same again.

ISBN 0 09 993190 7   £2.50

Other great reads *from* **Red Fox**

Enjoy Jean Ure's stories of school and home life.

JO IN THE MIDDLE

The first of the popular Peter High series. When Jo starts at her new school, she determines never again to be plain, ordinary Jo-in-the-middle.

ISBN 0 09 997730 3 £2.99

FAT LOLLIPOP

The second in the Peter High series. When Jo is invited to join the Laing Gang, she's thrilled – but she also feels guilty because it means she's taking Fat Lollipop's place.

ISBN 0 09 997740 0 £2.99

A BOTTLED CHERRY ANGEL

A story of everyday school life – and the secrets that lurk beneath the surface.

ISBN 0 09 951370 6 £1.99

FRANKIE'S DAD

Frankie can't believe it when her mum marries horrible Billie Small and she has to go and live with him and his weedy son, Jasper. If only her real dad would come and rescue her . . .

ISBN 0 09 959720 9 £1.99

YOU TWO

A classroom story about being best friends – and the troubles it can bring before you find the right friend.

ISBN 0 09 938310 1 £1.95

Other great reads from **Red Fox**

Leap into humour and adventure with Joan Aiken

Joan Aiken writes wild adventure stories laced with comedy and melodrama that have made her one of the best-known writers today. Her James III series, which begins with *The Wolves of Willoughby Chase*, has been recognized as a modern classic. Packed with action from beginning to end, her books are a wild romp through a history that never happened.

THE WOLVES OF WILLOUGHBY CHASE
ISBN 0 09 997250 6   £2.99

BLACK HEARTS IN BATTERSEA
ISBN 0 09 988860 2   £3.50

NIGHT BIRDS ON NANTUCKET
ISBN 0 09 988890 4   £3.50

THE STOLEN LAKE
ISBN 0 09 988840 8   £3.50

THE CUCKOO TREE
ISBN 0 09 988870 X   £3.50

DIDO AND PA
ISBN 0 09 988850 5   £3.50

IS
ISBN 0 09 910921 2   £2.99

THE WHISPERING MOUNTAIN
ISBN 0 09 988830 0   £3.50

MIDNIGHT IS A PLACE
ISBN 0 09 979200 1   £3.50

THE SHADOW GUESTS
ISBN 0 09 988820 3   £2.99